PRAISE FOR *PROMI*

"Gohlke tells a gripping tale of sacrifice, loss, love, and hope against the setting of familiar historical events."
PUBLISHERS WEEKLY

"This dramatic and heart-wrenching interpretation . . . will enthrall fans of character-driven Christian fiction and readers who enjoy Francine Rivers."
LIBRARY JOURNAL, starred review

"This grabs the reader from the first sentence. The characters are well-defined. . . . Readers will come away with a fresh understanding of that horrible day."
ROMANTIC TIMES, 4½ star Top Pick review

"A historic disaster becomes the crucible forging bonds of loyalty, love, and sacrifice between young Michael Dunnagan, Owen Allen, and his sister, Annie. The bonds are tested by grief, war, disease, and separation. Gohlke's attention to detail provides believable characters, good dialogue, and historical accuracy."
LIFE:BEAUTIFUL magazine

"Gohlke's historical romance . . . explores the depth of human nature and emotions through its three-dimensional, compelling characters. . . . *Promise Me This* will certainly satisfy romance readers who enjoy historical details and character-driven plots."
CHRISTIANBOOKPREVIEWS.COM

"Gohlke does not disappoint with her third novel, a carefully researched story full of likable characters struggling to cope with the difficult realities of grief and wartime. . . . [A] sweet, compelling story."
SHELF-AWARENESS.COM

BAND *of* SISTERS

CATHY GOHLKE

CHRISTY AWARD–WINNING AUTHOR

Tyndale House Publishers, Inc.
Carol Stream, Illinois

Visit Tyndale online at www.tyndale.com.

Visit Cathy Gohlke's website at www.cathygohlke.com.

TYNDALE and Tyndale's quill logo are registered trademarks of Tyndale House Publishers, Inc.

Band of Sisters

Designed by Ron Kaufmann

Edited by Sarah Mason

Published in association with the literary agency of Natasha Kern Literary Agency, Inc., P.O. Box 1069, White Salmon, WA 98672.

Unless otherwise indicated, all Scripture quotations are taken from the *Holy Bible*, King James Version.

The Scripture quotation in the dedication is taken from the Holy Bible, *New International Version,*® *NIV.*® Copyright © 1973, 1978, 1984, 2011 by Biblica, Inc.™ Used by permission of Zondervan. All rights reserved worldwide. www.zondervan.com.

Band of Sisters is a work of fiction. Where real people, events, establishments, organizations, or locales appear, they are used fictitiously. All other elements of the novel are drawn from the author's imagination.

Library of Congress Cataloging-in-Publication Data

Gohlke, Cathy.
  Band of sisters / Cathy Gohlke.
    p. cm.
  ISBN 978-1-4143-5308-1 (sc)
1. Sisters—Fiction. 2. Irish—New York (State)—New York—Fiction. 3. New York (N.Y.)—History—1898-1951—Fiction. 4. Ireland—Emigration and immigration—Fiction. I. Title.
  PS3607.O3448B36 2012
  813'.6—dc23   2012011647

Printed in the United States of America

18 17 16 15 14 13 12
 7   6   5   4   3   2   1

For My Mother

Loving, Courageous, Inspiring

Whose name, Bernice, aptly means "Bearer of Victory"

In celebration of your eighty-fifth birthday

She is worth far more than rubies. . . .
She opens her arms to the poor
    and extends her hands to the needy. . . .
She speaks with wisdom,
    and faithful instruction is on her tongue. . . .
Her children arise and call her blessed. . . .
"Many women do noble things,
    but you surpass them all."

PROVERBS 31

ACKNOWLEDGMENTS

This book was born of a passion to end modern-day slavery and most of all to ask: What can I do to help in a need so desperate?

I'm not the first to ask this question and am profoundly grateful to and inspired by those who have gone before, the countless men and women who have forged trails of hope and established organizations—visible and underground—that work for the abolition of slavery and the healing of its victims. It is a privilege to join my voice with yours.

In the research and writing of this book I am deeply grateful to . . .

—the late Charles Sheldon, author of the novel *In His Steps*, which posed the question, "What would Jesus do?"—a book given to me by my mother one Easter Sunday long ago, a book and a question that changed my life.

—Daniel, my son, who challenged me to write about a "current need." You planted a mental seed that inspired me to address modern-day slavery through a historical setting, enabling me to participate in this platform to raise awareness.

—Natasha Kern, my agent, for fearlessly championing books of strong spiritual and moral purpose, for sharing the vision behind this book and your insights on this manuscript, and most especially for your understanding, friendship, and wise counsel.

—Stephanie Broene and Sarah Mason, my gifted editors, for convincing me that while my heart is steadfast, my first draft is not, and for helping me bring to the page my heart's intent; Babette Rea, my innovative marketing manager; Christy Stroud, my enthusiastic and dedicated publicist; and the wonderfully creative design, PR, and sales teams, and all the others at Tyndale House Publishers who've worked so diligently to bring this book to life and to readers. You are amazing!

—Dan, my husband, who read this manuscript in its early stages, gave me insights, and enthusiastically shared treks through Ellis Island by day, less enthusiastically trudged through the Battery with me by night, hoofed through parts of Manhattan's Lower East Side in all kinds of weather— including the steep and winding stairs of aged tenements and old churches. You even combed a Brooklyn graveyard with me in search of the graves of Triangle Waist Factory fire victims. I love you, and I love exploring the world together.

—family, friends, and writing colleagues who have shared this story's vision and unique journey, sometimes generously brainstorming plotting dilemmas with me and sometimes faithfully praying when the research became too dark to traverse alone: Elisabeth Gardiner, my daughter (who also read and gave valuable insights bathed in prayer through the manuscript's first draft), Bernice Lemons, Gloria Delk, Rachel Kurtz, Carrie Turansky, Terri Gillespie, Dan Lounsbury, Angela Wampler, Reverend Karen Bunnell, Connie Wilkinson, Ed and Betty Sprague, Barb Tenney, Andee McKenica, Carol Sise, Kimberly Artrip, Liz Hook, Patti Lacey, my Elkton United Methodist Church family, writing colleagues through ACFW, and the amazing women I met through Proverbs 31. I know I don't walk alone, and I am grateful beyond words.

—park rangers and historians of Ellis Island, the committed and enthusiastic staff of the Lower East Side Tenement Museum in Manhattan, newspapers and archives of old New York, and the wonderful people I met in Greenwich Village and from NYU who were willing to share their stories and insights into the life and history of New York City. I couldn't have created this story without you or the wonderful books, maps, and news articles you brought to my attention.

And thank you, always, Uncle Wilbur, for reminding me that a sure way to know if I'm working in the will of God is to ask, "Do I have joy? Is this yoke easy? Is this burden light?"

My answer is "Yes! A thousand times, yes!"

PART ONE

CHAPTER ONE

OCTOBER 1910

Widowed crones, their ragged skirts and shawls flapping in the rising gale like so many black crows, threw back grayed heads and keened a wild lament. Though slow of gait, they kept a dozen steps ahead of Maureen O'Reilly, the eldest daughter of their dead neighbor. Not one dared walk beside the "Scarlet Maureen," no matter that they'd been handsomely paid for their services from the young woman's purse.

Maureen didn't care so much for herself. She expected nothing more or less from the village gossips. But she did care for the heart of her younger sister.

She pulled Katie Rose, the lily flower of her family, close. Together the sisters trudged up the rocky hill, part of a bleak and broken parade, toward the stone-walled churchyard. Twice they slipped, cutting their palms, the path muddy from the morning's rain. Once past the churchyard gate, Maureen pushed to the front of the troop, lifted her chin, and set her lips tight as the prow of a ship, daring the women to snub her sister.

The Keeton brothers had dug the grave that morning, and Joshua Keeton, the second eldest, nodded respectfully toward Maureen—an act so out of village character that Maureen turned away without acknowledgment.

The priest intoned his series of Latin prayers into the wind, finishing with the "Our Father."

The Keeton brothers lowered the wooden coffin into its bed.

The priest sprinkled its top with holy water and resumed in his monotone, "Grant this mercy, O Lord, we beseech Thee, to Thy servant departed, that Margaret Rowhan O'Reilly may not receive in punishment the requital of her deeds . . ."

Maureen had attended enough wakes and burials in her twenty years that she could recite the passages by heart. But she'd never buried her mother—and that made this day different from all the rest. Shunned from normal attendance at the village church, she'd wanted this service to penetrate her heart; she'd wanted to repent and mourn the loss of her mother as deeply as Katie Rose mourned—Katie Rose, who could barely stand for the grief of it all.

But the lowering of the coffin spelled only relief for Maureen. For the seven years since her father's death, Maureen had served at the landlord's grand house as the only means of support for her mother and young sister, first as a scullery maid and later, because of her earnest work and graceful ways, as a parlor maid. When the landlord's eye fell upon her, she was barely fourteen.

His mother, Lady Catherine—a good and godly woman—had seen the lust in her firstborn's eye and taken Maureen under her wing. For six of those years she'd employed her, trained her in the ways of a fine lady's maid, kept her as safe as she could. But even Lady Catherine could not outlive her strapping, willful son. Once she was gone, so was Maureen's protection.

And that was what Maureen thought of as the priest droned on. Not so much for herself—she was beyond safety, beyond redemption—but protection for Katie Rose.

Maureen pulled a tear-matted wisp of chestnut hair from her sister's pale cheek. *Thirteen and so beautiful—too beautiful not to be noticed.* The thought pierced Maureen's heart. The sooner Katie Rose was placed under the protection of someone good and kind, someone strong and not beholden to or at the mercy of the landlord, the better. Their mother, in her last years of consumption, had not been willing to hear of it, not been willing to part with the jewel of her life. But it was up to Maureen now, and she knew what must be done. If only she could make her aunt agree.

Maureen started as Katie Rose pulled from her side, lifted a clod from the earth, and dropped it atop the lowered coffin. Maureen winced to hear the finality of the thud—earth on wood—but did the same, and the village followed suit.

The keeners began again their long, musical wailing. The small band retreated down the hill, the men stopping at the pub to drink to Margaret O'Reilly. "A fitting end," they solemnly chorused, "to a great lady's passing."

But the women, expecting a well-laid tea, followed the road round to the cottage of Verna Keithly—aunt to Maureen and Katie Rose and sister of dead Margaret O'Reilly. When the troop reached her cottage door, Verna pulled the door handle, and her nieces passed through.

The band of women, having lingered a few steps behind, hesitated, stopped, and the leader, the blacksmith's wife, whispered loudly, "She'll not be staying, will she?"

Maureen looked back to see her aunt's spine straighten as she removed her gloves.

"You'll not be expecting us to join her for tea, Verna Keithly," the cooper's wife admonished. "Surely not!"

Aunt Verna tilted her head, smiled, and said simply, "No, Mrs. Grogan, I don't believe I will" and quietly closed the door.

Maureen felt her own eyes grow wide. But her aunt smiled, wrapping a work-roughened hand round Maureen's wrist. Maureen bit her lip at the sign of affection. But the tremble threatened anyway, so she turned her face aside, whispering, "You'll live to regret this kindness to me. They won't forget, you know."

"My only regret is in not being kinder sooner." Verna turned her niece to face her and hugged her properly. "I'll do better before this night is through. I promise."

Her aunt's words quickened the hope in Maureen's heart. Perhaps she'd grant her wish, after all. Surely she'd see the need, the urgency, once Maureen explained her plan.

"Shall I set the kettle, Aunt?" Katie Rose sniffled from the kitchen.

"Please! Tea first; I'll cut the cake directly. But let's get a bit of something warm going for later. I've a good shank of lamb already roasting." She hung her damp cape on the hook nearest the door. "Good food—that's what's needed. Maureen, you scrub the potatoes. Katie Rose, cut the bread."

As Maureen passed, her aunt whispered, "Once Katie Rose is abed for the night, we'll talk. We need to talk before your uncle comes home."

Maureen looked at the clock. "He'll be closing soon, won't he?"

Aunt Verna harrumphed. "Not tonight. First round's on him—'tis the first one that loosens purse strings for all the rest. So kind and generous of the grieving brother-in-law, wouldn't ya say?" She raised her brows in sarcasm, knotting her apron strings behind her. "They'll drink and sing and smoke and dance their hearts out. He'll *cha-ching* his till the whole night long. By then we'll have things settled."

―――――――――❧―――――――――

After the washing up, when her sister finally yawned with the weariness and emotion of the day, Maureen sat by Katie Rose as the girl knelt to say her prayers, then tucked her sister in herself. Maureen knew that Katie Rose had spent the last year doing all the cooking and sewing and tucking, ever since their mam became too ill to care for either of them. No matter that her sister was nearly grown—it was good to do for her now, if only for this night, their last together.

When Maureen returned to the little parlor, Aunt Verna had stirred the fire and laid more peat, indicating a long chat was in the offing. Maureen sat down, less certain now the time had come. But she could not miss this opportunity to sway her aunt to her thinking, and so she began before Aunt Verna had taken her seat. "I've been thinking of Katie Rose and what's best for her."

"Good, then, as have I," her aunt returned.

"If Katie Rose could live with you—" Maureen began, but her aunt cut her off, shaking her head.

"Katie Rose must go—leave the village—and she must go now. Gavin Orthbridge has set his eye upon her."

Maureen felt the blood drain from her face. "He's a boy!"

"He's fourteen and Lord Orthbridge's son. He's only bided his time for Margaret's death, till the girl has nowhere to go. He's already told her he can assure her of a job in his father's house. You know what that means."

Maureen knew exactly. It meant the same for Katie Rose as it had meant for her, and there would be no escaping, not once the disgrace came upon her.

"If she stays with me, there'll be no way to save her. The Orthbridges or your uncle will see to that—especially if it means security or gold." Her aunt spread her hands. "I've never been able to change that man's course once the drink or the gold has him in its grasp."

Maureen felt that vile truth rumble in her stomach, sensed the floor drop beneath her chair. She could not imagine a life like her own for Katie Rose. It was not to be borne. "I'll take her with me, though I don't know how. Every penny went to Lord Orthbridge to pay for Mam's rent and their food. I'd thought to go to Dublin, where no one knows me, and begin again, maybe work in a shop."

"With no references." Aunt Verna laid a practical hand upon her hip.

Maureen's shoulders drooped. The only letter of reference she'd ever possessed was from Lady Catherine—a last effort to protect Maureen from her son. But when Maureen had given her notice, Julius Orthbridge had rooted through her things, found the letter, and burned it. *Foolish, foolish me for not simply runnin' away!* The plan Maureen had laid such hope by now sounded feeble in her mouth. "I'd hoped to start over," she whispered. "I wanted Katie Rose here, safe with you. Uncle owns the tavern. I thought—"

"You're not listenin'. She'll not be safe with me."

"I am listenin'." Maureen stood, angrily. "I said I'll take her with me, then. I'll find work for us both. I'll go into service once more if I have to but never to be used like that again. And Katie Rose must never go into service! Never!" She bent her head into her hands. "Dublin's not far enough to hide us both. I know Julius Orthbridge. He'll come lookin'. And his son's of the same cloth."

"Sit down and calm yourself, Maureen." Her aunt spoke sternly. "There's another way."

But Maureen could only see in her mind the image of a drunken, bare-chested Julius Orthbridge, could only relive that first dark and fearful night. The night Lady Catherine lay dying, when he, reeking of whiskey and bearing a globed lamp that cast its shadows up and down the walls from the open window's night breezes, had barged into her servant's quarters and thrown her roommate to the hallway.

No matter that her screams had rent the night and were surely heard throughout the estate, they'd brought no one—no one to help her, no one to save her from the animal intent on relieving his lust. Not then, nor any night thereafter. They were all too afraid or too beholden to the English lord.

But neither fear nor debt had bridled their tongues, and within the week the entire village had heard the gossip. Whether or not they'd pitied her, they'd openly shunned her. The image of Katie Rose facing such a night, such a life, clawed through her brain.

"Take hold, Maureen! Take hold!" Her aunt shook her, forced her into a chair. "Drink this." Aunt Verna forced something strong and vile-smelling between Maureen's teeth, something that shot a hot path down her throat and shook her awake, making her sputter and cough.

"That's better. You need your senses about you. We've not much time. You must listen carefully."

Maureen tried to focus her brain.

"Do you remember the tale your da told over and over when you were but a girl?"

Maureen barely remembered her da, though she'd loved him with all of her heart. He was part of another life, a good life she could hardly claim as her own. She shook her head.

"About the war in America—the war between the states, north and south—the American Civil War, they called it," her aunt coaxed. "He'd gone to America to make his fortune—worked in service as a groomsman for some wealthy family in New York. They had some sort of falling-out, though your da never said what. When the war called for soldiers, he served with the Union, and he saved a man's life—an officer. The game leg your da hobbled upon came because he took a Confederate bullet meant for the American."

Maureen blinked.

"I can't believe ya don't remember." Aunt Verna waited, then went on. "The officer was so grateful that when your da came home to Ireland, the man wrote him a letter, offerin' to set him up in business if only he'd return to America."

Yes, Maureen remembered. Half-fantasy, half-real—she never knew where the truth lay . . . or the letter. And what good had letters done her?

"That letter was the talk of the town, the first letter straight from America to be found in the village, and an invitation to streets paved in gold. And though never said aloud, 'twas the reason his first wife married him; God rest both their souls."

"What?" Maureen tried to push the web from her mind. "Mam said the letter was Da's fireside tale."

Aunt Verna pressed on. "Your da and his first wife were expectin' their first child. They planned to sail for America as soon as the babe was weaned. But she labored early, and mother and child died before the midwife reached them."

"I never heard that."

"It was never talked about. But your da grieved mightily and walked very near the abyss for seven years or so. It would have been better if he'd returned alone to America, but he hadn't the heart. Then, finally, Margaret caught his eye and lifted his spirit. Though I think he never loved her as he did his first."

Maureen bristled. It was not a thing to be said the day of her mam's burial and surely not by her mam's sister.

"Don't look at me so. You were not there. You did not see." Aunt Verna sighed and stood to stir the fire again, though it needed no stirring. "Your da had saved the letter, and once he and Margaret married and were expectin' a bairn, he wrote to the man in America again, seein' if he was still of a mind to make good his offer." She set the poker down. "And the man heartily replied to come on, to bring his new bride and their babe, as soon as he was born. Promised to set him up in business and treat Morgan's firstborn as his own son. He even sent money for the passage, first class."

"And is this another tale for a winter's night? Because if it is, I—"

"I read the letter with my own eyes. I read it to your da because he could not read and Margaret was visitin' our folks when he came with it from town." Her aunt returned to her seat. "They laid their plans, and after the babe came, hale and hardy, your da sold most everything but his good name. Most importantly, he sold his land. They waited until sweet William turned three years old, to be sure he was strong enough for the voyage, and set off for Dublin. Three weeks they waited for the ship to sail—some problems with the keel that needed mendin'."

Maureen knew the rest by heart.

"Cholera swept through the city—a plague on two feet. William died, and they buried him there." Her aunt stopped and stared into the fire. A moment passed before she lifted the corner of her apron and swiped her mouth. "A sweet and lovely lad." She tucked her head to one side, and Maureen caught the shine in her eyes.

"The great ship sailed for America without your mam and da. Your mam could not bear to be parted from the country holdin' William's grave, and she convinced herself that God had cursed your da and his letter and the entire scheme of goin' to America—that the Almighty made him pay with the lives of his children for the notion of risin' above himself. She'd have no more to do with it, no matter how your da begged, no matter how he reasoned. She was sure they'd both die before reachin' the golden shore."

"Da owned his own land?" It was the part of the tale that Maureen could fathom least. None in the village owned so much as a grave plot, save her uncle, who owned his tavern. Lord Orthbridge owned all the rest.

"And he could have bought it back with the money saved from the voyage, but Margaret hid it, convinced as she was that it was cursed; your da became just as enslaved as all the rest to Julius Orthbridge. She was not a good wife, my sister."

Maureen did not stir. The story rang true with every memory of her da's bent back and white hair, of his sad retelling of the tale as he knew it—stolen gold and the lost letter—minus his wife's deception.

"She could not risk Morgan's findin' the letter, so afraid she was of goin' to America. So she asked me to destroy it and give the gold secretly to the church—none to know the giver. She said I dared risk Morgan's wrath if ever he learned the truth—and risk the curse of death, better than she; I was barren anyway."

Heat raced up Maureen's neck. She hated her aunt's accusing tone but understood. They'd both known the pain and betrayal of her mother's selfishness. She was certain her mother had known the price Maureen paid for rent for their cottage and food, but never once had she questioned her. Maureen thought of herself as her mother's workhorse. Her aunt must have felt something of the same.

"I didn't do it."

Maureen looked up. "What?"

"I didn't give the gold to the church and I didn't destroy the letter." Aunt Verna stood and clasped her hands. "I knew that one day she would rot in her selfishness and that your father would need the money and the hope. He was a good man, your da. But working for the Orthbridges did him in—that, and . . . well, the rest."

Maureen stood. "You kept the gold? Then why didn't you give it for our rent and food when Da died? Why did you let Mam send me to the grand house, into service?"

"I didn't know what it would mean. I thought only that it would get you away from her. She would have turned you into herself, and I could not bear it—not for you. I didn't know Lord Orthbridge would . . . would hurt you."

Maureen sat down again. "Hurt me." What could she say? "Yes, he hurt me."

"I swear by the Virgin Mary that I never imagined it." Aunt Verna sat down heavily. "I was foolish. I'm sorry, Maureen. I'm so terribly sorry. Margaret would not have taken the money, she was that sure it was cursed. But I should have stolen you away, sent you to America or London, to start fresh."

The idea was so big and unbelievable that Maureen laughed, one helpless, soulless laugh. "I couldn't have gone. I was obliged to help Mam. I would have stayed—for her and for Katie Rose." She looked at her aunt. "There's no way out—no end for me. First it was looking to Da's needs after his stroke; then it was providin' for Mam, and now I must protect Katie Rose." How could she have hoped to escape?

"You'll go to America and Katie Rose with you. You'll stand up to that man and have him make good on his promise to your da. You're Morgan's firstborn now—his firstborn livin'."

Maureen laughed bitterly. "You're crazy, Aunt Verna."

Aunt Verna's lips pulled grim. "I'm not accustomed to bein' told I'm crazy by a slip of a girl, and never under my own roof."

"I'm a soiled woman, Aunt. I'm nobody's 'firstborn son' or 'slip of a girl.' I'm near crazy myself."

With a toss of her hand, Verna waved her niece's melodrama aside and bent to the hearth, prying a stone from the space nearest the fire. "You should go on the stage for all of that, Maureen. You sound as dark as your mam, but there's more to you than she ever reckoned. You've just forgotten what it is to hope, to have a chance at life. You'd best set your mind to put that life to good use."

Maureen watched as her aunt pried a second stone, lifted out both, and wedged a poker beneath a third. From their opened graves, she pulled a rectangular metal box, dusted the dirt with her apron, turned a key set in the lock, and removed a small pouch and twice-folded paper from inside. She laid both on the rug by the hearth, then replanted the box, easing the bricks into place.

"There, now." Aunt Verna looked up, smiling, and knelt before Maureen, cupping her hands. She spread the neck of the pouch, turned it upside down, and spilled gold coins into her niece's palms. "What do you think of that?"

CHAPTER TWO

OLIVIA WAKEFIELD'S MAID pulled the last pearl button through the loop of her mistress's deep-apricot watered silk. She dusted a faint, shimmering powder across her shoulders and pinned the best and last of the autumn's garden roses in her upswept hair. Then she stood back, critically examining the masterpiece from coiffed head to slippered toe, and smiled. "Perfect, miss."

"Thank you, Mary. You've outdone yourself."

"You're ready for the ball, miss." Mary tucked a wayward wisp behind her mistress's ear.

"Now or never." Olivia smiled, then sobered. "I'm not much for balls."

"But this is your birthday, miss. Mrs. Meitland said that everyone who is anyone in New York will be here. The Ascots, the Vanderbilts, the—"

"Please, Mary." Olivia raised her gloved hand to stop the outpouring. The less she knew or thought about the grand event her sister and brother-in-law had orchestrated, the better chance she had of pretending a composure she did not feel.

Mary curtsied again, a habit that made Olivia want to bob up and down, too.

"Please tell Dorothy I'll be down directly."

"Yes, miss." Mary curtsied once more but hesitated. "The guests are arriving. There's already a dozen carriages by the—"

"Dorothy and Drake will greet them."

"Yes, miss." Mary bobbed less certainly but obediently pulled the door behind her.

Olivia sighed, relieved to be alone at last. She blinked at the softly powdered oval in the looking glass above her dressing table, recognizing the face but unnerved by the lackluster eyes reflected there. She hated this vulgar display of wealth and eligibility Dorothy and Drake had concocted. She'd argued and pleaded but in the end hadn't known how to stop them.

"Father, I miss you tonight most of all," she whispered. At last she breathed deeply, straightened, took up her dance card, and marched toward the battle.

Along the upper hallway, she paused and turned the brass knob of her father's study. *One moment. Just one moment.* Olivia slipped inside and leaned against the closed door, breathing in the faint, lingering scent of his tobacco. She strolled the perimeter of the room, running gloved fingers over his collection of stones chipped from the bases of pyramids in Egypt, tracing long shelves of leather-bound volumes. She smiled as she spun his globe—something she was ordered not to do as a child—and smiled again as she blessed the marble busts of his literary trio, Athos, Porthos, and Aramis—*"Tous pour un, un pour tous."* She ran her fingers for the hundredth time over the last stack of books he'd been reading. *All of it yours a year ago. All of it mine now.*

Olivia sank into the leather chair behind his mahogany desk, turned her face to the moon-filled window behind her, and fingered the string of pearls at her neck—his last personal gift given on her last birthday, a quiet and earnest family affair that he'd understood she loved so well. *You understood so many things.*

And she had understood him—understood what he was about to say, about to dictate, even before he'd formed the words. She'd been his protégé in travel and research for historic articles ever since her disappointment—ever since she'd sworn off men, a determination her father had assured her would pass with time. She'd been his secretary and typist for treatises on issues of social justice. She'd embraced the causes he'd espoused, and that had been enough for her—to work at his side—until last year.

With his first sign of heart trouble, he'd stopped traveling and insisted that she embrace a cause of her own, a life of her own. That was when she'd taken up with other young women from her church, forming a circle. They'd embraced the garment industry workers' strike, hoping that wealth could influence where desperation and a righteous cause could not. But the crusade was short-lived, at least for her.

When her father suffered a massive heart attack, Olivia had given up her crusade for social justice to nurse him. He'd lingered three months, arguing all along that her time with him was too great a sacrifice from her own life and aspirations.

Oh, Father. It was so little.

He'd encouraged but never pestered her to marry. Now that he was gone, it seemed the topic of every conversation with her sister and brother-in-law.

They've tried to assume the position of father, mother, and matchmaker—all in one. It does not suit them. It does not suit me.

"I thought I'd find you here." Dorothy, magnificent in ivory silk and diamonds that sparkled in the light of the hallway's chandelier, stood, eyebrows raised and hand on hip in the doorway. A perfect halo of electric light spread round her. "Hiding, Miss Liberty?"

Olivia smiled at their father's pet name for her—a title bestowed when she was born the same day Lady Liberty was dedicated in New York harbor. "Seeking courage, I'm afraid."

"You're not a coward," her sister chided.

"I miss him, Dottie," Olivia pleaded, hating her own pleading.

But it softened her older sister, if only for a moment. "I miss him too. But that's why you need someone, Livvie. You're turning into a recluse, shut up in this house."

Olivia turned away. "While he was alive, I had a purpose. I felt more alive—a part of something greater than myself."

"Father had that way about him."

"But now—I don't know. I feel . . . adrift." Olivia raised her shoulders helplessly.

"A ship without its mooring?"

"Yes . . . exactly."

Dorothy sighed but stayed by the door as if coming into the room might draw her into something too deep. She squared her shoulders, and Olivia recognized the subtle change as her sister's retreat to safer territory.

"There are things I want in life—things I need, things I mean to do," Olivia went on. "I just don't know what they are."

"I only want what's best for you."

"I know that. But I don't think I'll find what I'm looking for tied to a man I don't love and a silly social calendar. You, of anyone, should know that of me."

Dorothy looked away. "It's not all silly."

"I'm sorry," Olivia stammered. "You know I didn't mean that for you."

But Dorothy forged ahead. "Drake has invited some charming and eligible men to the ball. You can take your pick—railroad, real estate, banking. You're a wealthy woman."

Olivia's nerves pricked. "A perfect merging of bank accounts—how good of Drake."

"You need a husband. You can engage in all those causes you're mad about inside marriage, provided your scribbling about them doesn't create scandal. But Drake says you must have someone to direct your business affairs, at the very least. And if you won't allow him to take things in hand, well, then . . ."

Olivia closed her eyes at the unspoken but repeated topic of every conversation: *money, money, money.* Sometimes she envied people who had none to fight over.

"Drake said you really must be settled before . . . before long."

"Before I'm a crotchety old maid?" Olivia smirked.

"Let us say, more kindly, before the bloom leaves the gilded lily," her brother-in-law countered, standing suddenly behind his wife.

Dorothy started, clasping her hand to her neck.

Olivia, too, felt her breath catch but stood, determined to regain her composure. She did not want Drake in her father's study. He had no right, though he acted as if he possessed everything. Nothing could have moved her to her detested birthday ball so quickly as his presence.

"We mustn't keep our guests waiting." Olivia squeezed her sister's hand and pushed past Drake into the evening ahead.

CHAPTER THREE

MAUREEN KNEW her aunt was not one to waste words or actions, so it was no surprise that she'd set well-laid plans in motion within the hour of Mam's death.

Maureen argued that such a trip on short notice was impossible. She sputtered at the very idea that the American Colonel Wakefield might yet be willing to help them, insisted they were begging a fool's errand—a fool's irretrievable mistake. Still, she knew her aunt was right—this might well be the last night before the Orthbridges' minions pounded the door for Gavin's new toy. So Maureen numbly followed her aunt's orders, cutting bread and cheese and wrapping thick slices of roasted lamb in cheesecloth for boxed lunches.

Aunt Verna divided the gold coins, stitching some in the hem of each niece's skirt and tucking one in each girl's shoe. She placed the rest—all but one—in Maureen's purse.

"You should keep some," Maureen said, looking up from her task and wiping her hands down her apron. "I've never seen so much money. I'll not know what to do with it, and it's all foreign, beside."

"It won't be foreign once you get there, and you'll need every penny. There's the passage to be bought and more food for the trip. You can't trust the shippin' company to provide their due. This last coin—" she tucked it into Maureen's coat pocket—"you're to give to Joshua Keeton."

"Joshua Keeton? Whatever for?"

"You'll be needin' a ride to Dublin if you're to sail, won't you? He's goin' there himself, isn't he? And hasn't he agreed to meet you and Katie Rose at the crossroads beyond the hill, two hours before dawn?"

"You've already asked him, then? You were that sure of yourself—of me? And how can you trust anyone in this village?" Maureen wondered if she should be vexed.

The huff and puff left Aunt Verna's face. "Joshua Keeton is a good man—the only man I'd trust with both my nieces in the dead of night. And if you had eyes in your head, you'd see he's been taken with you since you were twelve. You could do worse, but I doubt there's a better man."

Maureen turned away, not willing to believe any man did something expecting nothing in return.

Her aunt crossed the room, taking Maureen in her arms. "You've no choice, Maureen, nor does Katie Rose. If you both stay, you're both doomed. If only one of you goes to Dublin, they'll track that one down and likely take it out on the one left. You, of all in all, should know that of the Orthbridge men. You must both go—you're best off together—and you must both live and thrive. Set your face to it, girl."

"I'm afraid," Maureen whispered in her aunt's hair. "And I'm not afraid of much."

"Do it for yourself, if you can. If you cannot, then do it for love of Katie Rose." Aunt Verna pushed flaming tendrils past Maureen's temples. "May America be good to you, Maureen O'Reilly. May every road rise to meet you, and may the good Lord hold you in the palm of His hand."

Nearly three hours before dawn, Maureen and a sleepy, bewildered Katie Rose hugged their aunt good-bye and stumbled through her dark cottage garden, out onto the moonlit road.

No candles to guide lost souls burned in the windows they passed. No dog ran to bark or give them away. Hard frost had settled on the fields, causing their boots to slip and their footsteps to echo brittle in their ears. Maureen wondered if she'd ever walk this pasture or that field again, if she'd ever sit to rest on any stone wall in Ireland.

She could not understand why Katie Rose walked along without speaking, why she allowed herself to be led so easily through the cold and dark with only a promise of going abroad. All Maureen had said to her younger sister was "Do you trust me?" And Katie Rose had simply nodded. It would not have been enough explanation for Maureen, and it nearly vexed her that it was enough for Katie Rose. How could a girl, especially a girl of thirteen, be so trusting? But, Maureen remembered, she herself had trusted at that age, and it had been her doom. *Never again. Not once.*

They were early by a good half hour, but Joshua Keeton, with his cart and his horse pawing the ground, stood patiently waiting in the cold.

"Miss O'Reilly." In the pale moonlight, Maureen could see that he tipped his hat and offered his hand to help them over the wheel. But she ignored his hand, pushed Katie Rose ahead of her, and climbed up to take the outside seat.

She wrapped her arm round her sister to keep her warm and steady and as far from Joshua Keeton as she could.

The Keeton men were not known for useless speech; Joshua's even pace and silent forward slump with traces loosely held betrayed nothing unusual in his midnight errand.

By the time gray dawn softened the sky, Katie Rose was fast asleep against her sister's shoulder, and Maureen's chin had begun to bob very near her chest.

"You'll not want to fall off, Miss O'Reilly," Joshua Keeton whispered.

The sound of a human voice jerked Maureen awake, and she shifted in her seat, adjusting her hold on Katie Rose. "Thank you, Mr. Keeton."

"It's an early ride. Once we're settled, you'll have a chance to sleep."

"'We'?" Suddenly alert, Maureen felt the cold creep through her.

"Did your aunt not tell ya? I'm sailin' too, bound to make my way in America." Joshua glanced proudly in her direction, then back to the road ahead. "When I told your aunt last week I was goin', she said you'd been waitin' to go yourself—you and your sister—until your mother passed, but to keep it to meself. 'Tis a fine and grand thing—a fresh start—good for the both of you."

Maureen felt her face flame. *She's tricked me! Did she think I'd not go alone—or that if she told me he was goin' too, I'd back out? I've half a mind to jump out of this cart and drag Katie Rose with me!*

"I mean," Joshua stammered, "I mean I only wish you could have gone sooner—for your sake, Miss O'Reilly. The good Lord bless you in your new life."

Maureen didn't know what to say. She was furious with her aunt and didn't know how to take Joshua's words—kindly, at face value, or as an insult, deep and abiding. *The good Lord's not blessed me so far, Joshua Keeton, and I'm not expectin' His ways to change in America!* So she said nothing at all, and the miles passed.

When at last the sun spread its golden orb over the horizon, she mustered a civilized tongue. "Why would you leave County Meath, Joshua Keeton? You've a good job, have you not?"

He clicked the reins and the horse stepped up. "I'm beholden to Julius Orthbridge just for livin' on his land." He grimaced as if he'd swallowed vinegar. "He's got us all under his thumb one way or another. 'Tis a shame, to be sure, but no shame to those who've no choice."

Maureen blinked, still uncertain as to his meaning. *Does he think I had a choice and made it?*

Joshua stared down the road. "I admire you for takin' your leave this way, and I'm proud to be of service, Miss O'Reilly—now, and in America."

So, there it is. A man in search of an easy woman. She didn't give Joshua Keeton the courtesy of a reply. For the sake of no other choice, she would ride with him to Dublin. But once they reached the wharf and she paid him his due in gold coin, as Aunt Verna had likely promised, she'd walk away. *I'll never leave this past if weaselin' men with tales of my sins trail me to America. I'll trust no one, least of all a man from County Meath!*

Katie Rose woke when at last they clattered over the cobbled and rutted streets of Dublin.

Maureen inhaled the sea air. Anticipation of change quickened butterflies in her stomach.

"I see the ships!" Katie Rose pointed, speaking for the first time.

"I've promised my horse and cart to a farrier near the docks. If you ladies will wait while I make the transaction, I'll—"

"No, Mr. Keeton. Thank you for the ride, but we've no mind to wait. Katie Rose and I'll go on alone. Drop us near the shippin' office, if you please." Maureen looked straight ahead but could sense the turn of Joshua's face.

"I'll not drop you alone at the docks, Maureen O'Reilly. You must wait for me."

"We'll be makin' our own way, and we'd best begin. We'll no longer be needin' your assistance, Joshua Keeton."

She felt him straighten, felt the air charged with his confusion and displeasure, but refused to look him in the face.

"I'll not—"

"You will!" She glared at him and pushed a gold piece toward him. "You've earned your gold coin, and that's the end of it." *Your fine shoulders and unruly black hair might have wormed their way into Aunt Verna's senses, but they'll do no good with me!*

Joshua, his jaw set and his eyes dark, guided the cart to a walkway across from the shipping office door. He made taut the traces and steadied the cart but did not get down, did not offer his hand to either woman as they descended. With a curt "God go with you, Maureen O'Reilly," Joshua seemed about to say more but instead picked up the coin, flipped it through the air toward Katie Rose, lifted and slapped the reins, clucked his tongue, and clattered down the wharf.

Maureen grabbed the coin from a startled Katie Rose and threw it into the back of the cart. *Take your fine baritone voice and pitch it in the sea.* With one strong spit to the back of his wagon, she gave her final good-bye to Ireland and all thoughts of Joshua Keeton.

And yet, several times over the next two weeks, Maureen wished she'd not sent the man away so hastily. For one reason or another she was not able to book passage: the ship she'd hoped to board was standing in dock in need of repair; a second ship was waiting until the full complement of steerage was booked—"Sardines in a tin," the ticket holders complained. Still, Katie Rose never protested, never questioned Maureen's decisions.

Crossing the western sea was not as easy as their aunt had believed, nor was the wait at third-rate rooming houses in Dublin cheap. Maureen spent first the gold coin in her shoe, then the one in Katie Rose's. By the time they'd bought a nightdress apiece, a comb and bag between them, the barest of lodging—a warehouse with sleeping pallets where they were locked in with others at dusk and let out at dawn—and food and tickets for a ship that would finally, truly sail, Maureen's purse was empty. They were down to two coins sewn into their hems.

To stretch the money, Maureen had bought tickets in steerage—four women to a cabin with a tiny washbasin in between.

"Aunt Verna said that God will help us through—if we trust Him," Katie Rose ventured when Maureen's spirits sank low.

Maureen smiled. She rumpled her sister's hair until Katie Rose smiled, too, but thought, *I'll not be trustin' what I cannot see.*

The crossing was storm-tossed rough, the bowels of the ship dank and putrid from vomit, urine, unwashed bodies, and voyage upon voyage with nothing but a splashing down for cleaning. The cabin doors bore no locks, and there was no privacy from drunken, leering men or curious boys.

"Here, then, let's pile our bags in front of the door, so we can at least hear if those ragtags push open in the night," the oldest of the cabinmates ordered, a stout woman with iron-gray hair greased back into a tight bun.

Maureen was grateful for someone else to take charge, if only for the night. Still, to be sure and safe, she and Katie Rose slept in their dresses and fastened cloaks, leaving them crumpled and dirty.

The next morning, after a too-salty herring and biscuit breakfast they couldn't keep down, a rousing melody of Irish pipes and drums drew the sisters to the swaying deck.

"How is it," Katie Rose, half-green, stammered, "that they're singin' their hearts out—not the least bit sick. How can they?" She dry heaved over her elbow.

"Riverboat hands, lass." A knowing voice spoke over the wind behind the girls as the man handed Katie Rose his handkerchief. "Doesn't matter if they've never set foot upon a seagoin' vessel. They've the needed cork in their legs and bellies to keep steadily afloat." He swatted the air whimsically, dismissing the musicians and the twirling, fancy step dancers. "They'll be larkin' about clear to New York, full of their own bravado, singin' up their courage!" He laughed. "Like as not they'll need it."

Maureen and Katie Rose exchanged envious glances and, clutching the back of a ship's bench for dear life, turned to make their way below deck.

In that moment a new high-stepping couple twirled to the center of the dancing ring. Spinning broad shoulders and a familiar mop of flying black curls caught Maureen's eye.

"Joshua Keeton!" Katie Rose called.

Joshua looked up, bright-eyed and laughing, and waved at Katie Rose as he spun his fair colleen.

Maureen gritted her teeth against the sudden drop in her stomach and the fury that raced up her neck. She grabbed Katie Rose's hand, pulling her quickly below deck and back to their cabin.

"Why did you do that?" Katie Rose demanded. "He's been nothin' but a friend to us, and you run from him like the plague!"

But Maureen refused to answer. She couldn't explain how desperately she wanted to leave all of Ireland and its memories behind. She had no reason to believe that Joshua Keeton would keep her secrets from America's shores—shameful secrets known by the entire village—if he could not curry the favors from her he wanted. *And surely,* she thought, *that's what he wants. Why else would he be carin' about me, about us? Why couldn't he have sailed on a different vessel?*

She kept her distance. It wasn't hard; the seasickness never left either sister, and they were rarely fit to take the sun on deck.

For that reason the simple food ration included in their ship's fare proved more than ample. What little they'd bought and stowed to supplement their meals was pilfered first by small boys and then by ship rats.

The last day, as the ship sailed through calmer waters nearing the American coast, they were simply too weary to eat.

"Will the pitchin' never end?" Katie Rose moaned from her bunk.

But by that time the pitching and rolling had truly stopped. All sailing was smooth.

"What is it, Katie Rose?"

"It's freezin' in here, and I'm just so weary of the motion. I'll be grateful to stop."

Maureen checked her sister's brow. "You've a fever. Eight days at sea and now the fever?" She thought it worse than bad luck.

"It's nothin', just a sore throat," Katie Rose assured her, sniffing, but didn't open her eyes.

"Keep her turned to the wall," the gray-haired leader ordered. "We don't want whatever she's got."

"It's a throat raw from the damp, nothin' more," Katie Rose whispered.

"Scarlet fever or influenza or raw throat—no matter. They'll not allow fever of any kind off Ellis Island. They'll send her back—and anyone catchin' it." The woman ignored Katie Rose but warned her cabinmates, "You'd all fare better on deck than in this tin can."

"Back?" Maureen could not believe her ears.

"To Ireland—in two shakes of a lamb's tail, and no regrettin'. I've heard Americans claim they're not the world's hospital, after all—that's what me brother wrote. You must stay well, strong, to make it through the medical check. They'll take no public charges on American shores."

"I'll not go back," Katie Rose whispered. "I'll not. I'll jump overboard first."

"Hush! There'll be no such talk, Katie Rose O'Reilly—never!" Maureen pinched her arm.

Katie Rose grabbed the neck of her sister's dress. Strong in her desperation, she whispered fiercely, "I heard what Aunt Verna said that night—that last night you both thought me sleepin'. I heard what she said about Gavin Orthbridge. He'll not touch me. I'll kill him first. I'll kill *me* first."

Maureen's heart nearly stopped. She had underestimated her sister. No wonder she'd never once complained; no wonder she'd never once challenged leaving everyone they'd known, everything she'd held dear, despite the trouble, the weariness of the journey. Maureen felt she'd been running uphill all night. "You knew, then?"

"I've known everythin', all along. I'm not stupid. I know about Gavin and I know about his father." Katie Rose struggled for her breath. She spoke so quietly that Maureen could hear only by placing her ear next to her sister's mouth. "I never would have done it."

❧ CHAPTER FOUR ❧

THE SHIP DOCKED at four o'clock Tuesday afternoon. By half past six, first- and second-class passengers had been treated to a medical officer's cursory glance and walked ashore.

But steerage passengers were held aboard for a trip to Ellis Island, for close questioning and a more thorough going-over. No matter the delay, no matter the sickness, there'd be no more ferries to Ellis Island until the next morning.

Rumors sped through the offended ranks during the wait: no carriers of disease and no vermin would be admitted among the poor, no immigration for anyone who might become a public charge—anyone too poor, too sick, too lame, too elderly, too deaf, too simple—and certainly no women traveling alone.

"Close, just not close enough. Ach, I s'pose the personal ailments of the swells is better than ours—venereal disease and all," groused a nearby voice at the ship's rail bright and early Wednesday morning, carrying with his foul humor the smell of sour ale and an accent Maureen did not recognize. "S'pose a bit of loose change in the pocket makes all the difference, no matter what the trouble." The man stepped closer, removing his tweed cap as if to speak to the sisters directly.

But Maureen, her instincts rising and her heart beating an unnatural rhythm, pulled the collar of her cloak higher. She turned aside with everyone on board to stare at Lady Liberty, fired by the rising autumn sun, and tucked Katie Rose into her embrace. She pointed to the statue and a bit too loudly urged her sister, "She's that lovely, isn't she?"

Maureen knew that Katie Rose, her shoulders weak and trembling from fever, was beyond answering.

The man beside Maureen took up the conversation as if it were meant for him. "Aye." He nodded toward the statue and stepped closer still, until their elbows touched. "Regal and majestic, that's what she is. Green, like she's risen straight from the sea to welcome us to her shores."

Maureen braced Katie Rose against the railing. She hoped with all her heart that the Statue of Liberty was welcoming, that the officials of Ellis Island were welcoming, that they would let them pass. But Katie Rose's fever had spiked in the night, and scarlet splotches had appeared on her neck and arms that morning. Maureen had covered them as best she could, pulling Katie Rose's shirtwaist higher round her throat. Still, she knew it would take a miracle for the officials of Ellis Island to let her sister pass. And Maureen had stopped believing in miracles long ago.

She could hardly bear to look at the magnificent skyline opposite the great statue—the skyline behind South Ferry that meant New York and all of America beyond—not if they would never be allowed to see it, to walk among its buildings.

"Are you well, then, Maureen O'Reilly?"

Maureen had not seen Joshua Keeton approach. Hearing her name spoken quietly in the familiar baritone, very near her ear, caught her off guard.

"There'll be a medical inspection, I've heard, and questions against the ship's manifest."

She could not let him see Katie Rose's splotches, could not let him call attention to them in any way. So she turned her back, keeping between them, and did not reply.

"You should have listed as comin' with me. It would have gone better for you."

What was that supposed to mean? *Are you pushin' your last chance with me, or do you mean to help?* She didn't know, and she couldn't risk making a mistake, not when they were so close.

A minute later she regretted her high hand and considered that perhaps Joshua would be willing to help them, to help her get Katie Rose off the ship and through the lines that surely awaited.

She turned, opening her mouth to speak. But Joshua was gone. No matter which way she looked, she saw no sign of him. Maureen drew a deep breath. "Well, then," she whispered, "we're on our own." *That's best. That's what I want.*

At last a strange, flat-bottomed boat—a barge, strong and big enough to carry hundreds at a time—pulled beside their ship.

"You don't suppose we're bein' made to 'walk the plank,' do you?" Maureen tried, to no avail, to tease a little life into her sister as they crossed to the barge that would ferry them to Ellis Island. The deck was so tightly packed with bodies and hand luggage that there was no place to sit, no shelter in any form; passengers stood shoulder to shoulder, front to back.

"If one takes a tumble, we'll all be in that frozen slop," a woman near Maureen fretted.

Perhaps in the cramped quarters no one will notice if Katie Rose cannot stand alone.

In only minutes they were moored before the grandest building Maureen had ever laid eyes upon. Redbrick with high, arching windows framed in white stone—something akin to towers, but fabulous beyond her imagination. She'd never been to London but doubted if anything there could be so grand.

The thrill was short-lived when they were told they must wait as an earlier barge unloaded its immigrants for processing. More than three hours later, still on their feet, still in the cold and wind, sheltered only by bodies before or behind or beside, they waited. And then it was noon, and men in uniforms streamed out the great doors.

"Where are they going?" a woman screamed, very near the end of her tether.

"They're leaving! Don't they see us waiting here?" another called, pulling her wrap tight over her head.

Maureen thought a riot stood in the offing. She didn't know what she'd do with Katie Rose, how she'd get her to safety, for her sister was sound asleep and only on her feet for being wedged between the railing and Maureen.

"Calm yourselves! Calm yourselves!" a voice with a nasal accent called from the landing, speaking English so foreign that Maureen craned her neck to see what manner of person spoke. "It's dinner, is all, and we've got a bite for you. But you must stand back so we can board! Stand back!"

Maureen dared not leave her post, but a woman nearby pulled a small box from the delivery wagon and handed it over Maureen's shoulder—a slice of brown bread, more salted herring, an apple. Maureen bit into the red apple. With juice dribbling down her chin, she retrieved the apple chunk and tried to press it between her sister's lips. But Katie Rose numbly shook her head. Maureen ate the apple herself, though it didn't sit well on the turbulence in her stomach.

By two o'clock they'd filed ashore to be tagged with their ship and manifest number, to wait yet again in an out-of-doors line. Maureen found a spot on the pavement for herself and Katie Rose; they slept, sitting back-to-back, despite the cold and biting wind. At last they were roused, allowed through the heavy doors of the imposing building, and directed to a long flight of stairs.

Doctors in uniform stood on the top landing, staring down into the maze of immigrants. Maureen felt rather than knew that they assessed each weary immigrant who climbed toward them. She did all she could to rouse Katie Rose, even pinched her to put a spark of life in her step. Ahead, she saw a young man favoring his lame left leg, and then an older woman, short of breath, pulled to the side, where officials chalk-marked large letters on their lapels. The two were pointed away from the group, and Maureen's heart sank into her shoes. She pinched Katie Rose again. Her sister slapped her hand.

"You there—one moment." A doctor, chalk in hand, reached for Katie Rose, but Maureen wriggled between them and pushed Katie Rose forward.

"How do you do, sir?" She smiled, not a foot from his face. "It's more than pleased I am to be makin' your acquaintance. How good and kind of you to welcome us to America! I'd no idea the doctors in America would be so fine and gracious." Maureen stroked his cheek in a brazen flirtation that astonished the doctor nearly as much as it astonished her. "I hope I'll be seein' you again, sir." She flashed a smile she knew would dazzle, then demurely lowered her eyes and moved forward with the orderly surge of the crowd. *Please, God, don't let him call us back,* she prayed—and that prayer was a wonder greater to her than any flirting she'd conceived.

The stairs opened into the center of a great hall. A moment of awe

28

swept through the crowd as a sea of caps slipped respectfully from heads before the gigantic American flag.

Maureen caught up with Katie Rose and placed a supportive hand on her sloping shoulder. They filed through a maze of metal railings, benches, high wire cages, and holding areas overflowing with group upon group and line upon line of jabbering humanity—some laughing self-consciously, some tearful, all crowding, talking loud enough to make themselves heard above the great din.

Maureen caught snippets of conversation, guessing at their general meaning by the inflection and tones of voices, the physical movements of hands and creases in brows. She never knew there were so many languages on the face of the earth and wondered how the people of America were able to understand one another if all these strangers with their strange words poured onto her shores.

She'd begun to rub her temples in weariness and worry when a little girl with coarse raven curls and eyes browner than any Maureen had ever seen smiled up at her. Maureen stared. The child reached out her hand. Something in that happy, trusting gesture pushed the strangeness of the din away. The little girl's open smile was infectious and sprang a return from Maureen—a smile that, this time, played naturally about her lips, pushing quibbles of fear and anxiety from the ache in her head. Refreshment seeped into her bones.

For the first time she paused and dared look forward to stepping into New York, to exploring that city of tall buildings set against the skyline opposite the Statue of Liberty—the one she'd been too frightened to more than glimpse while holding Katie Rose.

She drew a deep breath, looked about her with unveiled eyes, and suddenly wished she could understand the feminine voices two lines away—women in full, embroidered skirts—and the young men who spoke with their hands nearly as fast as they spoke with their mouths. She wondered what country they'd sailed from, how they meant to get on in America. This was, after all, the land of hopes and dreams—her aunt had said so. Her da had sworn by it.

But when she looked again at Katie Rose to share this sudden hope and saw that the clusters of scarlet splotches had sprung in a garden across her face, Maureen realized anew that they might never know.

"Chicken pox," the doctor pronounced not an hour later. "You should have reported this right away. Highly contagious."

Katie Rose looked too frightened to speak, like a small child disciplined for stealing biscuits from a crock.

"She's my sister, sir." Maureen intervened, as if that explained everything.

"How old is she?" the doctor demanded.

"Thirteen—just," Maureen hedged. "Please let us go through, sir. We won't be any trouble. I had the chicken pox when a bairn and I know just what to do."

"If you'd known what to do, young woman, you should have reported this! No telling how many have been infected from your negligence."

Maureen felt the hair on her arms prickle. "Well, she got it from somewhere, now, didn't she? She certainly didn't have it when we boarded ship! 'Tisn't like we brought the plague as a gift!"

Now the doctor did look at Maureen. He spoke evenly, and Maureen knew that flirting was out of the question. "Your display of temper will help neither of you."

"Please don't send me back," Katie Rose whispered. "I'll do anythin'. Please."

"Quarantined." The doctor marked Katie Rose's cloak and motioned for a nurse to come forward. "Chicken pox."

The nurse took Katie Rose by the arm and began to pull her away.

"No!" Maureen pulled Katie Rose by the other arm.

"Please." Katie Rose began to cry.

The nurse looked expectantly at the doctor, but he said nothing. She pursed her lips—appearing as disapproving of the doctor's callous behavior as of the girls' outburst—and took Maureen aside. "It only means that we'll keep her here in the hospital until she's well. Because she's contagious, she'll have to be in a ward with other patients with chicken pox. If all goes well, and if she has no further complications, she'll be released."

"Then you'll let her go to America?" Maureen begged.

"Then we'll see." The doctor spoke now. "She'll be eligible for further examination."

Katie Rose's eyes filled with terror, and she reached for Maureen's hand.

"I want to be here—to be present—durin' all my sister's examinations," Maureen said stoutly.

The doctor laughed. "Only if we detain you for idiocy."

The nurse's lips pursed again. "You'll have to go through, my dear. We'll take good care of your sister. Once you've settled, once she's past the point of contagion, you may come back to visit her. If she passes her examinations, she'll be free to immigrate."

"But how will I know?" Maureen persisted.

"You're holding up the line. Move along." The doctor pushed the women through, barely glancing at Maureen.

"Let me get your sister settled. I'll make sure you have all the information you need." The nurse checked the watch pinned to her uniform. "I'm going off duty soon, but I'll make certain someone from the next shift speaks with you. Is someone meeting you both?"

"No," Maureen said miserably, holding Katie Rose's clutching hand.

The nurse pulled the girls aside. "They'll certainly not let you through alone, my dear," she admonished. "Have you no one?"

"What?" Maureen could barely focus. The day and its emotions had become a murky swamp in her brain.

"The letter," Katie Rose whispered.

"The letter," Maureen repeated, as if all the world should understand completely.

"You have a letter of sponsorship?"

Maureen realized she was skating precariously. "Yes." She nodded and, unbuttoning her cloak, pulled the letter from its hiding place. "We've been invited, you see." She waved the page before the nurse, hoping she would not read it closely, hoping she would not focus on the letter's details or notice its date.

But the nurse was thorough. She snapped the letter from Maureen's hand and just as quickly copied the return address onto a new chart for Katie Rose.

Maureen tried to lift the page from her fingers, but the nurse turned aside, reading every word. "My dear, this letter of invitation was written twenty-eight years ago! And it mentions a son." She stepped back, eyeing

Maureen hard. Her action raised the eyebrows of the official in the next line. "This paper will never get you through Ellis Island," she whispered.

Katie Rose moaned, snapping the nurse to attention.

"It's all we have. I know it's good. Our father saved Colonel Wakefield's life; he's pledged himself to help us." Maureen was too old to cry but felt very near it.

The nurse shook her head. "Well, it's not my affair. You'll have to take it up with immigration." She tapped her chart with her finger. "You understand that your sister's care will not be free."

Maureen felt the room begin to spin. Beyond embarrassment, she lifted the edge of her skirt and searched for a weight, holding it up to the woman in white. "We've each a gold coin left. Is that enough?"

The nurse's eyes softened in pity. But she shook her head. "You'll need that and more. They won't let you go through empty-handed, you know." She sighed, and Maureen saw the weariness of futility settle upon the nurse. "Whatever happens later, I must get this girl to the ward now." Wrapping her arm round Katie Rose, she sternly whispered to Maureen, "But if you don't want to be sent back, I advise you to come up with a better plan than this—and quickly."

CHAPTER FIVE

MAUREEN BARELY NOTICED the succession of doctors prodding her with their tongue depressors and stethoscopes. Even the dreaded eye exam, when her eyelids were quickly flipped inside out with a wicked buttonhook in search of the fateful trachoma, seemed as nothing compared to her worry for Katie Rose.

And then a woman, a pert official, asked her, "And how do you expect to earn your living here? Do you have a job waiting for you?"

"Not yet, but I'm willin' and most able to work."

It was a question the woman aboard had warned her about. She mustn't be seen as taking work from another.

"What sort of work have you done? In the town? In the tavern?"

Maureen straightened, uncertain what the woman was asking, but fairly certain she understood the implication. "I've served seven years in domestic service, mostly as a lady's maid."

"Mostly?"

Maureen lifted her chin but felt her face flame and hoped the shame of her past did not paste itself across her brow. "I began in the scullery and then as a parlor maid. I attended the person of Lady Catherine Orthbridge of County Meath." She'd not say that Lady Catherine died a year past.

The woman seemed satisfied and motioned Maureen down the line, where she was directed to stand with a small group and await her turn yet again.

She'd not thought her nerves could be wound tighter, but when she heard women called up by turn and pounded with a barrage of questions, she thought she might snap. Most of the questions she recognized from the documents she and Katie Rose had completed as best they could before sailing from Dublin—a list of questions she'd answered with as much truth as she knew and telling as little as she thought they could get by with. She'd not considered the questions terribly important at the time but realized now that any conflicting answers might keep them both out of America. Maureen no longer cared so very much for America. But the thought of going back to Ireland, penniless and with a reputation more shamed for rejection at Ellis Island, was too much. *Joshua Keeton, if you were here now, I'd not be refusin' your help!*

"In a bit of a jam, are you, dear?" a young uniformed man whispered to Maureen in an accent so familiar that her heart raced. It could be a voice from the next county back home. "There, there now. They're a rough lot, right enough." He stood, looked around as though he was keeping an eye on the orderliness of things, then whispered again, "I couldn't help but overhear your troubles with your poor sister. A rotten piece of luck."

It was the first word of sympathy Maureen had heard since landing, and her lip quivered once, a thing she despised.

"Well, then, perhaps I can help."

"I'd be grateful, sir." Maureen could be polite. She would have been polite to the king of England if it would help Katie Rose.

"Would you, then?" He pulled her papers from her hand and looked them over. "Would you be grateful, Maureen O'Reilly?" He lingered over her name and eyed her carefully, returning her papers.

Maureen stepped back. "Is this a trick you're about?"

"No. Why, no, of course not!" He looked so offended that Maureen felt contrite.

"Beggin' your pardon. Everything's so—I don't know what to think."

"Or who to trust?" He nodded sympathetically.

"Aye, or who to trust." She sighed, glancing from side to side.

"Well, I'll tell you this: you can trust me. You're an Irish lass, for all of that, and we've got to help our own, now, don't we?" He pulled a small wad of bills from his vest pocket and passed them to Maureen as though he were shaking her hand.

She pulled back, but he pressed her palm between his two and whispered into her ear, so close she smelled his onion and cheese breath upon her cheek. "Now, not to worry. They'll ask if you have money and how much. They'll be wantin' you to have twenty-five American dollars to pass through so they know you're not about to become a public charge. I've given you thirty."

Maureen stopped pulling. "Thirty dollars?"

"Shh, then," he whispered. "I've not enough to do for everyone. Just one here and there as I can help a fellow countryman—or woman." He smiled.

Maureen did not like his smile. "I don't know what to say, sir."

"Say only that you'll make a fine American and a good friend." He squeezed her hand.

Maureen tried to decipher his meaning and her instincts—so hard to do with the desperation racing through her veins.

"You can give it back when you're through the lines or pay me back as soon as you're able. It's always good to have friends from the old country. We help one another with jobs and such. And if it comes to needin' someone to meet you or claim you're a relative, just leave that to me."

"Maureen O'Reilly!" Her name was barked by an official at the desk.

"Jaime Flynn—that's my name. Don't forget. I can send a friend round to meet you if they give you any trouble—someone to vouch for you. I'll make sure he sees you safely into the city." He winked—barely.

"Maureen O'Reilly!" The call came again, and Maureen, not knowing what to do, pulled away and stumbled toward the desk.

The man at the desk fired one question after another, checking her answers against the ship's manifest, until Maureen's head spun. When he asked how much money she possessed, she forgot about the gold coin sewn into her hem and dutifully opened her palm, displaying thirty American dollars folded into a slip of paper. From the corner of her eye, she saw Jaime Flynn raise his brow, smile again, and nod. Maureen felt a seasickness fill her belly.

Miraculously, the official seemed ready to pass her down the line and through the doors to freedom. But at the last possible moment he said, "Oh—nearly missed this," pausing his pencil over the printed form. "What is your final destination, and who is expecting you?"

Maureen swallowed hard.

"Do you have family here? Someone to vouch for you?"

"I have a letter," she stammered. The letter seemed completely foolish and impossible now.

"Well?" he demanded.

Maureen slowly handed him the letter and watched as he unfolded it, her heart pounding. In that moment two junior officials came to her interrogator with a question about another passenger; the man set the letter down and turned away. Maureen quickly stole the letter, licked her thumb, and worried the paper's edge, half-smudging and half-fraying the date in the upper right-hand corner.

Which was worse—to be sent back with an old and useless letter or to be sent back for deception? *Please,* she prayed, *blind his eyes to what I've done.*

Joshua Keeton stepped from the immigration center into the late-November sunshine. Getting through Ellis Island had been quicker and easier than he'd dared hope. Good health, a strong back, quick answers, and the requisite finances had stood him in good stead.

He stepped onto the ferry just before it pulled from the dock. He looked about but saw no sign of Maureen or Katie Rose among the passengers. Disappointed and a little unsettled, he found a seat, reminding himself that Maureen had made it clear she wanted nothing to do with him. He pulled from his pocket the rough map a fellow traveler had drawn for him, highlighting places he might find a room for the night. Long after he'd digested its information, he continued to stare at it while he prayed.

Thank You, Lord, for this new beginning in this new land. Guide my footsteps, keep my path straight, and make me a blessing to those I meet.

Joshua nodded to the Green Lady as the ferry passed her in the harbor. *Give Maureen and her sister the fresh start this good land offers and the liberty they've never known. I'd hoped to be of service to her in makin' that fresh start, thought that was what You had in mind when Mrs. Keithly asked me to watch over them. I'd hoped . . .* But he didn't finish. He looked away, shrugging the disappointment aside. He was used to forging a different path from those around him, both in his thinking and praying and in his doing. Still, he knew some honest confession was in order. *She'll not be needin' me when she has the Wakefields and all their wealth at her beck and call. And maybe that's as it should be, but I'm disappointed, Lord; I won't say I'm not.*

Just before the ferry docked against the pier of New York's Battery, he squared his shoulders and hefted his bag. *I ask that You keep her in Your care, Lord. And if she needs me, let me know.*

When the interrogator returned his attention to Maureen, he took up the letter, squinting as he read. "This letter is written on your behalf?" The official looked skeptical. "It mentions a son."

Before Maureen could answer, a short and thickly set middle-aged woman with gold wire-rimmed glasses and slate-gray hair fluffed into a soft bun interrupted. "Excuse me, Mr. Crenshaw. Nurse Harrigan asked me to see to this young lady."

"Mrs. Melkford." The official tipped his hat.

She smiled. "I see that cold has gone by the way, thanks be to God."

"As has your chicken soup. Does the trick every time."

"You let me know whenever you feel a sniffle coming on and need another dose of good medicine, and I'll cook you up another pot."

"In that case, I'm thinking I might be sick straight through the winter!" he teased.

"Then I'll see you with a crock next trip." She patted his hand. "Now, about this young woman. The Missionary Aid Society and I will vouch for her. We'll make sure she reaches her destination or finds a job, whichever we can accomplish first."

"That would be fine, but she's put forth a letter." He turned aside so Maureen wouldn't hear him, but she heard just the same. "She may be trying to pull a fast one—pinched some other fellow's letter."

"No, no, Mr. Crenshaw, it's her letter—a long story, no doubt. It will all work out in the end. You have my word for it—mine and Nurse Harrigan's."

"Well . . ." He hesitated, scratching behind his ear.

She smiled winsomely and laid a hand on his arm.

He shook his head, stamped the paper, and handed it to Mrs. Melkford. "With friends like the two of you, the woman's standing on gold." He looked hard at Maureen. "Don't make me live to regret this."

"No, sir. I won't, sir." Maureen wasn't certain what had just transpired, but she lifted her bag and dutifully followed the woman with her letter and papers, down the stairs and through a set of doors into another sea of humanity.

"Stay close beside me, dear," Mrs. Melkford ordered as she wove through piles of luggage, squirming children, and tableaux of joy and misery. "This is the waiting area for immigrants to meet their families and sponsors. And that—" she pointed across the room—"is known as the kissing post."

As if to demonstrate her meaning, a middle-aged man, dark, wiry, and heavily mustached, dashed through a gate at the end of the room, wove through a small crowd of bystanders, and whooshed into the air a woman at least his age. He twirled her twice around and kissed her lips and eyes and cheeks until Maureen thought he might eat her alive. Two children hung on to his coattails for dear life, and when he was finished kissing their mother, he tossed them high by turn. Maureen didn't need to know their names or jabbering, lilting language to envy their reunion.

"It's not always so happy." Mrs. Melkford tipped her head toward a tearful young woman just meeting her husband. By the empty baby blanket the young woman held, the child's tiny portmanteau with no child at her feet, and by her fearful looks and gesturing toward the doors through which Maureen and Mrs. Melkford had just passed, it was clear that something had gone terribly wrong.

"No." Maureen spoke to Mrs. Melkford for the first time. "'Tisn't always happy." She thought again of Katie Rose. "You've seen my sister and Nurse Harrigan, then? Can I see her? Will they let her come with us?"

Mrs. Melkford shook her head. "Goodness, no. Nurse Harrigan said your sister has the chicken pox! She's been quarantined. They won't release her until she's well. But if all goes as expected, she should be up and right as rain in a week or two at most." Mrs. Melkford nodded to this official and that, showed them her own papers as well as Maureen's, and waltzed the two of them through the doors into the biting wind and November dusk. "Come along," she chirped, half-running. "We'll want to catch that ferry!"

Maureen grabbed her arm and dragged her to a stop. "But I cannot leave this island without Katie Rose!"

"Oh, child! Have they explained nothing to you?" Mrs. Melkford wrenched her arm away.

But Maureen wasn't a child; she was a grown woman, and she was sick to death of Americans stomping on her life. *I never should have let them take Katie Rose! I'm her sister—she needs me.* She dug in her heels as the final whistle blew for the ferry.

Mrs. Melkford, stronger than she looked, jerked Maureen's bag from her grasp and headed down the planked dock. "It's up to you now!" she called back to Maureen. "If you want to stay in America, if you hope to see your sister again, you'll come with me!"

Maureen did not want to follow, but she didn't want to be left behind. Mrs. Melkford, whoever she was, had her bag, her letter—her only feeble claim to being allowed in America. Just as the dockhand was pulling up the gangway, Maureen dashed aboard, nearly knocking him over.

He swore in words familiar to Maureen, but she didn't stop. She'd heard them all in the Englishman's house and out the back door of her uncle's pub in the village. Even so, she felt the heat bathe her neck as she searched for Mrs. Melkford among the groups of passengers. A handkerchief and sheaf of papers waved through the air near the back of the ferry. Maureen followed their signal, hoping that Mrs. Melkford would be attached.

"I've saved you a seat, Maureen O'Reilly." Mrs. Melkford patted the bench beside her.

Maureen plopped close, too weary and exasperated to more than follow orders. "What did you mean, it's all up to me? What can I do to get Katie Rose out of there? When can I see her again?"

"I'll check on her next week when I come across. As soon as they're willing for her to have visitors, I'll let you know and will make sure you see her. But you'd best hope they keep her a time."

"And why should I be hopin' that?"

"Because you've got to make certain you're settled and employed, with a place to live, that you can take care of her—or that someone can. I can help you with that—the Society and me, that is."

"We've an invitation," Maureen said weakly.

"Yes." Mrs. Melkford raised her brows. "Nurse Harrigan told me about your 'invitation.'"

Maureen straightened, indignant. "It's perfectly real. My father saved Colonel Wakefield's life once. Colonel Wakefield is an officer and an honorable man—Da always said. He pledged to help Da, to help his child. He'll not let us down."

Mrs. Melkford turned her face toward Maureen and her back on the gentleman seated the other side of her. "Be that as it may, Nurse Harrigan said the letter is nearly thirty years old. Do you even know if Colonel Wakefield still lives in New York? If he's still alive?"

Maureen looked away.

"Well—" Mrs. Melkford sat back—"tomorrow is Thanksgiving Day. If your Colonel Wakefield still resides at the address on his letter, he'll surely be celebrating the feast at home with his family. We won't ring or send word; we'll just go along and see what we can learn." She shook out the letter and read. "Hmm. Morningside . . . this address is in Gramercy Park—much closer to my home in Greenwich Village than to the Aid Society. Perhaps I'd best take you home with me, just for the holiday. We'll be a mite cramped, but you could sleep on the settee in my parlor. I wonder if this could be—" Mrs. Melkford's brow creased and she bit her lip. "Oh, dear—my neighbor's grandniece. I promised her I'd come round early and help with her turkey. She's just married, and it's her first time cooking it on her own. Her mother's away, and my neighbor simply can't see well enough anymore."

Maureen could not imagine a new bride not knowing how to roast a fowl but knew it wouldn't do to say such a thing. "I can find my way."

Mrs. Melkford looked doubtful, then brightened. "I suppose that's so. If you can find your way across a vast ocean, you can manage a couple dozen New York City blocks. We're laid out on a grid, so it's simple enough." She smiled, then patted Maureen's hand sympathetically. "I'll draw a map. But we must consider the very real possibility that things will not turn out as you anticipate."

Maureen couldn't think about that now. She knew she should be grateful for help, and at least Mrs. Melkford seemed an upstanding sort of lady. "Thank you for helpin' me, mum."

Mrs. Melkford half smiled. "You'll need a job before you can afford a place to live." She lowered her voice. "Nurse Harrigan said you came with no money."

"I have money! Katie Rose and I each have a twenty-dollar gold piece Colonel Wakefield sent our da." She felt along the front of her hemline and, finding it, whispered, "They're sewn into our hems. He sent us more, but I needed it for the fare and food and—everythin'."

Mrs. Melkford looked at her steadily. "You sewed a twenty-dollar gold piece into your sister's hem?"

Maureen nodded.

Mrs. Melkford sighed. "Well, it's not enough. Even so, you might as well say good-bye to that."

"What do you mean?"

"They'll wash her clothes in the hospital, my dear." She studied Maureen, hesitated, and looked away again. "I'm sorry to say that not everyone is honorable—even in America."

Maureen groaned inwardly, knowing precisely what she meant; it was one more strike in a miserable day.

She slumped back, thrusting frozen hands into her pockets. And she felt the dollars—thirty American paper dollars—she'd completely forgotten. Surprised, she started to show them to Mrs. Melkford, about to explain about Jaime Flynn and his offer. But something about the memory made her uncomfortable; something about it felt dishonorable in its own right, and she hesitated.

When she looked up, she saw Jaime Flynn watching her from the next aisle of the ferry. He winked, tipped his hat, and turned away.

CHAPTER SIX

OLIVIA'S OCTOBER BIRTHDAY BALL had been grueling enough. But Thanksgiving marked the first major family holiday without her father and the foretaste of a long winter.

Dorothy and Drake had offered to celebrate the feast at their home, but Olivia insisted that they sit down at the Wakefield family table. She could not imagine spending their father's favorite holiday elsewhere—and Olivia knew that if Dorothy and Drake hosted the day, they would parade yet another entourage of would-be suitors before her. She craved a quiet time with those who'd known and loved her father well.

But when they waltzed through the front door, late by nearly an hour, Dorothy and Drake were not alone.

"Olivia, dear." Dorothy pressed her sister's arm in greeting. "I meant to tell you that we've compelled Mr. Morrow to join us for the day."

Olivia could not muster a smile.

Dorothy pulled her aside as the men handed coats and hats to the parlor maid. "He's a business associate of Drake's—all alone today—horrendous! I knew you wouldn't mind." She whispered, "I sent word to Cook. We all know how she hates surprises!"

"You didn't send word to me!" Olivia hissed.

But Dorothy shot her sister a warning glare as Drake introduced Mr. Curtis Morrow.

"We're so glad you are able to join us, Mr. Morrow," Olivia lied.

"It's most kind of you to invite me, Miss Wakefield. I feel I may be intruding on a family holiday." He bowed slightly. "Please allow me to express my belated condolences on the death of your father. I understand your loss was great."

"Yes, it was. It is," Olivia returned, trying to keep the irritation from her voice, wishing Dorothy would take up the conversation. "Did you know my father, Mr. Morrow?"

"I'm sorry to say I never had the pleasure."

She nodded again and looked away, relieved when Grayson, the butler, appeared at the dining room door.

"I believe dinner is served." Olivia hesitated only a moment before taking the arm that Drake offered and leading her guests to the table.

The Thanksgiving meal, which had normally included more than a dozen guests, celebrated with such joy when her father was alive, dragged into the late afternoon. Dorothy and Drake kept a lively conversation running with Mr. Morrow concerning the rising opportunities in real estate investments. The two men congratulated one another heartily on their business acumen and strokes of genius but deplored the lack of new investors willing to realize the market's potential.

Olivia silently marveled that there was no mention by Drake of the missing founder of their feast and fortunes or her father's lifelong custom of asking those around the table to share what they were especially thankful for. She sighed inwardly, supposing they'd already rejoiced in the treasures of their hearts. She resigned herself to tight smiles and polite nods when necessary, but her real appreciation was for the change of light and shadows that crossed the table as the day waned.

"You're very quiet, Miss Wakefield," Mr. Morrow observed as Grayson lit the candles.

"Am I? I beg your pardon." Olivia laid her napkin upon the table. "Perhaps I'm a little tired."

"We've overstayed our welcome." Mr. Morrow was quick to lay aside his own napkin.

"Nonsense, Curt," Drake insisted, waving him back to his seat. "It's just that Olivia has no interest in business. We've bored her."

"My apologies, Miss Wakefield." Mr. Morrow gave her his full attention. "We've been rude and neglectful. May I ask what interests you especially?"

Olivia hesitated, but Dorothy did not. "She's mad about causes, Mr. Morrow. My sister bears the weighty heart of a reformer." Dorothy smiled.

"You exaggerate, Dorothy," Olivia protested feebly.

"Not at all," Drake interrupted. "Give credit where credit is due. Olivia was a veritable pillar in last year's mink brigade with the shirtwaist workers' strike—rode in the backseat of her father's touring car in the parade and everything."

"There was more to it than that, Drake," Dorothy chided.

"Oh yes, she wrote a letter to the editor of the *Times*." He smiled condescendingly, took a sip of his wine, and set the glass down. "But I don't believe they printed it."

Olivia's fists clenched beneath the table, but before she could speak, Mr. Morrow intervened.

"I understand the women won their point. I believe I read about an hourly wage increase and a reduction in working hours."

"Too small a victory," Olivia argued.

"But you must have been proud that your efforts yielded success."

"I was not proud, Mr. Morrow," she countered, glad to disagree. "The women of the factory in question suffered much in their strike—no pay throughout the process, police and government brutality, arrests, beatings, humiliation paid for by powerful men who wanted to silence them. And in the end a paltry victory. No closed union at one of the biggest factories, no lasting 'success.'"

"But if they—"

"They, like the smaller factories that settled, desperately need a union. These women are largely poor immigrants." Olivia's righteous blood rose for the first time in months. "Their pay is not 'pin money' as the papers suggested, but the difference between food on the table and standing naked in the street."

"Olivia!" Dorothy reddened. "Your language, please."

"What did I tell you?" Drake raised his eyebrows in Morrow's direction.

But Curtis Morrow did not digress. "I confess to knowing little about the needs of New York City's garment workers."

"Then allow me enlighten you, Mr. Morrow. The owners have no reason to negotiate or properly treat their workers when they hold every ace in their poker game."

Dorothy looked as if fainting might be an option. "Mr. Morrow, please excuse my sister. She is—"

"She's quite right, Mrs. Meitland. I know practically nothing about the working poor of this city." He looked Olivia levelly in the eye. "And I should learn, now that they pay the rent and mortgages my investments depend upon."

"You own tenements, Mr. Morrow?" Olivia felt disgust rising in her throat.

"Apartment buildings, Olivia," Drake interjected. "Mr. Morrow owns apartment buildings throughout the city."

"Recently acquired," Mr. Morrow stated but shifted in his seat. "And please, Miss Wakefield, all of you, call me Curtis."

Olivia was about to speak when she felt her sister's foot connect sharply with her ankle. "Curtis is new to New York. Drake recently assisted him in some investments—real estate is simply booming in this city."

Olivia stared at Dorothy. It was the third time she'd emphasized the real estate "boom."

Drake's warning glare was unmistakable.

"And we're so glad he has joined us as our guest today," Dorothy finished graciously, meekly, and went back to her wine.

Olivia did her best to withhold judgment while she processed the trio. "Does that mean real estate is not your primary business, Mr. Morrow?"

"Curtis, please." He smiled evenly.

She did not blink.

"No—not until recently. I'm just up from Washington. It seems the literary world is bustling in New York—and that is my primary business. So I'm considering making a permanent move to your fair city." He raised his glass. "That would mean, of necessity, changes in the major areas of my life—not least of all, my investments. Your brother-in-law has been good enough to guide me in areas I know nothing about."

"And that includes the purchasing of tene—"

"Apartment buildings," Drake amended.

Dorothy coughed. "Curtis, tell Olivia about your publishing business. I know she will find that fascinating. She's something of a writer in her own right."

Curtis Morrow raised his brows appreciatively, but before he could set down his fork to speak, Grayson stood beside Olivia. "Begging your pardon, Miss Wakefield, there is a . . . a woman to see your father."

"Father?" She was taken aback. "Does she not know—?"

"What does she want?" Drake demanded.

Grayson stiffened, clearly uncomfortable speaking between his employer and Drake Meitland. "She claims to possess a letter assuring his assistance."

"Not another charity beggar!" Drake stormed. "Tell her to go away; the estate is settled."

"A letter? From Father?" Dorothy asked.

"She said it is an old letter, ma'am—an 'old obligation,' she said, to be precise." Grayson straightened, waiting upon Olivia.

But Drake threw back the rest of his wine and stood. "It's my concern; I settled the estate. I'll get rid of her." He tugged his vest into place. "Please, go on with your meal. I won't be a moment."

But when he'd left the room, silence reigned. Two full minutes passed. Grayson poured coffee.

"Who could be claiming an obligation after all this time?" Olivia wondered aloud. "Is it anyone we know, Grayson?"

"I think not, ma'am. She said her name is Miss O'Reilly. She recently arrived from Ireland—this week, I believe she mentioned."

"This week?" Dorothy gasped. "What business could Father have had in Ireland?"

"None that I know, madam," Grayson answered respectfully, but Olivia suspected from the squaring of his shoulders and pulling back of his chin that there was something he was not saying.

"O'Reilly," Olivia mused aloud. "What is there about that name that sounds familiar?"

Dorothy shrugged and bit into a morsel of apple pie, moaning in pleasure. "Father's favorite! I'm glad you had Cook make it, Livvie. It wouldn't be Thanksgiving without it!" She smiled. "But we're neglecting our guest. Please, Curtis, you were about to tell us—"

"Please excuse me." Olivia rose from the table. "Don't think me rude, but I would like to meet Miss O'Reilly."

Curtis Morrow stood.

"Drake will take care of her, Livvie; there's no need," Dorothy urged.

But Olivia was nearly to the door. As she reached it, a woman's anguished cry came from the drawing room at the end of the hallway. Olivia stopped short, feeling like a child caught spying on her elder, but reminded herself that she was mistress of the house, that if anyone should feel out of place, it should be Drake.

She mustered her courage and pushed open the drawing room door.

A flame-haired woman bent over the hearth, beating her purse upon the open fire, crying, "No! No!"

"What—?" Olivia gasped.

Drake grabbed the woman's arm and jerked her back, but she wrenched away and fell to the hearth, raising her purse to beat the fire again. It was no use; the hungry flames shot high, consuming the paper she sought to reclaim. The woman sat back, covered her face with her hands, and sobbed aloud.

"What has happened?" Olivia demanded. "Drake, what is the meaning of this?"

"He's burned the letter! He's burned Da's letter!" The woman lifted her face to Olivia's, her green eyes wide and stricken.

Drake's face reddened. "I told you I'd take care of this, Olivia."

"I don't understand. What justification can there be for such treatment of a guest in this house—ever?" Olivia stared from Drake to the disheveled woman, who could have been no older than she, and back to Drake.

But Drake, clearly working to control his fury, did not answer, and the young woman apparently could not. Olivia pushed between them and helped the woman to her feet. She felt not much more than skin and bones.

"Miss O'Reilly was just leaving." Drake spoke with authority, taking the broken woman's arm from Olivia to escort her roughly from the room.

"But what is this about a letter from Father?"

"Your father?" The flame-haired beauty turned, wrenching her arm from Drake. "Is Colonel Wakefield your father?" she nearly begged.

"Co—Colonel?" Olivia stuttered, as taken off guard by the question as she was by the woman's thick brogue. "Yes, yes—well, he was. Drake has told you that my father passed away?"

The woman's face fell and her breath caught in a sob. "Then it's true. Then it's no matter."

"What is no matter?" Olivia stepped closer, wishing to help.

"Enough of this," Drake insisted. "Miss O'Reilly has another appointment and must be on her way." He ushered her to the front door, ignoring Dorothy and Curtis Morrow, who had emerged from the dining room.

Stepping across the threshold, the woman turned again to Olivia with eyes empty as the sudden dead of winter.

Drake closed the door.

CHAPTER SEVEN

MAUREEN HAD NOT FELT the damp and raw of New York's bleak November as she'd made her way along cobbled and paved streets to the address printed on her da's precious letter. She'd felt only the warmth of hope, hope, hope beating in her chest.

But with the all-important letter reduced to ashes in the Wakefields' grate, and with nothing better than a shove and a kick through the front door, the cold seeped through Maureen's woolen shawl and skirt and chemise, right down to the chilled bones beneath her flesh and the feeble heart they covered.

The late-afternoon mist became a frigid drizzle. Shivering against the dampness that trickled down her neck, she pulled her dripping shawl over her hair, adjusting the wet, woolen weight across her shoulders. The miserable turn of the weather reflected the miserable turn in her soul.

She'd tried to prepare herself for the possibility that Colonel Wakefield, like her da, might no longer be there. She'd never prepared herself for the rough treatment of the man called Drake.

She supposed him Olivia Wakefield's husband. If so, she pitied her yet wondered that American women were so outspoken to their husbands in front of strangers. Still, Drake's actions and wishes had prevailed.

"Katie Rose," she whispered as she trudged through rain-wet leaves and muddy gutters, "what will we do now? What will become of us?"

The very whispering aloud made Maureen shiver. It gave her fear voice.

"There must be another way," she spoke louder. Those words heartened her a little, so she tried again. "Of course there's another way. There's never only one way." It sounded fine spoken into the rain, but she didn't believe it and walked a little faster—down East 20th, across Park Avenue and Broadway—as though she could outrun the inevitable.

What if I told Mrs. Melkford that I have a job—that the Wakefields gave me a job in their great house? Maureen turned down Fifth Avenue and crouched on a low stone wall beneath a tree—the first she'd seen surrounding a residence more modest than the Wakefield mansion. Dusk settled heavily. *She'll know I've lied when I come back with no money and no place to live. They'll not let me have Katie Rose if I've no job.*

Maureen buried her head in her hands. She would have sobbed if she'd been able to muster the energy. But she was too worried to sob, too frightened at the thought of losing Katie Rose to Ireland and Gavin Orthbridge.

When she lifted her head without inspiration, the night had truly come. Without a map she'd be fortunate indeed to find her way back to Mrs. Melkford's.

Just keep walkin', Maureen O'Reilly. You must have come halfway. Washington Square . . . Washington Square . . . It's bound to be straight ahead, and West Fourth is just a bit from there.

Twice she tripped, the weight of her sodden skirt stretching inconveniently over her boots. A sudden weariness made her clumsy, but she pushed that away, willing herself forward.

By the time she'd traipsed another four blocks, she began to slow.

As the rain had slackened, fog had settled in across the ground, as thick as any Maureen remembered over the lakes of Ireland. But suddenly the scene changed. In one swift breath, as though a magic fairy's wand swept the night, lights, evenly spaced along the street, created a glow like stars hanging above her reach. Maureen gasped. She'd never seen anything so bright and beautiful, so close at hand.

She looked up and down Fifth Avenue, as far as she could see, through the fog that lay beneath her waist. She'd seen electric lights, but never like this—not out-of-doors and framing a street. "It's a sign—a sign that somethin' good will come." She dared say the words.

Maureen stood and shivered all the more, realizing she was soaked through. She stuffed frozen hands into her pockets, hoping to warm them, and felt something crumpled there. Digging deep, she pulled out the bills the man, Jaime Flynn, had given her. She wondered if it was enough to rent a flat, to buy food, and how long it could last in New York. She unfolded the bills from the paper that enclosed them.

Something was written on the paper. She stepped beneath a streetlamp and in the pool of electric light held the paper close. "'Darcy's—34th Street, Manhattan,'" she read aloud.

"What did he say?" Something about knowing of a job and a friend—a friend who would act as a relative? Maureen frowned, her heart quickening. *Who is Darcy—his friend? What sort of job did he mean?*

Fear and hope alternated in her mind. He didn't seem like someone she should trust. *His eyes held that lustful light that kindles in men's eyes—not quite like men of Lord Orthbridge's cloth, who've nothin' and none to fear, but men who know how to take possession of what they want.* She swallowed. *But he offered to help. And the Wakefields, though they surely have aplenty, refused.*

She dared not presume that Mrs. Melkford would produce a miracle— she'd only helped because Maureen was so certain things would work out with the Wakefields. *No. I must convince Mrs. Melkford that I've worked it all out, that Katie Rose and I have a certain future and are in good hands.*

Maureen tucked the paper and the bills inside her purse and drew in her breath. *But what if this man Darcy wants references? Everyone wants references—hard work, character, length of term.* She pondered the improbability of surviving an interview without them.

"Well," she said aloud, "I'll just have to get references, then, won't I?"

But what if he wants what I'm not willin' to give? What if he's like Lord Orthbridge?

Maureen cringed at the thought. *But what choice do I have? If I go back to Ireland, I've nothin', and Katie Rose is lost. If I stay here, at least we have a chance for a different life—eventually. 'Tis a big country.*

She sighed, hoping she was only borrowing trouble that she'd never have to face. *Still, I've done what I had to before to survive and care for my family. Whatever it means, I'll see it through.*

Maureen closed her purse decisively, the click of the clasp sounding too loud in the lonely street.

❧ CHAPTER EIGHT ❧

"AT LAST! I was ready to telephone the Wakefields!" Mrs. Melkford exclaimed. "They made you walk in this weather?" But she didn't give Maureen time to explain. "You must get out of these wet things, child! Oh, I should have never let you go alone. The idea!"

Maureen could not remember having been fussed over, could not have said that anyone had ever drawn a hot bath for her, rubbed her hair dry before the stove, or made her sit while she was served a steaming bowl of turkey soup that tasted so delicious, so nourishing. No matter that the long day had proven disastrous, no matter that her nerves had been stretched taut and wound tight as a child's top, she giggled at the kindness and grandmotherly warmth of Mrs. Melkford.

"And I'd just like to know what is so funny, Maureen O'Reilly?" Mrs. Melkford stood in the midst of her small kitchen, her nightcap askew and her hands clamped to her hips.

"I'm sorry—truly, I am." Maureen coughed to constrain her giggles and wiped a laughing tear from her eye. "It's just that you're so good to me—so very, very good, and I love the pleasure of it."

Mrs. Melkford colored in return. "Well, it's nice to be appreciated, but I'd prefer that you'd been better treated. The thought of sending a young woman out alone after dark, let alone this time of night, is appalling—and in such weather! Whatever could they have been thinking?"

Maureen sobered.

"What is it, child? What did they say?"

Maureen drew a deep breath and spun a lie. "The comin' home in such weather was fully my fault. I told them I was stoppin' nearby."

Mrs. Melkford opened her mouth to speak, but Maureen rushed on.

"I didn't want to seem a burden the first time I met them. I wanted them to understand that I can manage on my own, with just a little help."

Mrs. Melkford's eyes softened and she took Maureen's hand. "But you can't manage alone, my dear."

"As soon as I've begun a proper position, everythin' will be fine."

"They offered you a place, then? In service? In their home?"

Maureen shook her head. "I told you I don't want to go in service—never again."

"But that's the occupation you gave for the ship's manifest. It's one of the best paying, most secure jobs a single woman in New York can take. Your lodging, your meals are provided, and the pay is—"

"No. No, I won't do it." Maureen could not keep her voice from rising. "I must provide a home for Katie Rose. I can't do that if I'm housed in the servants' quarters of some great house. And I was given an address—an address for a position."

"Oh, that's something, at least." Mrs. Melkford poured them each a cup of tea. "What is the position? Where are they recommending?"

Maureen opened her purse and offered the paper Jaime Flynn had given her. Mrs. Melkford squinted at the paper. "'Darcy's, 34th Street, Manhattan.'" She frowned.

Maureen held her breath, hoping Mrs. Melkford would confirm the safety of the area.

"Darcy's Department Store," she said, tapping the paper. "That's just off the old mile-long shopping district." She stirred her tea, took a sip, and placed her cup in its saucer. Then she brightened. "I suppose that's all right!"

"Department store?" Maureen didn't know the term.

"Yes—oh, it's like a group of shops, but all in one very large store. Ladies' hats and gloves and shoes and day wear and undergarments. Jewelry and linens, children's clothing, even some things for men—all under one roof."

"I've always wanted to work in a shop." Maureen could not believe her fortune. Perhaps Jaime Flynn was a good man, as good as his word, after all.

"It's hard work, mind you," Mrs. Melkford cautioned. "On your feet ten, twelve hours a day, running to and fro and waiting on customers—not really good for a woman's health. And with the Christmas season upon us, the work will be ferocious."

But it seemed wonderful to Maureen. "I've worked as a lady's maid, and in service before that, I was on call day and night, with only a half day off on Sundays."

"The pay is not much, and they'll expect you to dress well—respectably and somewhat fashionably—to represent the store."

Maureen's heart fell. "I've only these things I came in."

"Did you tell the Wakefields that?"

"No, I couldn't." Maureen drew in but honestly said, "I couldn't bear to say such a thing."

"A little pride is understandable, my dear, but it well may be your undoing." She stood and brushed off the crumbs from their late supper. "Well, at least we can do something about that. The Missionary Aid Society has charity bundles—cast-off shoes and clothing and the like from society matrons. They're not very practical, but we'll likely find something suitable among them." She eyed Maureen's figure critically. "You're a tall one, but there's not much meat. We can make do."

Maureen sighed. It was more, by far, than she'd expected.

"I suppose Monday's soon enough to apply. That gives us a day or two to fit you out." She placed the dishes in the sink. "Are they expecting you tomorrow?"

"The shop?"

"The Wakefields. Are they expecting you to move in with them tomorrow?"

Maureen hesitated.

"They are expecting you to live with them, aren't they? At Morningside? Gramercy Park is fourteen or so blocks from Darcy's, but you're young; you'll have no trouble with that. You'll not make enough to live on your own, let alone to support your sister, you know."

"No, no of course not."

"Sunday? Monday?"

"They'll not be expectin' me before Monday." Maureen checked her clothes to see if they were dry. She couldn't bear to look into Mrs. Melkford's eyes and lie outright. *And after all, I only said they're not expectin' me before then. I didn't actually say they're expectin' me at all.*

"Well, I'm just as glad to have you here for a few days more." She patted Maureen's hand. "Henry and I never had children of our own, and I do enjoy you girls." She straightened to the business at hand. "The Society's running on light duty through the weekend, thanks to the Thanksgiving food donations from churches and donors. I'll not be needed there before Monday. We can outfit you, and you can rest up a bit before your big day. That will surely give the Wakefields time to contact Darcy's owners and clear your way—unless they gave you a letter of reference to present directly." Mrs. Melkford tipped her head. "Did they?"

"Did they?" Maureen repeated.

"Did they give you a letter to present to Darcy's?" Mrs. Melkford repeated patiently.

"No, but—I suspect you're right. They'll send word round."

"Hmm. Yes, I suppose that is how they'd manage things. Though it would be nice to have something in hand when you go." Mrs. Melkford smiled tentatively. "Well, I imagine they know best."

Maureen sighed in relief. She knew she should feel shame and remorse for misleading Mrs. Melkford. She knew she should be worried about Katie Rose and all that lay ahead. But for now, she could rest and sleep, knowing no harm would come to her while under Mrs. Melkford's watchful eye.

"Yes," she breathed. "Oh yes, I'm sure they do."

It was a small matter for Maureen to wait until the clock bonged twelve and until she was assured of Mrs. Melkford's even breathing, of her deep sleep. Maureen rose from her place on the settee and crept on bare feet to Mrs. Melkford's desk, turned up the lamp, and twisted the small brass key, left trustingly in the desk lock. Inside the drawer she found the impressive Missionary Aid Society letterhead—letterhead entrusted to Mrs. Melkford's care and for her use on behalf of the society.

In her best hand, the hand tutored by Lady Catherine herself, Maureen wrote a fine letter of recommendation for the recently immigrated Maureen O'Reilly—not glowing, but credible and substantial, detailing her excellent character and past service to Lady Catherine Orthbridge of County Meath, Ireland. She signed the letter with a modest flourish, *Mrs. Florence Melkford.*

❖ CHAPTER NINE ❖

THE DOWNSTAIRS CLOCK struck twelve, then one and two. Olivia punched her pillow twice, adjusted her comforter, and turned to her other side, but it did no good. Each time she closed her eyes, the stricken face of the O'Reilly woman rose up before her. She saw again the light fall from luminous green eyes—as though a sharp wind extinguished a brightly flaming candle.

And then she thought of Drake—red-faced and obstinate—never giving the explanation she'd demanded, saying only that the woman was a temptress, trying to wheedle an inheritance to which she was not entitled.

Olivia acknowledged that Curtis Morrow and Dorothy had tried valiantly to keep the conversation going, but she'd been too furious to participate. The moment Olivia begged excuses, the party ended, to the apparent relief of every member.

But Olivia had not retired to her room. After closing the front door upon her guests, she'd stepped immediately into the drawing room and searched the fireplace grate for some remnant of the woman's destroyed letter—a letter that she'd dared hope was from her father. To see his words on paper this day would mean the world, a reason for thanksgiving, no matter the outcome.

Stirring the ashes of the still-smoldering fire, she'd found nothing. Disappointed, she'd just replaced the poker when from the corner of her eye she caught the edge of a page, scorched but unburned, beneath the back end of the grate. She'd grabbed tongs from tools stored inside the screen and gingerly, hoping it would not crumble, pulled the stray piece to the far side and across the hearth.

There was little writing unscathed by the fire. Even the legible bit was browned, as though a pot of Earl Grey had been spilled across its surface. She'd blown ashes from the page and carried the scrap to the lamp, holding it close.

Olivia had squinted, trying to read. No sentence was complete—only word fragments remained. But the script was even, the penmanship nearly perfect, except for a backward cut in the tail of the letter *f*—a telltale sign of her father's fine hand and the cause of the catch in her breath. She'd smiled, holding the paper near her heart, and, biting her lip, turned out the lamp.

It was enough. It didn't matter in that moment that she could not read the letter, did not know its intent. This small scrap was a much-needed gift.

"Thank you, Miss O'Reilly," she had whispered into the darkening room. "Whoever you are, whyever you came, you are my angel this day."

But now, as the clock struck three, Olivia threw back the comforter and sat up in bed, still as wide awake as she'd been at ten. She swung her feet over the bed's edge and pushed cold hands through tangled ropes of hair. She wished for the hundredth time that she knew Miss O'Reilly's first name, how she came by her father's letter, and what it meant to her.

She was so distraught, so hopeful of finding Father. Olivia slipped her feet into her bedroom shoes. *What did she want from him?*

The burned scrap of paper bore bits of phrases that she'd been able at last to decipher: *firstborn* and *passage* and *new life*. But she had no idea what those words meant, what her father intended, who he could have been writing about or to. *Did she say it was "Da's letter"? Did she mean her father's letter? Or that the letter came from my father? She surely doesn't think we have the same father!* Olivia shook her head. *How can I know what she meant?*

That the woman was desperate, Olivia had no doubt. But Drake's implication that the pitiful Miss O'Reilly was a fraud and a swindler seemed absurd.

She knew from surety of the letter's handwriting that it must have been written some years before, when her father was a younger, stronger man. The very fact that Miss O'Reilly had referred to her father as "Colonel Wakefield" was telling—he'd not gone by his military title in all the years of Olivia's memory. *She could not have known him then. She looked younger than I. What made her come now?*

Drake was right; she sounded "just off the boat" with her thick brogue.

And her clothes . . . Olivia raised her brows in the dark. *That heavy woolen skirt and shawl—she's not been in New York long.*

"O'Reilly" niggled at the back of her brain. *Where have I heard that name?*

She could almost hear her father saying the name aloud, almost see him form the *O* with his mouth and playfully imitate an Irish brogue, but not for years and years. She held some vague recollection of sitting on his knee—she could not have been more than four or five—and rummaging through his desk drawer, playing with a wooden box she'd found there. A box that smelled of Christmas, and inside it a leather pouch. She remembered turning, seeing her father make the *O*—but she could not remember the story that accompanied it.

Olivia closed her eyes, trying to recapture that long-ago picture. She opened them suddenly. "His war buttons," she whispered to the moon. "His Civil War buttons."

She wrapped her dressing gown round her shoulders and padded down the hallway to her father's cold study.

White moonlight poured through the arched window behind his desk, illuminating stacks of books, the literary busts, the Persian carpet spread across the floor. Olivia turned the brass switch of the desk lamp, turned the small brass key in the drawer, and pulled. She smiled, feeling the mission and delight of a snooping child.

There, in the back of the center drawer, was the small cedar box. The moment she lifted the lid, her nostrils appreciatively drew in the memory of Christmases past, of happy days spent in this room. She pulled the leather pouch from its home and poured its contents onto the blotter. She could still see her father polishing those buttons as he mulled things over in his mind—a habit she'd come to love. More than a year had passed since they'd felt the soft cloth. Some were a bit faded, not quite tarnished, yet when she moved them, they winked at her in the lamplight.

Before dawn, Olivia, fingering the buttons as her father had done before her, had recaptured from her memory bits of the story—something about an Irishman who'd taken a bullet in her father's place.

She remembered another occasion when her father had mentioned an O'Reilly. She'd been paging through the family photograph album and had asked him why beautiful Aunt Lillian had never married. He'd not answered directly but had muttered, "I should have been the brother to Morgan O'Reilly that he was to me. Lillian deserved that and more."

Morgan O'Reilly. But that was all Olivia could remember, and she'd no idea what he'd meant or if the two O'Reillys were connected.

There's a way to find out.

She opened the glass doors of the second bookcase by the fireplace and ran her fingers over the Moroccan leather volumes, tracing the gold leaf inscriptions on their bindings. Neither she nor Dorothy had been privileged to read their father's journals. He'd not forbidden his daughters; privacy was simply understood. After his death they had agreed to leave them in his study, intact.

But that was before Miss O'Reilly. Were Father alive, he would honor any obligation—even an old one. As his heirs, Dorothy and I are bound to honor that as well.

Though the moon still cast its halo round the busts of the literary trio, Olivia returned to her room and washed and dressed in the pale lamplight. She freshly braided her hair, leaving it in a long rope over her shoulder, slipped back down the hallway, locked the door of her father's study, and took down the first volume.

❖ CHAPTER TEN ❖

By Sunday morning Olivia had read through her father's teen years and into his early twenties. She found his first mention of Morgan O'Reilly two months before South Carolina fired on Fort Sumter.

> *February 15, 1861*
>
> *What now? Our fool groomsman, that strapping Morgan O'Reilly of County Meath, Ireland, has professed himself in love with Lillian, has dared ask Father for her hand in marriage. Of course, Father refused and sent the leech out. He'll be replaced as soon as we find a suitable groom. But Lillian is beside herself with grief. The notion of her marrying an Irish off the boat is absurd. And yet what is more absurd is that she's come begging me to intercede with Father and Mother on their behalf, insisting she truly loves this man. She begged me to make Father relent—as if such a thing were possible! They're both mad.*

Olivia winced, finding her father's words uncharacteristically harsh. Then she gasped when almost immediately she read of her aunt's diagnosis from the family doctor: "consumptive and failing."

In little over a month Lillian was moved to a sanatorium, but not before renewing her plea that her brother intervene with their parents.

> *March 25, 1861*
>
> *She claims she's told Morgan everything and that he still wants to marry her, that she wants to marry him. I can well imagine he does—with visions of inheritance dancing over her deathbed! I hate*

to break her heart, but I can't in good conscience encourage this travesty.

Before Lillian had forgiven her brother's refusal enough to write him, President Lincoln called for seventy-five thousand Union troops. Neither Douglas Wakefield, the strongest member of a long-standing abolitionist family, nor Morgan O'Reilly, who even her father admitted had embraced the freedom America offered him, waited for the draft.

Olivia turned the pages of another year and then another, shaking her head. If her father had imagined that soldiering would relieve him of his sister's iron will or her pleas, he was sadly mistaken.

May 21, 1863

Lillian's letter came today, begging me again to watch out for her Morgan, telling me that she's asked the same of him—to treat me like the brother she hopes I'll be to him one day. I wish to God the man had been assigned to another regiment. It puts me in a tight situation. I received a letter from Father last week, saying that Mother is beside herself with Lillian's decline in health, exacerbated, they're certain, by her pining for O'Reilly. Father suggested, in thinly veiled jest, that I put the man in the line of fire—let Lillian mourn her fallen hero and be done.

July 1, 1863

I am ashamed to write this. For obedience to Father, who'd written again, and love of Lillian—misguided though it was—I nearly sent O'Reilly to the front lines yesterday in a plan that would have put David's conspired murder of Uriah to shame. But for the onslaught of paperwork suddenly demanded of me, I might have done.

This morning, just after dawn, the Confederates surprised us, first with snipers, then rousing us with their bloodcurdling Rebel yell. Before we could muster troops, they were upon us. An explosion near my tent knocked me senseless. I was just gaining my feet when O'Reilly plowed into me, covering my body with his, taking a minié ball in the leg and a grazing in his chest, both surely meant for me.

Even now, he lies in the surgeon's tent. I've pleaded for the saving of his leg, but it will be a feeble leg at best. God forgive me!

July 9, 1863
A week has passed since O'Reilly's surgery. He's barely conscious, in and out, and weak—not a good sign. He's lost much blood, and the infection has spread. The doctor does not believe he'll rally.

I've misjudged the man. We've spoken twice during his conscious hours, and his only thought, his every hope, is for Lillian's good. If Morgan lives, I pledge upon my life that this man is my brother. I will do all in my power to persuade Father to give him Lillian's hand.

Olivia skipped ahead, and her heart broke as she knew it would. Aunt Lillian died in a sanatorium, alone—apart from her family—a year before the war's end.

Morgan O'Reilly survived but never again saw the dying woman he loved. Even after saving their son, Morgan was treated worse than an enemy by Douglas and Lillian's parents and blamed for Lillian's death. Because she'd loved him? Because he was poor? Because he was Irish? In a family of abolitionists—a family determined to fight for human rights and freedom?

Olivia closed the journal and returned it to the bookshelf. It was a side of her father and family she'd never known, and she didn't know how to bear its weight.

She barely remembered her grandparents. They'd lived north of the city, and her father had not fostered a close relationship between them. Perhaps this was why. She shook her head. *It's too harsh, that Aunt Lillian was denied the only love offered her.*

But Olivia knew such contrariness was not only possible, it was accepted business every day in New York City. Prejudice and class systems had not died with the war.

The downstairs clock struck eight. Olivia had barely time to dress for church. But she couldn't push the story from her mind. *What became of Morgan O'Reilly, and how does Miss O'Reilly fit into the puzzle?*

Olivia wanted only to return to her father's study and journals, so she was more than vexed to learn that Dorothy and Drake had invited Curtis Morrow to join them in their family pew, then to spend Sunday dinner and half the afternoon with them.

"How could you invite him again, after that scene at Morningside?" Olivia hissed from the side of her mouth, eyes on the pulpit ahead.

"Why are you so rude?" Dorothy returned beneath her breath. "We're only entertaining him."

"With no ulterior motive?" Olivia folded her hands in her lap but would have liked to cross her arms.

"Yes, of course there's a motive. Drake and I both hope you'll fall madly in love with him, and then we can stop this charade!" Dorothy pretended to pout. "You can't imagine how tedious it is, inviting every eligible bachelor in New York to dinner. If you'd simply pick one, we could all get on with things."

Olivia's mouth formed a grim line.

Dorothy smiled. "Stop being such a fussbudget." She pinched her sister as the congregation rose for its call to worship. "What better things do you have to do?"

But Olivia could not tell her sister that she'd begun the diaries. Even she felt she was treading on forbidden territory. Still, her heart told her their father would approve. She couldn't help thinking there was something that he'd want her to do. But she didn't know what. Not yet.

❖ CHAPTER ELEVEN ❖

FOR THE HAPPINESS and laughter the two women shared, for the delights of stories and kitchen, of hearth and home, Monday came too quickly.

Maureen tugged her lawn shirtwaist, with the smallest of stains upon its embroidered cuff, beneath her navy woolen skirt. She buttoned the matching jacket—secondhand but new to her, altered by Mrs. Melkford's pinning and her own needle to fit her figure perfectly.

Mrs. Melkford stepped back and clasped her hands with all the pride of a loving mother. Maureen pinned the neat hat she'd fashioned from bits and pieces in the bags of cast-off clothing over her curling, upswept hair. When she gazed in the looking glass, she felt for the first time as she imagined a princess might feel, going out into the world, blessed by mother and priest. But when she took up her purse, the hold and hiding place of her forged letter, she felt as though something foreign and dirty mucked her boots and soiled her jacket. She looked twice in the glass to make certain nothing showed across her cheek.

Could she have stayed and worked with Mrs. Melkford in her kitchen forever, Maureen would have been more than content. But she could not ask. *Everythin' for Katie Rose and myself depends on this job. I've spun too many lies for the sake of securin' stability and a home for us; I daren't go back now.*

"Everything will go well, my dear; you'll see. You look the perfect American." Mrs. Melkford brushed a stray thread from Maureen's sleeve and shook her head. "Oh, my. It does not do to get so attached to you girls. You come and go, and we old ladies never see you again."

Maureen caught Mrs. Melkford in a quick embrace before hefting her carpetbag. "I could never forget you nor your kindness. I'll come to you again and again once I'm settled. I promise."

"Stuff and nonsense. You'll be too busy with your job and sister and the Wakefields—all as it should be. But I'll see you next Saturday, and we'll go together to see how your Katie Rose is doing. If they release her, well and good. If they don't, perhaps they'll let you see her. And I expect to see you in church on Sundays—you mind that." She looped the button beneath the collar of Maureen's coat. "Now be off with you, child." Mrs. Melkford hugged her again quickly and closed the door.

Determined not to look back, Maureen drew a deep breath and covered the two blocks to the trolley stop. Reading Mrs. Melkford's directions, she smiled. The dear lady had detailed everything—from the cost of the trolley ride right down to turning in the front door of Darcy's Department Store.

Despite her nervousness and the regret that nipped her heels, Maureen loved the trolley ride—*a miracle in the midst of the street*—but her breath caught as she stepped from the car. Darcy's sign stood out in great black letters against its storefront, which covered most of the bustling Manhattan block. *How many hundreds of things can one of these department stores possibly sell that they're housed in a place so huge and grand?*

The flush of confidence she'd felt upon leaving Mrs. Melkford fell away, and all the worries of looking old-fashioned, provincial, and fully Irish swam like minnows in her stomach. She shifted the carpetbag clasped between her palms, sure she looked thirteen and poor and shamed all at once. She wished mightily for the safety of Mrs. Melkford's kitchen and nearly turned back.

But her feet carried her forward, and when she reached the plate-glass door and passed through, she caught sight of a tall, redheaded woman reflected in a large mirror on the far wall—someone dressed as neatly and fashionably as the women clerking behind the counters and wearing the hat she'd fashioned herself. Tentatively Maureen set her bag at her feet and touched the feather near her temple, just to be certain she was truly that woman.

"May I help you, madam?" a clerk in a slim skirt, white shirtwaist, and dark jacket asked, just as if Maureen were there to buy something, as if she could buy something.

But Maureen was dazzled by the sheer size of the store, by its counters of gloves and rows of hats and displays of ruby brooches and sparkling earrings and watches. Each way she looked, there was more to see and more of everything in the world than she had ever dreamed. Maureen clasped her throat and swayed slightly.

"Are you all right, madam?" The clerk reached her hand to steady Maureen.

"Yes, yes, thank you, miss. A bit warm, I am." Her brogue came thicker than usual.

The clerk drew back and sniffed.

Maureen sensed the snub and straightened. "I'm here to apply for a shop position."

The clerk smiled condescendingly. "I believe there are no sales positions available at this time."

"I've been referred." Maureen refused to act cowed, though she felt it entirely. "By the Wakefield family and Mrs. Melkford of the Missionary Aid Society." She had no idea if those names would mean anything to the woman but thought they sounded imposing.

"The Wakefield family?" The woman blinked, looked momentarily uncertain, turned on her heel, and whispered to an older woman behind the nearest counter. Both women scrutinized Maureen from head to foot. Maureen stared boldly in return. Now was not the time to falter.

"You'd best come with me," the second woman said, not pausing to see if Maureen would follow.

But Maureen, grabbing her bag, did follow, through a maze of counters, clear to the back of the store. They stopped before a wall, and Maureen wondered if the woman had lost her senses, until the wall opened, revealing a tiny room with a man inside.

"Fourth floor, Eddie." The woman stepped inside the minuscule room, then said impatiently, "Are you coming?"

"Yes, yes, of course." Maureen stepped into the tiny room, feigning understanding.

The young man swung a lever; a caged door closed. He pushed a button, and the wall slid shut before her. Maureen gasped as immediately the tiny room jolted and jerked. She felt as if the floor might be falling beneath her feet. She grasped the wall, feeling the blood drain from her head and her stomach plummet to her toes.

The woman and the young man glanced her way, exchanged a quiet snicker between them, and turned their faces toward the gate. She saw the woman turn slightly, mouth "greenhorn" to the man called Eddie, and he grinned again.

Maureen clenched her jaw.

Suddenly the little room stopped, jerked, and jolted once more. Eddie pulled back the accordion gate, and the wall opened before them. "Fourth floor, ladies," he announced.

The clerk walked out, her head high. When Maureen felt certain the tiny room would no longer move, she followed, straightening her skirt. The young man winked appreciatively, and Maureen felt the heat rise in her face.

"It's an elevator, that's all," he whispered. "Nothing to worry." And he winked a second time. Maureen fastened her eyes straight ahead and quickened her step.

The hallway opened into a series of rooms. As they passed open doors, Maureen glimpsed men and women bent over long ledgers with pens in hand, and others hunched or sitting straight before a half-dozen metal machines that shouted *clackety-clack* as their operators punched raised buttons. Farther down the hallway they passed a room of tailors, straight pins between their lips and cloth measures round their necks. She heard a more familiar hum from somewhere beyond, and though she couldn't see them, she envisioned treadle sewing machine operators—something modern but familiar from her days at Orthbridge Hall.

At last they came to a closed door. The woman knocked and, not waiting for a reply, walked in, Maureen at her heels.

A graying and middle-aged man with a loosened tie hanging over a paunch stomach sat behind a desk, banging away on one of the *clackety-clack* machines Maureen had seen through open doors.

"Well?" He didn't look up.

"Excuse me, Mr. Kreegle; this girl says she's come with references." The woman spoke loud enough to be heard.

The man barely glanced at Maureen, never breaking rhythm on the machine. "Send her to Bert."

"Not those references, Mr. Kreegle." The woman fidgeted. "The Wakefields sent her—and some missionary society woman."

The clacking stopped. The man studied Maureen, his eyes lighting on her carpetbag.

Maureen felt the warmth shoot up her neck but lifted her chin and set her bag squarely at her feet, as if it was perfectly proper to apply for a shopgirl position with all her worldly goods in tow.

"You can go, Mrs. Gordon." He leaned back in his chair as the door closed. "You say the Wakefields sent you?"

"Yes, sir, for a sales position."

He looked doubtful.

"The Wakefields of Morningside, sir."

"A bit out of their line, I'd imagine." He frowned, looking her up and down but resting his eyes in places that flustered Maureen.

"I'm a friend of the family," she lied and felt the heat rise up her neck again. "Our fathers were friends." That felt more natural.

"I see." But clearly he didn't. Still, he pulled a printed form from his desk drawer. "Fill out this application and bring it back tomorrow."

"I could bring it back today," Maureen offered quickly.

"Eager little thing, aren't you?" He grinned. Maureen hated his grin.

"It's just that I need to begin, sir, to establish my employment," she stammered.

"Just off the boat?"

Maureen thought she'd best be clear, lest she lose her nerve and the opportunity to speak with someone in authority. "My sister has been detained at Ellis Island until I can provide proof of my ability to care for her." *No need,* she thought, *to mention the chicken pox.*

"I see." He leaned farther back and swept his eyes over her again. "Is she, by any chance, as good a looker as you?"

Maureen shifted her purse to her other hand. "I'll need a letter statin' guarantee of employment and my wages. I'll need to earn enough to live on and to support us both."

His brows arched. "Bold, too."

Maureen astonished herself with her boldness.

"Sales clerking's not the highest-paying job." He stood and walked clear around Maureen, eyeing her up and down, then leaned against the desk, bringing his height more in line with hers, his eyes close to her face.

"There're jobs that pay better. Some jobs pay much better." He smiled and moved closer, pulling a tendril from her upswept hair to her neck.

Maureen stepped back, but he stepped forward again, until she pressed against the wall.

"I want to be a shopgirl. I've always wanted to work in a shop." Her nerve was fading fast and her brogue thickening.

He leaned closer, almost smirking. "A shopgirl?"

She shoved her purse between them, pulling out the letter with Mrs. Melkford's signature. "You see, Mrs. Melkford of the Missionary Aid Society knows I've come, and she's written this letter of recommendation."

He hesitated but took the letter, running his eyes over the page.

"And I'll be seein' the Wakefields this evening. They'll be eager to know who carried out their wishes so quickly."

He stopped smiling, seemed to reconsider, and stepped back. "Sit down." He pointed to a chair against the wall. "Fill out the application. I'll have one of the girls start you on the floor."

"Do you have a pencil, please?" Maureen regained a measure of composure. "And my letter of employment. I'll be needing that."

"Stop by before you're through for the night; I'll have it then."

She straightened.

"Never mind. I'll send it to you on the floor." He lit a cigarette, threw the saving, damning letter on a pile of correspondence, and went back to punching buttons on the machine.

Shaken, Maureen took up the pencil. She carefully completed her application, boldly printing the Wakefields' address as her place of residence and Mrs. Melkford as her secondary character reference.

By midday, Maureen had been given a tour of the store and cloakroom by a junior clerk, a rundown on company rules and regulations as they affected salesgirls by the floor supervisor, and a station as something of an apprentice beneath a weary clerk named Alice in the department of ladies' hats.

Maureen didn't know if her placement was a random choice on the part of Darcy's staff or because they'd noticed her smart, deep-blue hat on the way in. She hoped the latter. Regardless, she was determined to make a good showing—a hard worker and a personable, fashionable salesgirl.

"What do you mean you can't read the prices?" Alice snapped when Maureen made her first sale. "Don't you read and write?"

"Yes, surely!" Humiliated, Maureen dropped the sales pad and pencil and whispered as she retrieved them from the floor, "It's just that I don't know American money yet." How had she not thought to ask Mrs. Melkford? "I'll learn ever so quickly—I promise—if you could just explain it to me, please."

"Well, I like that. Girls smart as a whip apply here six days a week, and you waltz in off the boat with not a brain in your head!" Alice muttered, whispering the price to Maureen. "You're lucky clerks don't make change! Pretend you know what you're doing!"

The afternoon wore on with no breaks; Maureen was loathe to ask even about visiting the washroom.

"There's no sitting down, you know," Alice admonished when Maureen perched on the stool behind the counter during a slow period. "They'll dock your pay for that—didn't Old Blood and Thunder tell you?"

Maureen stood immediately. "Blood and Thunder?"

"That's what we call Mrs. Gordon, the floor supervisor," Alice whispered. "Suits her, don't you think?"

Maureen watched from the corner of her eye as Mrs. Gordon severely reprimanded a quivering and shame-faced clerk for not clearing her counter of unwanted merchandise quickly enough after a sale. Maureen thought it a perfect name.

Before the end of the day, Maureen had learned to read a sales slip aloud to customers. But at closing she still did not completely understand the money and was thankful beyond words that all transactions were carried out on the floor below. Her too-small secondhand boots had rubbed blisters across her toes, and the backs of her heels bled until raw. Mrs. Melkford's breakfast seemed but a dim and distant memory.

"You'd best bring a lunch with you tomorrow," Alice advised. "You can eat in the cloakroom. If you're here for the whole day, you'll get a lunch break—but only half an hour. There's hardly enough time to go out, and besides, bringing it along will save you."

Maureen had not thought that far ahead. "I'm wonderin' if you might know of a house of lodgin' for ladies—something nearby that's not too dear."

"Why on earth do you want to know about lodging? I heard you're living with some high-and-mighties."

"Word travels quickly." Maureen looked away and folded the cover of her sales book over. "It isn't for me. No, it's for my sister, you see. She'll be comin' to stay soon, and we thought we'd like a place of our own—eventually."

"Well, I don't blame you." Alice sighed. "Sometimes I think I'd like to live up with the swells or over in Gramercy Park." She looked pointedly at Maureen. "But then I wouldn't want them telling me this and telling me that. We get enough lording it over in the store."

"It's nice to have a bit of privacy, isn't it?" Maureen confided.

Alice nodded, the first hint of camaraderie between them. "Here." She tore the bottom off a sales receipt and scribbled a name. "Mrs. Grieser owns a tenement on Orchard Street—ask anyone; it's a couple buildings past the corner of Orchard and Delancey, down on the Lower East Side. You'll have to watch out for the fellas in the Bowery, and it's a bit of a hike in bad weather, but not so far you can't manage. You can take a trolley if you must." Alice passed her the slip of paper. "Tell her that Alice Draper sent you—she'll give you a good rate and a safe room." She hesitated. "Just use her side door. The front opens a few doors from a bar. Make no mistake."

"Thank you!" Maureen nearly hugged her.

"You might not thank me—it's not the Ritz, and it's certainly not the Wakefields. But it will do for a place of your own to start. If your sister's working too, you'll do all right."

The front doors were closed and locked; a bell rang through the store.

"That's it for today!" Alice sang over her shoulder, already trotting toward the cloakroom. "See you tomorrow—soak those feet!"

Maureen smiled as she buttoned her very American secondhand cloak. Her feet ached, her stomach gnawed and growled, and she had blocks and blocks to walk to find Orchard Street in the hope of sleeping a few hours before starting it all again. But she was gainfully employed in a fine and respectable department store, she had the letter in her pocket that she needed to have Katie Rose released into her care, and she'd spent her first day dressed not as a lady's maid, but as an American shopgirl.

Pinning her hat in place, she whispered to the mirror above the dressing room shelf, "Well, then, Maureen O'Reilly—shopgirl." Maureen turned her head from side to side, smiled at the attractive young woman smiling back, then hurried down the stairs and toward the side door, behind the other chattering women.

She'd reached the door when a nervous, girlish laugh and a deep but vaguely familiar Irish brogue made her turn back toward the nearly deserted store. Beyond an aisle displaying scarves and handkerchiefs, a raven-haired girl no older than Katie Rose, in a simple woven dress and tattered shawl, blushed prettily as she stepped backward into the elevator. Pressed too close to her chest, one hand round her back and the other clutching a small knotted bundle, like those of the poorest immigrants just off the ship, stepped a too-eager and attentive Jaime Flynn.

CHAPTER TWELVE

"I'm SORRY, DEAR. We're full up. I won't have another vacancy for a month, at least." Mrs. Grieser shook her head. "Such a pity. You've come all this way, and it's dark as pitch out there. I don't know what to tell you."

Maureen refused to cry. She'd been so certain the room would work out. "I understand, mum." But she didn't leave the step. "It's just that I've only arrived, you see, and I've nowhere to go."

"Dear me, I can't think why Alice would send you all this way on such a night. She should have sent a note by day."

Maureen couldn't tell her that Alice had no idea she'd traipse more than three dozen blocks in the raw wind that very night. She'd considered weaving a story to satisfy Mrs. Melkford, to allow her to return to her home for another night. But after seeing Jaime Flynn with the young girl in the elevator, Maureen felt a greater urgency to establish herself legitimately and quickly.

"The only thing I can suggest is Mr. Crudgers's tenement." Mrs. Grieser stepped outside the door and pointed down the street. "You see the bar? It's not a place to send a young lady, but he might have a vacancy above stairs. He lets out rooms and half flats." She eyed Maureen uncertainly. "But I wouldn't stay any longer than you have to, and keep your door bolted at night."

"Thank you, Mrs. Grieser."

The lady shook her head sadly but closed the door on Maureen.

Maureen wearily, warily hefted her bag and picked her way down the street. The November cold had more than seeped into her bones, and the cup of tea and ham sandwich she'd stopped for sat like a lump in her stomach.

"What have I done?" she whispered into the dark. *Oh, Mrs. Melkford, I wish* . . . But there was no point wishing and no one to call upon but herself. Maureen was sure of it.

"Twelve dollars a month—in advance." The bartender and landlord pushed a half-smoked cigar in his mouth, lit up, and inhaled deeply. He ran his eyes over Maureen appreciatively.

"Twelve dollars," Maureen repeated, trying to avoid his eyes. "That's awfully dear." Though she didn't know if it was. "I'm only wantin' the flat for a week. I'll not be stayin'."

The man shrugged. "Take it or leave it. There's them that'll take it for that—and more." He pulled the cigar from his mouth and smiled—yellowed teeth with dark spaces between. "We could make another deal. Maybe you have somethin' you'd like to barter, Red."

Maureen shook her head, pulling bills from her purse, willing her fingers not to tremble. At least the bills had numbers on their faces. "Twelve dollars it is, then. One month."

He stepped closer.

"My sister is joinin' me—and perhaps another friend."

He grunted. "Won't matter to me. Toilet's down the hall." He pulled a suspender to his shoulder and stepped into the hallway. "Use the back stairs, unless you've a mind to join my customers." He laughed down the hallway.

Maureen closed the door and braced her back against it, her heart beating its way to her throat. Never had she planned to live above a pub. Never had she so brazenly bluffed her way through an entire day. The weariness of it all came suddenly upon her.

But it was a place of her own. A place she could pay for—or would, as soon as she'd earned and returned the loan to Jaime Flynn. A loan for which she was, at this moment, most grateful. Maureen slid to the floor, tired beyond words, and pulled her hat from her head. She'd close her eyes for a minute, no more, and then find the bed and set things to rights for the morning.

Maureen jumped at the crash of breaking glass; raucous laughter bubbled from below. *The first thing I'll do is buy a latch for this door and then a . . .* But her eyes, heavy beyond memory, fluttered closed, and that was the last she knew.

A predawn clatter of the milk wagon outside her window pulled her from sleep. Maureen found herself still on the floor, her backside braced against the door, though she'd fallen to her side in the night. She pushed herself to her knees, to her feet. Her neck creaked and all her bones ached. Her feet complained, and she realized she'd not even removed her too-tight boots.

She'd no idea of the hour, but there was the barest of gray lights through the window. Whatever the time, there'd be little enough to wash and straighten her clothes for the day. She'd nothing else suitable to wear, and she dared not show up at Darcy's Department Store crumpled.

The toilet down the hall stank before she ever reached it. Maureen held her breath and, after the briefest of visits, fled back to her room.

The water ran in red tint from the pipe, and though the flat had been described as "furnished," there was no kettle or pot for boiling water.

Maureen tore her petticoat to wrap her bleeding feet and stuffed them back inside her boots. She made herself as presentable as possible, then limped to the street, hoping to reach Darcy's before the majority of the staff. She needed every precious minute to repair the night's damage to her face and hair.

She reached the sales floor as the bell rang to open the doors.

"Ohhh," Alice cooed, her brows raised as she took in Maureen's rumpled skirt and waist. "You look a bit worse for wear."

Maureen straightened but could not deliver a smile. "I had a time with the water this mornin'."

"At the Wakefields'?" Alice tipped her head to one side. "Don't they have maids to draw your bath and fetch and carry your breakfast?"

Maureen turned away, closing her eyes to muster courage. *If only I'd had breakfast!*

"Listen, I don't know what you're up to with that Wakefield story, and I don't really care. But you can't show up in the same skirt and waist every day, and you must polish your boots." She eyed Maureen critically. "You'd do better with proper shoes. This is a ladies' store, after all."

Maureen bit her lip.

"They'll fire you first thing if you don't measure up." Alice stood back. "Is this the best you've got? Have you no money to buy something new?"

Maureen was too tired and hungry to think of a lie, so she tried confession. "I've no idea how to count the money here—I mean, what's reasonable and what's dear. I'm sure I haven't enough to buy the clothes Darcy's sells. I looked at some of the prices yesterday." She bit her lip and smoothed the sleeves of her waist. "These are the only American-lookin' things I have."

Alice frowned.

"I just arrived; I've had no time to shop." Maureen could see that Alice didn't believe her. "Please, please don't ask me more. I'll figure somethin' out."

Alice blinked and turned her back on Maureen. She dusted the counter but didn't say a word. Maureen watched from the corner of her eye as Alice diligently fanned pairs of navy silk gloves around feathered felt hats on a low table between the counters. She stood back critically, then tucked white lace handkerchiefs between the sets in a striking display.

"Nicely done," the supervisor commented as she strode through the store with her checklist. "Very nicely done, Alice."

"Thank you, Mrs. Gordon. I'm glad you're pleased."

Mrs. Gordon tipped her head in acknowledgment and smiled.

"I was wondering, Mrs. Gordon, if you'd mind if Maureen—the new girl—and I took our lunch break together today. Mary could cover our counter along with hers, and I could show Maureen a place or two to buy a bite to eat."

Mrs. Gordon frowned. "Well, that is irregular . . ." She glanced at Maureen, who tried to look hopeful and professional at once. Mrs. Gordon leaned closer to Alice and whispered, loud enough for Maureen to hear, "Perhaps you can see that she finds another waist—or an iron, at any rate."

Maureen felt her face flame and turned away, polishing the counter with a fury.

"Thank you, ma'am. We'll be prompt."

"See that you are."

When Mrs. Gordon had gone, Maureen felt Alice close behind.

"I'm sorry if that hurt, but it's best we go at noon. The stores will be closed by the time Darcy's closes."

"I don't have much money," Maureen confided miserably.

"As long as you have a little. That's all you'll need. I know a place," Alice whispered. "Now, smile, for pity's sake. You'll scare the customers."

The morning wore long. But at noon, Alice was better than her word.

The girls raced down a side street. Less than three blocks from Darcy's Department Store, they stepped through the door of a dimly lit second-hand shop.

Alice expertly pulled embroidered and finely laced white and cream and navy shirtwaists and neatly tailored skirts from the racks, holding them critically at arm's length for inspection. "This was last season's design, but it will do. Stay away from those ridiculous puffed sleeves. They're years old and will never do for a salesgirl. You want something smart and attractive, but you must never outshine the customers."

Most were gently worn, but even those with well-placed stains or an awkward hole held promise for Alice's critical eye and Maureen's practiced needle.

They were in and out of the store in seventeen minutes. Maureen's arms were loaded with brown paper packages, including a pair of leather shoes that fit.

"Three dollars!" Alice crowed. "It's a steal! You'd pay thirty-five for all of that—easily—at Darcy's!"

Maureen clapped a hand on her hat to keep it from flying and ran to keep up with Alice. "How can I thank you, Alice? It's more than I ever imagined."

"Just do your job." Alice stopped so abruptly that Maureen ran into her. "Do your job and stay—stay at the store." She gripped Maureen's arm so tightly she winced.

"Yes, yes, of course I'll stay." Maureen could not understand the look of distress Alice gave her. But the cloud fled as quickly as it had come.

"Yes, well—never mind." She checked the watch pinned to her jacket. "Oh! We've got seven minutes. Come on!"

It was just enough time to grab a frankfurter slathered in mustard and a mug of hot coffee from a street vendor. "American delicacies." Alice laughed.

Maureen laughed, too, glad to run, to eat and sip hot coffee in the wintry sunshine, glad to feel the flush of roses in her cheeks, and glad to have made a friend.

Alice poked Maureen in the ribs. "Don't look behind you now, but there's Officer Flannery. This is his beat, and he's the heartthrob of every girl at Darcy's."

Maureen couldn't imagine what a "heartthrob" might look like.

"Good day to you, ladies." The Irish officer tipped his hat and winked.

Alice's color rose three shades, Maureen was certain, and she nearly curtsied. "Good afternoon, Officer Flannery."

"A fine day to be out and taking the air as ladies of leisure." He smiled, eyeing Maureen from head to toe and back again.

Alice laughed. "Only when we're protected by New York's finest!"

"Always glad to be of service, ladies. Good day to you, then." He tipped his hat again before strolling down the avenue.

"I do believe you're smitten!" Maureen vowed.

Alice stuck her nose in the air but laughed. "As is every girl on Flannery's beat!" And then she became earnest. "But if ever you need a friend, if ever you need help, Flannery's your man. You can lay money on it."

Maureen looked after the policeman, hoping she'd never have need of him but glad to know the stalwart officer was there, a man to trust.

The girls skidded behind their counter half a minute before the floor supervisor walked by, her brows raised at the giggling young women.

CHAPTER THIRTEEN

NOVEMBER'S BLEAK, rain-wet skies drifted toward December's clouds, pregnant with snow. Olivia turned the gas heater higher and neared the close of another decade in her father's journals.

She'd come to think of her father as a young man—not really as her father at all. She'd read early of his humbling change of heart toward Morgan O'Reilly. Olivia shivered at the depth of his anger toward his parents in those years, in what he'd perceived as heartless treatment of their only daughter. She felt keenly his loss of his sister in the years that followed and his disappointment that O'Reilly, despairing, had returned to Ireland shortly after the death of President Lincoln. Grief upon grief.

Her father's own despair only seemed to lighten when he met Maud Markham. Olivia felt for the first time that she was intruding where she had no right, a trespasser of the worst sort. But she didn't stop reading. She'd never known what it was to love or be loved by a man in the way her father wrote of his attraction and devotion to her mother or her responses to him.

Olivia had grimaced with his first mention of love. Her only experience with men she considered nothing short of disaster. At barely eighteen, a man ten years her senior had swept her off her feet. She'd loved him with all her young heart, though she realized now there was no similarity to the love her father wrote of having for her mother.

You were so gentle with me, Father, even though you didn't approve. Do I have Aunt Lillian and Morgan O'Reilly to thank for that?

Olivia could still hear her father's words. *"I promise to reserve judgment if the courtship lasts a year."*

It hadn't, and only in hindsight did she understand her father's great patience; within the year she'd understood his wisdom. The suitor had proven himself a cad, intent on her money and careless of her heart to a point very near scandal.

It had been a long time since she'd thought of herself as lovelorn. Olivia shook her head and returned to the journal.

Her father wrote to Morgan repeatedly, encouraging him, begging him to bring his wife and child to New York. He vowed to embrace him and his family as his own—to be a brother to Morgan and an uncle, a second father, to his son—for Lillian's sake and for his own.

But when he wrote of the death of Morgan's family and dream, Douglas Wakefield's tears had smeared the ink on the page. Olivia's joined them.

A year later a son, Peter, was born to Maud and Douglas but died within the day. Olivia never knew her parents had had a son. *How Father must have grieved!* But he gave the grief to God, as he prayed through his pen, and in four more years looked forward to the birth of another child, though with trepidation. Dorothy was born.

When Olivia finally came to another mention of Morgan O'Reilly, it was short. The man had married again, years later, and his new wife had given birth. The little family determined to sail for America.

Her father was glad—his pen showed it.

I heard from Morgan this morning. He and his wife and son will be here by spring, thank God. I posted funds to him this noon and can only hope he's as glad to come as I am to have him. I'll see my attorney this evening to set up a trust for young William, the equal of the son that could have—should have—been Lillian's.

I must have Waverly inquire of the owners next door. If they can be persuaded to sell, we could adjoin our properties as well as our businesses. I could have the house readied by the time they arrive.

Thank You, Father in heaven, for this opportunity to redeem some part of my past. I vow to forge the family we should have been.

Olivia rubbed the throbbing in her temples. *Father intended to make William O'Reilly, for all practical purposes, our neighbor and one of his heirs—as real a brother to Dorothy and me as we could ever know. And I've allowed the woman O'Reilly to be thrown from my door!*

She closed the journal and groaned, "Father, if only we'd known."

The horror of what she'd done, or allowed to be done, haunted Olivia through the night. Dawn had not come when she gave up tossing and turning and rose, tied her dressing gown round her waist, and crept back to her father's study. She adjusted the globe of the electric lamp and opened the journal again.

Months later, long after the little family was due to arrive, came another entry regarding the O'Reillys. The child, William, had died of fever just before sailing; the grieving parents stayed in Ireland. And that was the last mention she found of Morgan O'Reilly.

The next entry that made Olivia's heart race was October 26, 1886. After months and months of the public collection of funds for a pedestal, New York at last "unveiled" the Statue of Liberty in New York harbor. Her father had written that it was a momentous day and predicted that his own child would be born before the sun set.

But his reaction to her birth was written two weeks later.

My sweet daughter did not disappoint. I shall christen her "Olivia," as Maud wanted, though in my heart she will always be our "Lady Liberty."

Would that my sweet wife were here to hold her, to raise her in her likeness. Could it be, I would wrench her from heaven's gates.

Olivia swallowed when she saw that his tears had run the ink, his pen had torn the page. How long he'd waited to write the next lines, she could not guess.

God, forgive my folly. I love my precious wife too well to call her back, and hers is the greater liberty—not to be found in New York harbor.

Olivia swiped at her own tears. She had wondered, as long as she could remember, if her father had blamed her for her mother's death. She'd wondered, too, if he was disappointed that she was not a boy but could find no hint that he'd been less than thrilled with his new daughter. He'd loved his daughters—both his daughters.

Through the morning, Olivia read of the years of her childhood and the pleasure that childhood had given her father. By the time the journals reached the 1890s, Olivia began to recognize and remember the events of which her father wrote, and loved the familiarity.

Just before dinner, she replaced 1895 on the shelf and took up the following year's volume. A sheaf of bundled papers fell from the journal's binding. Olivia stooped to retrieve them, but her fingers fumbled, and she dropped them once again.

"The *Chicago Advance*? Why would Father keep a year's worth of weekly religious papers?"

The moment she turned them over, the memories came in a rush. Long Sunday evenings when she and Dorothy sat, spellbound, by the fire or in the back garden as their father read the serialized story aloud, the timbre of his voice rising and falling with emotion.

It was the beginning of his eternal life—he'd always said so—no matter that a lifetime had been lived before and that he'd always known the Lord.

She set the papers in order, week by week, and sighed. "Charles Sheldon—you'll never know how you set this family's head on end."

Dinner was served, but Olivia ignored it until Grayson knocked and set a tray at her elbow.

She read until midnight, until she could no longer hold up her head, then turned off the lamp and sat in the moonlight as it streamed through her father's window. She would finish tomorrow. But she knew how Sheldon's story ended, and knew what she must do.

CHAPTER FOURTEEN

ON WEDNESDAY MORNING Maureen purchased a sturdy bolt and a lock with key from a street vendor. During her lunch break she returned to the secondhand shop and purchased a kettle, one cast-iron skillet, two cracked plates, two forks, two knives, and two chipped mugs. On Thursday she purchased a flat iron, a length of toweling, and a blanket for the lumpy tick mattress in her flat. On her way home she stopped at the corner store for a small supply of potatoes and onions, half a loaf of brown bread, a half pound of cheese, and a tin of tea. She couldn't afford the sugar, though she would have dearly loved some. She eyed the eggs but decided to wait until Katie Rose joined her; Katie Rose would need the nourishment, and they could share the luxury.

"Is that all you're eating?" Alice demanded when she saw the little packet of bread and cheese Maureen pocketed to take to the lunchroom on Friday.

"It's quite enough," Maureen said stoutly, leveling her stare. "I had a lovely dinner last night—can't possibly eat more."

Alice frowned, and Maureen knew she didn't believe her.

Between her rent, the clothes for work, the expenses to set up a meager housekeeping, and the trolley and ferry fees she must set aside to visit Katie Rose on Saturday, she found she'd spent all the money Jaime Flynn had loaned her and nearly half of her last gold piece. She prayed that Katie Rose still had her gold piece sewn into her hem, that it had not been discovered. She prayed that the hospital fees would not exceed her pay envelope on Saturday. And then she stopped and reminded herself that she did not believe in praying, did not believe the Almighty listened to her.

She cut her lunch ration of bread and cheese in half and drank a cup of weak tea for breakfast. Potatoes and onions boiled in water sufficed for supper.

Despite being dead on her feet each night, Maureen had washed and mended and ironed each piece of secondhand clothing. She'd done her best to style the pieces necessary for work in the department store—enough to put together two outfits beyond what Mrs. Melkford had given her. But what had pleased her most was that she'd finished making over a woven skirt and waist suitable for school for Katie Rose. She hoped her sister would be just as pleased.

Saturday's workday, though shorter, dragged for Maureen. She was surprised when Alice placed a hand over her fingers to stop her from drumming the counter.

"Anticipating that first pay envelope, are we?" Alice teased.

"It's my first, indeed," Maureen confessed, stilling her fingers but unable to keep the smile from her lips.

"Didn't you work in Ireland?" Alice looked as though she couldn't believe it.

Maureen felt her face pale and turned away. "My pay went to my mother and sister." And then she squared her shoulders. "This is the first that's all my own."

"Good for you," Alice said; Maureen knew she meant it. "Enjoy today. We'll all be working extra hours beginning Monday—Christmas shopping season, you know."

"Does the store stay open longer, then?" Maureen had not considered that.

"Not open to the public longer, but we'll all be staying after to restock shelves and make up displays." She shrugged. "It's expected, and Old Blood and Thunder won't let anyone off 'less they've been struck dead. We don't get paid for the extra hours." Alice straightened a hat on its form and nodded meaningfully. "But it's no time to test her. All of management is wound like a clock straight through Twelfth Night."

Maureen couldn't think how she'd handle the extra hours or what she'd do about Katie Rose. She dared not leave her alone for hours in the evening above a bar.

As the clock neared closing time, Maureen's heart flip-flopped. It skipped a beat at the thought of seeing good Mrs. Melkford, then quickened for the shame of the lies she'd told. It lifted again with hope that Katie Rose was well and growing stronger and then fell with a thudding wish that she might remain at the hospital one more week, until Maureen could save more money.

How she would pay daily for two, how she would traverse the difficulty of enrolling Katie Rose in school and ensure her safety each afternoon until returning home from a long day's work, was more than Maureen could imagine. There were so many things made difficult by being alone. And yet there was no one she could trust to ask for help. Surely Mrs. Melkford would be obliged to report their need if she knew. And that could lead to deportation.

Even work, no matter how grateful she was for the job, posed its own threats. Each afternoon Maureen scanned the stairwell before descending and kept her eye on the front door, lest Jaime Flynn surprise her. She hated being beholden to him in any way; she wanted, more than anything, to hand him his thirty dollars the next time she saw him. She could imagine half a dozen explanations for his generosity to her and for his interest in the young girl in the elevator, but none of them comforted her.

❖CHAPTER FIFTEEN❖

OLIVIA HURRIED to Meitland House early Saturday morning, intent on arranging fresh centerpieces from the crates of evergreens and roses Dorothy had ordered directly from the docks and the cranberry-scented candles railroaded in from Pennsylvania.

Dorothy brought out their mother's silver tea service, had it polished to a sheen worthy of catching the late afternoon sun's gleam across its surface, and instructed the Meitland housekeeper and cook in every detail for the preparation of a spectacular December tea for the Ladies' Circle from church.

"Perfect," the sisters sighed in unison as at last they surveyed their combined efforts.

"Did you remind Julia to bring the minutes from last month's meeting? You know her head's in a thousand different places."

Olivia saluted. "Yes, O drill sergeant sister. The remainder of troops will arrive in good order momentarily."

Dorothy gave Olivia a testy slap but smiled. "I just want everything—just—"

"Just so?" Olivia queried, too innocently.

"Yes." Her sister smiled. "You know I do."

Olivia wrapped her arms round Dorothy's waist in a great and uncharacteristic hug. "I love you."

"Well, I love you, too." Dorothy laughed nervously, straightening her brooch. "The bell! They're here!"

Olivia was relieved that the tea went according to plan; she understood what order and beauty meant to her sister, especially when it came to the attention of their peers. As the meeting was called to order, Olivia hoped that Dorothy would be just as happy when the day was over, when everyone had had their say.

Julia Gresham read the minutes from last month's meeting, and the floor was opened to the twelve women of the circle.

"We must decide on our focus for the new year," Agnes Mein, the circle's leader, ordered. "We've foundered a bit since joining with the shirtwaist workers' strikes last year. It's time we took on a new project. Now, I think we ought to—"

"I didn't think much of being branded with the 'mink brigade,'" Julia interrupted.

Olivia sat straighter. She hadn't liked it either.

"No," Agnes allowed. "But I suppose it's natural that the papers aligned us more with society matrons than with the factory girls." She raised her hands. "That is why—"

"That is why we need to make our position clear," Julia insisted. "We're committed to helping those who need help, not to hosting fashion parades."

Olivia couldn't have agreed more but kept her peace to avoid adding to the growing tension.

Agnes's color rose, but she pressed on. "We'll open the floor for suggestions for next year's projects. Now, a number of concerns have been put forth, but we must join forces on one cause or nothing will be accomplished. Carolynn, you have the proposed list."

Carolynn Gilliston stood and cleared her throat. "We've been asked to consider the library's need for more books, especially in the New York history section. I've also noticed," she said quietly, "that the children's section could use a wider selection."

No one responded. Olivia felt a slight pity for her friend, knowing how Carolynn loved children. *But other needs are more desperate now.*

Carolynn continued. "We have a request to supply the Immigrant Aid Society with more gently worn clothing, especially things the women coming into New York can use in public employment while the weather is cold and then again, in a few months, some things more suitable for warmer weather." She glanced about the room. "The aid societies have asked that we consider the more practical needs of the women."

"Practical needs," Isabella Harris repeated. "What do they mean?"

"They mean," Julia answered for Carolynn, "that workingwomen do not need last season's ball gowns. They need skirts and shirtwaists, undergarments, sturdy shoes for walking the streets of New York to work because they can't afford trolley fare. They mean—"

But Agnes interrupted her. "We understand, Julia. Thank you. Carolynn, please continue."

"There have been numerous suggestions that we align ourselves with the movement for suffrage and encourage the men of the church to do the same." She paused. "And then there's the ongoing plea to assist the garment factory workers and department store clerks—in particular, in their call for higher wages and shorter working hours. A boycott of stores and brands unwilling to unionize or negotiate has been recommended."

Several women raised their eyebrows significantly and peered at Julia as Carolynn forged ahead. Olivia bit her lip to keep from shouting, "Hear! Hear!"

"We have the proposal, once again, to deliver food and clothing to the tenements, including—"

"As we made clear last year," Miranda Mason interrupted, "our husbands will never allow us to visit the tenements—never to so much as walk into the streets of those slums. The reverend himself doesn't go down there!" She drew herself up. "I motion we strike that suggestion from the record."

To Olivia's surprise, Julia did not say a word.

"And . . ." Carolynn colored miserably but did not go on.

"What is it?" Agnes demanded.

"And there is a suggestion to boycott the natural wishes of our husbands—those of us who have husbands—until they put forth a political motion to raise the age of consent."

"The what?" Miranda gasped.

"Oh, don't be silly," Julia fumed. "The age of consent—the age a man can force a girl to do his bidding."

The women stared.

"His sexual bidding," Julia spelled out.

"We know what it is, Julia!" Agnes gasped. "We simply cannot believe you—"

"We're gasping over words while ten-year-old girls are forced into prostitution to pay a family's rent—to survive! The immigrant women pouring into New York don't make enough money in the factories or the stores to keep body and soul together, much less put food in their children's mouths once their husbands die or are injured or run west to make their fortune and are never heard from again! No wonder so many turn to or are forced into prostitution. But if we can put the responsibility where it belongs—on the perpetrators—by raising the legal age of consent to—"

"Julia, I think we—" Dorothy began.

"I think we need to ask what is important here! New York history books or the health and safety, the very lives, of women and children!"

Olivia opened her mouth to second Julia, but Agnes overrode her.

"No one disputes the importance of protecting women or children, but we must ask what we, as a group, can do—which causes we can, with all propriety, embrace." Agnes drew a breath, and the women of the circle nodded in worried agreement.

"And what we, as a circle of churchwomen, can effectively accomplish," Dorothy added with authority.

Women nodded again.

But Olivia could remain silent no longer. "No." She spoke quietly but stood. "I don't think that is the question."

"Olivia?" Dorothy laid a hand on her sister's arm.

Olivia squeezed Dorothy's hand in return but let it drop. "As a group of women committed to helping those in need, I think the question is not what we can accomplish, but what Christ can accomplish through us and how we can follow in His steps."

"Well, of course it is," Agnes said. "We know that."

"Do we?" Olivia asked.

"You're questioning our sincerity?" Miranda lifted her chin.

"Not at all."

"Then I—"

"Let her speak!" Julia demanded. "Or I will."

Olivia suppressed a smile at the silence Julia's threat provoked. "Even that—how we allow Him to work through us—is the secondary question." She had their attention. "The most important question of all is, what would Jesus do—here and now?"

The women blinked.

"I don't think I understand the question," Agnes ventured.

"What would Jesus do if He were here—right now, in New York City—today? What would He, personally, seek to change, and how would He go about it?"

Women shifted in their seats, uncomfortably signaling their attention.

"Our cause has always been focused toward women and children," Agnes reminded her.

"Then," Olivia continued, "what would Jesus do for the women and children in New York?"

"Well, He certainly wouldn't allow them to be forced into prostitution!" Julia asserted.

"Nor would He want to see them starve for lack of nourishing food," Isabella admonished.

"Or freeze to death in those filthy tenements!" Miranda echoed.

"But He didn't address those things specifically in His time," Agnes insisted. "Poverty was all around Him. It's not as if we can do better than He! We can only accomplish so much."

"I'm not suggesting that we can single-handedly change the face of poverty," Olivia said. "But I am wondering, if we each asked ourselves, and committed to asking ourselves, 'What would Jesus do?' if we might not find clearer answers."

"I have no idea where this is leading," Agnes huffed.

"I do," Dorothy said softly, looking up at her sister. "I remember the story."

Olivia squeezed her sister's shoulder, then addressed the group. "When we were young, Father read us weekly issues of the *Chicago Advance*, and for a time, the paper ran a serialized story by Charles Sheldon." She paused, hoping there might be a sign of recognition from the ladies, but Agnes shook her head helplessly.

"In the story, the Reverend Maxwell had just preached a normal Sunday sermon in which he'd said that following after Christ requires obedience, faith, love, and imitation. The congregation sang a closing hymn, 'All for Jesus'—do you remember the words?

"All for Jesus, all for Jesus!
All my being's ransomed pow'rs:

All my tho'ts and words and doings,
All my days and all my hours."

Olivia warmed to her story. "Just as they finished singing, a man—a poor man who'd lost his job and family and was terribly ill—walked to the front of that wealthy, well-dressed congregation and asked what they meant by 'imitation' of Jesus."

An intuitive flush of color ran across the cheeks of several women.

"The man said that it seemed to him, if all those singing were truly living 'all for Jesus—every day and every hour,' there would be much less suffering in the world." Olivia glanced round the parlor. "He said that perhaps he didn't understand what they meant by following Jesus. They attended a big church, lived in nice houses, and wore fine clothes. They had money for luxuries and vacations, while the people outside the churches were dying in tenements, out of work, never owning so much as a piano or a picture for their home, and living in misery, drunkenness, and sin. He thought he simply must not understand. And then he collapsed."

"*In His Steps*," Carolynn said in a voice so small that Olivia barely heard her. "I'd quite forgotten. My grandmother gave me the book when it came to print."

Olivia smiled broadly. "Do you remember what happened next?"

Still seated, Carolynn clasped her hands. "Reverend Maxwell took the man to his home and cared for him. But the man died within the week." She leaned forward slightly. "I remember that the man thanked him before he died and said he thought that the care the pastor had given him was something Jesus would have done. The following Sunday, after the sermon, Reverend Maxwell set a challenge before his congregation."

Every eye was on Carolynn. She swallowed, twisting her handkerchief between her fingers. "He called to mind the words of the poor man from the week before and said he saw it as a sort of challenge for the church—a challenge to ask what it truly means to follow Christ." She stopped, drew in a breath, and finally looked round the circle, meeting the eyes of the women, just as Olivia had. "I've never forgotten it. He asked for volunteers to pledge for one year to do nothing without first asking the question 'What would Jesus do?'"

Dorothy sat straighter. "And then to follow Jesus, as best they could understand—do as best they could, no matter the result."

"No matter the result," Olivia repeated.

Julia whispered, "That's bold."

"Yes," Olivia returned.

"It's a fine story." Agnes stood. "But if I understand your proposal, I don't see how we can possibly carry out such a challenge as a group." She raised her brows and shrugged her shoulders. "We're clearly not all of the same mind as to what is the best cause to pursue, much less what Jesus might do."

"But if we each ask what Jesus would do," Carolynn persisted, "with all that He has given to equip us and with all that He lays on our hearts—if we each determine to carry that out, then perhaps those missions will intertwine and create something greater—something far beyond ourselves and our abilities, as they did in the book."

Carolynn's eyes flamed, and Olivia knew she understood completely, even as she wondered that the most naturally reticent in the group was the one in which the Spirit's fire so smoldered.

"I suggest we all read the book in the coming two weeks," Olivia urged, "and consider what it might mean for us. That's all I'm asking now. Read the book, and let's discuss it at our next meeting—before we choose our course of action for the year."

"If that's a motion, I second it." Carolynn spoke quickly.

Agnes, clearly not pleased at the turn of events, snapped, "We have a motion on the floor. Those in favor—"

The vote carried, nine in favor and three opposed. The circle broke up abruptly as Agnes called for her fur and swept from the room.

Carolynn kissed Dorothy lightly on the cheek, then clasped Olivia's hands and whispered, "We'll be transformed."

"Value," Julia said, pulling on her gloves. "Jesus valued women and children in a way no one else of His time did. He was an absolute radical."

"The Samaritan woman," Miranda remembered aloud, pinning her hat in place. "I've always wondered why He went to her, validated her, when He could have gone to women in His own community who needed Him."

"Maybe because she was not one of their own. A foreigner in need of belonging." Julia grinned and tilted her head pointedly. "As foreign and needy as those new immigrants pouring through Ellis Island and the Battery. Think on that." She arched her brows and swept out as regally as Agnes had done.

CHAPTER SIXTEEN

THE DEPARTMENT STORE DOORS locked and the bell rang at last. Maureen accepted and counted the wonder of her pay. Breathless, she pushed it deep inside her purse. She made certain she descended the stairs in the midst of the other girls, her face intent on the floor, then raced to the trolley stop.

At last she paid her coin and took a seat, grateful to be off her feet. Had there been enough time, she would have walked to save the fare. But she'd be lucky to reach Mrs. Melkford at the Battery's pier in time for the last ferry to Ellis Island.

She ran the last three blocks, rejoicing at the sight of the small but sturdy Mrs. Melkford scanning the distance with her hand to her eyes. She laughed to see her friend enthusiastically waving two tickets, motioning her to run faster. Maureen sprinted onto the dock just as the dockhands stooped to raise the gangway.

"I'm coming! I'm coming!" she cried, unmindful of the petticoat that flew behind her.

The dockhands, their eyes alight at the windswept Maureen, stood aside as she caught up with her feisty older friend, rooted to the center of the gangway. The dockhands tipped their hats and grinned as Maureen linked arms with Mrs. Melkford, and the two ladies, mismatched in height and age, waltzed on board as though the ferry had waited just for them.

"Catch your breath, dear," Mrs. Melkford counseled, then smiled and squeezed Maureen's hand. "It's good to see you!"

Maureen laughed. "And you!" It was the happiest she'd felt all week, snuggled on the cold ferry seat next to the motherly lady.

"Tell me about your week and about your new position and all about life at the Wakefields'."

Maureen's happiness burst. *How can I spin a tale to this good woman?*

"What is it, dear?" Mrs. Melkford frowned. "Don't tell me they're not treating you well. How could they not? Is it the store? The family?"

Maureen did her best to compose her face. "It's all lovely. My job is all that I'd ever hoped it would be! Today I collected my first pay envelope, and I've made a new friend—Alice. We share the hat counter, and she's helped me with my American wardrobe and learnin' what she calls 'the ropes'—that's everythin' about clerkin' that I need to know."

Mrs. Melkford pressed Maureen's arm. "You're rather thinner than when you left my kitchen."

Maureen mustered a laugh. "It's just that I'm a bit out of breath from runnin'. It's been less than a week . . . but perhaps you're right. Perhaps I need some fattenin' up with your good cookin'! I rather fancy a cup of tea and one of your puddin's!"

That brought a smile to Mrs. Melkford's face. "I was hoping you'd say that. When we return, you—and your sister, if she's released and able— must stay to supper. We can always telephone the Wakefields to send a car."

"Oh no!" Maureen stumbled over her words.

Mrs. Melkford raised a questioning brow. "You don't need to get back right away, do you? Oh, I suppose they will want to welcome and entertain your sister."

"No—I mean I would never ask them to send a car."

"But, my dear, your sister won't be well enough to walk or be out in the night air."

Maureen didn't know what to say. She couldn't tell her that she was not taking her sister to the Wakefield mansion, but to the Lower East Side, to what Maureen had learned was the least desirable part of New York.

"No, you're right. She mustn't be out in the night air." Maureen looked out over the water. "I was just wonderin' . . ."

"Yes?"

"I was just wonderin' what you'd think of us stoppin' for the night with you?" Maureen knew it was a bold question, a bold presumption.

"Why, I would love that!" Mrs. Melkford's eyes shone. "But won't the Wakefields be expecting you?"

"No—not tonight," Maureen stammered. She clasped Mrs. Melkford's hands between her own. "You've been so good to me. I know it's a great deal to ask, but I'd love for Katie Rose to know the warmth of your kitchen—just for tonight—as you've shown it to me. Tomorrow we'll be on our way, but . . ."

Mrs. Melkford glowed as if someone had handed her the moon. "And so you shall. As long as you're sure we'll not worry the Wake—"

"We won't," Maureen assured her.

"Well, then, that's settled." Mrs. Melkford sat back, satisfied. "You girls will stay the night and go to church with me tomorrow. Afterward, we'll have a fine dinner, and I'll send you on your way, so you'll get home well before dark. You'll need a good rest for your work on Monday."

Maureen sighed, relieved beyond words.

"Have you inquired about schooling for your sister?"

"Not yet; I'm not certain she'll be up to it straight away."

"Mmm, perhaps not. Best to have a full recovery first—perhaps another week. But from what Nurse Harrigan said last week, I'd expect her to be well on that road." Mrs. Melkford tucked her purse beneath her hands, clearly pleased. "At any rate, I'll keep you for the night."

The ferry docked before they finished making plans. Mrs. Melkford ushered Maureen through waiting stations and past officials that had loomed as land mines before her less than two weeks ago. When they reached the contagious disease ward, Maureen was told to wait in the hallway while Mrs. Melkford inquired.

Doctors and nurses, orderlies and staff members in white coats and uniforms paraded in and out of heavy doors on the side and end of the hallway. Only once did Maureen glimpse a patient on a gurney, and that from a distance.

The minutes of the hall clock ticked off, one by one. A half hour passed. Forty-five minutes. Maureen began to wonder what she would do if Katie Rose needed more care, if the chicken pox left her with some disability. She remembered a boy at home whose joints had swelled so that he went lame after the chicken pox and a girl who, it was whispered, had gone nearly mad before she died. Maureen tugged anxiously at her waist cuff. *Stop. Stop!* she scolded herself. *Don't be borrowin' trouble that's not your due. One blessed thing at a time!*

And then the door swung open, and Katie Rose, dressed in a navy American walking skirt and ivory waist, walked through, a bit tentatively, on the arm of Mrs. Melkford. When she caught sight of Maureen, a smile spread across her pale face, illuminating the scars of her illness.

Maureen jumped to her feet and, with a heart too full to speak, swooped her sister into a great hug. But Katie Rose was truly skin and bone, and Maureen stepped back quickly, lest she break her.

"There, now," Mrs. Melkford cooed. "She's all right, just in need of a bit of mothering." But she looked over Katie Rose's head and slightly shook her head at Maureen.

"They said the scars might not fade," Katie Rose whispered. "They said—"

Maureen couldn't understand any more, for the tears that laced her sister's words.

"For now, we're going home and have a good meal and a good rest," Mrs. Melkford asserted. "Everything will look brighter tomorrow."

Katie Rose, still fighting tears, bit her lip until it drew blood, and Maureen, not knowing what to say to comfort her, simply offered her handkerchief and wrapped her arm around her younger sister. The three walked to the dock and straight onto the ferry, taking a place by the stove. Katie Rose laid her head on Maureen's shoulder and, apparently weary from the short journey, fell asleep.

It gave Maureen an opportunity to scrutinize Katie Rose unobserved. The scars were dark, in various stages of healing, but white spots, like pocks, stood out on her face. She'd not seen this stage of the chicken pox in exactly this way and wondered what it meant. Whatever it was, it wouldn't matter. They would get past it. And yet Maureen knew how Katie Rose valued her beauty. *As would any woman,* Maureen thought, *especially one so young.*

She held her sister closer and kissed the top of her head, her gaze filtering through the faces crowding the rails. It was the last ferry of the day, and the day shift was traveling home. Maureen blinked at a familiar form across the wide deck. There stood Jaime Flynn, his back to her, but his accent carried on the breeze. He seemed to be introducing a lovely young girl at his side to a well-dressed gentleman standing before them.

Maureen pulled her hat lower and shielded her face with one hand but turned her ear to catch whatever of the conversation she could.

"My cousin, just over from Manchester," he said.

The Irish don't usually have cousins from Manchester!

"I'm sure we could arrange an outing, Mr. Whitson," Flynn nearly fawned, though the girl glanced—uncertainly and miserably, Maureen thought—between the men.

Maureen turned toward the water so that none of her face could be seen and cradled her sister protectively. Still, her heart beat quickly and her throat tightened. She pushed a stray hair from the young forehead and thanked God for her sister's face, just as it was. *Don't fret, Katie Rose, whatever may be. Scars are not the worst that could come. They may be a savin' grace.*

When all the circle women had gone and the parlor maid had finished clearing the tables, Olivia sat with Dorothy before the drawing room fire, nursing a fresh cup of tea.

"And what brought that on?" Dorothy asked, staring into the fire.

Olivia took her sister's measure and decided against telling her about the journals just yet. "The O'Reilly woman."

Dorothy's shoulders fell in a long breath. "I thought so. I've been thinking of her—and that day, too. Drake is determined to protect our inheritance—that's all." She blushed and looked away. "Sometimes I think he's rather overzealous."

Olivia agreed but would not wound her sister with the words she felt sure Drake deserved. "He takes too much on himself, especially in houses that are not his own."

Dorothy's color deepened. "He's my husband, Livvie." She picked at the upholstery on the arm of her chair, and the silence stretched between them. Olivia nearly spoke, but Dorothy lifted her eyes. "Do you think she might have had a legitimate claim?"

"Yes, I fear she may."

"But how can—?"

Before Dorothy could ask more, Olivia continued. "At any rate, her letter is gone, and Miss O'Reilly has disappeared." She set her cup in its saucer and massaged the back of her neck, wishing to alleviate the tension growing there. "And yes, if you're wondering, she is my parallel to the poor man in Sheldon's story. Only I didn't care for her as the Reverend Maxwell did for that man." She stared at Dorothy, feeling the miserable weight of her mission. "We, who were raised by a man who asked every day, 'What would Jesus do?' and who had apparently promised her or her family something, allowed her to be thrown into the cold." Olivia wrapped her arms round her shoulders, suddenly feeling the chill. "Did you see the emptiness in her eyes?"

"I can't stop thinking of it."

Olivia shook her head, frustrated that she could not turn back time to that Thanksgiving Day and rewrite the moment.

"Did you hear what Julia said about poor immigrant women?" Dorothy glanced at her sister, then quickly back to the fire.

"She's right, you know. I've thought of that a hundred times since Thanksgiving. What did we—what did I—send her to? Did she have anywhere else to go?" Olivia dropped her hands to her lap.

"Do you think she really could have known Father—I mean, how is that possible? What could he have promised her?"

"I have every reason to think I should have cared for her—every reason to regret that I didn't stand up to Drake on her behalf. And I'm thinking that it doesn't—it *shouldn't*—matter if Father promised anything or not." Olivia stood and picked up her hat and cloak. "We must find her, Dorothy, and we must find her soon."

CHAPTER SEVENTEEN

"YOU CAN'T EXPECT me to go to church—or school—or anywhere in public like this!" Katie Rose exploded at Sunday morning breakfast, the first spark of life Maureen had seen her sister exhibit.

"But, my dear, the Wakefields will be there. They could give you a ride home in their touring car," Mrs. Melkford insisted.

Maureen nearly choked on her tea. She'd not even thought of the Wakefields attending the same church as Mrs. Melkford. There were half a dozen churches in between Mrs. Melkford's and Morningside. "I didn't know you knew the Wakefields."

"I refuse to meet them for the first time in public like this!" Katie Rose fumed.

"I don't know them," Mrs. Melkford, her eyes confused by Katie Rose's outburst, answered Maureen. "It's a large church; I hardly know anyone yet. I just started attending there last month—it's so much closer to my apartment than St. John's, where my Henry and I used to worship—but I've heard the name. I didn't realize the father had passed until you told me. But surely they'd come for you girls; you're living with them."

"I won't go!" Katie Rose insisted.

"I don't think Katie Rose is ready to go out, Mrs. Melkford." Maureen pleaded her sister's case but knew she did it selfishly.

"I'm sorry, my dear," Mrs. Melkford said. "I know you've only just arrived and that you've been through a great deal. But Nurse Harrigan said that you're really quite well."

Katie Rose frowned, her lower lip protruding.

Mrs. Melkford smiled and patted Katie Rose's hand across the table. "You're tired, and here I am, eager to show you off."

"Show me off?" Katie Rose, her face splotched and red with astonishment and barely faded blisters, gasped.

Maureen sat close to her sister. "I know you don't want to go out today, but you must understand that Mrs. Melkford has been wonderful to us. If not for her, we wouldn't even be here. They might have refused us entry."

But Katie Rose was clearly not as taken with Mrs. Melkford as was Maureen. "We don't need her," she hissed to her sister. "The Wakefields—they're our sponsors."

Mrs. Melkford's color rose, but she sat back, straightening the napkin in her lap.

"Apologize to Mrs. Melkford!"

"Never mind." Mrs. Melkford's mouth formed a line as she picked up the breakfast cups. "Perhaps it's best if you gather your strength."

Katie Rose fled to the parlor. Maureen washed the dishes in silence. Mrs. Melkford dried and put them away.

"She'll need to come to terms with it sometime."

Maureen turned to her friend. "But the scars will fade in time, surely?"

Mrs. Melkford picked up another plate. "Some will. But Nurse Harrigan said it's too soon to know if they'll fade entirely. She's older than most children who contract chicken pox, and a woman's face is unforgiving."

"Did they tell her that?"

"Nurse Harrigan said she didn't take it well. She said I should tell you that the sooner Katie Rose accepts herself as she is and gets out into the world, the better." Mrs. Melkford sighed. "She's young, I know . . . but I rather doubt you were ever quite so young."

Maureen didn't know what to say. By the time she was Katie Rose's age, she'd been sent into service while Katie Rose stayed home with their mother. Maureen had envied her sister's opportunity to attend the village school, have friends, and drop by Aunt Verna's kitchen on a whim. But she later felt guilty when Katie Rose had to nurse their mother—a bleak and heavy responsibility for one so young. She watched Mrs. Melkford silently drying the last plate, sorry that Katie Rose's outburst had spoiled their cheerful morning.

"Well." With another sigh, Mrs. Melkford untied her apron strings.

"I believe I'll get myself ready for church. I don't want to miss Reverend Peterson's sermon. You and Katie Rose do as you think best. We'll leave the chicken roasting in a slow oven. It will be ready by the time I get back." Her voice was kind, but Maureen knew her friend was disappointed.

"I'd like to go with you—but I don't know that I should leave Katie Rose her first day here."

Mrs. Melkford hung her apron on the peg by the kitchen door. "It's only an hour or so. She'll be quite safe here."

Maureen hesitated. "Do you think we could sit in the back so if I get anxious about her, or if the service goes long, we might slip out?"

Mrs. Melkford brightened. "Certainly! I usually sit in the balcony. I can see everything from there." Her brow wrinkled. "The Wakefields have a family pew near the front of the church. I'm afraid you won't find it easy to speak with them."

"That's quite all right," Maureen assured her. "They're not expectin' me."

Mrs. Melkford looked as though she was about to say or ask something but stopped herself. She squeezed Maureen's arm. "I'll be with you here in ten minutes, and we'll be on our way."

It was the biggest church Maureen had ever stepped inside, and Protestant, besides. She'd only ever attended the old stone church on the edge of her village, and not that for years—except the day she walked into the church to make arrangements with the priest for her mother's graveside service.

Maureen followed Mrs. Melkford up the winding steps of the balcony, where, good to her word, she claimed two seats nearest the back.

Maureen held a bird's-eye view of the sanctuary. She scanned the parishioners for the two she'd confronted at the Wakefield house and the two who had stood aghast in the hallway. She couldn't be certain, but there was a pew, very near the right front side of the church, seating four well-dressed adults near her own age: two men and two women. She was fairly certain, once she saw his profile, that the one nearest the middle was the harsh man, Mr. Drake Meitland. She could not be certain of the women, whose faces were shielded by their hats.

"Do you see the Wakefields?" Mrs. Melkford craned her short neck to see around the sea of hats before her.

"Yes, I think so," Maureen admitted.

"It might be a good idea if you explain to them about Katie Rose's condition before you take her there tonight. Perhaps you can speak with them after church."

Maureen drew her breath in sharply, but it was lost in the organ's mighty prelude. She turned to take in the magnificent pipes, and that led her eyes to stained-glass windows, depicting Bible scenes that rang faintly familiar but that she could not place.

Maureen had heard of the grandeur of the cathedrals in Lincoln and London, of churches large and small through Ireland, throughout America, but this did not match any of the pictures her mind had conjured. The ceiling rose high, even above the balcony. Wood everywhere was polished to a lemon-wax sheen. But there were no statues—no Blessed Mother, no suffering Lord Jesus, no bleeding heart of Christ, no saints or apostles in the throes of martyrdom—save for the scenes of men and women dressed in Bible garb captured in the glass windows. She wondered what the parishioners worshiped as the glory of God if they'd nothing to see and touch.

Not that the images or fonts or kneelers had done wonders for her. But she'd assumed that was because she'd given up going to confession the day Julius Orthbridge had violated her.

At first she'd prayed, begging God to make him stop. But when the demon's strength increased, and her fear had burst its bounds, she grew convinced that it was all a judgment against who she was, what she'd become, and that there was no way out—not in this life and surely not in the next. Resigned, she'd stopped fighting—stopped fighting Julius Orthbridge and stopped begging heaven. Maureen knew she was smitten, despised of God, and that eternity could provide no hell worse than the one she'd lived day after day, night after night. She did not live in fear of the hereafter. She'd lived in the dread of Lord Orthbridge and the despair of the present.

Maureen swallowed a moan at the thought of what she'd done in Ireland, of the lies she'd already told in America, and the knowledge that she'd do it again because she didn't know what else to do. *For it all depends on me, doesn't it?* She glanced at Mrs. Melkford standing beside her as they sang from a shared hymnal. *If I'd told her the truth about the Wakefields, would she have turned me out—sent me back to Ellis Island from her own obligation? Or would she have helped me, let me stay with her until . . . until what? What is "enough" in this country? Wouldn't I have needed the signature of a man established to vouch for me?*

Maureen didn't know the answers, but in any case, the disappointment Mrs. Melkford had shown that morning in Katie Rose's outbursts made Maureen fear wounding her further.

And what of Katie Rose? She thinks we're leavin' Mrs. Melkford's for the Wakefields—for a grand life to be waited upon hand and foot! Wait till she sees where we're livin'!

The cold truth of their slope toward desperation and poverty chilled her. *It's one thing to do without, to live in a hovel, but another thing to draw Katie Rose in with me!*

Maureen drew a deep breath. This was supposed to be a fresh start. She'd never meant to spin and tangle such a ball of yarn.

The service was nearly over when Reverend Peterson coughed; that simple sound drew Maureen from her worries.

"It has come to my attention that there has been a revival of sorts among some of the ladies of our congregation regarding Mr. Charles Sheldon's acclaimed novel, *In His Steps*." Reverend Peterson paused, and Maureen noted a nervous shifting scattered among the parishioners, even in the Wakefield pew.

The reverend smiled, and Maureen thought it a wondrous thing to see a man of the cloth gaze so magnanimously upon his flock. She realized that she'd heard no condemning word through the entire sermon.

"I wish to commend this fine book to all and to encourage its reading, both in our homes and among our circles."

Mrs. Melkford clasped Maureen's hand. "Splendid!" she whispered.

"I look forward to hearing where Mr. Sheldon's challenge leads," he finished. "And now, let us close with hymn number 175, 'All the Way My Savior Leads Me.'"

Maureen did not know the book he mentioned, and she did not know the hymn, but she did her best to follow the tune as the great organ pealed its notes, resounding through her shoes.

All the way my Savior leads me;
What have I to ask beside?
Can I doubt His tender mercy,
Who through life has been my guide?

Maureen did not think that she'd been shown tender mercy by anyone other than Aunt Verna or Mrs. Melkford, or that anyone had been her guide. She'd survived by her wits, and that, barely.

Heav'nly peace, divinest comfort . . .
Cheers each winding path I tread,
Gives me grace for every trial,
Feeds me with the living bread.

"Living bread," Maureen whispered, wondering what that could mean. Mrs. Melkford raised her eyebrows toward Maureen but continued to sing.

Though my weary steps may falter,
And my soul athirst may be,
Gushing from the Rock before me,
Lo! a spring of joy I see. . . .
Perfect rest to me is promised . . .

Maureen could sing no more. *None of this is meant for the likes of me!* She'd have slipped from the balcony and the church had Mrs. Melkford not been there.

Why she couldn't stop the tears from slipping down her cheeks as the reverend prayed for grace and God's healing mercy through the coming week, for the restoration of relationships and the daily direction of his flock, Maureen could not say. She swiped at her wet cheeks, humiliated, hoping the men and women nearby would not notice when they raised their heads from prayer.

Mrs. Melkford ushered her out just before the benediction, as if she sensed Maureen's distress. "It was a touching service."

That was all she said, and yet Maureen chewed the inside of her cheek to keep from bursting into tears as they hurried along the sidewalk. "I don't know what's come over me. I don't normally carry on like this."

Mrs. Melkford smiled and patted her arm. "Faith creeps in unawares, betimes."

Faith? Not likely!

"Do you have a Bible, Maureen?"

Maureen shook her head. No one in the village, save the priest, had his own Bible.

Mrs. Melkford nodded. "We'll see that you have one today."

Olivia replaced her hymnal and gathered her Bible and purse.

"You'll join us for Sunday dinner, Curtis?" Drake shook Curtis Morrow's hand as parishioners filed from their pews. "Won't take no for an answer!"

"If you're certain I'm not imposing."

"Nonsense!" Drake clapped Curtis's back.

Dorothy smiled. "We're delighted to have you. And now that you're established in our fair city, we expect to see you often."

"That will be my pleasure, entirely." He tipped his head. "You'll be there, Miss Wakefield?" Curtis Morrow's dark-brown eyes found Olivia's, surprising her.

"Yes—yes, I will."

"Then I wouldn't miss it." Curtis offered his arm.

The foursome had driven only two blocks when Drake suddenly turned, staring after something or someone Olivia could not see.

"What is it, Drake?" Dorothy asked.

Drake didn't answer, but as he sat back, the cords in his neck rose taut.

Curtis leaned forward. "You all right, Drake?"

"What?" Drake's smile looked forced. "Yes. Sure, just thought I recognized someone. I was mistaken."

✥ CHAPTER EIGHTEEN ✥

Sunday dinner at Meitland House was traditionally an elaborate affair. Olivia expected nothing less from her sister. Dorothy's pleasure in welcoming and entertaining guests with her finest linens, crystal, and silver, and in sharing the bountiful gifts of her fine cook, was a thing of beauty.

Curtis raised his glass to his hostess. "A lady in her home." The others joined him, and Dorothy blushed prettily.

Drake raised his glass a second time, to Curtis, and winked. "May you be so lucky."

"That is not likely." Curtis's forced smile stole the moment.

Olivia felt her spine straighten of its own accord and was as quickly annoyed with herself that she'd responded at all.

But Dorothy diverted the topic by drawing attention to Reverend Peterson's morning sermon as the salad plates were removed in preparation for the next course.

"What was that about some book the ladies are touting?" Drake speared a slice of roast duck.

"*In His Steps*—I know the book," Curtis offered.

"Do you, Mr. Morrow?" Olivia asked.

"Curtis." He smiled. "Yes, I've read it."

"And what did you think of it?" Dorothy kept the conversation going.

Curtis placed his fork beside his plate. "One of the most challenging books I've encountered. Not for its literary merit, but for its personal and spiritual challenge. The idea of asking before every endeavor, 'What would Jesus do in this situation?' sounds trite." He hesitated. "It's anything but. It challenges every ounce of my moral fiber."

"I agree." Olivia sat straighter, astonished that anything of substance came from a colleague of her brother-in-law. "It makes me stop and ask if my preconceived notions and opinions are truth or prejudice."

"And then what do you do about that?" Curtis asked. "How do you proceed if you find that your thinking is 'weighed in the balances and found wanting'?" His eyes met Olivia's, but when he turned, she was certain they probed Drake's.

"Sounds deep for Sunday entertainment," Drake responded, visibly shifting in his seat.

"It's not intended as entertainment," Olivia pursued. "We're serious. I'm serious."

"Ah!" Drake laughed, raising his knife to point toward Olivia. "I should have known it was you who put the good reverend up to challenging the congregation!"

"I've taken the challenge too," Dorothy said quietly.

Drake stopped laughing. He set down his knife, and though his mouth registered good humor, his eyes spoke sternly. "And what, exactly, does this mean?"

Dorothy's chin rose, but when her eyes connected with her husband's, they seemed to falter. Olivia was about to come to her sister's rescue when Curtis stepped in.

"I think that has to be different for each individual, doesn't it? In the book, Sheldon makes clear that no person can interpret the direction Jesus would take in the life of another—they can do that only for themselves, as the Spirit leads them." Curtis picked up his glass. "The wonder is how those purposes seem to overlap, to create greater impetus for a common cause."

"But is it a wonder?" Olivia warmed to the subject for the second time that week. "Shouldn't it be just that way—if the Spirit is truly leading? Shouldn't it happen that the Spirit would direct multiple lives to accomplish a common goal? Like the work of the revival meetings and the settlement house activities in the book?"

"Providence," Dorothy spoke, and a light shone in her eyes.

"You're talking about a novel!" Drake interrupted, laughing.

"But a novel that reveals truth in a way that is easily understood!" Olivia felt her heart awaken, shaking off a long winter.

"That's the scribbler in her, Curtis. She fancies herself a writer," Drake mocked.

"That's right." A light of memory sprang to Curtis's eyes. "Dorothy mentioned that before."

Olivia was caught off guard. "My love of writing has nothing to do with this."

"Why not?" Curtis asked. "Why would God gift you with a love of something—and an ability, I have no doubt—unless He intended for you to use it?"

Olivia felt heat rise to her face. "I don't know that I have ability. And I don't know what to write, what would be of use."

Curtis smiled. "Isn't that the point?"

"The point?"

"The point of the challenge," Dorothy injected. "What would Jesus do with this gift of writing, this God-given love of writing? What would He write?"

Curtis nodded. "In this place, in this time—just as Sheldon did in his."

Olivia felt such a rising in her chest, she thought she might be lifted from her seat.

"I'd be glad to take a look at your writing, if you'd permit me," Curtis offered.

Olivia sat back, certain she did not wish to share her private thoughts on paper with Curtis or with anyone else—not yet.

"Curtis is in publishing," Dorothy reminded her sister, leaning toward her to add, "Right here in New York now. His advice could be most valuable."

"When you're ready, the offer stands." Curtis smiled.

Olivia nodded, uncertain what to say.

"So if you're not penning the great American novel," Drake took up, "what's the mysterious project you and your ladies have decided to tackle this year?"

"We don't know just yet," Dorothy answered. "We're all reading Mr. Sheldon's book and praying about the challenge. We'll discuss our mission at our next meeting."

"You're looking at this as a group decision?" Curtis asked, his brow furrowed.

Olivia swallowed. "We'll certainly ask what Jesus would have us do as a group, but first, we ask that question individually."

"So you are thinking about writing the great American novel after all," Drake teased.

"No," Olivia answered evenly. "I'm thinking of looking for the O'Reilly woman who came to my home on Thanksgiving."

Drake stopped chewing. "I took care of the matter."

"I wish you hadn't."

Drake turned his head. "I have every intention of protecting both you and *my wife*."

Olivia did not take the bait. "Do you know her first name? Or where she's staying?"

"No. She showed up on our doorstep with a fraudulent letter and some cock-and-bull Civil War story about her father."

"It was true, and it was my doorstep."

"What's true?" Dorothy asked.

Drake's glare gave Olivia pause, but she continued. "Morgan O'Reilly saved Father's life during the war, and Father pledged to do all he could for Morgan and his child."

"The war? But that was so long ago!"

"It doesn't change Father's promise." Olivia squeezed her sister's hand across the table. "Or our obligation to carry forth his wishes."

"This is ridiculous!" Drake fumed.

"How do you know, Livvie?" Dorothy asked. "How do you know Father promised? Did he tell you?"

Olivia hadn't wanted to tell Dorothy that she'd broken their pact to leave the journals alone, but she could see no other way. She smoothed the linen napkin in her lap. "I read the story in Father's journal."

Dorothy merely blinked, but Olivia sensed her sister's feelings of betrayal.

"I'm sorry; I should have told you. But I had to know. I had to know why she came, why she had a letter from Father." She wanted so much for Dorothy to understand.

"The woman was a fraud. That letter was a fake!" Drake insisted.

"It was real," Olivia countered, indignation rising. "I saw a scrap of

Father's handwriting—a bit you failed to burn. And that is what made me go looking."

Drake glanced at Curtis with barely controlled fury. "My apologies. This is not a matter that should be aired in front of our guest."

"What did the journals say Father intended?" Dorothy asked quietly, ignoring her husband.

"Dorothy!" Drake warned.

But Olivia ignored him too. "He intended to buy the property next to ours for Morgan's family, to set him up in business, and his son, as well." She paused, but when Drake seemed intent on interrupting, she rushed on. "I think he hoped Morgan's son would be another heir for him, and Morgan's children would be siblings of a sort for us."

"There you have it—it was a woman who came to the door, certainly not a son." Drake tossed his napkin to the table. "Mystery solved. Case closed."

"You said you hope to find Miss O'Reilly?" Curtis surprised Olivia by taking up the thread.

"Yes, I do. I want to know if she's truly related to Morgan O'Reilly and if there is some way I can help her." She glanced at Drake. "It sounds as though she may be his daughter. She looked to be about my age." Olivia sighed and bit her lower lip. "But I don't know where or how to begin looking for her."

Drake stood. "Well, then, that's that, isn't it? 'Providence' has spoken. Shall we retire to the drawing room?" He offered Dorothy his arm and escorted her from the room, signaling an end to the conversation.

"Olivia?"

Olivia turned toward Curtis as he slowly pushed his chair to the table, lagging behind Drake and Dorothy.

"I'd like to offer my services," he said quietly, "to help you find her."

Olivia glanced uneasily toward the door, but Drake had gone. "Thank you, Mr. Mor—Curtis. Thank you." Her heart quickened. "I would be most grateful, but . . . I don't understand why. It's of no concern to you."

"Because you wish it and because you'll need help to find her." He offered his arm. "Reason enough."

But the set of his jaw told Olivia there was something more.

CHAPTER NINETEEN

"You must be jokin'!" Katie Rose stood outside the Lower East Side bar, her arm wrapped round Maureen's for support.

"No." Maureen had dreaded this moment all the way from Mrs. Melkford's kitchen. "I told you it's all I can afford just now." She pulled her sister toward the side door of the building. "It won't be for long—just until we can manage somethin' better." *Though I've no idea when that will be.*

"We should try the Wakefields again. Surely they wouldn't let us stay here if they knew. Surely they'd do somethin'!"

"You weren't there; you don't know. I told you—Colonel Wakefield's dead and buried. They've no obligation to us—none to Father, even if he were alive."

But Katie Rose stood rooted to the pavement. "I'll not live in a pub!"

"We don't live in the pub." Maureen dropped her arm. "*I'll* not stand in the street and argue like fishwives. I'm done in. Come up when you're ready; we're the third floor, second flat on the left." She stomped through the door and up the stairs, knowing she was behaving poorly. But more than that, she burned with humiliation before her sister's righteous glare. *What have I done? What have I brought us to?*

Maureen had barely unlocked the door before she heard her sister's footsteps on the stairs. She sighed in relief and lit the lamp. She placed the Bible Mrs. Melkford had gifted her upon the table, running her finger over its leather cover as if touching it could recapture the peace of that lady's presence. *We need peace.*

"I thought all of America had electricity now." Katie Rose stood in the doorway.

Maureen pulled the pin from her hat and hung her cloak on a hook by the door. "Apparently not."

Katie Rose lifted her chin and turned away. Maureen bit her lip, regretting her sharp answer.

"Mr. Crudgers said he'd deliver a bedstead, but I don't believe him." Maureen spoke to Katie Rose's back. "We'll share the pallet."

"Who?"

"Mr. Crudgers, the landlord. He tends the bar—the tavern, downstairs." Maureen pulled an apron round her waist and bent to start the fire in the stove. "There's a toilet down the hall. We can boil water if you'd like a wash. We've our own indoor pump in the kitchen." Maureen looked at her sister, hopeful. "That's more than we had at home."

"Not more than you had in the grand house," Katie Rose retorted. "Not more than they had at Ellis Island or even at that missionary woman's flat. We'd be better off livin' with her!"

Maureen slammed the skillet to the stove. "Well, we don't, do we? We live here. And you're a fine one to appreciate her now that you've not got what you want!"

"Not got what I want?" Katie Rose fumed. "Look at you, Maureen O'Reilly! You, in your fine American shirtwaist and suit! You, with your pert hat and stylish button boots! You've certainly got what *you* want!"

Maureen felt her blood rise. "I've to dress the best I can if I'm to keep my job in the department store. As it is, I'm not so stylish as the other girls. And for your information, miss, I've reworked every stitch I'm wearin'. I've even reworked a dress for you, for school."

"I told you, I'm not goin' to school!"

"Yes, you are."

"I'll not go about like . . . like this. Not until the scars have gone. Do you understand me? I'll not go!" Katie Rose crossed her arms.

If Maureen had not been so vexed, she would have laughed at her nearly grown sister planted in the center of the room with the face and stance of a pouting toddler. For the sake of sanity and civility, she dared not and couldn't muster the energy to scold. So she ignored her and dropped a dollop of lard in the skillet to sizzle. She chopped the onions and potatoes she'd hoarded for their first meal, tossed them in to fry, and set the kettle to boil for tea. If there was one thing Maureen knew, it was that the aroma of frying onions and the warmth of a kitchen signaled home—a sense of home that she hoped would bring peace. She must trust that Katie Rose would yield, and upon her yielding, they could work together.

By the time Maureen had laid the table and poured the tea, Katie Rose had uncrossed her arms and moved to the window to peer into the street. It was Sunday night, but the tavern below was already doing a lively business, and a Tin Pan piano player kept the beat livelier still.

"It's different than the pub in the village," Katie Rose spoke meekly.

"'Tis," Maureen acknowledged. "We'll not be wantin' to walk about the hallway more than we need to by night." She motioned her sister to the table. "Nor to be seen through the window."

"Why?"

Maureen sighed. She hated that she even knew the answer. "The men in the streets look up, and if they see a face or figure they fancy, they tell the tavern keeper."

"That doesn't mean anythin'."

"It means they think you're advertisin' yourself—sellin' yourself—and they expect to get what they want. If you don't give it freely, they'll come bangin' on the door to take it. Now come away from the window."

They ate in grim silence. Katie Rose had not removed her cloak, and Maureen did not push her.

"It will warm up before long, at least a bit. The stove helps some."

Katie Rose did not respond.

"Would you like to see the dress I've reworked for you?"

"I'm not goin' to school."

"Would you like to see the dress?" Maureen persisted.

Katie Rose didn't answer but pushed the last of her potato to the edge of her plate and back again—once, twice, three times.

Maureen knew she was afraid to give an inch and decided at last that another week at home might not matter so very much, not if it meant they could forge some sort of truce. "I suppose you could do with another week to regain your strength."

Katie Rose looked up.

"But you'll be terribly alone. I leave at dawn for the store and am not home again until seven. From now till Christmas I'll be called upon to stay longer; I've no idea how late."

"I don't mind bein' alone—not now." Katie Rose looked about the small room.

"You can't go walkin' about and gettin' lost, and you can't be down-stairs in the tavern. Do you promise?"

Kaite Rose nodded quickly. A minute passed. "It's just . . . I didn't think it would be like this."

"No—" Maureen reached for her sister's hand—"nor did I. We'll make the best of it, the best we can. And as soon as we can save some money, we'll move. We'll move to a place with our own tub and a real bed."

"And hot water in the pipes. And no tavern." Katie Rose did not pull her hand away.

"And no tavern!" Maureen smiled.

"Promise?"

"I promise."

"Then I'll do our housekeepin' and food shoppin'. I'll do the washin' and mendin' and prepare our tea."

"For this week."

"Until my scars are healed."

"We don't know how long that will—"

"And then I'll find a position, like you."

Maureen winced at the strength of Katie Rose's grip upon her fingers.

"I'm not goin' to school. I'd have only this year before I'm too old, any-way. I know enough of readin' and writin' and cipherin'. It's plain as plain we can't manage on your wages. I might not be able to work in a shop, but I heard at the hospital that there are sewin' factories all over New York. You know I'm good with my needle, and I'm dyin' to learn the new machines."

"But—"

"There're no buts." Katie Rose pushed Maureen's hand away. "You're not Mam, and unless you're ready for us to go beggin' at the Wakefields' door, we're both needed."

Maureen was taken aback by the obstinacy of the sister she'd supposed meek and mild, the sister who'd had so little to say until stepping onto American shores. She stood, too weary to argue, and placed their crockery in the dry sink. She changed into her nightdress, pulled pins from her hair, and brushed long tresses until they shone in the lamplight. Something about the rhythmic brushing of her hair had always given Maureen a sense of peace and balance. She braided it into one long coil and swept it over her shoulder.

Everything her sister said was true. There was no way she could pay the rent, buy their food, recoup the money she owed Jaime Flynn, pay Katie Rose's hospital fees, and save enough for them to move on her wages alone. *As long as Jaime Flynn doesn't know where I am, we have time.* But she closed her eyes, knowing it was a matter of weeks—perhaps days—until he did find her, until he saw her in the store he seemed to frequent too often.

Well, I'll not force Katie Rose back to school. I can't start our lives together with a daily struggle—I've not the energy or leisure. And I do understand what it is to face a new world at less than your best. What we'll do if her scars don't fade, I've no idea.

She'd heard from Alice and Mrs. Melkford both that night schools held classes in many parts of Manhattan, some especially for immigrants. *Perhaps I can convince Katie Rose to take evenin' classes together once we're better situated, once our lives settle into a daily pattern. We lost so many years in Ireland. It will be good to spend time together, to get to know each other and learn new things together. We're all the family either of us has. And after all, it's a new land, a new life for us both. There's no sense tryin' to hold on to the old ways. They didn't serve us well.*

She waited until Katie Rose had readied herself for bed. Before turning down the lamp, Maureen pulled her last three dollars from her purse and passed one to Katie Rose. "There's a grocer on the corner. He gets fresh bread and milk each mornin' and produce on Thursdays. Make this last, and mind he doesn't cheat you."

❖ CHAPTER TWENTY ❖

Two weeks passed. Maureen felt that she and Katie Rose were settling into something of a pattern. She'd worked late every night, restocking shelves and helping to arrange new displays, trying to keep pace with the Christmas rush. By the time she returned home, it was pitch-black, but the bar downstairs shone bright lights into the street, peddling a noisy trade.

Still, Maureen was relieved at how Katie Rose had taken over the cooking and shopping, even the housekeeping, with a vengeance. She'd even grown determined to "decorate" their flat for Christmas—a thing they'd never imagined back in the village. Maureen tried to nurture her sister's enthusiasm, but her own longtime association with Christmas was confined to the landlord's house, a memory that led from an ostentatious display of wealth, lavish gifts and banquets, scented candlelight, and yule logs to the abuse of wine and ale, and finally to nights of debauchery and misery that followed.

Maureen shook her head, pushing back the unpleasant and too-familiar trail of memory. She'd determined not to live in the regrets of the past but to make the most of their new lives. Some days that was harder to do than others, but she'd discovered an investment she could make in those lives today, when she heard one of Darcy's clerks talking during lunch about a Christmas tree market near the Battery.

"Oh, you'll love it!" Eliza had exclaimed. "It has every kind of tree imaginable! Evergreens, freshly cut and shipped from the Adirondacks, all in a giant lot; it's like walking through a forest!" She'd lowered her voice. "And even if you're not wanting a tree, there are branches free for the taking."

Maureen didn't know that New Yorkers gave away anything for free.

"Sometimes they have to cut the bottoms off the trunk, you see, so the tree fits a customer's foyer or parlor or drawing room—wherever they want to place it. All those branches are thrown in a heap. My neighbor goes round and collects what he can, fashions wreaths, then sells them on the street corner."

"People pay money for branches wound round into wreaths?"

Eliza had nodded enthusiastically. "New Yorkers own more money than sense!"

The girls had laughed conspiratorially, but that night, Maureen and Katie Rose fell asleep talking of the fresh scent of pine and spruce, the aroma of sticky cedar.

"It will be just the thing to fill our flat with fragrance—and pale the reek of the privy!" Katie Rose clapped. "Say we'll go!"

It was the first excitement Katie Rose had expressed for anything out of doors. Maureen sighed to think how her sister's hatred of her slowly fading scars had kept her from exploring the possibilities of New York and from applying for employment. *Perhaps this will encourage her.*

They were inching along, a bit hungry, and shivering from lack of food and heat by night. *But we're managin'. Still, a trip to the tree market will make a fine outin'; it will cost us nothin' but shoe leather. And we'll hope there're branches to be had.*

She hadn't told Katie Rose, but there were wonderful Christmas displays in the store windows of Manhattan's shopping district, some backlit by electric lights in the evenings. Maureen smiled to anticipate her sister's delight of standing in a dark world, suddenly surprised by Mr. Edison's lights along the streets, as she had been that dark Thanksgiving night.

Perhaps in another month or two, if nothin' unforeseen happens, and if Katie Rose gets the job she hopes, we'll be able to move to a flat in a respectable boardinghouse. Perhaps there'll be a light outside our window in a better street! Maureen breathed deeply to think of the peace a move might bring—no more bawdy drunkards below, perhaps a hot bath on occasion, and the friendship of other young women. And best of all, no reminders of her past.

Despite the cold and lightly falling snow, Joshua Keeton wiped the sweat from his brow. He still wasn't used to dodging automobiles, whose drivers swore they owned the slippery roadways, or weaving his bicycle in and out of throngs of New Yorkers at breakneck speed. Horses, country lanes, and wide-open spaces were more to his liking.

But he was grateful for the work—any work that kept a roof over his head, food in his belly, and padded his pockets with a bit laid by for a rainy day, precious little though it was. Still, he'd no intention of making deliveries for department stores forever.

I'll find somethin' more by and by. At least I've learned the highways and byways and all the back alleys of the streets of New York. That's bound to come in handy.

He hefted his bicycle and carried it up the outer back stairs of the boardinghouse, then straight to his room. He wasn't about to leave it against the building for the next petty thief; he'd suffered at the hands of a few in New York. He slapped his cap against his knee to shake off the late afternoon dampness and hung his coat on the peg.

His stomach rumbled appreciatively at the smell of the meal Mrs. MacLaren was preparing below stairs. He took the steps down to the dining room two at a time.

"You'll kill yourself trippin' up and down those stairs one of these days, Mr. Keeton!" the plump landlady admonished, but with all the fondness of a doting aunt.

"The fragrance of your kitchen draws every bit of sense from my brain, Mrs. MacLaren! I can't help myself or stay me soul!"

"Oh, you're a silver-tongued devil, you are." She dimpled. "One for the ladies, no doubt." She set a bowl of steaming corned beef and cabbage on each end of the table, with a bowl of potatoes and a loaf of brown bread between.

"Only for you, my gracious lady." Joshua bowed respectfully before taking his seat but knew his mouth turned up at its corners.

Mrs. MacLaren tucked her head to one side. "If I'm your one and only, then who's this Verna Keithly, I'd like to know?" She pulled an envelope from her apron pocket and waved it, teasing, in the air. "A lass from County Meath pinin' her heart out for the rovin' likes of you?"

Why would Verna Keithly write to me? Joshua's smile turned down. *Maureen. What's happened to Maureen?*

His heart stopped. He'd prayed for her every day since last he'd seen her, since last she'd spurned him. He'd even mapped a route to the Wakefields' address—the one Verna Keithly had given him when she'd asked him to escort her nieces to America. But wounded pride had kept him at least two blocks in every direction from Morningside.

No matter. It wasn't easy to forget a woman who'd set his pulse to racing—a woman whose heart he'd set out to win since she was a girl and he a lad hired to cart wood for the Orthbridge estate. He'd dared hope his dream might come true when Mrs. Keithly charged him with care for Maureen and Katie Rose. But Maureen had made her feelings clear.

Willing his hand and mouth steady, he took the half-crumpled letter from Mrs. MacLaren and nonchalantly stuffed it into his pocket. He'd wait, he decided, and read it after dinner, away from inquisitive eyes.

But the moment the prayer had been offered, Joshua mumbled his excuses and took the stairs back to his room, three at a time.

Closing the door, he ripped the letter's seal. A second envelope, addressed to Maureen, tumbled out. He read the first one twice, his brow furrowing deeper each time.

He pulled long fingers of worry and frustration through his hair. "Whatever have you done now, Maureen O'Reilly? Whatever have you done?"

Joshua stuffed the letters into his pocket. Pushing his arms through his coat sleeves, he pulled his cap over his head, wound his muffler round his throat, and hefted his bicycle, bumping it out the door and down the stairs into the street.

The snow came harder, but he brushed the sting of sleet away, gritting his teeth. "If they've hurt you, I'll—I swear, I'll—" But he didn't finish the thought, for it shook him to his core.

———————————————※———————————————

That afternoon, Maureen continued to freshen the Darcy's displays, no matter that she could hardly wait for the Saturday bell to signal her shift was done. It seemed that hats and other goods flew from the shelves and hourly needed to be replaced. *New Yorkers are absolutely besotted with Christmas!* She'd seen more women buy hats and dresses that flattered neither face nor figure than she cared to remember. Maureen shook her head and smiled at the predictable unpredictability of her customers.

"Well, well . . . I thought you'd forgotten all about your old friend from Ellis Island, but I see you're busy makin' your way in the world, pretty Maureen O'Reilly from County Meath." Jaime Flynn stood close behind, eye to eye with Maureen as she turned from her work.

She started, dropping a box of handkerchiefs. "Mr. Flynn."

"A fine memory." He smiled. "Here, let me help you." He reached for the box, pressing close against her.

"No need, I've got them." She stepped back quickly, an image flashing through her brain of Jaime Flynn entering the elevator, fondling a young immigrant girl no older than Katie Rose. Disgust and shivers shot up her spine.

"I trust my employment recommendation stood you in good stead." He moved closer, intimating a private conversation.

Maureen swallowed and held the box between them, stalling for time to think. "Yes, sir. . . . I thank you for givin' me the address of the store."

"I trust you gave your employers my name. You know we all work on commission, one way or another."

Maureen dared not answer.

"I see." His smile faded. "Did my little advance help you—and your sister? What was her name? Karen? Kate?"

"Yes, sir. It did, sir." She stepped behind the counter and pushed sweating palms down her skirt, conscious that Alice, clerking at the far end of the counter, looked their way. "And I thank you for it. I'll be able to pay you back soon, very soon. Things have just run a bit more dear than I'd imagined."

He nodded, searched her face and figure, then spoke softly. "Cash is hard to come by, especially this time of year." He tilted his head as if he'd just remembered something. "I'll be needin' my money back this week, you know, with perhaps a bit of interest for my trust and goodwill to you."

"I'll do my best, sir." Though Maureen knew there was no way she could raise thirty dollars within the week, much less whatever "interest" he wanted to charge, even if she gave him her entire pay envelope.

He tapped the counter. "This isn't the floor where I was expectin' you'd be employed. There's better jobs upstairs, higher pay. There'd be no lack of funds with a job like that. You could pay me back with some to spare. I can arrange it for you and your sister. It's not too late."

Maureen felt the heat race up her neck. "There's no need, sir. I've always wanted to work in a shop. And I fancy hats. This is grand, just grand."

He licked his lips. "As I said—"

"My good friends, Mrs. Melkford from the Missionary Aid Society and the Wakefields of Morningside—they're all so very glad for me."

"Good friends, are they?" Flynn frowned and narrowed his eyes as if considering whether to believe her.

"Yes, sir. They are indeed, sir. We're livin' with the Wakefields, you see, and . . . and we're all off to church tomorrow." Maureen's heart raced, and she knew her face must flame scarlet, but she braved on, despite the suspicion and irritation that flashed in Jaime Flynn's eyes. "Would you be interested in a hat for the missus?" She forced herself to smile. "We've a fine selection for the season."

Willing her fingers to stop trembling, she turned to gather a striking burgundy hat, the nearest at hand, and a pair of complimenting silk gloves, as though he were an everyday customer. But when she turned again, he'd gone.

She heard the bell for the elevator ring and looked to see the door slide open. Jaime Flynn stepped through.

Maureen willed her heart to slow. But the moment she returned to her counter, Drake Meitland, with two other well-dressed gentlemen, walked through the revolving front door of the store. They looked neither right nor left as they headed directly for the elevator and could not, Maureen prayed, have seen her duck behind the counter.

Agnes Mein stood and called the Ladies' Circle meeting to order. "Our first order of business is our only order of business." She glanced round the room of fashionable ladies, longtime acquaintances, if not friends, gathered in Carolynn's parlor. "We've each had two weeks to read Mr. Sheldon's book and to consider, in the light of his challenge, our mission for the coming year."

"Shall I read our original list of suggestions?" Carolynn asked.

"No," Agnes answered quickly. "That won't be necessary. I believe we all remember the list and have surely pondered—and prayed—over it." She laid her papers aside. "I'd like to focus our discussion on our relationship to the poor, rather than on our duty to the poor, our specific mission."

She saw Olivia sit straighter. Carolynn leaned forward. Julia raised her brows.

"As you may have realized by Reverend Peterson's sermon, I went to him after our last circle meeting." Agnes drew herself up, determined to proceed though humility tasted foreign in her mouth. "What you won't have realized is that I went to him with the express purpose of insisting that he call our circle into line. I was furious with the twisting-turning of events and introspection, and I simply wanted us to get on with it—to choose our mission and proceed 'full steam ahead,' if you will." She paused and moistened her lips. "But my motive was wrong, and Reverend Peterson helped me see that."

Agnes knew the women dared not breathe for wonder of what was coming.

"He told me to go home and read Mr. Sheldon's book and expect miracles." She clasped her hands. "I confess to you now that I didn't want to. I didn't want to consider miracles, much less another way of thinking. I cherish the old ways of doing, the old ways of thinking." She lifted her chin and smiled—a little. "And I like being in charge."

Agnes saw Julia bite her lip to keep from smiling in return.

"Yes, well, that may not be new information for some of you, but it was for me." Agnes paused, determined to repossess her temper though not quite certain how to proceed.

"What changed your mind, Agnes?" Olivia asked.

Agnes sat down and drew in her breath. "I realized, as I read, that I've been thinking of the poor we serve as those who need our grace, our cast-off clothing, our noblesse oblige. I've thought that we, who are privileged to possess much of this world's goods and fortune, are obliged to help those less fortunate. Although, I did quantify that obligation, and I know now that I extended grace, grudgingly in some cases, especially where I believed those in need brought dire circumstances upon themselves through wantonness or lethargy or frivolity, or where I saw little effort to improve themselves. . . . But more than that . . ." She looked down at her hands and her voice fell. "I realize that I gave from a sense of superiority, as if I could give because I had received more grace than they." She looked up. "No, that is not true. I believed I *deserved* more grace, and therefore I had been blessed materially. Before reading Mr. Sheldon's book, I never realized that . . ." She spread her hands helplessly.

"That 'there, but for the grace of God, go I,'" Carolynn finished.

"Yes," Agnes whispered.

A long moment passed.

"You're not alone," Julia took up the thread.

Agnes looked up, surprised that Julia, of all the women present, might come to her aid.

"I considered all my bluss and thunder about the desperate needs of women and children to be my cause, my personal crusade." Julia straightened her spine, and Agnes knew she was ready to march once more into the fray. "I realized this week that my insistence was more about me—Julia Gresham, the wealthy young crusader who openly disdained her family's wealth and despised convention—than about those I helped. But it's not about me; it's not even about fighting low wages or prostitution or poverty—not entirely, anyway." She shrugged, clearly trying to find the words. "It's about . . ."

"Embracing one another as sisters—as brothers and sisters," Dorothy finished.

"Yes," Agnes said, and Julia nodded.

"The story Jesus told of the Good Samaritan kept coming to mind as I read." Miranda spoke for the first time. "It wouldn't let me go. I think because it is the same thing—it wasn't really about who the Samaritan was or who he helped or even how he helped, but the fact that he cared for the man. He touched him, picked him up, no matter the ideas of uncleanness or whether the man deserved help or was beyond help. He treated him like . . ."

"Like a brother and not a stranger," Isabella said.

"A band of brothers," Dorothy whispered.

"What did you say?" Olivia clasped her sister's hand.

Dorothy flushed. "It's something Father used to say, when he was reminiscing about the men in his unit, from the war. He said they were like a family, as close as any blood tie—what Shakespeare called a 'band of brothers.' One would do whatever he could to protect and care for the man beside him, even to the laying down of his life."

"As Morgan O'Reilly did for him," Olivia said aloud, though it seemed to Agnes that she was talking more to herself.

"Who? Olivia?" Agnes asked.

"What? Oh, nothing. I'm sorry."

"A band of sisters," Carolynn said. "We are or must become for one another a band of sisters in this determination to walk as Jesus walked, to live as Jesus lived."

"Yes," Agnes said, glad for the women she loved more than she'd realized. "That's it. We must embrace our suffering sisters."

"To form a greater, stronger band with them on the inside, not outside," Julia affirmed, tapping her knee.

"Yes. Yes!" Agnes almost laughed with joy, knowing that the next miracle she experienced might well be she and Julia Gresham marching arm in arm into the fray.

CHAPTER TWENTY-ONE

"Well, now . . ." Alice tickled the back of Maureen's neck as they stood in Saturday's line to collect their pay envelopes for the week. "And who was your dashing Irishman? I'm sure I've seen him hanging round Darcy's before. Do tell all!"

But Maureen had no intention of "telling all," not to Alice or to anyone else. "He's not 'my Irishman,' and I've nothin' to do with him!"

"That's not the way it looked to me," Alice chided. "He seemed to think you're something to him."

Maureen glanced over her shoulder, desperately wishing the line would move more quickly, anxious to get out of the store before the elevator door opened and Jaime Flynn or Drake Meitland reappeared. *What goes up must surely come down!*

"Maureen—" Alice leaned nearer and spoke quietly—"you look absolutely petrified. What is it?"

But Maureen only shook her head. *Do they know each other? That man, Meitland, won't even remember me, surely. Will he? What if Jaime Flynn asks him if I'm really livin' at Morningside? Oh, by the saints, what have I done?*

"Has that man frightened you? What did he say?"

Maureen could not bear to admit she'd taken money from a strange man or lied about her whereabouts or references or any of it. *And do they even care upstairs? I do my work; isn't that all that matters? Is this my wicked imagination?* She shook her head again. She couldn't tell Alice. But there was something Alice might know, and if it could be innocently explained, it might calm Maureen's fears about a good many things. She turned and whispered, "What happens on the fourth floor?"

The light and blood drained from Alice's face as she leaned away from Maureen. "Did he tell you to go upstairs?"

"Not exactly, but . . ." Maureen knew this was neither the time nor place to confide her fears, and the look of horror—or was it anger?—on Alice's face told her that she'd already said too much. "I have to go." She looked back to the line ahead. "Oh, why won't they hurry?"

Three more minutes passed as the line moved slowly forward. The girls were only steps away from Mrs. Gordon and the pay envelopes.

"It's the 'floor of promotion,' they call it," Alice whispered behind her. "Some of the girls go for a time—always the prettiest ones. They don't say why, but they come back with more money and nicer clothes; that's what I know. I've never been asked," Alice huffed. "Suppose they think I'm not pretty enough with my crooked nose. Not that I'd want to go, anyway."

Maureen inched her way forward.

"See the girl just ahead, with the red beret? She's been upstairs, and I saw her once in Manhattan and dressed to the nines, with one of the gentlemen who comes in here every Friday night—like clockwork, he's so regular."

Maureen swallowed.

"Some go to talk to Mr. Kreegle in personnel, and then they're gone—fired, I guess, or sent to work somewhere else. I'm not saying there's anything going on that shouldn't, but—"

If Alice finished her confidence, Maureen didn't hear her. For in that moment, as she accepted her pay envelope from Mrs. Gordon, the elevator door slid open.

Maureen did not stop to see if Jaime Flynn or Drake Meitland stepped onto the store floor. She raced down the stairs and through the employee exit door into the shower of snow. She did not stop running, did not respond to Officer Flannery's wink or tipping of his hat, and never waited for the automobiles and horse carts to slow, but dashed across streets, weaving through the traffic—human, horse, and machine.

She'd never have considered paying for a trolley when she could easily walk the long blocks home, but she couldn't risk being followed, could not risk anyone knowing where she and Katie Rose lived. She hopped aboard the first trolley she came to as it pulled from the curb. Her imagination of

Jaime Flynn or someone like him finding Katie Rose at home alone while Maureen labored behind the counter of Darcy's Department Store made her head spin and her stomach lurch.

The trolley car took her directly away from her route home. When she thought she'd put sufficient distance between herself and the store, she hopped off and trekked a meandering path through deepening snow back to her flat, knowing she was probably behaving foolishly, risking her health and taking precautions that were not warranted. But each time the image of Jaime Flynn's lustful smile or Drake Meitland's fury and power rose before her, so did the memory of the hands and smell and temper of Julius Orthbridge.

She dared not voice her fear to anyone, least of all to Katie Rose. She simply knew she must repay Jaime Flynn, and quickly. *If I can do that, I'll owe him nothin'. I'll be in no way beholden to him. He can't touch us if we're makin' our own way—not here and not through his connections at Ellis Island. It will be no one's business who we know or where we live. Oh, please, God, let that be true!*

By the time Maureen reached her own block, she was breathless, drenched from the snow, and she'd quite forgotten her promise to Katie Rose to go window-shopping and to gather Christmas branches from the tree market. The innocent thrill of electric lights strung along the main streets of Manhattan seemed a world away. All she could think as she bumped her leaden boots against the doorway was that it was high time Katie Rose applied for the job she'd championed over attending school. She had to know that Katie Rose was with other women during the day, that she was not alone. *And we must pool our money and repay this debt before Jaime Flynn or his friends come callin'.*

CHAPTER TWENTY-TWO

THE CIRCLE MEETING ran late, but Olivia knew it was simply that the women were loathe to part.

"A new sort of fire is burning!" Carolynn, her smile radiant, pressed Olivia's arm on her way out the door; Olivia returned her friend's affection.

"Livvie!" Dorothy called. "Wait for me; we can walk together."

But Olivia didn't want to wait. She knew what Dorothy would ask, but she didn't know what she would—what she in good conscience *could*—tell her.

"Please wait!" Dorothy repeated, breathless, as the sisters hurried down the sidewalk. "If I didn't know better, I'd think you were trying to avoid me."

Olivia stopped on the spot, feeling as if she'd been caught with her hand in the cookie jar.

"What is it, Livvie? Whatever is the matter?" Dorothy's hand on her back did nothing to make Olivia feel less guilty.

"I should have told you. I should have told you from the beginning."

"Told me what?"

Olivia looked away.

"Come home with me," Dorothy ordered. "We'll talk."

"No." Olivia took her sister's hand, pulling her forward. "You come home with me. We can talk freely there."

"I should let Drake know I'll be late."

"I'd rather you didn't." Olivia feared she clasped Dorothy's hand too tightly. "This won't take but a few minutes, and it's . . . it's private."

"Ah, something to do with our handsome Mr. Curtis Morrow?" Dorothy teased.

"No." Olivia felt her face flush. "Well, not entirely, but yes, in a way. He's helping me, and I think he's on to something."

"Helping you?" Concern sprang to Dorothy's face.

"Let's not talk in the street," Olivia urged, aware that passersby were staring.

The sisters walked quickly, arm in arm, to Morningside.

Grayson took their coats and stirred the drawing room fire. "Tea, ma'am?"

"No," Olivia replied. "Just close the door, please, Grayson."

"You've held me in suspense long enough," Dorothy pressed. "Now what is it?"

"You remember the Sunday we talked about Mr. Sheldon's book and what happened at Thanksgiving?"

"Our stellar family holiday?" Dorothy's eyebrows lifted.

Her sarcasm grated, but Olivia pushed past it. "I told you I wanted to search for the O'Reilly woman."

Dorothy looked wary. "And Drake told you to leave it alone."

"You of all people should know I couldn't." Olivia gauged her sister's reaction. "Curtis offered to help me."

"To help you? You can't be serious! Besides, it would be like looking for a fallen leaf in autumn—or an Irish maid in Manhattan. There must be a million!"

"But not a million O'Reilly women who've probably arrived in New York within the last two months. You saw her—her boots, her shawl. She can't have been here long."

"Even so, where would you begin?"

"Curtis has hired a private investigator."

"A private investigator!" Dorothy drew back as if dirty water had been thrown at her feet.

"Stop repeating everything I say," Olivia countered. "He stopped by yesterday and said that the investigator has not found anyone matching her description yet—"

"Well, there you are!"

"But he believes that it will be a simple matter of tracing her through records kept at Ellis Island."

"Surely those records are not open to the public."

"I don't think the rules are evenly applied, especially when a few dollars change hands." Olivia sighed. "But that's not the point. The point is that Curtis and I will find her soon, and when we do, I will do all in my power to help her. . . . I will embrace her as the sister Father intended for us."

Dorothy sat back and frowned, though Olivia believed she was trying to absorb the idea.

"I want to know if you want to be part of this, if you want to meet her, embrace her, too."

"Embrace her? How can I after what Drake said?" Dorothy looked miserably into the fire. "And how can you ask me? How can you go against his wishes and put this divide between us? No matter what Morgan O'Reilly was to Father, this woman is not our sister. I'm your sister."

Olivia reached for her hand. "The very closest of sisters. Dottie, you know I love you with all of my heart." She squeezed the fingers she'd known and loved all her life. "But ever since I saw Father's handwriting again, since I read his journals, and especially since reading *In His Steps*, I've known that this is something I must do. I must find her and help her. I must be a sister to her . . . regardless of keeping Father's wishes. It's what I believe Jesus would do, what He would have me do. I'm sure of it." She let go of Dorothy's hand. "And no matter how much I love you—and you know I do—I love Him more. I'm learning, little by little, to love Him most of all."

Time spread between them before she asked, "Do you understand? Please tell me you understand."

Dorothy picked up her gloves and began pulling them on her fingers one by one. "I'm trying to." She stopped and laid her hands in her lap. Watery pools gathered in the corners of her brown eyes. "You know I want to do what our Lord would have me do. But I can't go against Drake's wishes. He will forbid me outright, and that will drive a rift between us all."

"I know. I understand that. Truly, I'm not asking you to do anything."

"But you see this as the thing the Lord would have you do. How can you not judge me harshly for not doing the same?"

"I've no right to judge. I'm only giving you the opportunity, if you want it. I don't want to do this behind your back."

Dorothy shook her head slowly. "You think me a coward."

"Never! We're each to follow the Lord as closely as we can understand Him to be leading us—there's no way for one to judge another or to say He's leading this way or that." Olivia stood and paced before the fire. "But there is something I must ask of you."

Dorothy looked up.

"Please don't tell Drake."

"He's my husband, Livvie; how can you ask that of me?"

"Because I've told you this in confidence." Olivia knelt before Dorothy. "Perhaps Drake is justifiably worried about protecting our inheritances. But there's no reason for him to fear that yours will be touched in any way. What I do with my share is up to me. I won't have him trying to keep me from doing what I believe—what I know with all my heart—to be right."

Dorothy sighed again and laid her hand on her sister's head. "I wish I could be so brave, so true to my convictions. But my time, my money, even my . . . my person . . . are not mine alone."

"Those are shared gifts of married life; I know that. I *honor* that, Dottie. But I'm not married. I may never be . . . but for this moment I'm called, and I'm called to help Miss O'Reilly."

It was nearly dark by the time Dorothy rose to go. Olivia accompanied her sister home in the family carriage, snuggled close beneath heavy steamer rugs, just as they had traveled together when young girls.

Though Olivia harbored no fondness for Drake, she momentarily envied the scene she witnessed through Meitland House's bright drawing room window, keenly aware that there would be no one to greet her at her own threshold. The return ride to Morningside was short but colder for the loneliness of it.

Olivia had just been served her evening meal when Grayson stepped uncertainly into the dining room. Olivia was glad for the interruption. "Yes?"

"Pardon me, ma'am. There is a man at the back door, a Mr. Joshua Keeton of County Meath, looking for a Miss O'Reilly."

Olivia dropped her fork.

Grayson lifted his shoulders. "He insists that she came here, that she lives here. He maintains that he won't leave until he's spoken with the master of the house."

❖ CHAPTER TWENTY-THREE ❖

KATIE ROSE RECEIVED her first paycheck from the Triangle Waist Factory on Christmas Eve. When she opened it and saw the seven dollar bills lying flat and neat, one behind the other, her heart and stomach tumbled with one another for the upper hand. *My first pay!*

"Wait till you work full-time on the machines next week," her new friend, Emma, whispered. "They might increase it to nine or even ten!"

Katie Rose could not imagine such wealth.

"Must you turn it all in to your mother, or can you keep a bit?" Emma pressed, then blushed. "It's none of my business, but I was just thinking, if you're allowed to keep a bit back, we could go to the nickelodeon. There's a special show beginning this afternoon." She leaned closer. "My brother said he'd come with us and bring a friend—a friend I've been dying to meet!"

Katie Rose instinctively covered the last of the scars on her face with her gloved hand at the thought of sitting with boys. She could hear Maureen's sharp orders ringing in her ears: *"Every penny! Remember, we pool every penny until we're able to move."*

But Katie Rose had seen Maureen's new shirtwaist last week and knew she'd ridden the trolley car partway home one night. *That doesn't sound like poolin' every penny to me! Besides, Maureen's not Mam. And my scars have nearly faded. I'm not horrible lookin', or Emma wouldn't want me to meet her brother.* "How much?"

Emma laughed and linked arms with Katie Rose. "We'll go straight to the matinee—that's cheapest—and we can be home before we're missed!"

Maureen had promised Katie Rose that the first Saturday after they moved, they would go to the nickelodeon together. *But Maureen's not been one to keep her promises lately, at least not in good humor. She was quite the wretch last week about the Christmas tree market! She promised we'd go but came home late and wouldn't go out at all. She oughtn't begrudge me this—it's Christmas Eve. Besides, I've worked hard for it, and I'd rather go with Emma and the boys.*

Even so, a shiver passed through Katie Rose as she handed over her first dollar bill and received a veritable pile of change in return. The heft of silver coins in her hand felt a cross between thrill and betrayal, but she pushed her fancies away as silly. *I'm doin' nothin' wrong.*

As soon as everyone had paid their nickel at the door and was seated in rows of hard wooden chairs, the gaslights were turned low. Emma's brother, Benjamin, sat on one side and Emma on the other, flanked by her brother's friend, Chris. Curtains were drawn back from the center of the stage, revealing a large white rectangle suspended from the ceiling and resting against the forward wall.

The piano player, stationed on a platform in the back of the room, began a lively ragtime tune. Katie Rose's heart skipped a beat when Benjamin passed her a cone of lemon gumballs and let her help herself, brushing her hand more than was warranted in taking them back. A *clickety-clack, clickety-clack* reverberated from the balcony above until it smoothed into a continuous hum. Light and dark flickered on the white screen before a banner with the title of the film spread across its surface. And then people appeared, as in photographs.

<hr />

"Only the photographs moved—the people moved!" Katie Rose recounted that night, swinging her arms to explain and doing her best to regale Mrs. Melkford and draw Maureen into her adventure as they walked to Christmas Eve services. "They spoke and motioned and shouted—though of course, I couldn't hear a word. But I knew what they were sayin' because the piano would thunder in the scary parts—I thought my heart might jump out my chest. Like in the chasin' scene and when the hero wrestled the train robber to the floor of the carriage. It would play so trickily up and down the high notes when the tension mounted—when the bad man crept up behind the beautiful lady and clapped his hand over her mouth. But near the end, when the hero and his fine white horse raced in and rescued

her, and he was kissin' her . . . oh, the music was ever so sweet and tender."
Katie Rose, who'd never seen a moving picture before, nor heard a piano
or organ except in church and from the pub beneath them, stopped only
to catch her breath. "I didn't know there was such music in all the world."

"Were there no signs to explain what was happening in the story?"
Mrs. Melkford asked, trying unsuccessfully to hide her smile.

"What?" Katie Rose asked, pulled from her rapture. "Signs? Oh yes,
but I don't know why they bothered. The music said everythin'!"

Maureen, Katie Rose observed, was quiet—had been quiet and with-
drawn and worried-looking all week. It seemed she disapproved of everything but gave her full attention to nothing.

Despite her conviction that the matinee was a well-deserved wonder
and sure in the knowledge that she would go again next Saturday no matter what Maureen had to say about it, Katie Rose desperately wanted her
sister's approval. "You should go with us next week," she told Maureen,
hoping her cunning might kill two birds with one stone.

"I'd rather save my nickel, thank you." Maureen's eyes stayed straight
ahead.

Katie Rose sighed, at once put out and relieved. *If Maureen doesn't go,
then maybe Benjamin will want to sit with me again.* "It's only a nickel, and
you'd do well to have a bit of fun. It's somethin' we could do together."

Mrs. Melkford laughed. "The little sage might just be right there,
Maureen. You'd best listen to your sister."

Maureen frowned, but Katie Rose beamed, glad to have earned Mrs.
Melkford's approval while anticipating next week's nickelodeon unchaperoned, and linked arms with her unwitting conspirator.

How was Maureen to smile, simply because it was Christmas Eve or because
Katie Rose demanded it? She dared not say a word to anyone but screamed
inside her head: *I don't care about the stupid nickel. I'm terrified that I'll
come home some night and you won't be there, that Jaime Flynn or one of those
dandies or that sickenin' Mr. Kreegle from the fourth floor will have come and
taken you away! And that's what I'm afraid happened to Alice.*

"Are you all right, Maureen?" Mrs. Melkford asked softly as they walked. "You look a bit pale and peaked. I should have insisted you eat before church."

Maureen blinked at Mrs. Melkford and turned quickly away. "Yes, I'm all right. I am, thank you."

And she would have to be; she must keep all her wits about her. But she couldn't keep her mind from Alice.

Alice had come to work in the beginning of the week all smiles and with a fine pair of new kid boots and matching gloves. She'd polished her counter with stars in her eyes and a smile about her lips but acted as nervous as a cat, keeping her eye on Mrs. Gordon and the staff elevator more often than her work. When Maureen teased that Alice had found a Christmas beau, Alice had taken offense.

"Why? Do you think I'm not pretty enough to catch the eye of a gentleman, Maureen O'Reilly?"

"Why, of course you're pretty enough—and all the prettier when you smile." Maureen had not known what to make of her friend. "But who is he? Where did you meet him?"

"Never you mind that." Alice had lifted her chin. "Some things are best kept secret."

Maureen hadn't terribly minded the rebuke but wanted to mend fences. "Shall we walk round to the secondhand shop at lunch? There's enough to cover the counters for us both to go at once."

"No, but I do need to do some shopping. I think I'll try that new silk in the window."

"The blue silk? The gown in Darcy's window?" Maureen had felt her mouth drop.

But Alice had laughed. "Yes, of course Darcy's, and why not? Do you think it suits me? I've a bit saved. And I might be needing something special."

"Whatever for?" Maureen could no more comprehend Alice's ability to afford such a frock than she could imagine where her friend might possibly wear it.

But her question had miffed Alice, and she'd turned away. "You might have the hair and skin and eyes men go silly over, but you never know what a gentleman looks for in a lady. There's no reason to think one might not look my way."

"I never meant such a thing, Alice. But—"

"But what?"

Maureen had stood nearer. "We've just never considered shoppin' here. Everythin's so dear."

"Well, I can afford to now." Alice had dropped her nose to its normal position then and leaned forward confidentially. "You could afford it too. All you have to do is agree to—" But she'd stopped abruptly as if she'd reconsidered whatever she was about to say, then whispered, her eyes twinkling, "I'm not supposed to tell anyone, but I've been promoted," and pointed upstairs.

Maureen knew her eyes went wide.

"It was all so innocent; nothing really." But Alice's cheeks had colored. "Just dinner with a gentleman. He's a good bit older, but that doesn't matter. Everyone gets lonely sometimes."

When Maureen didn't respond, Alice had defended herself. "My mother, God rest her soul, used to say I have a tender heart, that I know how to make someone feel cared for and important." She folded her polishing rag and set it beneath the counter. "Mr. Kreegle paid me well and said the gentleman—whose name I'm not to know—might ask me dancing this week, and I should be ready with a proper gown." Alice's eyes danced as Maureen had never seen them. "I think the blue silk would be perfect with my eyes!"

Then both women realized Mrs. Gordon was near, making her rounds of the store floor and counters, and Maureen had the distinct feeling they'd been overheard. How much, she couldn't guess.

But that was Tuesday and the last day Alice had been to work, no matter that it was the week before Christmas, the busiest days of the retail year. When Maureen had asked the clerk who'd replaced Alice at her post where she was, the young woman had simply shrugged. Maureen had asked Mrs. Gordon if Alice was ill, and Mrs. Gordon had tersely replied that Alice was gone.

When Maureen pestered further, Mrs. Gordon had retorted sternly that it would have been better if Alice had minded her own affairs and that Maureen should take warning.

But what does that mean? Is that a threat? And if it is, what's happened to Alice? She's a hard worker, always on time, always very good with customers, and one of the top salesgirls on the floor. I don't believe for a minute that she's been fired! She said she'd just been promoted!

To be certain, at lunch on Friday Maureen had quietly questioned one of the clerks who'd normally walked to work with Alice. Uncertain how directly she dared ask, she'd confided that Alice had promised to speak with her landlady about a flat coming available for rent in her building January 1, but that she'd forgotten to ask the address.

Eliza had paled, given her the address, but whispered, "I don't know what's become of her. She wasn't down to walk Wednesday or Thursday, and you know Alice—she's regular as the morning mail. Last night I stopped in to see if she was unwell. But her landlady said she'd not come home Tuesday evening—figured she'd run off with some fella for the night based on the way she was dressed last Saturday. Some special date, she suspected, or . . . you know." Eliza had looked over her shoulder and whispered, "But that's not like Alice—not at all. She's not that kind. Something's happened to her. I feel it."

Maureen felt it too. *But who can we go to? Who can I trust? Who dare I trust? Not Mr. Kreegle or Mrs. Gordon.*

She'd been able to think of little else all day.

The church loomed suddenly before the trio, its gigantic front doors wreathed in spicy evergreen with pinecones wired into its swags. Maureen inhaled as they stepped through the vestibule, drawing in the fragrance of beeswax and cranberry-scented candles. She was no longer afraid of the church, and the smell of scented candles had begun to make her think of Sundays with comforting Mrs. Melkford, which had helped her push back her past associations. She'd begun looking forward to the church services, as long as she could avoid the Wakefields.

"Shall we see if we can sit downstairs tonight?" Mrs. Melkford began leading them down the center aisle. "I'm sure someone will share their pew."

"No!" Maureen was but an echo of Katie Rose. "Please, let's sit in our regular seats in the balcony."

"We'll see the candlelight better from there," Katie Rose added.

Maureen squeezed her hand in gratitude, and Katie Rose, clearly surprised by the sign of affection, squeezed back. They dared not risk running into the Wakefields with Mrs. Melkford; she would expect an introduction, only to let all the cats out of the bag. And regardless of her ruse, Maureen had no desire to cross paths with Drake Meitland. She didn't know if he or the men who'd followed Flynn to the fourth floor that day were connected to the strange happenings and services of Darcy's or not, but she knew from her meeting with him at Thanksgiving that he was a cruel sort, and she'd no desire to draw his attention to her sister or herself.

"Yes, that's true. The candlelight service will be wonderful from the balcony." Mrs. Melkford smiled. "But let's sit near the front if there's a seat. We'll see all the more!" If Maureen didn't know better, she would have suspected ten years had fallen from that dear lady's grayed head as she climbed the winding stairs.

"I'm delighted you girls are staying the night! We'll have a late night tea, and after a good sleep we'll have a sumptuous breakfast. I've found the most delicious Christmas bread. . . ."

As Mrs. Melkford prattled happily on, Maureen sank into the balcony's front pew beside her friend and let out the breath she'd been holding. She would have preferred her normal seat, a nearly sequestered spot and sanctuary all her own where, unobserved, she could hum along with the hymns, even if she didn't know the words. She could listen to the readings, drink in the stories and Psalms, and hear, for the first time, the life and words of Jesus in a language she could understand.

From the last pew in the balcony, no one saw if her mouth dropped in astonishment at the reverend's declarations that God hates cruelty and selfishness, that He expects His children to serve and love one another as if they were loving or serving Him. No one saw if her lip trembled at declarations of Christ's all-pursuing love, His ready forgiveness. She still didn't think it was meant for her, though there was no denying its comforting fascination.

But sitting in the front of the balcony for one service, Maureen decided, was little enough to gift her friend this Christmastide.

The evening's music began. The resounding pipes of the organ swept the worries of Maureen's life gently, temporarily, to one side. Despite her fear for Alice, the chorus of Handel's *Messiah* transported Maureen to a realm she'd never visited, as the choir's triumphant voices proclaimed, "King of kings! and Lord of lords! And He shall reign forever and ever. . . ."

Maureen listened as Reverend Peterson read from Luke 2 of the birth of the baby Jesus. She slipped into the picture, envisioning herself as a shepherdess, asleep on the barely moonlit hillsides of Bethlehem, awakened in the night by an explosion in the sky, an angel heralding, "Fear not: for, behold, I bring you good tidings of great joy, which shall be to all people."

What would it be to "fear not"? Did the angel know what he was sayin'? Did he have any idea what "fear not" could mean to poor people who ate and slept and woke to nothin' but fear—fear of poverty, fear of homelessness, fear of bein' sent back to Ireland, fear of men who forced their will?

"Tidings of great joy . . . to all people"—me, too? What would it mean to belong to someone who brings peace and only goodwill? Peace? Oh, God, how can I find peace and safety?

"Oh!" Katie Rose gasped when the lights were lowered and the flame of one small candle was passed from one person to another and another and another, until all the church glowed in the bath of flames raised high. And then the organ began the low, sweet strains of "Silent Night."

At last, a hymn Maureen had known as a child. From deep within her, the memory of words and music grew, rising, swelling.

Maureen closed her eyes and sang with the congregation to the rafters, every note proceeding from her heart as a longing, every word a praise for this merciful God the reverend had preached of—this merciful, loving, pursuing God she'd never known, yet yearned to know.

"'Sleep in heavenly peace . . .'" *How I need peace!*

When she opened her eyes, the heads of parishioners nearby had turned, smiling appreciatively. Maureen felt a deep blush rise from her toes, up her legs and torso, through her neck and to her hairline. She lowered her eyes from the men and women standing near her, down into the sanctuary, directly into the astonished upturned face, dark-blue eyes, and wide smile of Joshua Keeton.

Joshua Keeton, who stood beside an openmouthed Olivia Wakefield.

"For safety's sake, please snuff your candles before leaving the pews" was the last thing Maureen heard from the pulpit. While the flames were extinguished, and before the lights were raised, she grabbed her purse and cloak in one hand and Katie Rose with the other and made for the winding stairs. Stumbling once, she sped through the vestibule and out the heavy church door, into the dark, scarcely mindful that they'd deserted Mrs. Melkford without a word.

What is he doin' here? With Olivia Wakefield? What has he told her about me, and why would he do such a thing?

Maureen groaned to think of the tangled web she'd so quickly woven. *It will all come out eventually—secrets always do! Maureen O'Reilly, what a fool! What an absolute fool!*

CHAPTER TWENTY-FOUR

MRS. MELKFORD walked alone to church Christmas morning, her steps a little tentative and without the buoyancy of the night before.

I don't know what got into Maureen, Lord. First she's standing in church singing like the archangel, and next thing I know she's a whirling dervish, and Katie Rose with her. She shook her head. *I know You're pursuing that girl. And it's plain she wants to come to You with all her heart. Why she doesn't relent, I just don't know. But something happened last night. Something happened. I simply don't know what.*

Mrs. Melkford nodded absently to the man who tipped his checkered flat cap to her just outside the church door.

She climbed the steps to her seat in the balcony. The empty places beside her were easily filled that morning by strangers. Mrs. Melkford smiled, doing her best to show herself friendly. *But they're not my girls, Lord. Here, they're missing this lovely service, and I don't understand why. I can't imagine Maureen's stomach was really so poorly she had to run home first thing this morning. That girl's got an iron constitution.* She sighed. *I shouldn't get so bound up in the lives of these young women. It's not like they're my daughters.* Mrs. Melkford sniffed, pulling her handkerchief to her nose. *It's just that they seem so, Lord.*

Mrs. Melkford looked down into the sanctuary and noticed that the Wakefield family pew was more full than usual. A young man had been added to the group, this one tall and broad of shoulders, a thick crop of curly black hair above his collar. Perhaps a relative? But he looked strong, like an outdoors laborer. And handsome, she noticed, when he turned and swept his eyes across the balcony as if searching for someone. She wondered if Maureen knew him. If he attended church with the Wakefields, she must surely have met him.

It occurred to her to ask the Wakefields if Maureen made it home all right, if there was anything she might do to help.

She shook her head. *Mind your own business, Florence Melkford. For whatever reason, Maureen has not introduced you to her benefactors. This is not your affair . . . unless Maureen's in trouble.* And then she knew she'd move heaven and earth to make things right.

No matter that the sun was shining, Mrs. Melkford felt the cold right through to her bones as she walked home.

In her kitchen she drew water and set the kettle to boil. She'd just filled the basin to wash the morning's dishes when she glanced through her window and found the man from church, the one who'd tipped his cap to her outside, standing across the street, leaning against the lamppost, and staring directly at her.

Startled, she clasped a soapy hand to her chest and stepped back. Though she knew it might seem rude and though it was broad daylight, Mrs. Melkford quickly drew the curtain closed.

It was nearly five o'clock on Wednesday afternoon, and Mrs. Melkford had just set her kettle to boil for tea when three distinct knocks came at her door.

"Yes?" Since the Christmas Day surprise outside her window, she'd been cautious, a little frightened, and reluctant to open wide her door. But something about the young woman looked vaguely familiar.

"Mrs. Melkford?" the pretty, well-heeled woman with dark upswept hair and brown eyes asked hopefully, or so Mrs. Melkford thought.

"Yes," she replied hesitantly, trying to place the face.

"Good afternoon, Mrs. Melkford. I'm Olivia Wakefield, and I'd like to ask—"

"Miss Wakefield!" Mrs. Melkford pushed wide the door. "Come in, come in! Oh, my, is Maureen worse? I told her she shouldn't walk home feeling so poorly. I knew you'd send a car. I've wondered about her all week." Mrs. Melkford pulled Olivia through the door, barely noticing the two men standing on the stoop behind her.

"Maureen O'Reilly?" Olivia repeated. "With me?"

"Yes, yes, of course." Mrs. Melkford couldn't understand the woman's expression. "She is with you, isn't she? The girls made it home all right?"

"The girls?" Olivia's confusion confused Mrs. Melkford. "Please, Mrs. Melkford, allow me to explain and to introduce my friends, Curtis Morrow and Joshua Keeton."

"Mrs. Melkford, it's pleased I am to make your acquaintance." The moment Joshua Keeton, the black-haired, blue-eyed man from the Wakefields' pew at church, opened his mouth and swept his cap from his head, Mrs. Melkford knew he hailed from the same Irish county as Maureen and Katie Rose.

"We've been looking for Miss O'Reilly for the last few weeks," Olivia explained.

Mrs. Melkford felt her head spin and her heart race. "But she's living with you—she and Katie Rose."

"Katie Rose?"

"Her sister." Mrs. Melkford stopped, momentarily annoyed that the woman repeated everything she said, then alarmed that she might as well have been speaking a different language for all Olivia Wakefield seemed to comprehend her words.

"May we sit down?"

Mrs. Melkford felt the blood drain from her limbs. *Something's not right, Lord!*

"Please, may we get you a glass of water or a cup of tea?"

Mrs. Melkford shook her head, intent on entertaining her guests properly. She moved to the kitchen but hesitated when her head began to spin again and sat down heavily at the table. "The tea is above the stove," she said weakly, fearing the worst. *But what would that be, Lord? Oh, take care of them, please!*

Joshua worked his way through the kitchen as if he'd been born to it, warming a brown Betty, measuring the tinned tea, pouring the boiling water, stirring the leaves, setting it to steep, and wrapping the pot in a tea towel. Watching him calmed her heart. *If a person can still make tea, still behave so normally, it must not be so very bad.*

But it was incomprehensible. By the time Olivia Wakefield explained that her brother-in-law had turned Maureen away Thanksgiving Day in a terrible mistake and that Olivia wanted only to find her and help, that Olivia and Curtis had tracked Maureen to this address through a private investigator's search of Ellis Island's records, Florence Melkford was drained, right down to her toes.

"Does your private investigator wear a checkered cap?"

"No," Curtis spoke up, "a brown derby, I believe. Why?"

Mrs. Melkford placed her hand over her heart. "Never mind."

"Until Mr. Keeton came to my door with a letter for Miss O'Reilly, I didn't even know Maureen's first name or that she'd come to New York with her sister. That information helped Mr. Morrow's man locate the proper O'Reilly."

Mrs. Melkford was still trying to take it in. *Maureen lied to me and from the start, but why? Why would she keep up such a pretense? Where on earth is she living, and how has she managed all this time? However did she obtain her position at Darcy's Department Store without the Wakefields—and with no references?*

"Please believe me when I say I want to make amends, to help her and her sister, in any way I can." Olivia's clasp of Mrs. Melkford's hand seemed earnest to the older woman.

"It's hard to know what to believe." Mrs. Melkford drew her hand across her brow. *Though this explains why neither of them look as if they've eaten a smidgen from week to week. To think I'd thought them feasting and living comfortably and securely with this very woman!*

Joshua stirred two cubes of brown sugar into a cup of tea and slid it across the table to her.

"And how do you fit into this?" she asked the Irishman.

Joshua blushed. "I'm a friend of the family from home, from County Meath." He pulled an envelope from his pocket. "I've had a letter from Maureen's aunt, worried because she's not heard from her and because her letter to the Wakefield address was returned." He glanced toward Olivia, and Mrs. Melkford saw accusation there.

"Please believe me; I didn't know anything about the letter," Olivia pleaded.

"But why would Maureen keep up such a story?" Mrs. Melkford felt the weight in her heart.

"She's proud, mum." Joshua spoke quietly. "She's doing her best to care for her sister, to make sure they can stay in America."

"But I would have helped her. She could have stayed here with me for as long as she needed—if she'd only told me."

"Did she know that?"

Mrs. Melkford straightened at the impertinence, nearly said yes, but remembered, "I told her that someone must vouch for her. I took responsibility for her at Ellis Island."

"Have you been through the rigors of Ellis Island, mum?"

"I was born here." She hated that she sounded offended.

Joshua sat back. "They're not an easy lot, those immigration folk. Especially for women. Perhaps she was afraid you'd send her back if she didn't have a place."

Mrs. Melkford allowed, "They don't permit women to enter alone."

"And she won't return to Ireland," Joshua said.

"Surely that would be better than being on the streets here?" Curtis asked.

"No!" Every eye was on Joshua now, and Florence Melkford thought his mouth turned grim. "We don't leave everything—we don't emigrate—because things are good at home." He crossed his arms, daring anyone, she thought, to challenge Maureen's decision or behavior. She couldn't help but like him.

"Well, what now?" she asked, believing but praying for affirmation.

"Help me find her," Olivia begged. "I want to invite her—both sisters—to live with me. If that's what she told you, it must be what she'd hoped."

"She'd hoped to become independent," Joshua asserted. "Her aunt only thought you'd help her get started."

"I will," Olivia promised. "I will! But I must find her before I can do anything!"

"Does she work? Has she given you any clue where she lives?" Curtis probed.

It was Curtis Morrow who gave Mrs. Melkford pause. Why would such a finely dressed gentleman be interested in Maureen? He seemed attached to Olivia Wakefield, but not in a terribly personal way. *Give me wisdom, Lord.*

But Joshua won her over when he sat down, took her hand, and looked directly into her face. "I saw Maureen in church Christmas Eve. She sang like an angel—she is an angel, though she does not know it. I understand you're wanting to protect her, and I thank you for that, for all you've done for her and Katie Rose." He placed the letter on the table between them. "If you can just give her this letter from her aunt and tell her that Joshua Keeton wants to help. If she wants to reach me, she can send word to Miss Wakefield or to Mr. Morrow. I'm working for him now, and even if I'm not available, he'll know where to find me."

Mrs. Melkford doubted, after the way Maureen had taken off that morning, that she'd be seeing either girl for some time—certainly not until next Saturday afternoon. She prayed she was doing the right thing, and that if she wasn't, the Lord would overrule her naiveté and fight for Maureen. "Darcy's Department Store," she whispered. "She works at Darcy's Department Store, here in Manhattan."

CHAPTER TWENTY-FIVE

Maureen remained stoic, though Katie Rose badgered and berated her stupidity all of Christmas Day and each day after.

"Joshua Keeton won't hurt us, Maureen. He's been nothin' but kindness!" And she'd begun to tick off the ways he'd helped: the trip to Dublin, how he'd meant to watch over them on the ship, if only she'd not been so rude. "We'd never be in this mess if you'd trusted Joshua and let him list his name as comin' with us on the ship's manifest. But no, you with your high-and-mighty ideas and letter from a dead man, you had to—"

"Shut up!" Maureen had shouted when she could take no more. "You've no idea what you're talkin' about. We cannot have any connection to Ireland; do you not know that?"

"You mean *you* cannot! You're afraid of what he knows about you, aren't you? Afraid he'll tell what you did with Julius Orthbridge." Katie Rose had sneered at her, and that, of all things, had taken Maureen aback, made her sick to her stomach. "Well, I'm not afraid. In fact, I fancy havin' a friend from home." She lifted her chin. "I'd be proud to walk out with Joshua Keeton."

"He's a grown man!"

"And I'm a grown woman," Katie Rose asserted, though her color rose. "It seems a fine arrangement."

"You're a child!" Maureen had spouted, regretting the words before they'd escaped her lips.

Katie Rose's blush had turned to fury. "A child? A *child*? You think you're so grand and desirable, men would fall all over themselves for you, Maureen O'Reilly! Well, we'll see about that, won't we?"

And she'd left for work, slamming the door behind her, not waiting for Maureen to walk with her.

All that Thursday morning, behind the counter at Darcy's, Maureen castigated herself for the way she'd handled the situation with Katie Rose. *I remember what it is to be thirteen—nearly fourteen. How I was dyin' to be thought grown-up and beautiful. I suppose her scars make her more sensitive; why did I not take all of that into account?* But Maureen also knew she'd never displayed the temper Katie Rose had; she'd not been in a position to. *Perhaps that's my satisfaction—or should be—that Katie Rose has the freedom to shout and rage. She believes she's safe, that I'll take her temper and still love and care for her.* Maureen sighed and polished the counter.

At lunch she looked for Eliza Farnham, Alice's friend, but didn't see her, hadn't seen her all week. She sat beside Eliza's counter mate, asking if she'd seen or heard from her. But the girl's eyes widened; she glanced at the lunchroom monitor, scooped up her half-eaten sandwich, and without so much as stuffing it back in its bag, walked quickly from the room.

If Maureen didn't know better, she'd think she had the plague or that chicken pox had broken across her face. Not one of the girls seemed to want to sit beside or talk with her, not even the normal chatter about sore feet and backs.

Maureen finished her bread and cheese and washed it down with tea, though that did little to dislodge the lump in her throat. She stepped back to her counter a few minutes early.

She glanced around the floor as the girls returned from the first lunch shift. There were fewer girls on the floor than usual, though that might be because fewer were needed after the season's push. Still, Maureen realized that some faces were new to her and that, besides Eliza, two more girls she'd known as regulars were not there. *Could they all have taken holiday or come down with something?*

Maureen did not want to draw attention to herself in any way, did not think she had, and yet she realized that Mrs. Gordon and Mr. Kreegle conferred twice through the afternoon by the elevator and kept a close eye on her. She checked her hem, the buttons of her waist, and smoothed her hair to make certain no tendrils had escaped. Everything seemed in order;

she could not imagine the reason for their keen interest, but the knowing made her uncomfortable.

It was nearly half past four when Mrs. Gordon—"Old Blood and Thunder," as Alice had called her—stopped by Maureen's counter. "Everything is in order, Miss O'Reilly?"

"Yes, Mrs. Gordon," Maureen answered respectfully. "Excuse me, ma'am . . . but I've a question, if you please."

"Yes?" Mrs. Gordon's nose seemed to rise.

"I was wonderin' if Eliza Farnham is ill? I've missed her this week."

Mrs. Gordon tilted her head. "You take an unhealthy interest in your coworkers, Miss O'Reilly. I'm sure you realize that for some of our young ladies, this position is a stepping-stone in their working careers."

Maureen blinked. "I know Eliza is content here." And she could not resist adding, "As was Alice. Have they found employment elsewhere?"

"What is your keen interest in these ladies?"

"I—I'd simply like to stay in communication with them," she said but thought, *I'd be ever so relieved for them, just to know they're all right.*

Mrs. Gordon stepped closer and spoke softly but with a severity that Maureen had not felt directed toward her before. "I've told you once that what the other girls choose to do is none of your affair."

Maureen swallowed.

Mrs. Gordon turned to go, stopped, and faced Maureen directly. "Precisely what did Alice say to you before her departure?"

Maureen felt her stomach drop.

"Or Eliza? Do you think we do not notice?" Mrs. Gordon's voice lowered yet again and she stepped closer. "You may have the advantage of wealthy friends, Miss O'Reilly . . ." She paused. "Or you may not, but I would advise you to put your house in order."

"Put your house in order! What a clever expression for a counter clerk's display!" An impeccably dressed Olivia Wakefield interrupted with gritted-teeth cheerfulness, standing just at Mrs. Gordon's elbow. "How do you do, Miss—?"

"Mrs. Gordon." The woman looked mortified.

"Mrs. Gordon, employee of Darcy's Department Store? I'm Olivia Wakefield and so glad to meet you." Olivia tapped the floor supervisor on the arm and whispered loud enough for the stage, "You're so lucky to have Maureen working at Darcy's. I've told her a dozen times she needn't work at all, but she's quite the progressive, independent woman."

Mrs. Gordon drew back, pasting her smile into place. "Miss O'Reilly is most fortunate to have such friends."

And then it seemed to Maureen that Olivia dropped her pretenses. "On the contrary, it is my family and I who are most fortunate to have Maureen's friendship and good company."

Mrs. Gordon's eyes registered uncertainty. Maureen saw her glance toward the elevator, then reply, "Please excuse me, Miss Wakefield. I must return to my work."

"Of course." Olivia touched the other woman's arm again and whispered, "Simply know that my friends and I will shop here often, as long as Maureen can attend us."

Mrs. Gordon nodded sharply. Maureen would not have been surprised to see her run as she made headlong for the elevator.

When she was gone, the two women left standing stared at one another.

"Thank you," Maureen whispered.

"It looked like a tight spot," Olivia returned. "I owe you this and so much more." She placed her hand on Maureen's arm, but Maureen dropped her arm to her side, not knowing how to respond.

"You've certainly no reason to trust me, not after the way you were treated in my house. But I beg you to forgive me and allow me to do better."

Maureen shook her head. "Why would you? Your husband said—"

"My husband? No, oh no! Mr. Meitland is my brother-in-law and the executor of my father's estate; he thought he was protecting me—"

"Your brother-in-law?" Maureen could barely take that in. "And protectin' you? From me?" She found that incredulous.

"I'm ashamed, Miss O'Reilly, and I don't really know what to say. But he behaved shamefully, and I was wrong to allow him to send you away." Olivia laid her purse on the counter and took Maureen's hands. "I know what your father did for mine, and I know what my father promised. I'll keep that promise."

Maureen could not stop the beating of her heart or the onslaught of memory.

"Come home with me—you and your sister, please. Let's begin again."

Maureen felt as much as saw the eyes of the other clerks upon them, until the front revolving doors began their turn, and three well-dressed gentlemen walked through the main aisle of the store and toward the back elevator, reminding her of Drake Meitland and his visit to the fourth floor. Recognition of any kind was not helpful.

Maureen pulled back her hands. "I don't know what you're about, Miss Wakefield, but—"

"Olivia, please, and I only want to help," Olivia stammered. "Mrs. Melkford said—"

"Mrs. Melkford?" Maureen gasped. "What has she to do with you?"

Now Olivia colored. "We found her through the records at Ellis Island, that she had helped you and Katie Rose, had vouched for you. And Joshua Keeton told us—"

"Joshua Keeton?" Maureen felt as though someone had punched her in the stomach. *I can well imagine what it is that Joshua Keeton's told you!*

"Yes, he came to my home looking for you." She pulled an envelope from her purse and held it out to Maureen. "He brought you this."

But Maureen didn't take it. She'd as soon pluck hot coals.

Olivia looked confused and set the letter on the counter, pushing it gently toward Maureen. "I suppose all this is rather sudden," she said at last. "I don't blame you that you don't trust me."

Trust you? You've tracked me down and surely convinced my one friend in New York that I'm a liar! And how can you speak so daringly toward Mrs. Gordon? Do you and Drake Meitland run Darcy's Department Store that everyone kowtows to you so? What becomes of the women and girls you befriend? Maureen narrowed her eyes, trying to focus, to register Olivia Wakefield in the foreground of her brain and Drake Meitland in the background. *Are they connected by more than marriage? Do they work together, or are they completely ignorant of one another's intentions?*

She stepped back and spoke softly. "I thank you for standin' up for me with Mrs. Gordon, but I don't think I want to know you, Miss Wakefield." She hesitated. "And I'll thank you not to come again."

She turned her back on Olivia Wakefield and drew in a ragged breath.

"I hope you'll reconsider, Miss O'Reilly. I'd very much like to know you."

Maureen waited a long minute until Olivia's footsteps faded but turned in time to see her exit through the revolving door. On the counter lay the letter. Maureen thought she might toss it into the trash, but with nearly every eye in the open room upon her, she swept it beneath the counter and into her bag. She could dispose of it later.

The finishing bell rang at six. Maureen's head was pounding and she could think only of the long walk home in the cold and dark. She had no fear that anyone would bother her now, not with the Wakefield stamp of approval resting on her forehead. She'd seen the fear and humiliation in Old Blood and Thunder's eyes.

In the cloakroom she avoided the chatter around her. She grabbed her cloak and hat and hurried from the store.

Maureen had walked ten blocks through ice and snow when she realized she'd left her purse, with the letter, in the store. She groaned aloud. *If anyone opens it, even to see whose it is, and reads Joshua's letter . . . No tellin' what he said, what he wrote! I can't believe I walked out without it!*

She stood a full five minutes, arguing with herself. *The store is surely locked by now. Perhaps no one will find it before mornin'. Perhaps they've already found it. And if they read it, they'll know I'm not the respectable clerk I maintain. Oh!* She groaned again. *That will mean deportation! And Katie Rose left here alone.*

All the way back to the store, she rehearsed her plea for the night watchman. But to her surprise, the employee door was not locked; a stone had been placed between the door and its jamb. *Thank You, God,* she found herself praying, then caught herself, wondering at her audacity.

Quietly she climbed the dark back stairs, keeping to the balls of her frozen feet. She slipped into the employee cloakroom and pulled the light cord with numb fingers, but her purse was not on the shelf where she thought she'd left it. *Downstairs, behind my counter? Could I have been so stupid?*

She knew it was no small thing to creep through the darkened store at night. But she dared not use a light. If the night watchman found her, she'd have no adequate explanation. They'd not consider her poor purse worth breaking into the store to retrieve. And who would believe the door was left ajar?

But the fear of Mrs. Gordon or anyone finding and reading Joshua's letter propelled her feet forward. *Curse that man!*

She'd just opened the cloakroom door to venture out when she heard a scuffling. Maureen froze, though she told herself it was rats. *Very big rats.* She shivered. The scuffling came again, this time accompanied by what sounded like a sob, nearby. She closed the door again softly and pressed her ear against it. The sobbing came louder, followed by a loud crashing sound, then stopped abruptly.

Maureen knew they were sounds that didn't belong in the department store. But she also knew that whatever it was, it was not her business, could not be her business unless she wanted to be discovered and dragged from her hiding place. She pressed a hand to her throat.

But what if someone needs help? I can't just walk out.

Voices, all of them familiar, argued in her head. She crept out into the center of the hallway and listened. But nothing more came.

It had to be my imagination—this big, empty building at night. She shook her shoulders as if to rid herself of a bad dream and headed for the stairs.

Making her way down the pitch-black stairs was not hard; she braced herself against the wall. But the main floor was a maze of counters and displays. *It would be so easy to bump a hat stand or design pyramid and send everything clattering to the floor!* Maureen took baby steps, still on the balls of her feet. She guided her steps by holding fast to counter edges until she grasped familiar dress gloves, the rounded shapes of hat crowns, and finally her counter with the fanned display of handkerchiefs.

At last! She stooped behind the counter, ran her hands along the shelf beneath, and found her purse. She opened the clasp, reached in, and recognized the shape and feel of the letter. *Still here! Thank You! Thank You!*

She'd risen and stepped from behind her counter into the center aisle when she heard a scream, followed by sobs and pleas.

"No! Stop! Don't—please don't!"

Maureen froze. *Eliza?* She couldn't tell from which direction the cry had come, except that it was above her. She stepped further into the empty, darkened store. The whimpering continued, muffled, but just the same.

The bell on the elevator dinged. Maureen's heart stopped. As the elevator door slid open, Maureen ducked behind her counter, knocking hats to the floor with her purse.

"Who's there?" It was Jaime Flynn's voice, plain as plain to Maureen's ears.

But the whimpering was louder, the cries of protest more intense. "Please! I won't tell; I'll never say a word. Please let me go!"

"Shut up!" And the sound of a slap so sharp it rattled Maureen's teeth.

The whimpering stopped abruptly. A light played crazily over the store floor, coming to rest on the tumbled display of hats very near Maureen's foot. She drew in her arms and legs, folding them beneath her, and crouched behind the counter, holding her breath, willing her teeth not to chatter.

"Somebody's here. Somebody's here, I tell you!" Jaime Flynn's voice barked again, and the light danced over the floor a second time.

"You'd best hope not." The second voice—deep, impatient, and cultured—sounded vaguely familiar. "He won't tolerate any more of your messes; do you understand?"

"Yes—yes, sir." Jaime Flynn's humble reply startled Maureen.

"Help me get this one to the truck. Then you go back for the other. We've got to get them out of the city tonight. Stupid of you to bring them here!"

There was no mistaking that superior tone. Images of an arrogant Drake Meitland, his cruel burning of her letter and his coarse jerking of her arm, ripped through Maureen's brain. Afraid to move, afraid to breathe, she tucked herself as small as possible and waited until the elevator dinged and the torchlight disappeared. Certain she would stumble into another display, Maureen caught her skirt between her teeth and crawled toward the exit. She'd almost reached the stairwell when the elevator bell sounded again and the door slid open. In the pale light of the lamp she caught sight of a grim-faced Jaime Flynn, a long burlap bag hefted over his shoulder. Two smart kid boots dangled from its open end.

❦

The policeman—the Irish policeman walkin' the block! He was the only help Maureen could imagine, the only possible salvation for Alice and Eliza.

The moment the delivery door closed and the lock clicked into place behind Jaime Flynn, Maureen had raced out the side employee entrance. Now she slipped round the corner, ran through the dark, skirting the pools of light from the electric streetlamps, searching for the foot policeman on patrol. *Where are you, Flannery? You're everywhere when I don't need you, but now . . . when I do!* Tears of terror and frustration coursed down her face.

She heard a metal door slam in the alley behind the store. *How do I stop this? How?* But there was no one in sight. The streets were dark and deserted.

At last she caught sight of the stalwart figure of Officer Flannery, very near the corner of the store, and made a mad dash back in his direction. In the same moment, the motor and headlights of an enclosed-bed truck roared to life behind the alley. Officer Flannery disappeared down the alley, toward the truck.

Thank You, Lord! He'll stop it—he'll stop them sure!

But Flannery emerged from the alley half a minute later, looked both ways, up and down the street, and motioned the truck forward.

Maureen pressed back into the building's shadows in time to see Officer Flannery give a nodding salute to Jaime Flynn, the driver of the truck of stolen women.

CHAPTER TWENTY-SIX

MAUREEN POUNDED FRANTICALLY on the only door she trusted.

When Mrs. Melkford threw wide her door, Maureen nearly fell into her arms, and with her the howling January wind.

"Whatever are you doing out on such a night?"

"Please—can—can we stay the night?" Maureen begged, her teeth chattering so she could barely form her words.

"Of course! Come in! Come in! Why, you're soaked clear through. Give me your coats."

"It's snowing to beat the band." Katie Rose stamped layers of white from her boots.

"Did you get stuck along the way home from work?"

Maureen shook her head but couldn't speak, had not formed, even in her mind, what explanation to give. "We can't stay alone." It was all she could say, all she could think to say.

"She came dashin' in—in a whirlin' tizzy—and dragged me out the door again." Katie Rose unwound her muffler and unbuttoned her coat. "She wouldn't even stop to eat the supper I prepared! We left it cold on our plates. She's in an absolute state, and I've no idea why."

"I don't know what to do," Maureen whimpered at last, her best attempt at explanation.

She saw Katie Rose and Mrs. Melkford exchange worried glances, but she couldn't help it. *I can't tell them. It will put them in danger, just like Alice and Eliza! There's no one to help! Oh, God, what am I to do?*

"Sit down, my dear. Sit here, near the stove."

Maureen was grateful that Mrs. Melkford guided her. Now that she was safe, she felt as if she couldn't have found her way across the room, and she couldn't stop the tears that streamed down her cheeks.

"I'm afraid this is my fault." Mrs. Melkford poured each girl a mug of steaming coffee and pressed buttered rolls into their hands. "I told that Wakefield woman and the others where you worked, Maureen. I never should have done it without asking you. I'm so sorry."

Maureen shook her head. Olivia Wakefield? That was a lifetime ago.

"That's not it?" Mrs. Melkford looked more concerned than before. "Then what has happened? Has someone hurt you?" She looked to Katie Rose, who shrugged again, this time helplessly.

Maureen closed her eyes. *How can I make them understand without tellin' them? Look what my simple questions did to Alice and Eliza! There's no one I dare tell, no one I dare risk, and no one I dare trust, none to help! Even Officer Flannery is party to their stealin'! Oh, please, God!*

All her foundations felt like melting snow. Never had Maureen felt so entirely, absolutely alone, not since the night Julius Orthbridge first threw open her door.

Maureen woke Friday morning, exhausted, only to find the sun streaming through the window and Katie Rose gone to work.

"We didn't want to wake you, dear," Mrs. Melkford said when she peeked in the door midmorning. "You moaned through the night in your sleep, and you're still running a fever." She pulled the quilt up to Maureen's neck. "I sent word to Darcy's Department Store that you're ill and won't be in today or likely tomorrow. That should give you a good rest."

Maureen sat up, knowing she should protest, worried that Mrs. Melkford had associated herself with any employee of Darcy's, especially one who might be under suspicion for protesting so much—who might have been seen by Jaime Flynn. But the room began to swim and her thoughts with it. She laid her head back down on the pillow.

"That's better," Mrs. Melkford cooed. "I'll bring you some breakfast. Just you wait here."

But when Maureen closed her eyes, she saw the faces of Alice and Eliza rise up before her. *Where are you now? Oh, where have they taken you?*

She couldn't seem to hold the thought steady in her brain. Her mind was about to drift to dreaming when she remembered why she'd returned to Darcy's last night.

Maureen forced her eyelids open and willed strength into her limbs. She dropped her feet over the side of the bed and tiptoed across the cold floor to find her cracked leather purse laid squarely atop her neatly folded shirtwaist and skirt and stockings. She pulled Joshua's letter from her purse, intending to throw it on the fire without reading it. As she prepared to toss it into the flames, she realized the address wasn't from Joshua Keeton in America. The postage was Irish. *Aunt Verna?* She pulled the sheet of paper from the envelope.

> *Dearest Maureen and Katie Rose,*
>
> *It has been over two months since you left County Meath, and I've not heard a word as to your health or whereabouts. My letters to the address of Colonel Wakefield have been returned, marked "Unknown," and when I wrote directly to the colonel himself, my letter was returned, "Deceased." I am at my wits' end and regret the day I urged you to go.*
>
> *I learned of Joshua Keeton's whereabouts through his mother and took the liberty of writing to him, hoping that he will find you and see that you are both well. Please, please, dear nieces, if this reaches you, write and let me know where and how you are getting by. If the colonel is truly dead, I fear for your safety.*
>
> *I've asked Joshua to help you, so be good to him, Maureen. He's doing my bidding. I know your nasty temper, child.*
>
> *All my love,*
> *Aunt Verna*

Maureen refolded the letter and returned it to the envelope. She crept back into bed and pulled the covers high about her neck, pushing away the chill that raced upward from her cold feet. *You're right to fear for our safety, Aunt. This is no better than Ireland. It's hidden and secret and more violent in the stealin' of its women—at least more violent than I've known. But it's stealin' and coercin' and no doubt rape just the same. And who is there to stop it?*

CHAPTER TWENTY-SEVEN

MAUREEN'S TIME OF REPRIEVE nestled in Mrs. Melkford's gentle care passed quickly. Fever and sore throat were little price to pay for the mothering she craved and received in abundance.

But she worried that Katie Rose walked to and from work with no more protection than other girls her age; she feared for her sister's boasted brazen flirting with the policeman in Washington Square, near the block of the shirtwaist factory, knowing Katie Rose had no idea the fire she toyed with.

And yet telling her still seemed the greater risk. Katie Rose would never be able to keep such knowledge to herself or the knowing from her face. She'd make herself a target by her fear.

Maureen worried that she would lose her job at Darcy's for being out sick. She worried that she would keep her job—and leave the company not because she was dismissed, but in a burlap sack or the back of a truck, as Alice and Eliza had.

She tried to remember the other girls who'd disappeared. *It's not possible that they were all stolen away and that no one has noticed or said anythin'.* And then she remembered Eliza's fearful glance over her shoulder in the lunchroom and Alice, the first day they went shopping together, when she'd begged her not to leave the store floor.

Maureen sat up in bed Saturday morning. Every word, every glance took on new meaning. Had they known there was more going on than escorting lonely gentlemen to dinners or dances? Alice had seemed so pleased to be asked to escort, had seemed to think it was not so bad after all. But Maureen did not believe such "escorting" could be innocent— certainly not for long.

Did the girls know about this other—this horror? What had she read in the newspapers? What did they call it—this stealing of women?

When Maureen had read the headlines, she'd thought it simply sensationalism—a crude tactic to sell papers. But she'd heard things whispered in the cloakroom—something about the passing of the Mann Act. Only she'd overheard a discussion on the trolley that made it clear the act had nothing to do with men; it was all about preventing the transport over state lines of women and girls intended for prostitution and the selling of human beings for sexual purposes.

Slavery—they called it "white slavery" and "modern slavery."

When the girls in the cloakroom talked about it, they hadn't been whispering for sake of embarrassment or impropriety of the subject at all—they'd been afraid! Afraid they might be next!

The knowledge sat like a brick in her brain. *But won't their families miss them? Won't they inquire?* Maureen bit her lip, and that made her remember. She'd asked Alice about her Christmas plans, and Alice had looked away, saying she had no family. And what of Eliza Farnsworth? Did she have family, or was she, too, a young woman on her own?

Maureen didn't know, but she did not doubt the answer. *Young women no one will miss.*

Katie Rose had gone to finish dressing when Mrs. Melkford laid a cool hand across Maureen's forehead Sunday morning at breakfast. "At least the fever's gone. I'd surely like you to stay here a bit longer."

"You've been so good to us, but we can't keep takin' advantage of your generosity." Maureen's green eyes looked bigger in her too-thin face.

"I'd dearly love to keep you both permanently; you must know that. But the Missionary Aid Society provides my small apartment in exchange for the bit of work I do for them, and . . ." Mrs. Melkford didn't finish. It was the first time she resented giving up her own home after her husband's death. *If only I had those two stories now!*

"It's all right, truly. We must manage on our own; we'll be fine."

Mrs. Melkford knew Maureen did not believe that. She didn't know what had happened, could not understand why Maureen's confidence had suddenly flown, only that it had. "Won't you reconsider Olivia Wakefield's offer? You and Katie Rose would be no farther from your work, and you'd be safe and warm and well fed."

But Maureen shook her head. "I can't. It's impossible. Please don't ask me."

"I just don't want to see you go back to your flat alone." Mrs. Melkford worried her lip. *What is it she's not telling me? Whatever kept her from telling me the truth in the first place?* "Is there someone you're afraid of? Has someone threatened you?" She knew by the widening of Maureen's eyes, though she clearly tried to hide it, that she'd stumbled on the truth or some semblance of the truth. The man in the checkered hat came to mind. *But Maureen was not here when he . . .* "If that is the case, you girls mustn't be alone."

Maureen shook her head again, and Mrs. Melkford could see she was very near a new fount of tears.

"If you're not able to confide in me, and you don't feel you can trust Olivia Wakefield, perhaps you should talk with that young man Joshua Keeton. He seemed so concerned for you."

"Joshua Keeton is concerned for himself and his wants."

Maureen's sourness startled Mrs. Melkford. "I didn't see that at all. He's worried for you and only wanted me to give you your aunt's letter and his offer to help should you want it. He asked nothing in return."

Maureen turned her head away, but Mrs. Melkford was certain she caught a shade of doubt cross the younger woman's features. "He called you an angel but said you didn't know it."

"Joshua Keeton called her an angel? Maureen?" Katie Rose stood at the door to the kitchen. "Was he jokin'?"

The look that passed between the sisters told Mrs. Melkford that it was anything but funny and that all was not well in the O'Reilly home. She couldn't help but wonder if it had more than a little to do with the handsome Irishman.

Maureen had not planned to go to church that morning. She'd wanted only to write Aunt Verna—lie outright and tell her everything was fine and not to worry—and rest one more day, hide from the world long enough to gather strength for her return to Darcy's on Monday. But Katie Rose's remark had stirred the dreaded war between shame and ire within her breast. And Maureen, despite her fears of the future and failings of the past, still rose for the battle.

Puttin' it off won't help. It will be best to test the waters with Mrs. Melkford there. Though what can that dear soul do to protect me? And the thought came as clearly as any she'd known: *She can pray, and I will . . .* But Maureen cut off the stirring in her soul before it was fully formed, certain it was not real.

The walk to church was quiet, and Maureen knew Katie Rose was miffed that Joshua should mention her older sister in anything but derision. *In fact, I'm not certain his words were anythin' but a cruel joke, no matter what Mrs. Melkford thinks of him.*

They'd reached the church and were about to climb the front steps when, from the corner of her eye, she saw a lady's hand reach for her arm.

"Miss O'Reilly," Olivia Wakefield pleaded, "I would be honored if you and your sister, and Mrs. Melkford, would sit with us." She eyed Katie Rose as though awaiting an introduction. "You know Mr. Keeton, I believe, and this is Mr. Morrow—Curtis Morrow."

Just behind her stood Joshua Keeton, and at her side, the man Maureen had seen at the far end of the hall at Morningside that hateful Thanksgiving Day tipped his hat.

But all Maureen could see was her shame before Joshua and her fear of Olivia's connection to Drake Meitland. She began to decline.

"Please, Miss O'Reilly, I'd be honored." Joshua offered his hand.

"No, no thank—" Maureen tried again.

"But we'd love to join you, and isn't that kind?" Katie Rose pushed between them, introducing herself and taking Joshua's arm.

Maureen couldn't miss Olivia's glad surprise or the light in Joshua's eyes.

"There won't be room for all of us in one pew," Maureen stuttered, grasping at straws.

"You young folks go ahead," Mrs. Melkford urged. "I'll be fine in my usual seat."

"No!" Maureen felt panic rising in her throat. "I'd not think of leavin' you. Katie Rose, you must stay with us."

"There's room enough," Olivia assured. "Dorothy isn't well this morning, and Drake is away on business."

I know exactly what business! Do you?

Olivia paused a half breath. "It will be a new beginning for us all."

Maureen couldn't seem to make her mouth protest as she wished.

"Truly, we never use all the seats in our family pew." Olivia laughed nervously. "It's silly to have it all to ourselves." She stepped nearer Maureen. "Please, Miss O'Reilly."

"Thank you, Miss Wakefield," Katie Rose affirmed, guiding Joshua into the church.

Maureen couldn't stop the rapid beating of her heart, couldn't think how to regain control of the situation.

"Come, my dear, we'll all go." Mrs. Melkford took Maureen's arm and smiled at Olivia. "It will be a nice change to sit with a family."

Olivia Wakefield looked to Maureen as if someone had handed her the sun and the moon.

Is it possible she truly knows nothin' of her brother-in-law's wickedness or what goes on above stairs at Darcy's? How can that be, when her sister is married to the man and he administers the affairs of their father?

Maureen was still trying to slip the mental square pegs into round holes as they found their seats. She sat between Katie Rose and Mrs. Melkford, with Joshua on one end of the pew and Curtis Morrow and Olivia on the other. Uncomfortably near the front of the church, Maureen would have much preferred to be tucked in her secluded spot in the balcony, able to safely observe everyone and everything without being observed. She closed her eyes against the all-devouring tension, hoping to keep her hands and voice from trembling.

As the congregation softly shared their greetings and morning gossip around her, Maureen coaxed her nerves to settle. *Is it possible I've misjudged Joshua Keeton? Olivia Wakefield would never pull me to the front of her church and sit me in her family pew if he'd told her of my past. But why wouldn't he tell?* She shook her head, trying to dislodge the cobwebs that fought to take over. *Mrs. Melkford is convinced he's a good man, that he truly wants to be my friend. But why would he?* She stole a glance at his face—one of calm assurance. He stared straight ahead, not trying in the least to catch her eye, or that of Katie Rose, his expression displaying peace and something Maureen could barely describe.

Contentment. He looks content.

And then the organ with its wondrous pipes began the service's prelude. Notes danced and swelled in patterns, trilling up and down scales Maureen had never heard. She sensed Katie Rose's intake of breath beside her and tentatively smiled for her sister's newfound pleasure in music, a joy that neither of them had known except for the drums and pipes and flutes of Ireland and the simple pump organ at the church—a beauty to be sure, but nothing like this organ with its great reverberations that spun through the floor and up their legs, into their hearts.

The reverend welcomed the congregation, then called for moments of silent prayer and meditation, urging his flock to praise God for His goodness, thank Him for His mercies within the past week, and pray that the Holy Spirit be present in the service ahead.

Maureen kept her eyes closed as the white-robed choir made its slow entrance down the aisle. She knew, without looking, that they divided right and left at the altar rail, as usual. Their many-ranged voices joined with the praise of the congregation. For the first time, by the very nature of her seat, Maureen was caught in the midst of that heavenly host, that angelic choir she'd heard of on Christmas Eve, praising God and singing, "Peace on earth, goodwill to men."

Only this day the hymns were about determination to forgive and new beginnings. The sermon echoed the theme, both in the new year and in individual lives. The reverend called for belief in a God who loves and pursues, a God willing and eager to forgive and to accept all into relationship with Him through Christ—a relationship that fully embraces.

He spoke of a woman named Rahab—a harlot and spy who was an ancestor of Jesus. Maureen felt her face flame and glanced at the listeners beside her to see if they'd get up and leave at what must surely be blasphemy. But they stayed.

And then he told of Bathsheba, who'd slept with King David in an adulterous relationship, saying that she, too, was in the bloodline of Christ. She listened for murmurs of complaint but heard only an uncomfortable shifting in seats among the congregation.

He listed five women in all, women of strange and suspect character in the eyes of the world—a scheming widow, a harlot, a foreigner, an adulteress, an unmarried teen mother—but women God loved, forgave, and honored in the maternal bloodline of His Son.

It was not a picture that coincided with her image of the blessed Mother or the demanding, damning God she knew.

A wild Protestant tale, surely! What did he say—that once they'd sought forgiveness and reconciliation, God blotted out their sins as though they'd never been? That He loved them as daughters?

Could He possibly love such as these—these women who lived the picture of my own desperation? And if He did, if He does . . . could He love me?

But the idea was so big, so preposterous, so presumptuous.

Where is the beatin'? Where is the ramrod of shame? Maureen opened her eyes. Reverend Peterson lifted high his arms, invoking the blessings of God. *Where is the wrath?* she asked again as if to trip him up, as if to cause the hidden rod to fall.

But he called for the passing of the peace—a welcome shaking of hands and embracing of parishioners and strangers alike, an event unknown to Maureen and Katie Rose. Maureen stayed seated, though Olivia and Mrs. Melkford, even Curtis Morrow and Joshua, reached out to her and Katie Rose. And then, when she thought she'd survived all the foreign impossibilities, the reverend called for Communion.

"Must you be Protestant?" Katie Rose whispered to Mrs. Melkford as ushers shepherded people forward by pews to the Communion rail.

Mrs. Melkford shook her head. "It's open to everyone, everyone who believes that Jesus is their Savior."

Maureen sat back, mortified. *I cannot go. Even if He could save me from what I've been—like He did those women—He can't change what I've failed to do for Eliza, for Alice.* A sob escaped her throat; she felt Katie Rose's elbow in her ribs. She closed her eyes, and the faces of her friends loomed before her. *No, He can't want me, can't save me. And I can't save myself!*

When the usher came to their row and opened the little gate at the end of their pew, those on either side of her stood. Maureen didn't know what to do. She pulled her knees to the side to allow Katie Rose and Joshua to pass.

"Get up," Katie Rose hissed and pinched her. "You'll shame them!"

And so Maureen did. She filed to the center aisle behind Mrs. Melkford. But when they reached the altar rail, just before they were to kneel to receive the bread and wine, Maureen turned and, eyes to the floor, followed the group of men and women who were leaving the rail—those she'd seen approach the Almighty to eat His body and drink His blood, no matter that there'd been no talk of confession beforehand, nor so much as the sign of the cross made after. She followed them back to her own pew, struggled with the catch on the little gate at its end until an usher came to help her, then slid in and kept her head down. She could not hold back the tears betraying her shame.

You're not my Lord, and I've no right to partake. Oh, God! Why do You call me to this possibility and then send me away in public humiliation?

❖ CHAPTER TWENTY-EIGHT ❖

To Maureen's relief, Katie Rose did not interrogate her about why she'd not partaken in Communion. Her sister alternately bubbled and fumed throughout the afternoon and evening about Olivia Wakefield's smart hat and stylish fur coat and her invitation to an undoubtedly lavish New Year's dinner—a dinner she boasted she would have gladly and thoroughly enjoyed had Maureen not spoiled everything by "being impossibly rude in church."

By the time Maureen walked into work on Monday morning, she never wanted to see or hear of Olivia Wakefield again.

The store opened on schedule despite a heavy snow that began in the early morning hours. Maureen stood anxiously behind her counter, freshening her display, ten minutes before the bell rang and the doors opened. She noticed that the girls who'd staffed the floor last Thursday were on duty. *No one else is missin'. Oh, Eliza, Alice—where are you? What's become of you?*

"Good morning, Miss O'Reilly." Mrs. Gordon stopped by Maureen's counter. "I trust you have sufficiently recovered from your sudden illness." Her tone was snide.

"Thank you, ma'am. I'm much better today." Maureen looked away, wondering if Mrs. Gordon helped to choose the girls who disappeared, if she was an integral part of the racket—for she'd come to think of it as just that—or if the woman was simply a miserable employee who ignorantly pressured working girls under the orders of the store's management. *But you work with management; how could you not know? How could you know and turn a blind eye? But isn't that what I've done—because I'm afraid?*

Maureen didn't try to communicate with the girls at lunch. She did not think it her imagination that the room was quieter, the girls more subdued and less talkative than usual. Nor did she think she imagined that they were all watched more carefully than usual by the floor supervisors. Even Mr. Kreegle walked through the room once, and Maureen felt certain he searched the faces and posture of the young women. *For what? Signs of knowin'? Is knowin' grounds for being stolen away or dismissed, or is there somethin' else they're lookin' for?*

By the end of the workday, Maureen's nerves were ground raw and her head ached. She gathered her hat and cloak and purse from the employee cloakroom and headed for the stairwell, determined to take the trolley for once.

Such a relief it will be to ride through the snowy streets rather than plow my way on foot! I hope Katie Rose is home early enough to fire the stove and lay our tea.

Intent on her plans, she didn't realize until she'd reached the door that it had been closed, that Mr. Kreegle and Mrs. Gordon stood sentinel, cross-armed before it, or that the other girls hung back, whispering nervously.

"In a hurry tonight, Miss O'Reilly?" Mr. Kreegle challenged.

"It's snowin'," she said lamely, taken by surprise. "I'm anxious to reach the trolley." She stepped back, wishing she had the courage to press forward.

"You'll need to delay your travel plans, miss. You all need to delay travel plans." He barked, "Get in line and wait your turn."

Maureen drew in her breath. *What can he be thinkin'?* Neither she nor the other women had perceived there was a line, but they dutifully and quickly formed one.

Mr. Kreegle cleared and raised his voice. "There's been a rash of thefts from the store counters—a thing Darcy's will not tolerate, certainly not from our own employees." He nodded toward Mrs. Gordon; she stepped before the door. He made his way down the line, glaring at each young woman in turn. "From now on, before you leave each evening, purses, coats, and pockets will be searched."

A rush of indignation followed by a whisper of fear swept through the ranks.

"Let's begin with you." Mr. Kreegle spoke to the girl behind Maureen. "Mrs. Gordon?"

"Open your purse and turn out your pockets," Mrs. Gordon ordered the terrified young woman.

When the search yielded nothing, she proceeded to the next clerk.

Why did they bypass me? Maureen could not imagine.

"Feeling left out, Miss O'Reilly?" Mr. Kreegle asked. She hated the way he smiled at her. "Shall I search you myself?"

Maureen knew her face flamed, but she summoned her courage. "I've nothin' to hide, nothin' at all."

"Mrs. Gordon, perhaps you could search Miss O'Reilly. She has a trolley to catch." He snickered, stepping back, and a nervous twitter sped through the line.

"Open your purse," the floor supervisor ordered. "Turn out your pockets."

Maureen did as she was bid; both were empty of anything but her personal belongings. Mrs. Gordon lifted her brows and proceeded down the line.

"Why are you holding your cloak, Miss O'Reilly?" Mr. Kreegle challenged loudly. All nervous chatter stopped.

"I—I've simply not put it on," Maureen stammered.

"Every other young woman is dressed to go into the cold." He stepped closer. "Why, pray tell, are you different?"

"I'm not—"

"Hand me your cloak," he ordered.

Maureen, angry to be doubted, angry that any of the women would be subjected to his sneers or play for power, thrust her cloak into his arms.

As he lifted her cloak, Maureen intuited rather than knew he would find something. *'Tis a ruse—a play upon the stage! He's planted somethin'.*

Every eye turned upon Mr. Kreegle's searching, probing fingers, and Maureen knew she was not the only one who cringed at the way he clawed her cloak. *He's planted somethin' and now he can't find it.* Maureen nearly smirked in return, until an unholy light came into the man's eyes. Her heart sank.

"What have we here?" Maureen knew he feigned surprise as he fingered the hem. He manipulated something through the lining of the cloak, right to one of the pockets, until he was able to work it through a hole that she knew for certain had not been there that morning. "A hole in your pocket. Ingenious but futile, Miss O'Reilly." He held up the turned-out pocket and pulled a pearl necklace from its hiding place in the lining, displaying it high for all to see.

Horrified gasps washed over the group, then silence.

Maureen felt her head spin. "'Tisn't mine."

Mr. Kreegle smiled. "I'm sure none of us ever suspected it was." He hefted the cloak. "I believe we've found our thief, Mrs. Gordon."

"I never took—" Maureen could barely catch her breath.

"Save your lies for the police, Miss O'Reilly. The rest of you may go."

Maureen struggled against the growing tightness in her throat and chest as the women rushed past her and out the opened door, most not daring to look her in the eye.

"Close the door on your way out, Mrs. Gordon."

Mrs. Gordon flashed an uncertain glance between Maureen and Mr. Kreegle. "Shall I telephone the police?"

"Well, let me see." Mr. Kreegle walked close to Maureen, who instinctively stepped back. But he circled her, walking ever closer. "A police report would lead to trial. A verdict of theft would mean deportation as likely as imprisonment in this case, I imagine."

Maureen's senses flared.

"Now, I wonder . . . would that be deportation of Miss O'Reilly alone, or would that include her sister—her young, impressionable sister? What is her name? Ah, Katie Rose O'Reilly, employed by Triangle Waist Factory, I believe."

Maureen felt a gnawing terror rise from the pit of her stomach, swirling with the knowledge that she'd never given this man her sister's name or place of employment. "I didn't take it. I don't know how it got there, but I swear I did not take it." She turned to Mrs. Gordon. "Please, you must believe me."

Mrs. Gordon looked away, uncomfortable, Maureen thought, for the first time.

"But deportation won't be necessary, will it, Miss O'Reilly?"

"No." She shook her head. "No, please."

"No, I don't believe we'll need the police," he continued as if Maureen had never spoken. "I believe we can come to some agreement with our pretty little orphaned thief." He dropped his smile and all pretense of mercy as he circled Maureen a second time, pulling a long red lock of hair from her bun and trailing it with his finger down the back of her neck.

Maureen closed her eyes at his touch and held her breath, felt the air being sucked from her throat, felt her chest constrict.

"You may leave, Mrs. Gordon. I'll take care of this . . . situation."

"If you're certain?" Mrs. Gordon asked, hesitating at the door.

He pulled a pin and another tendril from Maureen's bun, tracing it down the other side of her neck, fingering the collar of her shirtwaist. "Quite certain."

Memories of Julius Orthbridge barging through her door late at night bullied their way into Maureen's brain. She felt the world and darkness closing in, began the intentional numbing of her heart. She heard the door open, sensed Mrs. Gordon passing through and with her any feeble hope of protection.

"We can, no doubt, reach an understanding," the man crooned, self-assured, arrogant, continuing his pulling of pins from Maureen's hair.

She could not reply but felt the dam behind her eyes begin to overflow. With each pull of the pin, he undressed her mind and all its bulwarks. Her upswept hair, symbol of refinement and womanhood, tumbled to her shoulders, leaving her naked, exposed of spirit.

The trickle down her cheek seemed only to inspire him. "We've much to discuss, don't we, Miss O'Reilly?" The timbre of his voice was oily, slick, like the rodents along the wharf in Dublin. His breath foul, smelling—tasting—of rotting fish heads and onions piled behind her uncle's pub. "Such a pretty face." His finger traced her jaw, her neck; his hand began its descent.

Maureen cried out, but he pressed himself against her and laughed. "Go ahead and scream. There's no one to hear you, little Paddy. No one to save you." He pulled at the buttons of her waist.

The horror and truth of his words drove a knife into her heart.

And then, unbidden, came words she'd read in Mrs. Melkford's Bible: *"When my father and my mother forsake me, then the Lord will take me up."*

She jerked away.

Kreegle laughed and jerked her back. "Feisty, are we? That's all right. I don't mind a little fight in a woman."

"Help!"

Kreegle laughed again.

From the recesses of Maureen's brain came another Scripture she'd heard in Mrs. Melkford's church: *"For the Lord your God is he that goeth with you, to fight for you against your enemies, to save you."*

You would fight for me?

As Kreegle ripped her buttons, a new strength flowed into Maureen's heart, through her core, and out into her limbs. She clenched her fists and pushed them both at once up and into Kreegle's chin, knocking him backward.

He regained his footing, and Maureen saw a familiar succession sweep through his eyes—anger, challenge, then lust with the thrill of the hunt, the determination to overpower his prey.

But refusal, rage, and a bewildered vestige of hope raced through her calves and into her pointed-toe boots, straight to his shins.

He swore, grabbed her again, and pinned her arms behind her. She kneed him, once and sharply, in his groin.

Kreegle doubled over but grabbed Maureen's skirts, pulling her to the floor with him. She kicked him in the face, a toe to his eye, a sharp heel to his nose. He covered his face and she kicked his hand, his head, the blood staining red through his thinning hair.

Maureen scrambled backward, across the floor and to her knees, her feet. Unmindful of her purse, heedless of her cloak, she wrestled with the knob of the door and, throwing it open, raced down the stairs and out into the freezing night.

CHAPTER TWENTY-NINE

"I'M NO LONGER a powerless village girl, but an independent, workin', wage-earnin' woman of New York City. And if I'm to be deported, I shall go havin' had my say, wearin' my dignity." Maureen spoke the words aloud as she marched to work on Tuesday, hoping for the courage she feigned. Her arms sore and bearing bruises from Mr. Kreegle's grip, her head weary from the cold and from the raw throat building there, she trooped on, determined to face her accusers.

Katie Rose had offered little sympathy at the loss of her cloak and purse, certain that whatever had happened, Maureen had brought it on herself. "You've no sense of propriety! After your behavior at church on Sunday, I'm surprised at nothin'! Besides, your tea is cold, and it's your own fault for bein' late. I'll not heat it up again." Katie Rose had turned her back on a shivering Maureen.

Maureen had laughed, very near hysteria, at the notion that she should care about the temperature of her tea after what she'd been through with the demon at the store—the demon she'd fought and bested at his own game. She'd laughed until Katie Rose had stomped out, slamming the door, on her way down the hall to the toilet.

And then Maureen had lain awake half the night, into the wee hours, alternately shivering in fear and wondering at the voice that had come into her head, the surprising flow of strength to fight that slime of a man. Most surprising of all was its clarity of vision and solidarity with her own spirit.

She longed to talk with someone, but who? She wondered if she should have confided in Katie Rose—about Mr. Kreegle, about her suspicion of Drake Meitland or her dread of Jaime Flynn, about her worry for the women who'd disappeared, about the new voice in her head. But

Maureen had heaved a sigh and turned over. *She's too young to hear such things. Someday, when it's settled, when we've made our way and have nothin' to fear, perhaps I'll tell her then—two grown women, together. But it's a burden she should not have to bear now. What could she do but worry and fear? And how will I protect her?*

Maureen had no idea what to do but knew she must stand up for herself. Fighting back against Mr. Kreegle had been the greatest revelation of her life. She could fight. She might not always win, but she could stand for herself, and although she dared not think that the Lord had accepted her, cared about her, He'd done something magnificent for her in bringing those Scriptures to mind, in infusing her limbs with strength beyond her own. He'd stood with her against evil. No one less could have done such a thing.

Perhaps it was a mistake, an automatic action on God's part—that answerin' of a prayer in a way I'd never imagined. He may never do it again, may be on His guard not to help me in future, but He stood with me last night. And that gave Maureen pause, courage, and the daring to hope—a little.

Clasping the edges of a woolen blanket thrown over her shoulders for lack of a cloak, Maureen stomped through the ice and slushy streets. She pulled open the employee entrance door and marched up the stairs. She folded her blanket and placed it on the cloakroom shelf as if she'd done it every day of her working life. She combed her hair into place, smoothed her skirt and waist, and walked, head high and fingers trembling, to her post.

"You've more nerve than sense to show up here today!" a girl who stood at the counter next to Maureen's whispered. "I thought sure Mr. Kreegle was going to fire you!"

Maureen smiled thinly and set to polishing her counter. The bell rang, the doors were unlocked, and Darcy's was opened for business.

Mrs. Gordon's pale face as she made her rounds told Maureen that she knew at least some version of what had transpired last night.

But Maureen banked on the hope that Mr. Kreegle would not want anyone to learn that he'd been pummeled by a woman. She hoped that his shame would stand between her and the upper management of the store. What could he say? What dared he say?

Two hours after the store opened, Mrs. Gordon appeared before her. "Miss O'Reilly," she began, standing in front of her counter.

"Yes, Mrs. Gordon?" Maureen straightened and looked her in the eye, no longer frightened by the woman who'd shown herself weak and intimidated before Mr. Kreegle, ready to abandon Maureen because she'd been told to remove herself from a room.

"Due to the uncertain nature of your indiscretion, management has decided to give you another chance."

Maureen squared her shoulders. "I've done nothin' wrong. I did not take that necklace."

Mrs. Gordon blinked in the face of Maureen's stare, focusing beyond her shoulder, but did not respond to her declaration. "I'm to tell you that you have been demoted to the stockroom and placed on probation for the next two weeks. If in that time you perform satisfactorily with no further complaints against you, you will be allowed to remain a part of Darcy's staff—in the stockroom, of course, and at that rate of pay. You will receive no pay for this week's work. If, however—"

"That isn't fair." Maureen felt new rage flow through her veins at the injustice, at the fear of no pay, and in the newfound strangeness of standing up for herself.

"Fair? Is theft fair, Miss O'Reilly?" Mrs. Gordon's voice rose enough to attract unwanted attention from the counter clerks nearby. She lowered it. "Mr. Kreegle said that if you and your sister would like alternative employment, you may have it, as long as you're willing to relocate across state lines. In that case you—"

"No." Maureen knew her voice faltered. "No!" came louder.

Heads turned their way.

Mrs. Gordon visibly composed herself. "You are most fortunate you have not been dismissed. I don't know why formal charges have not been filed against you."

Maureen leaned closer. "Yes, Mrs. Gordon, you do. You know precisely why."

Mrs. Gordon's face faded to white. "Mr. Kreegle has asked me to make certain you know that he has learned through one of our most reputable clients that you misrepresented your connections, your references." Her color lifted. "He suspects that further inquiry will lead to more damaging revelations—none of which will stand you in good stead in a court of law or with immigration." She paused. "Get your things and leave this counter at once. Take the stairs to the basement. You will be shown what to do."

Maureen stood, rooted, unbelieving.

"Do as you're told, Miss O'Reilly . . . unless, of course, you prefer to resign now." Mrs. Gordon lifted her brows and waited. "It's up to you, isn't it?"

But Maureen could not resign, not without another job and not without a letter of reference, a thing she knew was hopeless to ask for.

"Mary—" Mrs. Gordon turned to the clerk at the next counter—"attend to this station until a replacement can be found." And then she walked away.

Maureen stood but a moment, dumbfounded, then headed for the stairs, conscious of the stares of the surrounding clerks. But the moment she glanced in their direction, each head turned away.

CHAPTER THIRTY

"IT WAS A MINOR VICTORY—at least as far as Maureen is concerned," Olivia explained to Dorothy over tea, attempting to divert her sister's attention and soothe her apparently jangled nerves with the news that the O'Reilly sisters had joined her in the family pew on Sunday. "Wait until you meet the younger Miss O'Reilly. Katie Rose is very thirteen!"

Dorothy appeared neither interested nor well but declined an explanation.

Olivia tried again. "I hope you don't mind, but I've sent round an invitation to the O'Reillys to join our Ladies' Circle next Saturday."

At last she had her sister's attention. "Do you think that's wise?"

"I don't know if Katie Rose can convince Maureen to come, but I hope so." Olivia smiled. "They'll certainly liven up our group."

"Just the type to send Julia Gresham into a spin. You should have asked the other ladies first. You should have asked *me* first. You don't know what sort those O'Reilly women might be."

Oliva sobered. "They're just the sort of women we're anxious to help make a strong start in this country. And if you're concerned about entertaining two more women on Saturday, you know I'll help you—or we can have it at Morningside. I don't mind."

Dorothy looked away. "It's just as well," she sighed.

Her despondency felt contagious to Olivia. "What is it, Dottie? What's wrong? You're as off your kilter as ever I've seen you." She was surprised when something liquid trickled down her sister's cheek. "Now, enough of this. What's wrong?"

"It's just as well that you take up with them because you'll be needing company other than mine."

"What on earth are you talking about?"

Dorothy paled. "I can't bear to tell you. I can't bear *not* to tell you—I need to talk to someone."

"Dottie? Not another miscar—"

"No."

"Then what's Drake done?"

Dorothy covered her mouth with her hands. "I don't know. I don't know what he's done or who he's with or where he goes for his 'business.'"

"Is that unusual?"

"He's made it the norm. He's either down in those infernal tenements he sells near the Battery or hobnobbing with clients in Midtown or out of town—out of the state—doing who knows what with whom." Dorothy lifted her cup from its saucer, then immediately returned it. She sat back, pulling her hankie from her pocket and an earring from its folds. "This was found in Drake's trouser cuff when he returned from his business trip."

"It's not yours?"

Dorothy shook her head. "George found it when he was brushing Drake's suit. He naturally assumed it was mine and gave it to me after breakfast." She knotted her fingers. "You should have seen Drake's face. He was livid."

"But did he explain?"

"No. How could he?" Dorothy raised her chin as if facing a firing squad. "He shifted the attention with his fury at my implication that it was anything but a complete accident. As if I should believe a cheap earring jumped from a stranger's ear as he walked down the street." And then the fire left her eyes. "I don't trust him, Livvie."

Olivia reached for her sister's hands.

"I don't trust him and I don't believe him." Dorothy began to cry.

"I'm sorry. I'm so sorry." Olivia didn't know what to do or say. She'd had reasons of her own not to trust men, but Dorothy had been besotted with Drake from the beginning, absolutely sure of his love and devotion. Olivia had been too young to know better when they married, but she'd grown certain at least of Drake's love and devotion to Dorothy's money, though she'd never implied such a thing to her sister. And she'd never believed he'd betray her. "Do you suspect someone?"

Dorothy pulled her hands away. "You mean do I suspect his truancy is due to one woman rather than the smorgasbord offered through a brothel?"

"Dorothy! Surely you don't think Dra—"

"He's given me syphilis." Dorothy spoke quietly.

"What?" Olivia felt the room spin.

"Do you know what syphilis is, Livvie?"

"I don't—yes—it's a venereal disease." Olivia stumbled over the unfamiliar words. "But what does it mean?"

Dorothy stood and crossed the room to the window. "It means that the disease will rear its ugly head off and on throughout the rest of my life—that it may, and likely will in the end, take my mind and my life. It means that if I should be lucky enough to conceive a child through my adulterous husband, our child could be born deaf or blind or crippled or without a coherent thought in his head. Or he might not be born at all but be pulled dead from my body."

Olivia did not realize that she'd stood or that she openly gaped in horror.

Dorothy faced her again. "It means that good people, if they ever learn of it, will have nothing to do with me. They will look on me as a pariah, a prostitute, a leper. Those same good people will refuse to conduct business with Drake. He'll be finished—we'll be finished."

Olivia could not stop the pounding of her heart, the thrum in her ears. The idea was incomprehensible. *Good, loving, pure Dorothy. Why, Lord? Why?* "But surely there are treatments!" She reached for her sister. "Tell me there are treatments!"

The look in Dorothy's eyes did nothing to dispel her fears. "Mercury—that's what Dr. Blakely recommends, for Drake and myself."

"But isn't mercury—?"

"Poisonous in its own right?" Dorothy almost laughed. "Does it matter?"

"Of course it matters!" Olivia sputtered. "There must be something else. There must be other doctors, Dottie. Dr. Blakely is as old as Father was!"

"And just as wise. Father trusted him completely." Dorothy covered her face with her hands. "I was so embarrassed—so stunned and ashamed when he examined me. Oh, Livvie, I dared hope I was pregnant! I couldn't think what else it could be."

"Dr. Blakely will be discreet. You know that." Olivia thought it stupid to care about such things at such a time, but she knew it was crucial.

"And that's why I couldn't bear to go to anyone else. No one else can know."

"But what did Drake say? How long has he—? For surely he will seek the best, the newest treatment for you both!"

"He doesn't know I've spoken to the doctor. He doesn't know I have it. I've no idea if he knows *he* has it."

"But he must know. How could he not? Why haven't you told—?"

"I'd intended to confront him this morning. But when George presented me with the earring . . . it changed everything. I'd hoped the disease was at least from an old liaison. Now I don't know—new or old and new . . . daily? I don't know, and I don't know what I want." She hugged her arms to herself. "Except I don't want him near me or touching me." She looked up. "How can I believe anything he says?"

"You must allow me to do some research. There are new medical studies going on all the time—especially in Europe. I can—"

"No!" Dorothy's eyes flashed. "Don't be ridiculous! Where would you ask such questions? It's unthinkable!"

"It's unthinkable to do nothing!" Olivia retorted. "I did research for Father frequently on the most delicate of issues. Nothing is more important than your good health. Father would tell you—"

"Father is dead, Olivia! He can't tell me anything! He can't help me any more than the money he left behind, and neither can you!"

Dorothy's venom pulled the wind from Olivia, forcing her back into her chair.

Dorothy closed her eyes. "I'm sorry. I'm sorry I shouted." She turned again toward the window, her back to Olivia, and heaved a great sigh.

"Dorothy, I—"

"I think you should go now, Livvie. I'm tired."

Olivia stood. "But—"

"Please. Please, go."

Olivia knew from her sister's posture that all discussion was at an end—at least for today. She looked helplessly around the room, desperate for some response, some thread of hope in the nightmare. But there was none to be found. "I'll see you tomorrow, then."

Dorothy did not reply.

Olivia crossed the room and embraced her sister, but Dorothy stiffened, shrugging her away.

Undaunted, Olivia kissed her cheek, squeezed her arms, and stepped into the hallway. She closed the door behind her—*how loud and lonely that sounds*—then rang for George, who helped her into her heavy cloak and called for her car to be brought round.

Olivia waited patiently by the front door, mentally ticking through her list of medical resources and imagining all the ways she could reduce her brother-in-law to ashes.

CHAPTER THIRTY-ONE

KATIE ROSE FOUND the note the moment she returned from the Triangle Waist Factory. "It's like bein' invited to a ball!" She waved the invitation beneath Maureen's nose the second her sister stepped through the door.

"'Our next meeting of the Ladies' Circle will be held Saturday, at four o'clock, Mrs. Dorothy Meitland's home in Salley Square, Manhattan,'" Katie Rose read aloud, barely lower than a squeal, and fairly dancing across the room. "I'll be a bit late, of course, but as soon as I collect my pay, I'll take the trolley directly there!" She tapped her upper lip. "You take the trolley from Darcy's, and we'll meet on the corner of the block before Salley Square; we absolutely can't be later than we must. And, oh, I must tell Emma that I can't go to the nickelodeon with her on Saturday. Do you think they run the movin' pictures on Sundays?"

Maureen shook her head and turned away without answering, but Katie Rose did not care. "This is the beginnin'; you'll see."

"The beginnin'?" Maureen pulled the pin from her hat and hung it on the peg beside her cloak.

"Of our entrance into polite society, of course!" She stopped and admonished, "Really, Maureen, you must attend to that rip in your sleeve. You'll need to wear your best shirtwaist. I'll wash all our things this evenin' so they can dry overnight, then iron tomorrow as soon as I get home from work."

Maureen sighed.

"I know it's days away, but we'll want to be ready and no surprises. Everything must be in good order before the end of the week!"

"Don't bother," Maureen said wearily.

But Katie Rose laughed. "Of course I'll bother! We might not own the best—not like Miss Olivia—but we can turn ourselves out pretty well, at least the best we're able." She placed her hands on her hips and eyed her sister critically. "Now, change out of that skirt and let me have your waist. I'll put everything to soak before tea."

"I'm not goin', and neither are you." Maureen said the words, though Katie Rose was certain she'd not heard correctly.

"Of course you're goin'. We're both goin'." Katie Rose spoke with authority, but the first twinge of doubt scraped across her nerves. "It's the perfect opportunity."

"An opportunity we'll miss, then."

Katie Rose set the envelope down. "I'll not."

Maureen bit her lip, a sure sign to Katie Rose that her sister was struggling with words. But she determined to beat her to the punch.

"I don't know why you're intent on insultin' the Wakefields, or Joshua, for that matter. They've been nothin' but kindness—"

"Kindness!"

"That bad beginning with Mr. Meitland was an unfortunate misunderstandin'. Miss Olivia explained it perfectly, and it was nothin' to do with her, anyway." Katie Rose dug both fists into her hips. "She's done all she could to find us, to make amends. It's no good bearin' a grudge, Maureen. You'd best stop poutin' and mopin' about before you ruin things for the both of us."

"You don't know the Meitlands." Maureen drew out each word.

"No, I don't, nor do you. But I shall meet Mrs. Meitland on Saturday." Katie Rose drew her words equally long. "It's not right to judge Olivia's sister by the rudeness of her husband." She took up the teakettle and half giggled. "And if he's a problem, I've a feelin' Miss Olivia can well take care of him."

"You don't understand anythin'."

Katie Rose slammed the kettle onto the stove. "Then perhaps you'd best explain it to me. Because what I do understand is that I've been workin' like a scullery woman and cook after spendin' my long day at the Triangle, and you waltz in here like the queen bee with nothin' but frowns and grimaces for everythin' that's good or hopeful in our lives." Katie Rose felt her blood rising and only wished she dared fling harsher words at her sister.

Silence stretched between them as Maureen stood in the middle of the floor, her eyes closed, as though praying. Finally she said, "We cannot go to the Meitlands because we cannot, dare not, trust them. Mr. Meitland is . . . he's not a gentleman; he's a dangerous man."

"Not a gentleman? And dangerous? Says who?" Katie Rose demanded.

"Says I!" Maureen's voice rose and her eyes popped open. "And I don't say it lightly, but that's all you need to know!"

"That's not good enough. If you've somethin' sure to say, you'd best say it. Gone are the days when I follow you around like a whelp pup, Maureen O'Reilly. You've proven you're not thinkin' straight. You imagine fairies and leprechauns where there are none. Look how you took on last week at Mrs. Melkford's and your rudeness in the church." Katie Rose threw coal onto the fire. "You've left me little to trust."

Maureen turned her face to the wall.

Katie Rose, seeing her sister's shoulders slump in defeat, was moved to pity—a little. She knelt beside Maureen. "What is it? What's made you so dark?"

"I've been demoted. There'll be no pay this week and only half the next. I don't know if we'll be able to keep this flat, and there'll surely be no trolley fare to anywhere, least of all to the Meitlands'."

"What have you done now?"

The face Maureen raised to Katie Rose was not repentant but angry. "I've done nothin'! I stole nothin', but that wicked Mr. Kreegle planted a pearl necklace in my coat, sayin' I'd taken it, and . . ."

Katie Rose sat back on her knees in horror as the story poured from Maureen—details of the necklace, the fighting off of Kreegle, the shaming before the store. Rarely had she seen her sister cry and never in such a state. For the first time in memory, Katie Rose found herself in the role of comforter.

"How dare the man! But don't cry; don't take on so. There's no understandin' the gall of some of these Americans. We'll manage." Katie Rose pulled out her hankie and pressed it against Maureen's cheek. "We've almost the rent saved for another month. We'll just have to . . . to go Spartan on the tea for a while. And you're right; we'll walk to the Meitlands'."

But the fear in her sister's eyes did not subside. "They're tryin' to force me out of Darcy's. And you know what that means—no job and no references. We can't manage on your wages alone."

"But why? Why would they force you out? Has that Mr. Kreegle so much say, just because you wouldn't . . . wouldn't let him have his way?" Katie Rose looked at Maureen as though she'd not seen her before, trying to imagine why anyone would not want her beautiful, striking sister working at their counter. "Is it . . . is it because you're Irish?" she whispered.

"No!" Maureen threw up her hands. "I think it's because of what I . . . what I suspect. What I know of them."

"What on earth are you talkin' about?"

But Maureen put her face in her lap and covered her head with her hands, as near to keening as silent sobbing allowed. Katie Rose did not know what to do.

"Shall we go to Mrs. Melkford's, Maureen? Will that help?"

"No!" Maureen cried.

"Then let me get Joshua—or Miss Olivia."

"No!"

"Then tell me what's the matter!" Katie Rose was nearly frantic. "It's got to be more than a demotion!"

And so Maureen began her story with Jaime Flynn and his financial rescue and the job address given at Ellis Island. Before she could go further, Katie Rose cut her off.

"You took money from a strange man?" Katie Rose frowned, knowing such a thing was not to be done. "You shouldn't have. But it's all right now. It came out all right with the job."

"But I lied to get it. I told Mr. Kreegle that the Wakefields had recommended I go there. I forged a letter from Mrs. Melkford, saying she recommended my character and vouched for my workin' history."

"You never!"

"I did. I was desperate to stay in America and desperate to keep you here."

"Mrs. Melkford would have helped you for the askin', and Olivia would have helped."

"I didn't know that then! How could I?"

"How could you do that to Mrs. Melkford?" Katie Rose took her hands from her sister.

"It was wrong. I've nothin' to excuse it, and I've never told her. But Jaime Flynn has come and wants his money back—insists—and I don't have it." Maureen rocked back and forth in her agony. "The demotion is all part of a plan to force me into greater desperation."

"Greater desperation?" Katie Rose tried to understand. And as the possibilities dawned, she reclaimed her feet. "What do you mean?"

"I mean—" Maureen drew a deep breath—"that Jaime Flynn never meant me to be a shopgirl, a department store clerk. He meant me to work upstairs, where there's some sort of . . . sort of . . . ladies escortin' gentlemen about."

"You mean a . . . a brothel? Like the women downstairs?"

Maureen shook her head no, then yes. "I think so—or more likely some sort of escort service. But girls have been disappearin' altogether from Darcy's—at least my friend Alice and another girl. I know Jaime Flynn and others more powerful are behind it—Drake Meitland, for one."

"I don't believe it. Darcy's is a respectable department store."

Maureen's stricken face did not move Katie Rose.

"You've taken money from a man and accepted his help," Katie Rose recounted quietly, "just like you did from Lord Orthbridge. If you're up to your old tricks, I'll not be part of it."

"You don't understand!"

"What I understand is that you've not changed! All the village said you—"

"When the floor supervisor ordered me to leave my counter, she said that Mr. Kreegle offered to transport me and my sister across state lines for 'alternative employment'!" Maureen stood and faced Katie Rose. "Do you understand what that means?"

Katie Rose felt the blood drain from her face. "I understand what you think it means."

"Katie Rose!"

"Perhaps you're right about the man at the store, but I'll not do it—no more than I'd have done it with Gavin Orthbridge!"

"And I'll not have you do it! But I'm tellin' you the Meitland man and his friends may be part of the disappearance of those women. They may all be connected, these men who meet on the fourth floor. We can't have anythin' to do with him—not with him or his wife or her sister or any of them!"

Despite Katie Rose's nasty accusations, pouting lip, and obstinate silence through the remainder of the week, Maureen was certain she'd made her point, certain her younger sister would obey her now that she knew the seriousness of their plight.

But when Maureen returned home after a long and wearisome Saturday restocking shelves in the Darcy's Department Store cellar, she found the apartment empty, with only a note next to the table lamp.

I've gone to the tea. Will be back when it's done.

Katie Rose

Maureen dropped the paper, unbelieving. *How could she go when I told her . . . ? Foolish, foolish girl!*

But in her anger an image of her sister rose up before her. Young, flirtatious, smiling, trusting—so wanting to be noticed. An image of Drake Meitland followed closely behind, his superior smirk and the cultured voice she was certain was his that night in the dark of Darcy's Department Store.

Maureen had not unbuttoned her cloak. She grabbed her purse, dug a nickel from the pint jar on their bedside table, as well as the address for Dorothy Meitland, and raced down the stairs.

By the time Maureen reached the mansion in Salley Square, she was breathless, her frozen feet ached, and the rumble in her empty stomach had become a grinding churn. But she pounded on the front door with all the force of a judge's gavel, determined to rescue her sister.

✣ CHAPTER THIRTY-TWO ✣

Olivia had just poured tea for the Ladies' Circle when a frantic pounding began at Dorothy's front door.

Dorothy started. Several of the women raised inquisitive brows, but Olivia signaled for her sister to continue with her guests and discreetly slipped from the drawing room, closing the doors softly behind her.

By the time she reached the foyer, George, the Meitlands' middle-aged protective and vigilant butler, had planted himself firmly in the front doorway and was addressing the ruffian in quiet but not uncertain terms.

Olivia thought to step back, to allow George to attend to his business, but the brogue of the undaunted ruffian sounded surprisingly familiar.

"Where is she? Where is my sister?" The flame-haired, green-eyed monster pushed past George, nearly mowing him down.

"What is the meaning of this, miss, and to whom do you refer?" George, Olivia saw, could barely contain himself before the sprite now in his foyer.

"My sister, Katie Rose O'Reilly. I know she's here and you daren't deny it!"

Despite the impropriety of it all, Olivia Wakefield squirmed between them.

"Maureen! I'm so glad you came." Olivia pulled the irate young woman into the hallway. "George, please take Miss O'Reilly's coat. She'll be staying to tea."

"Where is she? Where's Katie Rose?" Maureen demanded shrilly.

"Please, lower your voice," Olivia whispered. "Katie Rose is in the drawing room, with the ladies from our circle, having tea." She smiled and confided, "I think she's having the time of her life—she's certainly the center of attention."

At that moment Katie Rose's tinkling laughter rang beyond the door.

Maureen visibly perked her ears toward the sound but demanded, "Is Mr. Meitland here?" Her green eyes were startlingly bright and wide.

"Why, no. He's away on business, and this, after all, is a ladies' circle." Olivia felt a little perturbed. *Why should she want Drake?* But her assurance that Drake was not there seemed to calm the trembling creature before her. At least she allowed Olivia to draw her into the hallway and take her coat.

"I'm sorry, Miss—"

"Olivia, please." Olivia reached for her arm.

"I beg pardon for burstin' in on you like this, but I'd no idea Katie Rose had accepted. I told her to decline."

"Well, she did—decline, I mean. But I'm so glad she changed her mind at the last moment. I'm so glad you both did."

"But I didn't . . . I . . ." Maureen looked desperate, frustrated, and very much like she was going to cry, as though she had been crying.

"It's a blustery day, I know," Olivia soothed. "Would you care to freshen up before coming in to join us?"

Maureen looked miserably self-conscious as she smoothed her skirt and tugged the cuffs of her crumpled waist. "No, I don't want to join you. I want Katie Rose—"

"Come with me." Olivia pulled her guest into her sister's downstairs powder room and opened a cupboard. She took out a brush, a comb, and a porcelain dish of hairpins. "Dorothy keeps these handy for her guests. You never know what the weather will be, and it does so wreak havoc with our hair."

But Maureen's hands trembled as she glanced frantically around the room, and Olivia knew the poor creature was very near the end of her tether.

"Please sit down." Olivia gently but firmly pushed Maureen to the seat of the vanity before an oval mirror. "Allow me." And she pulled the simple pins from Maureen's wild knot, combing the long and tangled tresses one by one until they shone like silk in the electric light.

The brushing and combing seemed to calm both women, though neither said a word. Olivia wound the thick cords of shining hair into an attractive upswept style, something her lady's maid would have done for her, and pinned it neatly into place. "There. You have such lovely hair, Maureen. Thank you for allowing me to help."

"I ran all the way from home. I was so afraid for her." Maureen spoke low, breathing more deeply now.

"Afraid for Katie Rose?" Olivia watched Maureen's face in the oval before them. "For coming here? But why?"

Maureen's wide green eyes held the same bleak expression they'd held Thanksgiving afternoon, when Drake had roughly ushered her from Morningside.

"Why would you—?"

But they were interrupted by Dorothy's knocking on the door. "Olivia? Are you there? What has become of you? We're ready to start the meeting."

"I'll be right there, Dorothy!"

Maureen's frightened look was a total mystery to Olivia, a mystery she determined to solve, but later.

"Come, sit with me, and I'll get you some tea. You must be starving."

"Please, don't ask me. Send Katie Rose out, and we'll go."

"No, Maureen. You're here now. Please, please stay. Sit with me. Nothing and no one will harm you here."

"But—"

"I don't think Katie Rose will leave willingly. She's so bright and eager to stay. Please."

From the look on Maureen's face and the change in her posture, Olivia knew she'd hit both a nerve and the truth. She took Maureen by the elbow and drew her gently along the corridor to the drawing room, smiling with all the loving care and happiness she could muster, until Maureen breathed almost evenly and gave a tentative smile in return. Then she opened the drawing room door.

For the sake of Olivia, who'd been so kind and reassuring to her, Maureen did not glare the daggers at her younger sister that she might have, that she determined to give in good measure when she got her home—not even when she was introduced as Katie Rose's elder sister to the ladies of the circle. Maureen thought the ladies welcomed her warmly in words, if a little awkwardly in spirit.

Still, the color faded abruptly from Katie Rose's cheeks, and while she'd apparently been the life of the tea party, she said not one more word as the meeting was called to order.

The order of business sped by as little more than a blur to Maureen, who, so relieved to find her sister safe, was truly grateful for the piping hot tea in the warm room, the dainty sandwiches and scones. *"A lovely English nursery tea,"* Lady Catherine would have said.

As Maureen's nerves calmed, she recognized the conversation around her—sometimes heated and passionate, sometimes calm and questioning—as a continued discussion of the book and its purposes that Reverend Peterson had commended in church some weeks before.

"Have you read *In His Steps?*" Julia directed her question bluntly toward Maureen.

"No." Maureen nearly choked on her scone for the sudden attention drawn to herself. "I've not." The women stared, seeming to wait for her to continue. "I'd not heard of it until Reverend Peterson mentioned it just before Christmas." Women nodded politely, still waiting. The silence was awkward, so Maureen offered, "We may not have it in Ireland, it bein' an American book."

"Well, I would like to read it, if I may." Katie Rose spoke up and basked in the approving smiles of the women around her. "Is there a copy I might borrow?"

"Gladly." Carolynn beamed. "You may take my copy with you today."

Agnes, the eldest and the leader of the circle, appeared to overlook Katie Rose and returned the conversation to Maureen. "Do you understand the question posed by the book and the purpose of our meeting, Miss O'Reilly?"

"I—I think so." She hesitated. "You're askin' each one to do what they think best for the poor."

"They're asking what *Jesus* would do for the poor," Katie Rose corrected.

"That's right," Agnes praised the girl, "and we're each taking a pledge to do just that—whatever we believe Jesus would do in every situation."

"Regardless of the consequences," Miranda added.

"But how do you know what Jesus would do?" Maureen asked. "How can you be sure?" She looked around at all the different women, twelve in all, wondering if they realized just how different they were from one another, from her—how different they all appeared from the radical Jesus pictured in the stories Reverend Peterson read about from his Bible in the Sunday pulpit. "And what if you disagree?"

"Maureen!" Katie Rose admonished.

"No." Julia jumped in. "That's a perfectly legitimate question, and I applaud you for asking it." She glanced round the group, daring them, Maureen thought, to contradict her. "We've been praying, asking the Lord to lead each of us individually, trusting that He will lead us in a similar direction to work with the . . ." She hesitated. "The poor."

Maureen forced a smile, realizing suddenly that she was not a guest and not an equal, but "the poor" and the cause of the forthright young woman's discomfort.

"The Holy Spirit leads us," Olivia offered. "We've no right to question the Spirit's leading of one another."

"The Holy Spirit?"

"The still, small voice of God within. The Comforter who leads and guides us," Carolynn explained.

Could that be the voice I heard? The voice that helped me battle Mr. Kreegle?

"But we want to do something that truly matters," Agnes intervened. "Something that makes a difference great enough to change the lives of . . . of . . . women who . . ."

"Women who what?" Maureen stared her down.

"Of women in need, especially those who come to this country with nothing," Miranda spoke plainly.

"Women like me and my sister?" Maureen asked quietly. "Is that why you've asked us here, because you want to give us tea?" She set her cup in its saucer. "Do you think tea will solve the problems of the poor?"

"No." Agnes took charge. "We know it won't."

"But we need to know what will, and we need to form a solidarity with the women of—the women in need." Julia regained her voice.

"Until there is no difference between us," Olivia offered. "Until we are sisters, a band of sisters, strong and united. That is why I asked you here, because I want us to be sisters in every way."

"A wonderful plan," Katie Rose enthused.

"It won't work," Maureen said flatly. "The poor don't go away rich. We don't stop bein' poor or uneducated or hungry because you want it. Our employers don't suddenly become generous or honorable or even fair."

Katie Rose bit her lip, and Maureen saw the daggers she'd intended to give her young sister spring from Katie Rose's eyes.

"It will work when we all come to know the Lord, to share fully and freely in the gift of life He died to give us." Dorothy Meitland spoke for the first time, lifting her chin, Maureen was sure, in some sort of barely perceptible snub.

"Jesus said that the reason some have wealth or earn an abundance is to share it with those who have none." Carolynn, who seemed to be the quiet one of the group, spoke up. "We just need to know how to best share it."

"To share it? Or to give it away as benefactors?" Maureen frowned. "No one wants a handout."

"Then why are there beggars in every street?" a woman named Hope spoke from the side of the room. "Help me understand that."

"Because they've figured a way to make themselves pitiful to you. Beggin's a job to them—some do it willingly, and some are forced by those greedier and more powerful."

The women looked astonished.

"You pay the hungry beggar for his beggin' through your coins dropped into his cup, and you both leave happy: the beggar, who's worked at beggin', is paid, and you, the 'employer,' who's paid so generously to feel good about yourself."

Spines straightened as if Maureen had bitten the women.

"But the ones in greatest need you never see. They're behind closed doors, in sweatshops, hunched over tables, workin' their hands to the bone—too cold to sit in winter and too hot to breathe in summer. They're down dark alleys, scroungin' through the leavin's behind pubs and stores, or hidden away, scrimpin' and starvin' or bein' threatened or beaten . . . or sold by the hour for another's gain. And their children are starvin' or sent to beg, dirty because they can't afford to ask their landlord to fix the water pipe—they daren't bring attention to their need when they can't pay the rent."

"How do you know?" Hope demanded.

Maureen stared at the young woman in blue silk, ivory lace, and pearl earrings. *She must be all of three and twenty, and she's never really seen the poor. She's never gone hungry. She can't even imagine it.* "Because I'm one of them. Because I've been one of them, and I've seen many worse off than me in Ireland and right here in your 'land of the free.' But it's not free—everything costs money, and those without it are enslaved to their poverty or to those who feed them—at whatever cost to their souls."

The only sound in the silence was Katie Rose's muffled sobs. And for those tears of humiliation and shame, Maureen pitied her sister.

"But how can we change that?" Julia persisted quietly.

And Hope echoed, "Please, tell us how."

"The problem you describe is monumental." Agnes spoke as though to herself.

"All I know is that if you want to help women, you need to help them find jobs—respectable jobs with fair wages so they can afford good food to eat and a safe place to live. Invitin' the poor to drink tea in your grand houses won't do that."

"We'd hoped to treat them as equals and then to draw them into the church, to help them spiritually and economically." Miranda spoke up.

"But you won't let the poor forget they've received a handout, will you?" Maureen replaced her teacup. "You'll invite us to your church, to sit in your pews and take Communion at your side, but you won't forget the next day, the next week, that we've come from someplace different, that we've had to do as you would never do, live as you have never lived, just to get by. You might not even notice us if we passed you in the street, say on Fifth Avenue. You'd not miss us if we disappeared entirely. We'd never truly be a part of your 'circle.'"

"I wouldn't have thought the poor would be ungrateful for help of any kind," Dorothy replied, not smiling.

Maureen stood.

"Please." Olivia stood too, her distress visible. "We're all missing something. This is not a 'them and us' question; it's a question of how we work together for everyone's good."

"Until we all go back to our places—all of you to your grand mansions in the squares with butlers and cooks and scullery maids, and Katie Rose and me to our hovel, our tenement near the Battery, our flat above a bar and brothel."

"Brothel?" Dorothy paled.

"It's not a brothel!" Katie Rose cried. "You're exaggeratin', Maureen!" Her eyes flashed desperately round at the women sitting tall in straight-backed chairs, women whose acceptance Maureen knew was her sister's heart's desire. "We're only there until we can afford somethin' better. We've nothin' to do with the pub downstairs! Tell them, Maureen—tell them!"

The women waited. Maureen finally spoke. "How can you talk of bein' like your Jesus and helpin' the poor when you've no idea what it is to be poor, to be powerless and hungry, unprotected and desperate? To be vulnerable all the time?"

"And what do you do in your desperation?" Dorothy asked coldly.

"You're right," Julia said, ignoring Dorothy. "We've no idea and no right. So help us, Miss O'Reilly. Tell us where to begin and what we can do."

But Maureen had had enough. *If sayin' we live above a brothel shocks them, what would they say to knowin' the number of their wealthy husbands and fathers and brothers who not only visit those brothels but buy and sell women—dupe or dope or beat them and take them who knows where, right under the nose and with the blessin' of Tammany Hall and "New York's finest"? What would they say if I told them Drake Meitland, the benefactor who housed and hosted their ladies' tea, may well be among those sinners?*

"Come, Katie Rose, we're goin' home." Maureen walked to the door.

"No." Katie Rose's voice trembled, but she stood firm. "I want to stay."

"Perhaps you should—" Olivia began.

"I want to take the pledge," Katie Rose interrupted. "I want to join you, just as you said, and follow Him together. I can help you help the poor."

Maureen stopped with her hand on the door, not looking back. *Katie Rose, you're simply curryin' favor with these women—women you don't know if you can trust beyond a pleasant afternoon with tea and scones. Don't pledge—not for that reason. Wait until you know you can trust this Jesus, until you know that He will help you, love you as you want, before you love Him.*

But no one said anything, so shocking was Katie Rose's insistence. *What can they say? They can't turn her away from their notion of the all-forgivin', all-lovin' Jesus. And perhaps, after all, I shouldn't. Just because He can't love me—want me—it doesn't mean He won't love her.*

Maureen sighed and turned the knob. "I'll wait for you in the hallway."

Such a simple, foolish girl. But I envy you, Katie Rose. What if this Jesus really loves you?

❖ CHAPTER THIRTY-THREE ❖

"I WONDERED if I might join you lovely ladies in your pew this mornin'?" Joshua Keeton tipped his hat as he met Maureen, Katie Rose, and Mrs. Melkford on their walk to church Sunday morning. He offered his arm to Mrs. Melkford, who smiled at his courtly manners and slipped her arm through his.

"You'll not be sitting with the Wakefields this morning?"

"I believe Mr. and Mrs. Meitland will have returned. It would make the pew a mite crowded with all of us, and after all, my connection with the family was only to deliver a letter to the Misses O'Reilly." He nodded toward Maureen and Katie Rose but didn't address them. "I'd be most grateful for the pleasure of your company."

Mrs. Melkford dimpled. "I'm not simple, Mr. Keeton. I know when my presence is a matter of convenience. Still," she sighed, "it's been quite a long while since I walked through a church door on the arm of a handsome gentleman, and I'm pleased to do it."

Joshua winked in return, knowing his eyes twinkled. But he kept them fastened on Mrs. Melkford and the sidewalk ahead.

He sensed more than saw that Maureen had stiffened in displeasure and that Katie Rose had melted at the sight of him. *Walkin' a precarious line, I am, but a line that must be walked.*

"What is it that you do, exactly, Mr. Keeton?" Mrs. Melkford asked. "Besides seek out missing ladies?"

"In Ireland I worked the land with my father and brothers. But here I've worked makin' deliveries for department stores, and now I've taken a position with Mr. Morrow in his publishin' firm."

"Oh?" Mrs. Melkford inclined her head approvingly. "What exactly—?"

"There's not much farmin' to be had in the midst of Manhattan." He smiled.

"No, no, I don't suppose there is," she replied. "But—"

"You're lookin' dapper today, Katie Rose. I believe this New York City air agrees with you."

Katie Rose blushed from her neck to her hairline. "I believe it does." She hesitated only a half second. "You know, I've a position too, Mr. Keeton."

"Have you now?"

"With the Triangle Waist Factory. I'm a seamstress—I operate one of the new machines at full wages."

"That's quite commendable. Perhaps I should be callin' you 'Miss O'Reilly' rather than by your Christian name." He tipped his hat to her. "Forgive me if I've been impertinent."

He heard Maureen snort.

"No, please call me Katie Rose; I love the way it sounds when you say it."

He nodded. "Katie Rose it is, then."

Maureen spoke at last. "Mr. Keeton, you were about to say what you—"

"Ah, here we are." Joshua walked Mrs. Melkford through the portal of the church with a flourish and guided her up the balcony stairs, Katie Rose at his heels and Maureen taking up the rear.

He stood aside as the ladies filed into the pew and was more than pleased when Maureen, in her lagging behind, ended up beside him.

"Oh, look! There's Miss Olivia and Miss Dorothy!" Katie Rose pointed into the congregation below.

"You mustn't point in public, my dear," Mrs. Melkford corrected softly.

Katie Rose sat up straight, and Joshua smiled his sympathies toward her.

"Don't you think they'll be expectin' us to sit with them?" Katie Rose whispered to no one in particular.

But Joshua answered quickly, "I think Mr. Morrow is glad for the opportunity to accompany Miss Olivia with none to distract." He leaned toward Maureen conspiratorially. "I rather think he fancies her."

Maureen shifted in her seat beside him. "You seem to have an opinion about everythin' and everyone, Mr. Keeton."

Joshua couldn't help the smile that grew inside him. "On the contrary, Miss O'Reilly. I've no opinion about you."

She shifted again.

"I'm at a loss what to think," he teased, but from the corner of his eye he saw her redden and her mouth flatten in a straight line.

Oh, will you never lay down your prickles and armor, Maureen O'Reilly?

By the service's end, Joshua's head was more filled with the nearness of Maureen than of the Savior he loved and served. Still, he wasted no time in hastening the ladies down the balcony stairs and out the door. He walked them all the way back to Mrs. Melkford's street and at a steady clip.

"You'll stay to dinner with us, won't you, Mr. Keeton? I'm serving roast chicken and gravy, potatoes, and—"

"If only I could, Mrs. Melkford, and it's very kind of you to offer. Very kind indeed. But I must be off. I've a bit of work to catch up on." And he stepped along more lively yet.

"Are you off to a fire, Mr. Keeton?" Maureen fussed as she caught Mrs. Melkford's other arm when the good lady nearly tripped over a cobblestone.

"Beggin' your pardon, ladies," Joshua apologized sincerely. "I'm used to bein' about my business, and my farmer's legs don't stride a lady's pace. Are you all right, Mrs. Melkford?"

"Yes, yes," she said, a little breathless.

"Exactly what is your business?" Maureen demanded.

Joshua tipped his cap as they reached Mrs. Melkford's door. "Seein' you ladies safely home at the moment, Miss O'Reilly." And he left just as quickly as he'd come.

For once, Maureen did not doubt Joshua Keeton's sincerity or word. *What was that about? Did Aunt Verna bid him watch over us?*

"I still think we should have stayed to speak with Olivia and Dorothy." Katie Rose pouted. "I don't know why Joshua rushed us out so, not if he wasn't goin' to stay to dinner."

"Nor do I," Maureen answered. *Not that I'm anythin' but grateful to avoid either one of the Meitlands. But I wonder . . . It's as though he didn't want us to speak with them—any of them. Why?*

CHAPTER THIRTY-FOUR

WHEN MR. CRUDGERS came to the door for the rent, Maureen was still at work, and Katie Rose was two dollars short.

"You'll have to make it up before the month is out, little missy." He stepped over the threshold and leered, his tobacco-stained teeth and liquored breath too near her face. "Unless you want to work for it." And he fingered the stand-up collar of her shirtwaist.

But Katie Rose, her senses screaming, pretended to see her neighbor from across the hall, just beyond his shoulder. She waved and called, "Mrs. Kaminsky! I'll be right there. Mr. Crudgers is just collectin' the rent."

He stepped back into the hall then and turned. Quickly, Katie Rose slammed and bolted the door in his face.

"You little minx! You think you're clever," he shouted through the door. "You get me that two dollars, or you and your sister get out!" He thumped down the stairs to the bar below.

Katie Rose wrapped her arms around her torso, going weak in the knees, and slipped, her spine against the doorframe, to the floor. In the minutes it took for her breath to come evenly and for her heart rate to steady, she tore the collar from her waist and threw it on the floor. Then she made three decisions:

First, I'll demand that Maureen take Olivia up on her offer for us to move into Morningside.

Second, if Maureen refuses, I'll go without her.

Third, I'll ask Joshua for help and company, no matter what Maureen says. He has demonstrated himself a protector—completely trustworthy and every bit a gentleman. A gentleman I'd be proud to walk out with . . . proud to marry. She felt the heat race up her arms and face at her own confession but did not repent the thought. *Perhaps he'll notice me more if I'm not forever standin' in Maureen's shadow.*

———————— ❦ ————————

"Absolutely not!" Maureen fumed that evening. "You've no idea what you're sayin'."

"He wanted to touch me!" Katie Rose shouted. "Do you hear me? That filthy, lecherous man wanted to touch me!"

Maureen pushed her tea away and leaned her elbows on the table, her hands covering her face.

"He said that we could 'work' for the rest of the rent! Do you know what he meant?" Katie Rose demanded.

Maureen felt the weight of the world descend. "Yes, yes, I know. Do you know?"

"Don't be stupid! Of course I know. I told you on the ship that I would never have done it in Ireland, and I won't do it now." Katie Rose stood before her, hands on her hips, but Maureen could not bring herself to speak.

How has it come to this?

Katie Rose slumped into the chair across from her and clasped Maureen's hands in her own. "We can't go on like this, Maureen. You must go back to your old wages and your old job."

"They'll not take me. I don't even know if I'll have a job at the end of my 'probation period.'"

"We'll never pay the rent at this rate, let alone eat. It's plain as plain we have to move somewhere, and Olivia's offered to take us in—rent free."

Maureen ran her fingers through her hair in frustration. "Yes, I know we have to move, but not there. We can't make ourselves beholden to her or her sister—none of them. We can't trust them. We must make it on our own."

Katie Rose stood again and pushed her chair beneath the table. "I thought you'd say that. And I'm tellin' you now that I won't move to some-place lower and cheaper and dirtier, with who knows what or who livin' above or beneath or beside us. Vermin live with vermin, and that's what we'll become if we go on like this. We've barely enough to keep body and soul together now—to keep ourselves clean and respectable enough to stay employed."

"It will only be for a short time, until I can find a different position." Maureen sat up. "What about the Triangle Factory? I could learn the sewing machines too. And I'm fair with fittin'—you said they needed more fitters. You could put in a word for me."

Katie Rose colored. "They need more fitters, but girls are standin' in line for those jobs. They pay better than runnin' the machines, and they'll not appreciate someone waltzin' in off the street and snaggin' the position from them—especially not Irish."

"Does it matter what they think?"

"It matters to me. Those girls are my friends. They and their families need the work as much as we do. And I think it's best if we don't work at the same place."

"But I'm your sister."

Katie Rose turned and crossed the room. She pulled back the tattered curtain and looked into the darkened glass. Maureen watched her sister's reflection as she waited, watched her features change, wondered what brewed in her thirteen-year-old head. She sighed at last, unable to guess. "Come away from the window."

"I've decided." Katie Rose spoke quietly. "With you or without you, I'm goin' to Olivia's. We came to America for a different life, and I mean to have it. I won't become like you. I won't crawl, and I won't do the things you've done to get what you want."

"The things I've done? What I want?" Maureen could not believe her ears.

Katie Rose faced her sister. "I saw you do it in Ireland. I know you took money from that man at Ellis Island—you told me yourself. And now, now that we can't make ends meet, you'd rather move into some deeper, darker hovel than take the decent hand that's offered us."

Maureen gasped, anger and shame both rising within.

"Well, I'll not do it, and if you persist, I'll not have anythin' to do with you."

Maureen stood. "What I did in Ireland I did so you and Mam could keep a roof over your heads and food in your bellies! I did it so you wouldn't be sleepin' in ditches and barns after Da died or be driven off to the poorhouse." She shoved the chair between them aside. "I did it because Lord Orthbridge was bigger and stronger than me and I had no other choice. And I did it with no thanks or pity from you or Mam! Not once!"

Katie Rose's face took an ugly, grim turn. "That's a lie, Maureen O'Reilly. May God strike you for such a lie!"

"Did you think Lord Orthbridge let you both squat in a cottage not our own because he took pity? He was not well acquainted with pity!"

Katie Rose began to tremble and shouted back, "He did it because Mam paid him with her body and soul, regular as clockwork every Monday and Thursday night that he stumbled home from the pub. She paid him in her bed, to keep us and to keep you in your fine, grand life—you with your feathered bed and painted walls and clothes and shoes and more food than we saw all the year!"

Maureen felt a rush of waters through her body, a dinning in her brain.

"So don't tell me that you did anythin' worth anythin'! Mam did it all, and you did whatever you did because you wanted it. You wanted him crawlin' over you and whatever luxuries he gave you for it!"

Maureen knew her head moved from side to side in sick denial. She knew that Katie Rose had it wrong—terribly, terribly wrong. *Unless . . .*

"And now you want to pull me down with you—when I've a chance to be good, to lead a good life, and an offer to help me have those luxuries you enjoyed. Only I'll have them without your sin!"

Lord Orthbridge played us all for fools, two ends against the middle, knowin'—bankin'—that we'd never confess the horror of our shame to one another. "It's not true . . . I never knew he went to Mam."

Katie Rose glared as though she didn't believe her.

"Those nights he frequented the pub—they were my only nights of reprieve after Lady Catherine died. But I never suspected he—he never told me, and Mam never did. He took my wages for your rent and food all those years, and he took me after Lady Catherine died because he said the money wasn't enough for—Oh, why didn't she stop him? Why didn't you tell me?"

"Mam made me swear." Katie Rose turned her face to the wall; Maureen could not tell if she cried.

"But how could she keep such a secret in the village?" *Everyone knew what he did to me. They never let me forget!*

"They knew."

"But they treated Mam with respect."

"Because 'a husband has his rights'—that's what Mam said."

"A husband . . . his rights?" Maureen could not believe her ears. "He had no rights to force her! Mam was Da's widow, alone and defenseless. He took his liberties because he was landlord and powerful, not his rights!"

Katie Rose stared blankly at Maureen a long time, so long Maureen whispered, "Katie Rose?"

"You don't know?"

"Know what?"

"That he was Mam's lover—long, long ago."

Maureen felt the blood drain from her face. "What?"

"Before she and Da—your da—ever married. They'd bed and wed in a makeshift ceremony in the woods. But Lady Catherine wouldn't have it, Mam being a country girl and no title, no dowry—a *nothin'*. Lady Catherine cast her out."

Maureen stood, the room falling around her.

"And so she married Da. But Mam said she still saw Lord Orthbridge from time to time." Now Katie Rose cried. "She said she could not help herself."

"No."

"And that's how it was that Da had his stroke—when he found them together. He'd not known before. All the village had known, Mam said, but Da had been too grateful to have a family of any sort to heed, and they'd had the decency not to openly shame him."

Maureen could not believe the slander, and yet it forced itself with steel-edged clarity into her brain.

"And that's how I was born."

Maureen sat down again, her knees weak, her stomach broiling, her wits seeking a mooring.

"Lord Orthbridge is my father, not Da. That's why Aunt Verna insisted you take me away. Because Gavin Orthbridge is my brother—my half brother." Katie Rose faltered, then went on. "Lord Orthbridge wouldn't touch his daughter, but there was no tellin' if he'd keep his son away or be able to."

A minute, two minutes passed as Maureen tried to put the tale in order, but it swirled and tumbled through her heart, her mind, her limbs.

"Did you not notice that my hair and eyes were nothin' like yours and Da's—nor even Mam's? Did you never wonder?"

Maureen swallowed, trying to push down the bile in her throat.

"Have you nothin' to say, then?"

"I didn't know." *All that time, all that time he used me night after night, he was sneakin' off to do the same to my mother—but no, he didn't rape her. She willingly went to him, let him come to her. She carried his child. Katie Rose is his child—and Da found them together! Da found them together, and it brought on the stroke that shaped the rest of his days!* She couldn't bear the tale; she couldn't bear to take it in but, unable to grasp it, did not dare to let it go. Aunt Verna's words coursed through her veins: *"She was not a good wife, my sister."*

"I won't allow myself to be caught in that tangled web that you and Mam wove—which is exactly what will happen if we stay here. We'll be workin' for Mr. Crudgers or someone like him. I won't do it! I won't!"

Yes, a web—so tangled, so convoluted. But I must protect her. She's his daughter . . . she's not Da's girl, but . . . I must protect her.

"You suit yourself, Maureen. I'm goin' to—"

"You can't," Maureen whispered. "You can't," she pleaded more loudly. "Don't you see that you'd become beholden to them as well? The Meitlands are the Orthbridges of New York City!"

"What I see is that you don't want to go—you and your pride—and you don't want me to go without you. You fear I'll come above you. And you don't like that, do you? You don't think I'm equal to you."

"Katie Rose! It's not like that!"

"You despise Mam's love for Lord Orthbridge. And now that you know I'm not Da's daughter like you—you so noble and high . . . but I'm the daughter of a lord! But to you, all you can see is that I'm his dirty leavin's! That's what you think, isn't it?" Tears streamed down Katie Rose's face.

"No! I never thought such a thing!"

"Are you goin' to tell Olivia?"

"Tell Olivia? Why would I—?"

"Are you goin' to tell her I'm not Da's daughter, that I've no rights to her protection?"

"Of course not. I'm just tryin' to take it all in—"

"Well, I don't care. I'll deny it. I've as much right to the Wakefields as you do—not by Da's blood, but by all Mam did." Katie Rose picked up her plate and threw her meal into the slop basin. "I don't know what to believe about you anymore, Maureen. You say one thing—as if you're so concerned about doin' what's right, what's best for us—and then you go and do another. You made us beholden to that Jaime Flynn, and you got us stuck in this hovel! You forged a letter and you lied about the Wakefields." She glared at her sister. "You lost your good job, and you refused to take the Lord's Communion, for pity's sake! You've spurned the best man we know, the man I . . . I love, and turned your back on good and decent people. And now that horrid man is comin' to our door for—for—" But she couldn't finish.

"Katie Rose, we'll move. I promise. But the Meitland man is mixed up with the disappearin' women; I'm sure of it. I don't want you near him!"

"So you said before, but you've no proof of it." Katie Rose stepped back. "How do I know that you've not spun that tale? People don't just disappear with no one cryin' the alarm." She tilted her head and looked squarely at Maureen. "You're tryin' to scare me. You are, aren't you?"

"What?"

"You're tryin' to frighten me from acceptin' Olivia's offer so I'll stay with you. Well, it won't work, and I won't stay."

Maureen saw the light of decision in her sister's eyes. *Whatever I say she will discount. Whatever I say will add fuel to her fire.* Maureen sighed. Her head splitting, she turned away, knowing that only a miracle could heal their breach.

CHAPTER THIRTY-FIVE

OLIVIA STEPPED into the motorcar. She knew it was totally beyond the bounds of propriety for her, unchaperoned, to invite Curtis Morrow to her home, but a midday stroll through Central Park seemed harmless enough.

And she needed to talk with someone about the O'Reilly sisters. She couldn't talk with Dorothy. Her sister had struggled with inviting the O'Reillys to attend the Ladies' Circle and tea in her home. How would she respond when she told her that Katie Rose had moved into Morningside?

But Curtis had helped her find Maureen, and from the beginning he'd seemed to grasp and support her desire to help the sisters—no questions asked.

Why can't Dorothy exhibit that same kind of faith? But Olivia knew the answer. It was all too close to her sister's heart and health. *Beautiful immigrant girls in need of help, perhaps desperate. Just the type of women Drake must see every day in the tenements he buys and sells.* Olivia sighed. *No, I can't ask Dorothy. And Joshua is busy working for Curtis—besides, he's too smitten with Maureen to be objective. Curtis is the only logical choice.*

Despite her conviction of the need for this meeting, the corners of her mouth tugged upward. She didn't mind seeing Curtis Morrow again, for any reason.

Ralph, her new driver, pulled the motorcar to the curb and ran round the back to open the door for his employer. He proffered a steady hand as she stepped onto the frozen ground. "You're certain you don't want to wait in the car, ma'am? It's biting cold, and the path to the pond may be slippery."

"Quite certain, Ralph, thank you. But you'll keep the motorcar here?"

"Of course, ma'am. I'll keep the motor running. But don't you want me to accompany you?"

"No. No, of course not." And she walked off, her head held as high as she dared while watching for icy spots.

Olivia had thought it brilliant and proper enough to meet Curtis in the open-air company of the colorful, swirling ice skaters in Central Park. Now that she was descending the slippery path in the cold, she wondered if it was the best location for a serious conversation.

By the time she'd reached the pond's edge, a tall and graceful skater had sped by, returned, and waltzing near the edge, tipped his black hat to her in a rakish grin. Not daring to return his forward glance, she turned aside, pretending she'd not seen. When she was fairly certain he'd gone, she turned again, wishing mightily that Curtis would come soon.

A few couples with heads close together, whispering and laughing, dominated the frozen landscape, gliding, twirling, cutting lavish figure eights.

When a handsome pair flew by in tandem, their arms and eyes locked, Olivia momentarily imagined herself being led and twirled round and round by Curtis in a Viennese waltz. So mesmerized was she by the idea that she stepped gingerly onto the ice and attempted a little glide in her shoes. Three feet from the shore she realized the impetuous folly of what she'd done and, clasping a hand to her chest, chided herself for behaving in such a schoolgirl fashion. One step toward shore and her feet flew from under her.

But Curtis Morrow was suddenly beside, behind, and around her in one smooth glide, lifting her to her feet. "Where are your skates, Miss Wakefield?" he teased, spinning her once.

"My skates? But I didn't come to skate!" Olivia slipped again, was caught again by Curtis and righted in one smooth swoop, and left breathless from the sudden nearness of the strong and confident man.

"No skates? For a skating meet?" Curtis swerved, digging his blade to a sudden stop.

"No!" she tried to laugh, doing her best to cover her heated face. "It's not that kind of meeting!"

"But you said you wanted to meet at the skating pond—oh—oh, I thought this was a social event." Curtis frowned, looking sincerely disappointed, though he couldn't seem to keep the grin from pulling up the corners of his lips. "At least, I'd hoped you wanted to engage me in a social event."

"No, I didn't. I don't. I mean, another time, of course, but—you see, it's about something else entirely. I need—" But Olivia could hardly remember what she'd wanted and couldn't remember feeling so flustered. *This is not at all how I imagined this!* She straightened her coat and brushed her gloved hands down the front to regain her composure, an action he apparently found charming from the twinkle in his eyes. "No, this is business. Well, not exactly business . . ." She couldn't stop the infernal blush from rising up her neck to warm her cheeks or the break in the rhythm of her heart. *If only you weren't so handsome!*

"Ah." Curtis stopped his teasing as quickly as he'd appeared. "This is about your book, isn't it?" He led her from the ice and toward the nearest bench. "It's high time we talked about your writing. I've been meaning to ask."

"No." She pulled away, annoyed. *As though I'd pull you from your work to talk about my scribbling! As if I'm a schoolgirl begging to show you my copybook!*

"You must take my arm, Miss Wakefield," Curtis admonished. "Those shoes were never made to traverse ice patches."

Is that a reprimand? She felt herself blush again at the chide. *Why didn't I wear a sensible pair of boots on such a day? You know why,* she told herself. *Because they simply weren't attractive enough.*

Her concern for the appearance of her feet made the purpose of her visit seem pure irony. But there was nothing to be done but to get on with it. Humiliated or not, she was completely at a loss to know how to handle the situation he'd helped her create by locating the O'Reilly sisters.

"If it's not your writing—and I'm sorry if it's not—then forgive my presumption and allow me to be of whatever service I may." He brushed the bench and saw her safely seated before taking a place beside her.

Olivia's bristles melted. She'd no desire to be contrary—indeed, had no sympathy with pouting females. "I must talk with you—with someone—about the situation with the O'Reilly sisters."

"Things have not gone well?" Curtis seemed confused.

Olivia lifted her hands. "I issued the invitation to Maureen and Katie

Rose in all sincerity, hoping they would join me at Morningside, hoping they would trust me to embrace them as the family Father intended and help them find solid footing in New York," she began. "But I never imagined Katie Rose would come alone—or with wild tales of Maureen losing her job for stealing and the most horrendous accusations against her character and behavior, both here and in Ireland."

"That seems most unlikely. Joshua Keeton speaks highly of Maureen."

"Yes, I've noticed that too." Olivia thumbed the clasp of her purse. "In fact, he seems rather infatuated with her."

"Is he?" Curtis looked mildly interested in the idea but more interested in her. "I hadn't noticed."

Olivia sighed impatiently. *How can someone so clever be so obtuse?*

"Even so—" Curtis pulled on the business face Olivia had seen before—"I doubt Joshua would be taken in; he's a good judge of character, as near as I can tell."

"Yes, I'm sure you're right. But why would Katie Rose say such things, and about her own sister?" Olivia implored. "And why would she abandon her to come to me?"

"Ah, I can answer your second question." Curtis smiled again, pulling his gloves from his hands and blowing on his fingers to warm them.

"Will you, please?"

"Haven't you offered her the world—your world? Can you imagine what that looks like to a young girl, practically a child, who's never had enough to eat or nice clothes to wear? Who's probably never ridden in a motorcar or eaten ice cream?"

Olivia drew back, confused and indignant that he'd think Katie Rose so shallow. Even so, her naiveté dawned slowly. "I'm ashamed to say I never thought of it like that. Maureen's so proud. When I visited her at the store, she'd take nothing from me—wanted nothing to do with me."

"But you said they joined your Ladies' Circle for tea. She didn't turn that down."

"Well—" Olivia nearly laughed—"she did, but Katie Rose came anyway . . . and then Maureen burst through the door as though she was sure we'd sold her sister to the gypsies!"

Olivia could not mistake the sudden flame in Curtis's cheek.

"Sold her? What do you mean?"

"Just that she came in forty or so minutes after we'd assembled, absolutely terrified for her sister's safety." Olivia lifted her shoulders. "In any other situation I should have been insulted, but I put it down to her fear of the unknown—her lack of experience in society, at least New York society."

"This was at Morningside?"

"No, at Dorothy and Drake's home."

Curtis leaned forward and took her hands. "What did she say—when she first came through the door? What were her first words?"

Olivia did not understand Curtis's sudden, intense interest. "She demanded to know if her sister was there."

"That's all?"

"Yes, that was her concern. Evidently, when she realized where Katie Rose had gone, Maureen raced across town as though she were being chased."

"And what did you do?"

"I tried to calm her, of course." Olivia replayed the scene in her mind, trying not to notice that he suddenly seemed far removed, no matter that he still held her hands. "Oh," she remembered, "and she asked if Drake was there."

"Was he?"

"No, of course not. It was a ladies' tea."

"But it was his house. She might have expected he'd be at home. And how did she react when you told her Drake wasn't there?"

"She seemed visibly relieved, almost to the point of exhaustion."

Curtis unceremoniously dropped her hands, sat back, and made a pyramid of his fingers. "She fears him."

Olivia shrugged slightly, trying not to let on that she felt . . . *That I feel what? What are his moods to me?* "It's a misunderstanding, I'm sure. But Katie Rose said Maureen claimed Drake is a dangerous man. All I can think is that she referred to her first encounter with him at Thanksgiving. He was monstrous to her."

Curtis looked at her steadily, enough to make Olivia tug the cuffs of her coat sleeves and shift in her seat. "Is Drake normally monstrous to attractive women?"

He's odious to every woman—especially to my beautiful sister, who he's infected with his nasty disease. But she would not betray Dorothy's confidence. She returned Curtis's probing gaze. "That's an odd question coming from his business associate."

"Not all businessmen conduct their business in the same way."

Olivia straightened. "No, they don't." *Did he just chastise me again?*

"I'm sorry," Curtis apologized. "That was rude and uncalled for. Drake is your sister's husband."

"Yes, he is," Olivia answered slowly, remembering Katie Rose's tirade of Maureen's accusations and fears. *But Katie Rose was in tears—hysterics. It was all too much, too melodramatic, too thirteen. The sisters probably had another falling-out, as they did in Dorothy's parlor. But what if it wasn't that?* She looked at Curtis as if she'd not seen him before. *And what is your position, your business with Drake, Mr. Curtis Morrow? What is it really? Why did you help me find Maureen and Katie Rose? Why are you interested in Drake's relationship to Maureen?*

For the first time, Olivia wondered if she should entirely trust Curtis Morrow.

WHEN JOSHUA KEETON answered the summons to Curtis Morrow's office, he detected a lingering hint of lily-scented perfume, reminding him of the fragrance Olivia Wakefield had worn to church.

Joshua was not surprised to learn that Katie Rose had run to Olivia for sanctuary and security. He didn't blame the girl. He was only mildly surprised she'd held out as long as she did.

But what of Maureen? It was bad enough the two of them livin' in the tenement together. Maureen in that rat hole alone is unthinkable.

"You're sure Maureen's not one to steal or to entertain men—that there's no justification for the girl's accusations?" Curtis's eyes probed Joshua's, but Joshua stood without flinching.

"She'd do neither." *Not willingly. God, please, no—protect her! Hasn't she been through enough?*

"Then there's something amiss—some missing piece. Katie Rose said Maureen is convinced Drake's a dangerous man. Put that together with her unreasonable fear of either of them living with Olivia—when help from the Wakefields is what she came for in the first place—and I have to think Maureen knows something about Drake. Something she's afraid to tell. But how could she be connected to him in any way? She was only days off the boat when she met him—any of them—and she came straight from Mrs. Melkford's."

"It cannot be from the church or either sister's house," Joshua considered. "Where else could she have seen him?"

"If it's not in her apartment—"

"It's not," Joshua interjected almost fiercely. *I've kept watch since the moment I found her again.*

"Then it must be work or some other public place—which leaves most of Manhattan." Curtis grimaced.

"But none that Maureen frequents without Katie Rose . . . except her job."

"Darcy's," Curtis murmured. "But we've found no direct link there." He stood, turned toward the window, opened the blinds.

"If Maureen's lost her position—if she's been accused of stealin', as you say, it may be because she wouldn't do as she was told."

"Is she normally obstinate?"

"Maureen?" Joshua smiled. "Obstinate as the day is long. But she'd do nothin' to knowingly jeopardize her position. Steady employment and her wages are what keep her in America. No—" he shook his head—"she'd not risk that—not without the best of reasons."

"Nor would she be able to quit—with no place to go—even if things weren't right there. I'd say divide your time between the sisters as best you can, with a focus on following them to and from work each day. See if Maureen stops anywhere else—who she knows or speaks to, what she does. And if you think she'll trust you, have a word with her."

If she'll trust me—that's the question.

CHAPTER THIRTY-SEVEN

KATIE ROSE FLOATED on air her first week with Olivia. Never had a lady's maid run her bath, let alone from a faucet in a room made for such a purpose. *A real claw-foot tub and not a tin tub in the kitchen—who could have imagined?*

"Miss Olivia indulges me as if I'm a princess!" Katie Rose gloated to Emma as they left work. "She gives me money for the trolley every day and bought me this fine pair of walkin' shoes—brand-new—and this woolen coat. Do you like it?" She did a little twirl in the midst of the sidewalk.

"Why are you working at all if the grand lady's looking after everything?" Emma asked.

Katie Rose slowed, sensing that her friend was miffed. *Well, I'd be too if she waltzed in with all this finery and no woes.* "Don't be cross with me, Emma. I'm sorry to boast. I know it's not right. It's just I've never had such things or anyone to look after me like this."

"It's like falling into a fairy tale, I guess," Emma sighed. "I'd like to fall into one of those myself. Someday I'll work in one of the stores uptown, like your sister, and wear pretty clothes and shoes that don't look like my brother's boots," she dreamed aloud. "But I've no rich American friends to take me in—not me and not my six brothers and sisters!"

Katie Rose linked arms with her friend. "Oh, but you have me! And look here." She dug deep into the pocket of her new burgundy coat. "I've not used the trolley once this week. I've saved every nickel Miss Olivia gave me. So what do you say that we stop at the nickelodeon on our way home—my treat! We've enough for two shows and supper between us."

"On a Friday night?" Emma gasped.

Katie Rose nodded eagerly. "We won't stay terribly late. I can't go tomorrow afternoon. The Ladies' Circle meets and I'm a member now. I must attend." She whispered, "I've taken the pledge," hoping Emma would ask her just what she meant.

"But tonight's the beginning of Shabbat. Papa doesn't mind so much that I go Saturday afternoons since I have to work on Saturdays anyway. But Friday night—he'd skin me alive, for starts." Emma's mournful gaze trailed from the coins in Katie Rose's palm to her face.

"Can't you go just this once?" Katie Rose begged.

"No." Emma shook her head and sighed again. "Can't you miss Saturday, just this once?"

Katie Rose pocketed the coins. "I'd better not. I don't think Olivia would understand after I took the pledge and all." She waited, but when Emma didn't ask her to explain, she pulled in her lower lip. "I don't want her to send me back to Maureen."

"How is your sister? Have you seen her at all this week?"

"No." Katie Rose lifted her chin. "And I don't mean to. She'd try to pull me back, and I'm not goin' into that hovel—never again."

"But she's your sister, and she took care of you when there was no one else."

"Well, there's someone else now."

But Emma, her lips pinched, had stopped walking. Katie Rose took that as a rebuke.

"You don't know what she's like," Katie Rose protested. "She—"

"Hush a minute." Emma tugged her arm. "Do you see that man? The one in the checkered cap over there—across the street?"

"What? Where?" Katie Rose turned to look, but Emma jerked her forward.

"Don't stare so at him. Pretend you're looking at something else!"

"Why? What's—?"

"I think he's following us. I saw him outside the Triangle, and he's walked these same three blocks."

"So have lots of people."

"But he stops every time we stop."

"You're crazy."

"I've seen him before," Emma whispered. "He comes round the Triangle and follows girls home sometimes. I've seen him walking through the neighborhood, but not for a while."

"He's handsome enough—probably just some fella that fancies a pretty smile." *Not that he'd be lookin' for that with me, though my scars have all but healed. Maybe he does* . . . "Or maybe he's lonely and—" Katie Rose turned again and stole another glance. The man smiled and tipped his hat. She whirled away, sensing a skip in her pulse.

"Mama says I'm not to speak to him, that all the girls should ignore him," Emma rattled on. "Come, walk faster."

After two blocks of fairly racing, Katie Rose panted, "Slow down, Emma! I can't keep up with you."

Emma stopped so quickly that Katie Rose pounded into her, knocking them both off-balance.

"I think it's okay; we've outfoxed him. Just watch as you walk home, especially along the darker streets." Emma straightened her hat and pushed the flying tendrils of her hair into place. "This is my corner. I've got to hurry; I'm to buy the candles for Shabbat, and it's nearly sundown."

"You're sure you can't come to the nickelodeon? Just this once?" Katie Rose begged. "I'm dyin' to see this week's film; tonight's my only chance."

But Emma shook her head. "I'll see you tomorrow. Maybe you'll be able to miss a Saturday meeting in a week or two; maybe the ladies won't mind so much by then."

"All right. I'll let you know what happens tomorrow."

Emma pulled her back. "You're not going on your own, are you? Nice girls don't go to the nickelodeon on their own!"

Katie Rose felt herself redden. *I'm a nice girl and that was exactly what I was goin' to do. Why not?* But she sputtered, "No, of course not. I just meant that I'd let you know how things go with Miss Olivia tonight. Though I don't think it should matter—boys go in alone all the time."

"But it does matter—boys are different!"

I don't see how. So many rules and regulations! If it's not Maureen or Olivia, it's you! "I'll see you at the machines, Emma."

Katie Rose lifted her chin at Emma's apologetic smile and watched her friend walk quickly away.

Maybe I should take the trolley after all. What's the point of savin' my nickels if I can't use them for what I want?

As Katie Rose headed for the trolley stop, the electric lights of the marquee above the nickelodeon two blocks down flashed on, advertising the evening show and winking against the growing dark.

Oh! There it is! I'll just stand outside and see what the billboard says. As though I've not read it every day this week!

But as she drew nearer the lights, her heart beat more quickly. When she was still half a block away, she caught the first faint chords of the tinny piano inside the hall, tripping up and down the keys in a lively quick-step. Energy, even after a long and tiring day at the noisy machines, crept through the thick soles of Katie Rose's new shoes and up her legs. It tingled in her fingers and up her arms. She hugged them round herself in a vain attempt to keep delight from springing from her chest and clamped her lips to keep from breaking into song.

"Catchy tune, ain't it?" a familiar brogue, but lost in the crowd around her, asked.

Katie Rose didn't turn at the question. A minute passed as men and women filed to pay their nickel at the door. She stood to the side of the line, tapping her foot and fingers to the music, just as enraptured as she'd been the first time she'd stepped into the world of moving pictures and player piano.

"Shame to listen to it out here in the cold when we could be sittin' inside and enjoying the show in the warm theater," the same soft tenor voice complained.

Katie Rose nodded in wholehearted agreement but couldn't bring herself to defy Emma's admonition. "My friend can't come tonight."

"More's the pity. Mine, neither," came the voice again. "We didn't have that sort of music in Ireland."

Katie Rose turned then and was startled to find the man in the checkered cap behind her. But he'd removed his cap and looked more handsome than he had from a distance—certainly no older than Joshua, nor so frightening as Emma had described him. *In fact, he looks quite humble.*

"Me name's James, miss." He bowed, just slightly, his brogue thick now and unmistakable.

"You're from Ireland, sir."

"Dublin, miss."

"Dublin? That's near County Meath!"

"Next door." He smiled. "You'd not be from thereabout, would you?"

"I am! I'm from County Meath! My sister and I sailed from Dublin."
It feels forever since I've heard anyone from home.

"Well, it's glad I am to meet you, Miss—?"

"O'Reilly." Katie Rose knew she blushed. She only hoped it was prettily. "Katie Rose O'Reilly."

James smiled. "A name like that can only fit a lovely wild Irish rose."

Katie Rose's hand instinctively flew to her cheek. "I'm not one."

But James's eyes widened. "Never one to contradict a lady, but I must this once, for you are, miss. Quite lovely."

Katie Rose looked away in misery, praying it was true. *Miraculously true.*

"Say, Miss O'Reilly, since neither of our friends were able to come tonight, and since we're both dyin' to hear the music and see the show, would you do me the honor of accompanyin' me?"

The air stopped short in Katie Rose's throat. "Accompany you?" *Emma would cut me off. Maureen would be furious! Olivia would say . . . she'd say, "Ask yourself, is that what Jesus would do?"*

"Aye, I'd be obliged, miss. I can always go in alone, but it's never so nice to sit alone, and it seems you're wantin' to see the show."

If I don't let him pay my way, it's just as though I was sittin' next to a stranger, but I'd not be unescorted, so Emma couldn't complain about that. Olivia won't be home until later. She's helpin' Dorothy this evenin'. I could be back to Morningside before she knows I'm gone. "Well," Katie Rose began, fingering the coins in her pocket, "I don't know."

"I hear it's a dandy of a show," James urged, smiling very near her face now.

Katie Rose could scarcely think with him standing so near—*so near and as though he doesn't see my scars! Maybe—*

"Is that you, Katie Rose O'Reilly?"

Katie Rose jumped at the familiar voice. "Joshua!"

Joshua tipped his hat. "Are you and Maureen here to see the evenin' show, then?" He looked about.

"No, no, Maureen's not here." Katie Rose's happiness evaporated.

"You're not out and about alone in the dark, are you?"

"She's with me." James stepped closer to Katie Rose. "We're off to see the show."

Joshua's eyebrows shot up.

"I was just on my way home when I stopped to hear the music." Katie Rose knew she said each word, but her mouth felt as though it were full of straw. "James is from Dublin, so close to home. We just started talkin' . . . and . . ." But the look on Joshua's face told Katie Rose that he saw something entirely different. *Don't look so, Joshua! It's not what you think!*

"James, is it?" Joshua didn't smile but stuck out his hand. "The name's Keeton. Joshua Keeton. I'm from Ireland as well. Where in Dublin are you from, then? I know it well."

The glint in James's eye was unmistakable, and Katie Rose saw that the hand he gave Joshua in return was a pump to test his strength. "The show's about to start, Mr. Keeton. I'm sure you won't mind excusin' us."

As James offered Katie Rose his arm, Joshua pulled three nickels from his pocket and plunked them into the palm of the ticket seller by the door. "You'll not mind if I join you—it's a rare treat to meet someone from home, isn't it, Katie Rose?" He handed a ticket to Katie Rose, one to James, and bowed to usher them through the door, close on Katie Rose's heels.

CHAPTER THIRTY-EIGHT

MAUREEN HAD HOPED, had dared to ask if she might leave work a few minutes early—early enough to apply elsewhere, though she dared not give her reason. But she was kept five minutes past quitting time, for the very presumption of asking, and treated as though her petition was nearly cause for dismissal.

Opening boxes in the stockroom and running sales tickets up and down the stairs was thankless and humiliating work after having clerked on the sales floor. *But that is what they're countin' on—that I'll be so demeaned I'll quit. And that's where they're wrong. I've been ground in the dirt far worse than the management of Darcy's knows how to do. I'll not quit until I've found another position!*

It was a fine boast, but Maureen knew it grew more feeble by the day. She could not pay the rent beyond the next week, not even if she limited herself to one meal per day. *How can I do such work on bread and tea?*

At least Katie Rose is safe—oh, I hope she's safe with Olivia. If only I knew! Maureen pulled her cloak—the cloak she'd found thrown into a corner of the stockroom the second morning of her demotion—tighter around her.

At least I can go to Mrs. Melkford's on Saturday. Maureen smiled into the upturned collar of her cloak at the thought. *A haven—a haven with food!*

The thought warmed her heart for more than twenty blocks, no matter that her toes numbed. She turned the corner at last, rubbing her fists together against the cold. The lights of the marquee above the nickelodeon halfway down the block flashed. In the blinking lights she saw a familiar form—two familiar forms. *It can't be. How dare he?*

Grim-faced and furious, Maureen marched to the nickelodeon door, but the ticket seller blocked her path. "That'll be a nickel, miss, and best be quick. Show's about to start."

"I don't want to see the show. I want my sister. She's in—"

"Nobody gets in without paying, miss."

"But I'm not stayin'! Do you not hear me?"

He didn't seem to.

Maureen rooted through the pockets of her cloak, but they were empty and holed. "Please, I haven't got a nickel. I just want my—"

"Close the doors, Joe! Curtain's going up," a deep voice ordered from inside the theater.

The ticket taker shrugged. "I gotta close the door, lady. Ya payin' or not?"

"I don't have a nickel." Maureen could not keep the quiver from her lip.

"Don't take it so hard, miss. There'll be another show next week." And he closed the door.

❧

Katie Rose could not believe her predicament or her exquisite good fortune. *Caught by Joshua in the act of goin' into the nickelodeon with a stranger! Escorted by two handsome gentlemen at once—Joshua Keeton himself beside me!*

The piano played, and Katie Rose's imagination raced faster than the pictures that flashed across the screen. *Wait until I tell Emma! It's all right now that Joshua's here. He's no stranger—an old family friend, really. Perhaps he sees me as more than a friend, more than a girl, after all. Perhaps now that he sees James takin' an interest, he will too.*

But what will I do when the show's over? I must get back to Olivia's before I'm missed. What if one or both of them ask me to stop for a bite of supper or a cup of tea? It will be dark as dark when we walk out. . . . I'll ask Joshua to walk me home—he knows Olivia. It will be all right. But what about James?

Katie Rose smiled in the darkened theater, sighed contentedly, and leaned closer to Joshua. *Such delicious quandaries!*

❧

An hour later the doors opened and a chattering Katie Rose, flanked by two handsome Irishmen in a cheerful crowd of theatergoers, waltzed onto the sidewalk.

"Did you hear the mournful melody when the soldier lay dyin'—and when his sweetheart found him? If only I could play a piano like that, I—"

But Katie Rose never finished. Blood drained from her face the moment her eyes caught her sister's. She watched in horror as Maureen, eyes blazing, stormed across the street and pushed through the crowd. Katie Rose slipped her arms from Joshua's and James's, wishing she could melt into the pavement for what was surely coming.

But Joshua stepped before her.

"Get out of my way, Joshua Keeton!" Maureen growled. "What do you mean takin' my thirteen-year-old sister about like a trollop?"

"Fourteen! I'm fourteen, though you never took notice of my birthday!" Katie Rose, her heat returning, shouted back.

"Ladies." Joshua spoke quietly as heads began to turn in their direction. "Perhaps we could talk about this over—"

"There'll be no talkin'. Katie Rose, you're comin' with me!" Maureen yanked Katie Rose's arm, but Katie Rose, to her own surprise, yanked back.

"You'll take your dirty hands off me, Maureen O'Reilly. You've no right and no say about me—not anymore."

Katie Rose jumped back as Maureen lifted her hand to slap, but Joshua caught it in midair.

"Maureen, Katie Rose is all right. No harm has come to her. You must calm yourself."

Katie Rose marveled that any man could stop her sister's tirades cold. And then she remembered James. *What must he think of my hellish sister? Now that he knows how young I am, he won't want anythin' to do with me.* But when she turned to speak, to explain, he'd gone. "There, Maureen. We had a guest and you've scared him off—you with your vile temper."

"Him?" Maureen was visibly shaking.

"A friend." Katie Rose lifted her nose. "A very nice friend and gentleman. But you've scared him off."

Maureen looked in horror at Joshua. "To think I nearly trusted you!"

"Joshua, I'm sorry Maureen has taken on so. But as it's late and I need to return to Morningside, would you please walk me home?"

"Home?" Maureen said feebly.

But Katie Rose ignored her. "Please?"

Joshua looked anything but comfortable, but he offered Katie Rose his arm.

Katie Rose nearly stumbled when Maureen jerked her quickly away.

"Don't you know he's usin' you? Don't you see he's no different than Mr. Crudgers?" Maureen pleaded.

Katie Rose pushed her sister's arm away and hissed, "That's a filthy thing to say, and 'tisn't true! What I see is that you're jealous. Just because a good man won't look your way, you can't imagine one would care for me. Well, I'm not you!"

Maureen stepped back, visibly stunned. Katie Rose knew she'd as good as slapped her sister. But she wouldn't take it back. She didn't want to take it back. Even now she saw the concern written on Joshua's face for Maureen. That was the last thing she wanted. "Come, Joshua. I must get back to Olivia's." And she pulled him away.

CHAPTER THIRTY-NINE

MAUREEN TOSSED AND TURNED until the clock in the bar below stairs bonged three. She gave up sleeping, washed and dressed, waited until the clanking milk wagon made its early rounds, then slipped downstairs before another soul stirred in the building. She walked the blocks toward Darcy's without bread or tea, stopping to knock at every shop that shone an early morning light behind locked doors.

"Please, sir. I'm lookin' for work. I'm a hard worker, and—" But each door, of the few that were opened to her, was closed in her face, most without pity. By the fifth closed door, Maureen passed her hand over her brow, dizzy from lack of sleep, lack of food, from cold so penetrating it numbed her feet and hands.

"Just somethin', Lord, anythin'! I'll do anythin'. Please, please take care of Katie Rose until I can find enough work to take care of her! Mend her foolish ways!"

She hardly realized she'd been praying, let alone aloud.

"He's takin' good care of her, the very best."

Maureen whirled round so quickly she slipped on a patch of ice. "What are you doin' here?"

Joshua extended a hand to steady her, but she slapped him away. He stepped back, reaching into his pocket. "I've somethin' for you."

"I want nothin' from you except a promise to leave my sister alone."

"Last night wasn't what you imagined."

"It's what I saw!" Maureen's blood rose to a furious boil. "I know about men like you—men who take young girls, and—"

"That's enough." Joshua's voice was low and nearly threatening. "I came upon your sister last night just as she was about to go into the nickelodeon with a man she'd met on the street."

"That's a lie. Katie Rose would never—"

"But she did! The man's a weasel, a con artist, a seducer of innocent girls. I broke in so she'd not—"

"A friend of yours?" Maureen knew the moment the biting words left her mouth that they weren't true. She knew from the white of Joshua's complexion as he stood beneath the streetlamp that she'd pierced him.

"Do you think that of me, Maureen O'Reilly?"

Maureen stood trembling, furious at Katie Rose, at Olivia, at Mr. Kreegle, Mrs. Gordon, Mr. Crudgers, at Jaime Flynn and Drake Meitland—at the whole world, except Mrs. Melkford. *But what of you? You were with Katie Rose last night! I saw you! She thinks you fancy her—she thinks she loves you!*

"I don't know what to think." Maureen put a hand to her head and swayed in her weakness.

"Trust your instincts, Maureen. Trust the God who made you, who wants to help you."

Maureen scoffed, "The God who—"

But she stopped midsentence when Joshua handed her a paper wrapper. "It's a mite smashed, but it will help."

"What?"

"A sandwich. Cheese and ham." He pulled an apple from his other pocket and pressed it into her hands.

She stared at them as if they were a gift too great, too precious to receive. "I don't know what to say." She could not stop the tears that fell.

Joshua guided her across the street and down a block into Washington Square. "How about somethin' like, 'Mmm, I didn't know you could whip up a feast like that, Mr. Keeton.'"

She fumbled with the paper, barely able to pull the wrapper back. He took it from her, opened it, and placed the sandwich in her hands, then gently pushed her to a seat on the first bench they came to.

Still she held it, her throat tight, her heart full, her mind awhirl.

Joshua clasped her freezing hands, bowed his head toward hers, and prayed, "For these Thy gifts, O Lord, we are truly thankful."

A peace, foreign to Maureen, fell lightly upon her, like an early morning mist on dry ground. Joshua let go her hands. She breathed, then breathed more deeply. She took a bite. He sat near, and his body blocked the rising wind.

The dawn had truly come when Maureen opened her eyes and lifted her head from Joshua's shoulder. Light poured through the winter-bare branches of trees. Men and women, on their way to work and market, walked the paths quickly, sometimes stealing a curious or reproving glance at the couple on the bench.

Maureen realized they must look like lovers spooning and sat up straighter, shrugging Joshua's arm away.

"'Twas only to keep you warm and let you sleep." He pulled his collar higher.

"I don't—"

"I want only to be your friend, Maureen. I've no desire for anythin' but your good and that of Katie Rose. It's all I've ever wanted."

Maureen felt her face flame, certain he'd read her thoughts. "You saw her back to Morningside last night, then?"

"I did. Safe and sound. And I've told her to send word to me when she wants to go to the pictures again. I don't want her goin' with that bloke I found her with."

"Who was he?"

Joshua shook his head. "Not sure. But I've seen him hangin' around the Triangle Factory as well as Darcy's for some time now. He follows girls. I don't know where or what he does. But I don't trust him."

"The Triangle Factory and Darcy's? You're followin' me? And Katie Rose?" Maureen felt a prick of alarm.

Joshua held out both his hands. "It's not the way it sounds."

"Then tell me, how does it sound to you?" Maureen tilted her head in frustration, digging her fists into her hips.

Joshua threw up his hands in surrender. "I'll explain everythin'—all you want to know and all that I know. I'll explain it this very day. Only, if

I do it now, you'll be late for work. I'll not have you blame the loss of your position on me as well."

Maureen realized the sun was nearing eight o'clock and that she was blocks from work. She grabbed her purse and fled, calling behind her, "I hold you to that, Joshua Keeton!"

CHAPTER FORTY

MAUREEN HAD BEEN AGITATED all day. When the closing bell at Darcy's finally rang, she was more than surprised and self-consciously pleased to find Joshua Keeton waiting for her two blocks from work.

She'd never been escorted to a restaurant, not even a delicatessen, by a gentleman, let alone had one hold the door or a chair for her. She wasn't sure she liked sitting across from a man in public when everything was dark outside, but she wasn't sure she didn't. She simply couldn't think what to make of Joshua Keeton.

Either he's tellin' the unvarnished truth, or he's an excellent liar. How can I tell which?

"But why would Curtis Morrow hire you to follow us? He barely knows us." Maureen's mind sharpened with the hot food and tea.

"I'm thinkin' it's partly that you and your safety matter to Olivia Wakefield. What matters to Miss Wakefield matters to Mr. Morrow." Joshua smiled—shyly, Maureen thought—as he placed his cup in its saucer. "But there's more." He sobered. "And that accounts for my work and Morrow's chief business in all this."

Maureen waited.

"It's a delicate matter to be speakin' to a lady about."

Maureen straightened, wary, not used to being referred to as a lady, but allowing the word to seep into her thinking.

"Have you heard the words *white slavery* and—?"

Maureen felt her spine go rigid. She stood so quickly that she knocked over her chair. Joshua caught it before it hit the floor. "You nearly had me fooled, fool that I am!" She grabbed her cloak.

Joshua leaned across the table and took hold of her wrist. "Maureen!"

"Let go of me!"

"Maureen, settle yourself and hear me out."

"You're like the rest of them!" She wrenched free and pushed toward the door. But then she turned, flaming in fury. "You've shamed your family name!"

From the corner of her eye, she saw Joshua throw coins to the table and tear after her.

Maureen knew she should run, but she was too tired, too disappointed, too broken. When he caught her as she turned down an alley, she clawed the air, aiming for his eyes. "I nearly trusted you!"

"You can trust me—you should trust me, you devil of a woman!" Joshua's voice broke, and he pulled a handkerchief to dab the blood her nails had drawn across his face. "I want to help you—you and Katie Rose—and those like you."

"Like me—prostitutes? Is that what you think me? Do you want me to say the word, Mr. Keeton?" She wondered if her mam's heritage was emblazoned on her forehead.

"I mean defenseless women and girls—immigrants and orphans and any woman desperate for a start in this land with no one to protect her." He ran his hands through his hair. "I don't want to traffic you, foolish woman—I want to save you from traffickers! I want—Curtis wants—to bring the monsters to justice. To see them hang!"

Maureen held her breath.

"When I saw that James character go after Katie Rose last night, I nearly lost my mind."

"James?" *He can't mean . . .* "What was his full name?"

Joshua, still dabbing at his cheek, waved aside the question. "Don't know, but I've seen him go after the girls. I've not caught him in the act, but I'm sure he's part of—of their disappearin'. We just haven't found his connections or where or when they're taken."

"Why? Why does Curtis Morrow care? Why does he do this? The police don't even care."

"Good men—police or no—care, and we mean to do somethin' about it." He pulled his jacket closed as if suddenly mindful of the cold. "But it's hard to get anythin' done with crazed women beatin' me off like I'm the enemy." He picked up the cap Maureen had knocked to the ground and slapped it against his knee. "Not every man is a cad. I'm not the one you should be afraid of, Miss O'Reilly." And he strode toward the head of the alley.

Maureen sank against the building, the fight gone out of her. In rapid succession, her mind ran scenes from the horrific weeks since Joshua Keeton, with his horse and trap, had rescued her and Katie Rose at County Meath's crossroads in the dark of night.

Rescued?

She thought again of the deception of her mother, of the manipulation and cruelty of Julius Orthbridge, of the threat of Gavin to Katie Rose. *Yes, you did rescue us. No matter this trouble, I've slept every night in America without fear the door would open and that monster would appear. What if you'd been there the night Eliza and Alice were stolen, instead of Officer Flannery? Would you have tried to stop them? Oh, God—dare I trust him? Who can I trust?*

Trust Me. There it was—the voice again. The voice that pushed itself past everything else in her brain.

The same peace she'd felt that morning, while sitting on the bench beside Joshua as he'd prayed, stole through her, a calm in her storm, a pause in her rapidly beating heart.

"Joshua." The word was a whisper. She knew he could not have heard it as he turned the corner onto the street. Maureen roused herself, steadied her feet, began to walk and gradually to run toward the head of the alley.

But when she reached the street, he'd gone, disappeared into the dark. *Joshua! I'm sorry—I'm sorry.*

Maureen covered her face with her hands.

At last she turned her feet toward the only home she knew—her flat in the tenement. *Mine for the remainder of the week. And then what?*

She'd not gone fifteen steps when a figure emerged from the dark, nearly upon her before she realized his presence. "Joshua!"

"I don't care if you don't trust me. I don't care if you swear nothin' to do with me. But I'll see you safely home and behind closed doors before I leave you standin' in the dark in the midst of this city, Maureen O'Reilly."

Maureen stared at him, unable to discern his features but knowing all she needed to know from his return, his presence, the obstinate tenderness in his declaration. A moment passed before she spoke. "Tell me why."

"Why?"

"Why you trust Curtis Morrow."

"He's a good man—an honorable man—and he's tryin' his best to do a good work. A work that you mustn't let on you know anythin' about—for your sake as well as those he's helpin'."

"But he's a friend of Drake Meitland."

"Not a friend—a business partner, and only that for show, for gettin' to know the man's business, whatever it may be. You've no reason to trust Drake Meitland, nor should you. Be careful of the man. Curtis is." Joshua breathed out. "But don't count the two men from the same cloth."

A memory dawned in Maureen's mind. "Is that why you kept us from the Wakefields' pew on Sunday? All that escortin' and la-di-da, that was more about keepin' us from them—from Mr. Meitland?" Maureen tried to conjure the picture. "And you, you didn't want him to see you. He—"

"That's all I can say for now. It's up to Curtis to tell you more, if you choose to trust him—if you choose to trust me. What I've learned from Curtis is that it's not enough to stop a bad man from doin' one bad thing. You have to stop him at his source—lest he prey upon thousands. And that takes time."

Maureen held her breath.

"You've been dealt with harshly by those who should've sheltered you in the past. You're right to be wary." Joshua lowered his voice. "If I could break the neck of the man who hurt you or the yoke of that past, I would. I swear it. But you're in a new land now—we're both in a new land. You must lay down that past if you're ever to go forward, to claim this new life." He looked away, hesitated, looked back. "You're a rare woman, Maureen O'Reilly. It would be more than a shame to miss all that lies ahead."

Maureen swallowed the knot that threatened to choke her. *He sees me?* She closed her eyes for a moment. *Not what Lord Orthbridge did to me, not the shame that covers me, the label the village cast upon me, not even the favors he fancies he can curry from me or my bed—but me. Can that be?* She ran her hands up the sleeves of her cloak, as much to see if she and the moment were real as to ward off the chill of the January night. She let go her breath, mindful for the first time that she'd been holding it too long, then drew in a clean one.

She shifted her purse slowly to her other arm. She looked Joshua Keeton in the eye, waited, and said in the steadiest voice she could muster, "Will you offer your arm, Mr. Keeton? Will you offer your arm as you walk me safely home?"

❖ CHAPTER FORTY-ONE ❖

JOSHUA'S PULSE THROBBED as he handed Maureen up the trolley steps Monday evening, as he paid their tokens, as he sat beside her on the ride through uptown Manhattan to Curtis Morrow's publishing house. He'd determined not to read more into her willingness to accept his help than was warranted, but his heart, a disobedient renegade, would not listen.

That her information about "James" was linked to their search for human slavers, underground brothels, and forced prostitution, he had no doubt. Nor did he doubt that she was holding something back.

Joshua stole a glance at Maureen while her gaze was fixed out the trolley car window. She bit her lip and puckered her brow in concentration, a habit he'd memorized. *I'll guard you with my life, if you let me, and defy any man to lay hands on you. But what is it you're not tellin' me?*

As they neared their destination, Joshua reached over Maureen's head and pulled the stopping cord. The trolley slowed. He jumped to the ground, then offered his hand to help her down. The flush on her face told him that she'd been treated like a lady too seldom. *A slight I'll gladly remedy, given the chance.*

The building they entered was five stories high, the publishing house claiming all floors. Joshua ushered Maureen through the firm's swinging door on the fifth floor. A male secretary, just locking his desk for the day, nodded Joshua through, with one curious and appreciative brow raised to Maureen as he eyed her from head to toe and back again.

As Joshua turned the doorknob, Maureen caught his arm. "You promise you'll take me away the moment I ask?"

Joshua put his face close to hers. "The moment you whisper."

253

She drew a deep breath and nodded. He pushed open the heavy oak door.

"Miss O'Reilly." Curtis Morrow, pulling his arms through his suit coat, rose from his seat behind a wide mahogany desk framed by a large picture window looking out on the darkened city. "I'm delighted that you're here. Please, come in."

Joshua felt Maureen stiffen, knew her senses stood alert. She turned to him, her eyes suddenly apprehensive. Immediately he opened the door to freedom and offered his arm. She hesitated, bit her lip, but remained where she was.

Joshua guided her to a deep armchair across from Curtis's desk and took the matching leather chair beside her.

"I'm grateful you've agreed to confide in us, to help us, Miss O'Reilly," Curtis began. "I understand Joshua has given you some idea of what we're about and that you understand the need for absolute discretion."

Maureen sat still as a statue.

"We have reason to believe that the man who calls himself James might have something to do with the disappearance of young women in the city. Joshua tells me that the man approached your sister the other night and that you think you might know him."

Maureen nodded at last but still didn't speak.

"Could you—could you tell us something about him? How you know him? Where you met him?"

Maureen locked her gloved fingers.

Joshua watched her face. "Can you assure Miss O'Reilly first that what she tells us will be in confidence, Mr. Morrow? That there will be no repercussion in any way for her or for her sister?"

"Yes, of course." Curtis frowned, clearly surprised by the question. He leaned forward. "What can you tell us about the man?"

"I didn't see him at the nickelodeon," Maureen began. "He'd gone. But if he's the one I think he is, his name is Jaime Flynn. He works for Ellis Island—somewhere in the Great Hall. I'm not knowin' his precise position, but that was where I met him."

"You're certain he was employed by the immigration center? Did he wear a uniform?"

Maureen nodded again. "Yes—yes, he did."

"And he interrogated you there?"

"He . . . befriended me." Maureen's color deepened.

"Befriended you?" Curtis repeated.

The misery in Maureen's face made Joshua pity her, but he could not help her—or any women—unless he and Curtis knew how Flynn and men like him operated, how they approached unsuspecting women in the first place.

"It all happened so quickly."

Joshua nodded, encouraging her.

"Along the way to America, Katie Rose came down with the chicken pox, you see. And when we got to Ellis Island, the doctor wouldn't let her pass—he insisted they keep her in their hospital, in the infectious disease ward." Maureen dug her thumb into her gloved palm. "And then I learned that they didn't want to let women in alone at all. They thought—" She bit her lip.

"It's a tough go for women alone," Joshua interjected. "They make it hard for respectable women like Miss O'Reilly and her sister to pass through." He drank in her glance of gratitude.

"I was terrified that I'd never see Katie Rose again, that they'd send her back to Ireland; the nurse said they might unless I could establish residency and employment and sponsorship."

Maureen paused for breath. "This man, this Jaime Flynn, overheard our dilemma somehow. He stepped along beside and sympathized with my plight." She shook her head. "I trusted him—a little. He'd the accent of a man born near County Meath." She looked to Joshua, whose jaw tightened at his imagination of the smooth-operating Flynn.

But he nodded. "That's exactly what Katie Rose said about him—that he was from home."

"That's all?" Curtis probed.

Maureen colored more deeply. "He gave me thirty dollars. And he said if they gave me any trouble about passin' through, he knew someone who would vouch for me as family. He could work it all out—even a job."

"I'll wager he did," Joshua murmured but caught Curtis's warning glare.

"How did Mrs. Melkford come into the picture, Miss O'Reilly?"

"She came at just that moment and vouched for me, offered to help me—saved me from goin' with him, really."

"That was the last you saw of the man?"

"Well, no." Maureen shifted in her seat. "That day—that day you call 'Thanksgiving'—I learned Colonel Wakefield was dead."

Curtis nodded. "And Drake burned your letter of invitation. I suspect that left you in a precarious position."

Joshua could see the wheels whirring in Maureen's brain.

"I'd no idea what would become of us, but then I remembered that Jaime Flynn had given me an address—for a place of employment." Maureen studied the hands in her lap. "I was afraid, not knowin' what position it might be, for I feared what sort of man he was." She looked up, and Joshua saw pleading in her eyes. "But I couldn't go back to Ireland or let Katie Rose be returned. I couldn't tell Mrs. Melkford that the Wakefields had refused to help. She might have been obliged to report me."

Joshua nodded his understanding.

"I led Mrs. Melkford to think that the Wakefields had recommended I go for a position to the address Mr. Flynn had written. Darcy's Department Store—a respectable store, she believed."

"So you applied on the recommendation of Jaime Flynn?" Curtis asked.

"I . . . I forged a letter of character recommendation from Mrs. Melkford and told them—told Mr. Kreegle, the man who interviews new girls—that the Wakefields had recommended I go there." Maureen looked from Curtis to Joshua and back again.

Joshua grimaced inside but forced his face to remain unflinching, encouraging, for Maureen's sake. *That she should be caught in such a need—I should have trailed her, spurned or not!*

"I told him that I lived with the Wakefields, at Morningside, and that my sister was bein' held at Ellis Island's hospital until I could establish employment." She shook her head. "Such a tale—and so many . . ."

"Necessity is often the mother of invention, is it not?" Curtis smiled sympathetically. "But you never mentioned Jaime Flynn to the management at Darcy's?"

"No. I wasn't certain what that would mean to them, but a missionary society lady and gentry—well, I hoped those recommendations would carry respectability." Maureen's eyes pleaded.

"Your instincts served you well, Miss O'Reilly," Curtis affirmed. "You're quick on your feet." He seemed to be thinking of something else but caught himself. "But what about Flynn?"

"He comes to the department store sometimes. He apparently has some dealin's with the owners and such, above stairs." Maureen hesitated. "One evenin', just after closing, I saw him enter the staff elevator with a young girl."

"An employee of Darcy's?"

"No." Maureen shook her head again slowly, as if trying to remember and state clearly what she'd seen. "No, I'm certain she was not. She wasn't American nor here long. Still in her native dress, she was. Jaime carried her bundle and . . . and behaved toward her as no gentleman would."

Curtis sat back in his chair. "He didn't seek you out?"

"Not then. But he came to my counter some days later. He pressed for the money I owe him, and he seemed angry that I was clerkin' at all. He'd expected I would be hired—that I'd be workin' upstairs, too."

"Upstairs? Is that another sales floor?"

Joshua's fists clenched, his instincts rising.

"No, it's nothin' to do with merchandise—at least not tangible goods." Maureen placed a hand to her reddened cheek. "They call it the floor of promotion."

Maureen knew she was in too deep to stop now. Either Curtis Morrow was completely trustworthy or Joshua had been completely duped. *I'm trustin' in your good judgment, Joshua Keeton. Do not fail me.*

She told of the girls coming and going from the fourth floor and out on the town, of the wealthy gentlemen who frequented the store, of all that Alice and Eliza had told her.

She told the mesmerized men sitting before her of her friends who were there one day and gone the next, of the night she'd gone back for her purse, of the crying sounds she'd heard beyond the wall. And that she was certain it was Eliza and Alice that Jaime Flynn and another man had dragged to a truck and stolen away in the night.

"Why didn't you tell me?" Joshua nearly shouted.

"Because I didn't know if I could trust you! I've not known who to trust. For the love of Mary and Joseph, the policeman on the corner helped the monsters get away!" She hesitated, knowing she sealed her fate, but pressed on. "I didn't see his face, but I'm thinkin' the other—the man who helped Jaime Flynn—was Drake Meitland."

She could not mistake the sudden fire in Curtis Morrow's eyes.

"How do you know?"

"I never forget a voice." She shivered at the memory.

"Where could he have taken them?"

Maureen shook her head miserably. "I don't know, but it must have been some distance. He was missin' from church that Sunday. Dorothy said he was away on business."

"I remember. Real estate doesn't take him out of New York. What night were they taken?"

"That Thursday evenin', perhaps forty minutes or so after closin'."

"Three days—time enough to go out of state and return by Sunday night or Monday morning. Any chance either of them saw you, suspect you?"

"I don't think so."

Joshua paced the floor behind her. She felt his growing frustration but didn't turn around.

Curtis stood, his mouth flattened into a grim line, and leaned toward the window. "Darcy's and Meitland. The link we've been looking for, respectable on the outside, rotten at the core—right under our noses." He slammed his fist into his hand. "Neither woman had family in the city?"

"Not that I could learn, so I'd no one to tell—no one who would listen."

"Girls no one will miss—at least not right away," Joshua pronounced angrily.

I miss them! Maureen swallowed her sob.

Curtis turned, his face a study of concentration. "Joshua tells me that you've been looking for a new position, Miss O'Reilly."

"I must pay Jaime Flynn back if I'm ever to be rid of him. But I was demoted, and they've cut my wages to a rate that I'll never be able to pay.

Finding another position without references . . . They said I stole, but I swear to you, I did not!"

"The necklace, Olivia told me. You were set up." Curtis waved the accusation aside. "They're determined to keep you poor and afraid, to force you into submission so you'll come willingly to their 'fourth-floor promotion.'"

Maureen sighed heavily, humiliated and frustrated that Katie Rose had shared such a tale with Olivia but relieved that at last someone understood, someone believed her. "Poor and afraid," she repeated. "I must tell you, Mr. Morrow, they are successful in their venture. For I am poor and very much afraid."

"I have a proposition for you, Miss O'Reilly." Curtis leaned across his desk.

Maureen pulled back, clasping her purse.

Before she could bolt from her chair, Joshua interjected, "Make plain your words, Morrow, or she'll be out that door and I with her."

Looking thoroughly rebuked, Curtis stuttered, "I beg your pardon, Miss O'Reilly. A respectable position is what I intended. Respectable, if unusual."

Maureen waited, not entirely at her ease.

"Continue working at Darcy's, doing just what you're doing. But keep your eyes peeled for anything that might have bearing—more women going to the fourth floor, Flynn coming or going, women disappearing. Pay special attention to the wealthy clients who walk through the store. Note who takes advantage of this escort service. See if you can learn their names, and report them to me."

"I'm in the cellar now. I don't see anythin'. And . . ." She faltered. "I don't know how much time I have. I think they're tryin' to . . . make me invisible."

"Invisible?"

Joshua turned to Maureen. "So no one would notice if you disappeared—like your friends."

Maureen nodded, worried.

"This has gone too far." Joshua stood as if to challenge Curtis. "It's too dangerous. Maureen cannot go back to Darcy's. We'll handle this."

"She's our only link, our only way to find out who's behind the disappearances. Flynn's not working alone—he's nothing, a tool. Even Drake has to be a pawn—or more likely a middleman. He's desperate for my investments, and I know the money's not going into real estate; two of my deeds are phony. There must be power—wealth—behind it all. Perhaps a network, a ring of some kind, but someone's at the top. We need to find where the girls are taken, if they're sold, what happens to them. If they're transported across state lines—"

"She can't—"

"One week," Curtis urged, cutting off Joshua's protest. "One week to watch, to wait, to learn whatever you can. During that week I'll get closer to Drake, push him to let me in on riskier, higher-paying investments. I'll let him know I've heard a word or two about his side ventures, press him, see where that goes. If he lets me into his confidence and I can do this without your help, Maureen, you'll be done. You can leave Darcy's without a word, and I guarantee you a permanent position here, in my firm. Or I'll work one out elsewhere, if you prefer. If we need more time, we'll discuss the next step, and that will be up to you. I can't deny that it might be dangerous, but we'll do all we can to watch and intervene if things get out of hand."

"They're already—" Joshua got no further.

"If I help you—now, this week, and later if needed," Maureen demanded, "will you find Alice and Eliza? Will you not quit until you find them? And will you protect Katie Rose—at all costs?"

"Maureen, it's not safe," Joshua interrupted, protection, frustration, pleading plaguing his voice.

"I swear it." Curtis extended his hand to seal the deal. "If Joshua is unable to watch over both of you, I'll assign someone else to watch over Katie Rose. She'll never know, but she'll be safe."

Maureen clasped his hand. *It's a firm grip—a good sign.*

Joshua threw up his hands.

"Two things," Maureen insisted.

"Yes?"

"Pay me now." Maureen felt her face warm. "I'm hungry, and my rent is due."

Curtis nodded, pulled out and opened his wallet. "And the second?"

"Tell me why—why are you doing this?"

Curtis folded dollar bills and placed them squarely into Maureen's outstretched palm. "Let's just say I have a vested interest in the whole affair and in Drake Meitland, in particular."

PART TWO

OLIVIA DIDN'T KNOW what to make of the note from Curtis Morrow. She wanted to trust him, to believe in him. Her every inclination was to do so after his help in finding Maureen and Katie Rose and after weeks of what must be considered more than friendship between them. But why he wanted Olivia to take Maureen in at a moment's notice when Maureen had flatly declined help before, and how he'd achieved with Maureen what she so clearly had not been able to do, Olivia could not guess.

It's what I've wanted, isn't it? It's what Father would have wanted. But how is it that Curtis is so involved with Maureen and her needs? Is that even appropriate? He's asked me not to confide his involvement to anyone, but should I not at least tell Dorothy and let her decide whether to talk with her husband about his business partner?

But Olivia knew that Dorothy was barely speaking to Drake and that he was absent from Meitland House more often than not.

Rather than respond by letter or telephone, Olivia met Curtis at a restaurant in the city, to speak with him in person. When they'd placed their order, Olivia leaned forward.

"I'm simply asking you to explain, Curtis. That's little enough under the circumstances, don't you agree?"

"Certainly, and I'll gladly explain everything when I'm able. But I cannot put you or Dorothy in the position of knowing more than is good for either of you to know now." He kept his voice low, and she matched it.

"Good for us? Is Maureen in some sort of danger?"

"She's not in danger if she's with you—but living alone, in that filthy tenement, is out of the question."

Olivia wouldn't let him off so easily. "I understand from Dorothy that you are now the proud owner of that filthy tenement."

"Then you can imagine why I don't think it a fitting place for your friend."

The waiter brought their first course, refilled their wineglasses, and stepped away.

"Dorothy also told me that you've been spending a great deal of time with Drake this week—business trips out of town. She said he's very pleased with your further investments."

Curtis did not answer but cut his meat with precision.

"And yet he refuses to discuss the details with her." Olivia waited.

Curtis raised his eyes to hers, then glanced away and down again to his plate. She saw the muscles of his jaw tighten. "Interesting that he mentioned my purchase of the tenement, nevertheless. I didn't realize that Drake normally consults his wife in his business dealings."

"He doesn't," Olivia admitted. "Someone delivered a group of leases to their home. Dorothy recognized the address because I'd told her the street Katie Rose gave me—the address of the apartment she and Maureen shared."

Curtis's shoulders relaxed. "I understand why Dorothy might question me or my methods. But I'm not the one Dorothy—or you—shouldn't trust."

Olivia could make no sense of Curtis's double-talk. "Do you mean Drake? If you do—"

"Please, Olivia." He reached for her hand but she pulled back. "Don't ask me now. I promise to explain when I'm able, and I vow that what I do puts neither you nor Dorothy at risk. But you must keep all this to yourself for the present. There's too much at stake for—" He stopped midsentence.

Olivia had never considered Curtis melodramatic. The earnest plea in his eyes told her that she should not now.

"Two weeks, that's all I ask. Everything I need to do can be accomplished in two weeks. And then I promise to explain everything."

Olivia prayed for the right words. "Curtis, I've spent a great deal of time in your company these past weeks."

"And I have cherished every moment." His eyes spoke sincerity.

"I have to ask . . . I think I have a right to ask, based on all we've shared—"

"You have every right, and because of all we have shared, I beg you not to ask—not now—but to trust me."

She bit her lip. "I must ask," she persisted, "if what you're doing, whatever it is that you're planning to do . . . is it what you believe Jesus would do?"

Curtis took her hands in his, not allowing her to pull away this time. "On my life, I believe that the Lord has brought me to this place to accomplish this purpose. On my life, I don't know if Jesus would do what I am about to do in the way I see to do it. But I know that I do this for the good of those who cannot speak for themselves. To protect God's little ones from the menace of predators who deserve to have a millstone slung about their necks."

"And be 'drowned in the depth of the sea.'" Olivia's breath caught in her throat as she quoted the last of the Scripture. *Not the answer I expected.*

She pulled her hands away, trying in vain to decipher whatever cryptic message he intended. Then she sighed softly. "I'll prepare a room for Maureen."

"I don't believe she'll be there long. But when she leaves, you mustn't let on that she's working for me or that we're in any way connected. In fact, it might be best if everyone thinks she's staying on with you."

"Will she be safe?"

"As safe as I can make her."

Olivia left their luncheon with little satisfaction, but having made the unsettling choice to trust Curtis as well as the small inner voice that persuaded her.

The days at Darcy's passed slowly. Sequestered in the stockroom, Maureen had no opportunity to observe the comings and goings of those using the elevator or visitors on the sales floor. And she heard nothing from Curtis. She might have believed that he'd forgotten her or that she'd imagined the entire conversation, except that each morning and evening she glimpsed Joshua faithfully following her, watching from a distance. The comfort it gave her to be watched over made walking to and from work in the bitter January cold her most pleasant time of day—that, adequate food, and the knowledge that she could pay her rent made the days pass more quickly.

Thursday night, Joshua passed her in the street, dropped a small brown paper package tied with string at her feet, nearly tripping her, then stooped to pick it up. "Begging your pardon, miss—my clumsiness." He tipped his hat and handed her the package as though she'd dropped it, then went his way.

Maureen was startled, especially by the sudden nearness of him, but played along. She could hardly wait until she reached her flat to pull the string and unwrap the small square box.

"Banbury tarts! Wherever did he find them?" She smiled. *A little worse for slamming on the ground, but no doubt just as tasty. When did I ever receive such a gift?*

Beneath the tarts was an envelope. Maureen pulled the notepaper from its hiding place.

My dear Miss O'Reilly,

> *Tomorrow morning, make a scene on the sales floor of Darcy's that no one there will soon forget. Complain about your unfair treatment—whatever you wish—but make certain you are fired or quit on the spot. Proclaim loudly that you've been offered a home with Olivia Wakefield whenever you want and that you intend to take her up on that offer. Under no circumstances allow yourself to be alone with anyone from management.*

> *Go directly to Morningside. Olivia expects you. Our mutual friend will collect your trunk.*

> *Confide in no one.*

Curtis Morrow

Maureen folded the letter, slipped it into the envelope, and placed it in her purse.

Katie Rose—I'll be with Katie Rose! And then she sobered. *But will Katie Rose want to be with me? Will she want me with her at Morningside? Will Olivia want me after the way I've treated her in front of her friends? And what's happened to make Curtis ask this?*

Maureen's heart beat steadily, faster, glad that something was happening, or about to happen, and at the same time fearful as to what that might mean. *What shall I say at the store tomorrow—and to whom?* She sighed. *High conflict is made for the stage—the last thing I want—and yet it seems that I'm forever on its sudden end.*

She looked round the sparsely furnished flat, mindful of how little there was to show she'd ever been there, and mindful that no matter how pitiful the room might seem to another, at least she'd been safe. *And that is beauty of its own.*

She rubbed her arms against the cold and drew a case from beneath the bed, pulling her extra clothes and the few things she'd brought from Ireland from their pegs. Among them she tucked her teakettle, the iron skillet she'd bought when first moving in, and Mrs. Melkford's Bible. She'd opened it only once to read, but she'd not consider leaving it behind.

She pulled Curtis's letter from its envelope again. *What if someone finds it?* She lifted the lid of the stove but hesitated, undecided. *What if he's not all he says? What if I need proof that he told me to do this?* Maureen bit her lip, remembering the devastation she'd felt at Drake's burning of Colonel Wakefield's letter to her father. *But Curtis is not Drake.*

Should I trust him? Joshua trusts him.

She thought of Joshua, of how he'd appeared outside the nickelodeon at just the moment Jaime Flynn had preyed upon Katie Rose. She thought of the next morning, when Joshua had appeared again, sandwich and apple in hand, and fed her body and soul in his caring.

That knowin' and helpin' at just the desperate moment, that trustin' that he's chosen wisely, it's not all Joshua's doin', is it? He's a good man, but just a man.

She swallowed, remembering the still, small voice that had directed her steps more than once. "So You're there, then, Father God?"

She drew her breath and lifted the stove lid.

Is this faith? And she dropped the letter into the flames.

❖ CHAPTER FORTY-THREE ❖

A FRIGID DRIZZLE stalked Maureen through the slippery city blocks to Darcy's Department Store the next morning. Even so, she could not convince herself that her knees shook from the cold.

She hung her dripping cloak and nearly empty rain-soaked purse on the peg in the staff room, knowing they wouldn't dry before noon. But she would don them wet rather than stay the entire day. She'd not decided just how she would stage her dramatic exit, only knew that as a stand for liberation and a thumb in the face of her oppressors, she would buy her lunch as a free woman from the frankfurter vendor on the street. No matter that it rained or snowed, he would be there to gain his livelihood. She drew in her breath, trusting Curtis that she, too, would find a new means of sustaining herself.

Maureen had run five sales slips and change up and down the steps before she saw Mrs. Gordon on the main floor, making her rounds.

It was barely ten thirty, but Maureen was weary from too little sleep, no breakfast that would stay down, and her cold walk. She stood at the top of the stairs and looked mournfully over the sales floor. She steadied herself against the banister and watched for a moment the clerk who'd taken her place behind the hat counter, lamely displaying a hat to a customer. *I was a shopgirl—a good one, for that little while. It wasn't fair, them pushin' me out and down the stairs.* She swallowed. *How is it that I'm slow to leave what isn't good for me? That counter with Alice was a little taste of heaven—at first. My first real job. But you're not here now, are you, Alice? Oh, where are you?* Maureen blinked back the pools that threatened to well.

"Miss O'Reilly." Mrs. Gordon stood suddenly behind Maureen and whispered sternly, "Move along to your duties."

Maureen, startled from her reverie, turned to face Mrs. Gordon. "Move along?" she repeated.

"Yes, of course! Get back to your duties below stairs," she hissed.

Maureen knew the woman whispered for the sake of customers on the floor. She glanced round, noting that the store was busy once again, having survived the early January slump. She also realized that a few of the clerks were new. *New clerks, who don't know the job nearly so well as I did! Who probably can't eye a lady's hat to fit her suit nearly so ably.*

"I think I've served below stairs long enough as punishment for something I didn't do," Maureen said quietly.

Mrs. Gordon blinked as though she'd not heard clearly. "What did you say?"

This is it. This is how it will go. I'd not planned it like this, but here it is. Maureen drew herself to her full height. She spoke clearly, loudly enough that she knew her voice would carry to the front of the store. "I said that I've been punished below stairs long enough for somethin' I didn't do. I'm ready to resume my duties on the sales floor—immediately and at full pay."

"How dare you!" Mrs. Gordon kept her voice low. "Get downstairs immediately if you value your job at all!"

"I did value my job—when it was the job I was hired to do. Work I did well." A thrill ran through Maureen's heart as she stood tall. "I've been insulted too long by you and by that filthy little Kreegle man who tries to fondle the salesgirls. I'll return to my counter now, if you please."

A dozen pairs of wide eyes fastened on the two women, and Maureen waited. *It's a dare, but however she takes it, I'll win. Win if she gives me the counter after all, or win if she fires me and I really do work for Curtis. What will it be, Old Blood and Thunder?*

"Lower your voice! Why Mr. Kreegle insisted on keeping you on is beyond me. Get downstairs, young lady, or you will never work in sales again."

"Work in sales?" Maureen screeched. "Do you call unpackin' boxes in a rat-infested cellar *workin' in sales*? How would you like to be demoted for somethin' you never did, Mrs. Gordon? Somethin' everyone—includin' the sales floor manager—knew you did not do but were all too afraid to speak up?"

"You're dismissed!"

She stepped closer to the shorter woman, trying to remember all that Curtis had bade her say, delighting in the strength rising from her anger, the voice it gave her words. "Dismissed, am I? I'll have you know I don't need you and I don't need Darcy's! Olivia Wakefield has begged me to come live with her for weeks! I'd never need to work again! I've a mind to take her up on it!"

"Get out!" Mrs. Gordon's eyes reddened. Her mouth quivered in fury.

"Firin' me, are you?" Maureen laughed. "Ha! Foolish woman—I quit!" She turned on her heel, stomped across the sales floor, and took the employee stairs two at a time for the cloakroom. She slammed her soggy hat to her head and pushed the pin through the wool with a vengeance.

Though Maureen knew she should run from the building before Mrs. Gordon contacted Mr. Kreegle or any henchmen he might have at his disposal, she pulled her cloak from its peg and buttoned it standing in the midst of the room. Glancing into the looking glass above the coats, she walked nearer and paused, just as she'd done on her first day, just as she'd done each day before leaving the store. The face reflected there did not look weak or terrified. It was an older face than the one that had been revealed to her that first day at Darcy's weeks—it seemed like years—before.

Maureen touched her reflection. The fury in her face fled. The lines in her forehead relaxed. She smiled, and a healthy coloring returned to her cheeks.

I did it. I stood for me, shouted for me, and she did not kill me. The ceilin' did not fall and the world did not end. I did not die. I did not die!

CHAPTER FORTY-FOUR

"WHAT DO YOU MEAN you've quit your job?" Katie Rose stood in the door of her sister's room at Morningside, her face a rush of anger and incredulity. "You can't stay here! You'll spoil everythin'!"

Maureen had not expected Katie Rose to welcome her with open arms, but she'd not anticipated her sister's venom. "What choice do you think I had? You know I couldn't pay the rent alone and on reduced wages."

"Well, it's your own fault, isn't it?" Katie Rose demanded. "You can't expect an employer to trust you if you take things that don't belong to you."

The smugness on her sister's face sickened Maureen, reminding her for the first time of their mother when vexed—something about the mouth—and chillingly, of Lord Orthbridge—something about the flash through her eyes. But she'd agreed with Curtis to keep counsel, and this, she knew, was her first test of that contract. "You needn't worry about your place with Olivia; I won't be here long. I'll find work and be on my way. We'd never planned to stay with the Wakefields forever, you know."

"And who do you suppose will hire you with no references—nothin' but black marks against you? Or are you plannin' to forge a letter from Olivia this time?"

Maureen bit back her retort, doing her best to ignore the gibe, and answered meekly, "I don't know who will hire me. Someone. Someone, I'm sure."

"She's on to your ways. I've told Olivia everythin' about you, you know—everythin'."

"I'm sure you have, Katie Rose. I'm sure you'll tell all you imagine to whoever will listen."

Her sister flushed, the first sign that Katie Rose recognized she'd gone beyond righteous anger and immersed herself in cruel betrayal.

"It's a credit to you that you can still blush," Maureen said quietly after her sister stormed away.

Curtis Morrow's note came during supper, a small envelope that Grayson delivered to Olivia, who passed it to Maureen. Katie Rose sat straighter, curiosity written on her face.

Maureen recognized the handwriting on the envelope but pocketed the note for later and fixed her eyes on the place setting before her.

"I've told Dorothy you are with us now." Olivia smiled at Maureen. "I do hope you'll join our circle meeting tomorrow. Mrs. Melkford has agreed to come. When I told her you were coming to stay, she was thrilled. We'll all be so glad to have you."

"Mrs. Melkford?" Maureen's heart tripped at the thought of seeing her friend, but she registered the dread on Katie Rose's face as her cream soup spoon paused in midair. "Thank you, Olivia. I know the invitation is kindly meant. But I've other plans tomorrow."

Olivia seemed, to Maureen, truly disappointed; Katie Rose, relieved but suspicious.

There's no pleasin' you, Katie Rose. Your fear and jealousy eat you alive. The thought surprised Maureen, making her, too, stop her spoon halfway to her mouth. *You've made a god of your fear and jealousy, Sister. For what is a god but what we go to again and again?*

Maureen placed her spoon beside her plate, thinking that through, as Grayson removed the soup bowls in preparation for the next course. *I want more for you, Katie Rose. I want more than shame and anger for me.*

She glanced at Olivia, almost surprised at the calm the other woman exhibited despite the palpable tension between Maureen and Katie Rose. *Even in the midst of our bad temper and turmoil, you've a peace about you. How is such a thing accomplished?* Maureen ran her mind through the list of outward gestures of refinement that Lady Catherine had taught her. *No, it's more than that—something abidin', somethin' not put on, but grown from within. I don't envy your carriage or clothes or fine house, Olivia Wakefield,*

276

though surely I'd love a roof over my head and food on a table I call my own, and I'd not mind fashionable waists and skirts and kid boots. But what I want, what I crave, is your sense of presence, that peace you possess.

Grayson served coffee and a light sponge cake smothered in sherry. Maureen marveled that Katie Rose had taken to this grand life so quickly and was so apparently at ease in the fine house.

At length Olivia stood, Katie Rose and Maureen following suit. The late January wind rushed past the windows and whipped round the corners of the sturdy chimneys as the ladies entered the drawing room, where a fire crackled, burning brightly. Despite Katie Rose's attempts to exclude her from conversation with Olivia, Maureen smiled and feigned relaxation as best she could. Finally Olivia chose a book from the shelves, extending an offer to Maureen to do the same. Katie Rose threaded a needle and took up her embroidery.

Maureen stole a discreet glance at Curtis's note behind the pages of her novel before slipping it back into her pocket. After its first line, nothing in the novel mattered.

Report to my home on Monday for training. Tell no one.

That alone was another exercise in faith—or foolishness. She wasn't sure which. But she'd stepped into the boat, and there was nowhere to get out now but the deepening sea. Maureen sighed. *I hope you're all you seem to be, Curtis Morrow.*

When her eyes grew heavy, she closed them and leaned back in the chair, letting the warmth of the fire infuse her bones, doing her best to decipher the remainder of Curtis's message, to guess at his meaning. The flames of the fire fell, burning low, its occasional hiss overshadowed by the intermittent turning of pages. The long hand of the clock swept its face twice.

The fire was little more than embers when Katie Rose, who had yawned herself nearly to sleep, at last excused herself from the company.

Despite her sister's persistent frost, Maureen had enjoyed the evening in the silent company of women. When Olivia made no move to go, Maureen remained opposite the fire, savoring the room's lingering warmth and the security of the deeply cushioned chair. She stared into the smoldering embers, waiting for the last to drop beneath the grate, all the while summoning her courage, knowing she must reach out to the woman who'd taken her in.

When at last Olivia closed her book, Maureen cleared her throat. "I thank you for takin' me in," she began. "I know Curtis—Mr. Morrow—asked you to do it, but you weren't obliged. And I'm grateful. I'd nowhere else to go."

"He needn't have asked. I've wanted you to come a long while. It's also what our fathers wanted—what they both intended." Olivia laid aside her book. "You could have asked or simply come."

Maureen raised her brows at the mild rebuke but remembered that Olivia knew nothing of Curtis's "project." For that was what she'd decided to call his proposed venture. She didn't know exactly what he'd planned, and what little she understood was frightening. *What does he mean in his note, that we will "sting the viper in his own nest"?* All she could think of was the sharp and sudden sting of a bee. *But what if the viper anticipates the bee? What if . . . ?*

"What do you want, Maureen?" Olivia's question held no malice, no judgment, but it brought Maureen sharply back to the moment and to the mental vision she'd conjured earlier that evening.

"I want what you have," Maureen answered simply, just as directly. "Not," she hastened to add, "your wealth or home. Not your inheritance."

"I never assumed that, though I think we should talk about that soon—about all my father intended for you and Katie Rose, what my father hoped for us as sisters."

Maureen momentarily closed her eyes. The pain of thinking of her father, her mother's cruel betrayal of so good a man, was still too near.

"But if that's not what you mean—what, then?"

"The peace you radiate. The inward calm that carries you." Maureen breathed, considering. "Whatever it is that makes you walk peaceably where others are afraid to walk. Yes, I want that—for myself and for Katie Rose."

"Why do you want it?"

Maureen felt mildly taken aback at such a question. "Because it matters. If I possessed such calm, I would—" She hesitated, closed her eyes again to concentrate, to summon the vision and form the words she intended. "I would not be alone. I would never be alone again."

"My peace, my companionship," Olivia said softly, "come from my surety that the Lord loves me. Surety that because I've asked, believing He's redeemed me, He's also forgiven me and accepts me—now, as I am. He lives inside me, walks beside me, in the form of His Holy Spirit. He holds my heart, my life. He *is* my heart, my life."

As Olivia spoke, Maureen felt a tiny flicker of hope rise within her chest. But the slumbering darkness rumbled. The shaming voice of her past and her recent failure to save Alice and Eliza taunted her heart, her brain, whispering that she could never claim such forgiveness, such acceptance, such friendship. Maureen clamped tight her heart lest the darkness overwhelm her. The last ember fell into the grate.

"I'm glad for you," she answered at last. "'Tis a beautiful thing." Maureen meant it, though she had no hope it could be hers. She rose and laid her unread book on the table. "Good night, Olivia."

"Maureen." Olivia stood and grasped her hand, contorting her head until Maureen was forced to return her gaze. "You can have it too. The same Holy Spirit, the same forgiveness, the same love."

Maureen pulled back, fighting the rising tide of darkness, the swell of futility. *You mean well, but you can't know; you don't understand.* "Good night, Olivia." Five steps brought her to the door.

"It isn't because of who I am, Maureen. It's because of who He is and what He's done—what He longs to do in you!" Olivia's voice carried into the hallway, but Maureen closed the drawing room door, cutting her off, and walked quickly toward the stairs. She stopped on the second-floor landing, heart thrumming as she gripped the banister.

If forgiveness is because of who You are, Lord, and what You've done—if You are willing to give it to those who cry out to You—then watch what I do. Perhaps if I'm successful in helpin' Curtis and Joshua, if we save others more worth savin', then You'll hear me—even me. Perhaps then I'll have a right to ask You too.

CHAPTER FORTY-FIVE

"Mornin' coat, afternoon coat, evenin' dress, cuff links for this, and cuff links for that! Brush this and polish that—I'll never remember this la-di-da!" Joshua slapped the pair of gentleman's riding gloves across his thigh.

"You will if you pay heed, Mr. Keeton. It takes a bit of practice and a great deal of patience," Evans, Curtis Morrow's manservant, responded to his unruly pupil. "The practice you may achieve by repetition, but patience is a matter of character gained by choice."

Joshua caught Maureen's smile behind her hand. "It's all well and good for you, Maureen O'Reilly. You've had years of chamber and lady's maid trainin' at Lady Catherine's knee! This is worse than Greek and Latin to me!"

"Well," Maureen taunted coyly, "I can't imagine what you're complainin' about. You've had all of an hour to learn the ways of a gentleman's gentleman. But if it's really too much, then I suppose I could ask Mr. Morrow to find himself another to play the role of manservant, and me another protector for his scheme."

Nothing could have given Joshua greater pause. He squared his shoulders and raised his eyes. Then he breathed deeply, gave Evans a curt, apologetic bow, and humbly asked, "Would you kindly repeat the process, Mr. Evans?"

"Evans will do for me, as Keeton will for you." The older man smiled, and Joshua was certain he winked at Maureen. "Now, let us begin once more with the morning coat."

───────────── ⚭ ─────────────

Throughout the next week Maureen and Joshua absorbed the instructions Curtis had detailed in his letter before leaving town. Over and over, hour after hour, in the sanctuary of Curtis's home, they trained and rehearsed until they knew backward and forward their responses to any summons or question concerning their roles. Never had anything so taxed or intrigued Maureen's imagination, and never had her brain felt so agile, so alive.

She was fitted with the tailored uniform of a wealthy American employer's private chambermaid and all the shoes and cloaks and trappings, as well as all the history such a woman might possess, just as Joshua was properly outfitted for his role. Her hair was combed and twisted and clucked over by Madame Sevier, a stout Frenchwoman of few words and many mumbles from a local theater company—and a woman whom Curtis evidently trusted. After making several notes, she slipped away, leaving Maureen less easy in spirit.

"You don't think he's plannin' to have that woman cut your hair, do you?" Joshua asked.

"I don't know," Maureen admitted. "I've no idea what he's thinkin'."

"'Twould be a shame, that." He reached a finger to catch a wayward tendril. When their eyes met, he dropped it and pulled back. "But whatever makes you safest, that's what's needed."

By the end of the week, she was confident in her duties, and Joshua, a quicker study than she'd realized, became fairly adept in his role as gentleman's gentleman. He mastered the details of valet with ease, along with the peculiarities of table settings, table service, and the expected seating for everything from intimate dinners to banquets. He could pass as a well-established butler. Only the vast array of cigars, wines, liqueurs, and brandies he might be expected to offer guests confounded him.

But Maureen knew, from her intense discussions with Joshua over pots of tea gone cold, and her own intuition, that each lesson must be so thoroughly absorbed that they could perform their duties in their sleep. She knew, too, that their hours of lighthearted jest and the growing camaraderie between them could not last.

On Friday evening, just before Joshua was to accompany her back to Morningside, a hastily scribbled note from Curtis arrived.

"He says we're to be ready by ten on Monday, packed and prepared to be gone a week, though it won't be any longer than absolutely necessary. He'll explain everything in person, Monday mornin'." Joshua spoke the words without emotion, but Maureen sensed his anxiety. "He says to make certain we're both seen in church on Sunday—to sit in the balcony with Mrs. Melkford. He'll be there, but we should in no way recognize him. He expects Drake to be there as well."

Neither spoke during the drive toward Morningside, though Maureen felt as if she could hear all their mental wheels spinning.

"We've been prepared for a purpose," Joshua whispered as he helped her from the car parked three blocks from the Wakefield mansion. He took her arm to walk the last blocks through back streets, careful they not be seen. "I don't know what it is we'll be doin' exactly, but my instincts say it won't be safe nor easy."

When have I been truly safe? When has life been easy?

He pulled her arm more surely through his own as they walked, a protection she leaned into, craving the warmth and solidity of his presence.

"I wish—I almost wish I'd not brought you into this, except for these days we've shared." His fingers tightened over hers. "I swear I'll do my best to keep you safe, but I don't know what is to come."

She squeezed his hand. "I know you'll do your best, Joshua Keeton. And I'll do mine." *And I would not trade these days for anythin'. You've been spring to me, carin' for me, respectin' me, doin' all in your power to prepare me for whatever lies ahead.*

They reached the back gate of Morningside, an entrance shrouded by an old holly weighted down in berries. In the darkness, beneath a three-quarter and faintly ringed moon, Joshua's finger lifted her chin. Tentatively, his lips touched hers.

Maureen's heart trilled and swelled. She stepped back in surprise, as much at her inner response as at his touch. Joshua did not pursue her but briefly raised her gloved fingers to his lips, to his cheek. He bowed, the gentleman he'd become. *The gentleman he's always been.*

———— ❧ ————

Katie Rose dropped the edge of her bedroom window drapery, letting it fall into place. A tear slipped down her cheek. Though it had been dark, her vision faint, she'd seen enough.

CHAPTER FORTY-SIX

"KATIE ROSE has not come down to breakfast?" Maureen asked Saturday morning, late though she was.

"Grayson said she left early for the factory and told Cook not to expect her for the evening meal." Olivia frowned. "She asked Grayson to tell me that she won't be attending the Ladies' Circle this afternoon."

"It's not like her to miss a good meal. Did she say why so early or so late?"

Olivia shook her head. "She said nothing to you last night?"

"No, but I was late comin' in. Her light was off." Maureen opened her napkin. "Did she ask for me?"

"She wondered where you were at dinner. I told her you were working and that your hours were uncertain." Olivia colored slightly. "I didn't know what else to say."

Maureen sat back, smoothed her napkin in her lap, and tried to view Olivia's words as her sister might. But she realized she knew exactly what Katie Rose would think of her "working" late hours. *At least she's trailed by someone who will see that she's safe. Curtis made certain of that.*

"Maureen?" Olivia sounded hesitant.

Maureen wearily lifted her eyes, wondering if she was looking for trouble where there was none or if she should go to the factory and ask Katie Rose directly what she was up to, where she went so early, and why she would return so late. *It's so hard to know with her.* "Yes?"

"Curtis has asked me not to question the work he's having you do—at least not for the time being."

"'Tis for the best, he said. For Joshua and for me." Maureen sat a little straighter. It felt good to link their names together.

"Yes, I understand . . . at least I'm trying to understand." Olivia appeared distressed, something that registered so foreign in her character that it captured Maureen's full attention. Olivia blushed. "I'm afraid this sounds . . . exactly what it is, but I must ask."

"Ask me anythin'. I'll tell you if I can."

"I just wonder, do you . . . love him?" Olivia looked to Maureen as though the asking had sentenced her to face a firing squad.

So unexpected was the question that Maureen could not control the unbidden rise of heat from her core to her hairline, the rush through her limbs. "Love him? No, of course not." *Does my turmoil show so clearly? If Olivia suspects, does Katie Rose? How could she when we've barely spoken a civil word since I moved in? But does Olivia think I'm betrayin' my sister's heart? Katie Rose is still a child!* "No—I don't think so." She remembered the warm flush of happiness as Joshua kissed her the night before and felt the sudden rush once more. "But how can I know?" she said aloud in contemplation.

The anguish in Olivia's eyes confused Maureen.

"Do you think it's wrong?" Maureen held her breath, wondering what it was she could not see, was too blind to see.

Olivia's forced smile unsettled her more. "No. No, of course not. Love between two people who care for and respect each other is . . . is wonderful." And yet her face looked anything but wonderful to Maureen.

Mrs. Melkford was delighted to have Maureen and Katie Rose join her on her walk to church Sunday morning, though it took less than a moment to realize that all was not well between the sisters. She looped Katie Rose's arm.

"I've seen far too little of you girls since you moved in with Miss Wakefield, though I suspect that's as it should be. I'm delighted you're there, safe and sound and well fed. You must enjoy lively evenings all together."

But the grim line where Katie Rose's mouth should have been told her they did not. Mrs. Melkford changed the subject. "Have you found new work, Maureen?" She immediately sensed that was not a safe topic, either.

"Yes, I think so." Maureen appeared to hedge.

"Not certain?"

"I begin tomorrow." Maureen walked briskly on.

Mrs. Melkford decided to mind her own business, but that some extra time in prayer for her young friends was definitely in order.

"I'll be away for a time." Maureen surprised Mrs. Melkford by slowing and speaking at last.

"Going away?" *Now that is not what I expected.*

"Yes." Maureen hesitated. "My employer travels for work, and I'm to attend him and his family."

Katie Rose stopped suddenly, wrenching Mrs. Melkford's arm so that they both nearly fell backward. "You've gone back into service?"

Maureen's face, a plum in the cool morning air, now blanched white. "It's the only work I could find."

"You said—you swore—you'd never—never in a million years!" Katie Rose exploded.

"Domestic service is perfectly respectable, Katie Rose," Mrs. Melkford admonished.

"Not with her it isn't!"

"Katie Rose! Apologize to your sister."

But Katie Rose dropped Mrs. Melkford's arm and pushed Maureen with both fists into the street, her words rushing out as though a dam had burst. "Who is he? Who is he this time, Maureen? Or is there more than one? Are you farmin' yourself out to the masses now—lettin' them take turns crawlin' all over you?"

Maureen slapped her sister and slapped her hard.

"You whore!" Katie Rose hissed.

Maureen raised her arm to slap her again, but Joshua, who'd joined the group unseen, caught her hand in midair.

"You're not wantin' to do that," he said quietly. "You love Katie Rose."

"But she loves only herself, and she uses you!" Katie Rose shouted to Joshua. "Don't you see? You're just another in a long line of—"

Mrs. Melkford grabbed Katie Rose by the arm and shook her. "Stop that! Stop before you say more than you can ever take back."

Katie Rose stopped abruptly, covering her face with her hands. The broken dam that had poured spite and venom now poured tears, great and wrenching.

Joshua took her in his arms. She beat against his chest and struggled to go free, but he held her and walked her down a side street, letting her cry and cry.

"Whatever has happened between the two of you?" Mrs. Melkford asked, very near tears herself.

But Maureen shook her head sadly, her eyes filled with such weariness and concern for Katie Rose that it made Mrs. Melkford's heart ache. And yet, as she watched Joshua cradle Katie Rose against his chest as an older brother would comfort his young sister, she could not see the same familial love in Katie Rose's face or in the fierce grip with which she clung to him.

Joshua motioned, above Katie Rose's head, for the two ladies to go on.

"Come, dear. He'll bring her along." Mrs. Melkford tucked her arm in Maureen's, squeezing her young friend's hand, and guided them slowly to church.

As they climbed the steps toward the vestibule, Mrs. Melkford turned once. Her heart caught at the sight of a familiar figure, a face she'd seen weeks before, staring from outside her window. "Do you see that man, Maureen? The one in the checkered cap, there, beside the tree?"

But as she pointed, the man stepped back, the tree between them, and the two ladies were swept with the tide of the congregation into the church.

Mrs. Melkford, unsettled by the stranger, was grateful that Maureen seemed to regain her sense of purpose and take charge of them both, shepherding her up the balcony stairs to their seats.

Such a strange and too-eventful morning. Mrs. Melkford sighed, sinking thankfully into their familiar pew, willing her heart to steady its beat.

The call to worship, the opening prayers, even the first hymn had finished by the time Joshua quietly ushered Katie Rose into the pew beside them. Neither removed their coats, and neither made eye contact with the women to their right. One glance told Mrs. Melkford that Katie Rose's eyes, though dry, remained glassy and that the girl's knuckles whitened as she gripped Joshua's hand beneath a shared hymnal.

CHAPTER FORTY-SEVEN

MAUREEN TOOK THE CHAIR beside Joshua, explaining to Curtis, as best she could, Sunday's fiasco with her sister and Mrs. Melkford's account of the man who'd watched them enter the church.

Curtis nodded as he spread a New York map across half the desktop between them. Madame Sevier, who'd returned to help Maureen and Joshua with their disguises, spread her wares across the other half.

"I understand your concern—" Curtis thumped weights on the map's corners—"but her outburst may work to our advantage. Unless I miss my guess, Mrs. Melkford's checkered cap man was your Jaime Flynn—and Katie Rose's nickelodeon predator. If he's been following you ladies, hoping to ascertain your current circumstances—your daily patterns—perhaps he's scheming to pressure you into working for him. Or more likely he's working for Darcy's, keeping an eye on you. They're probably uncertain how much you know and how far your interest into the disappearance of your friends goes. It's just as well he caught sight of Joshua and Katie Rose together again rather than the two of you. We don't want to supply fodder for any suspicion that you're especially connected.

"When he realizes Joshua is not with your sister, Flynn may keep himself busy trailing her for a few days rather than looking for you—at least if he thinks pestering her might give him or Darcy's some sort of insurance for your silence. They won't touch either of you, certainly not while you're living under Olivia's roof. The attention and scrutiny would be too great—the last thing they want. In any case, it might throw him off your trail just long enough."

"Olivia's agreed to demand that Katie Rose limit her comin's and goin's to daylight, but I'll not leave the city thinkin' Jaime Flynn will be pesterin' after my sister," Maureen retorted.

"I've got a man on it—a good man following her, someone neither Katie Rose nor Flynn will see or recognize. He'll not let Flynn get too close, and he's not afraid to step in if necessary."

"You're askin' me to trust you with my sister's life." She sighed. *Perhaps that will be safer for her after all. If I'm not at Morningside, at least she won't be leavin' early and returnin' late to avoid me. But how resistant to Jaime Flynn's wiles are you, Katie Rose?*

"Ouch," she protested, jerked from her reverie as Madame Sevier, wielding tools surely made to torture her clients, twisted and pulled Maureen's hair tightly into a bun, pinning it mercilessly against her scalp.

"Do not complain, mademoiselle. Were it up to me, I should cut it off." The fingers of Madame's right hand made one sharp snip in the air.

Maureen clamped her mouth. Joshua raised sympathetic eyebrows.

"That might be the most practical disguise, Madame Sevier—" Curtis smiled—"but we may need Maureen to reappear in the city at any time. She must have her normal hair."

"Her 'normal' hair, monsieur, would, in all events, twist high upon her head. To cut it eight inches or ten . . ." She shrugged, spreading her fingers. "No one would be wiser, and yet it would fit more securely beneath the wig." She pulled pins from her mouth. "If flaming tendrils spill from beneath these raven tresses—how do you say?—the jig is up!" Her finger swiped sharply across her throat.

Joshua pulled the pair of scissors from the table and placed them squarely in Madame's hand.

Maureen challenged Curtis, "I'd feel much better about havin' my hair cut if I understood the point of this disguise."

"There's a very good chance we'll encounter some of the gentlemen frequenting Darcy's fourth floor. They must not recognize you. Each of our lives—yours, in particular—depend on it."

Maureen bit her lip and nodded once. *My hair will grow back; my neck will not.*

Madame whipped the pins from Maureen's hair, brushed it sharply, and began to snip.

Maureen cringed, watching locks of hair fall around her. *You snip, snip with relish, Madame, and your "eight inches or ten" look more like a baker's dozen!*

"With a bit of financial persuasion—including the outrageous purchase of two more tenements I neither wanted nor needed—last week I convinced Drake Meitland to introduce me to the man above him, a Victor Belgadt." Curtis leaned back in his chair. "I'm not certain if he heads the organization or is just another rung in the ladder. But I've convinced Belgadt and Drake that I'm an asset—that I can match any financial backing he can cultivate and that I already oversee lucrative mines—and moles—in Washington from which he can glean property."

"Property?" Maureen's mouth felt suddenly dry.

"Girls, women. Either kidnapped outright or more likely lured in with promises of good jobs, marriage, bribes—whatever it takes. Then they're sold to the highest bidder to be used in brothels, sold as sexual escorts here in New York, or shipped to private buyers elsewhere." Curtis stopped, nearly breathless from his intensity. "You do understand this is what's been happening?"

Maureen nodded solemnly. *I do understand. But I've never heard the words said aloud, as though it's some master, manipulative plan—all supply and demand.* Her spine pressed into the rungs of her chair. Madame gave her hair a tug, making her sit up straight once more.

"And they trust you?" Joshua asked.

"Enough that Belgadt's invited me to an event he's hosting at his estate outside Cold Spring—a few days of wining and dining other potential investors." Curtis pointed toward the map. "The estate lies sixty, possibly sixty-five miles from Manhattan, just off the Hudson, opposite West Point."

Joshua nodded. "Far enough to be out of the city's news and patrol, but close enough to make a river run out and back before daylight."

"Exactly, which is what I'm guessing happened with your friends from Darcy's." Curtis glanced at Maureen. "I can't say for sure, but I'm banking on a hunch that he holds women captive somewhere on or near the estate until they can be transported. No doubt it's rigged to look like just another night fisherman or something entirely legitimate. In and out, no questions asked."

"Or someone there is on the take." Joshua crossed his arms.

Curtis shrugged. "There are enough tributaries in the area to mask any method. But this is the plan." He leaned forward. "I've convinced Belgadt that I never travel without my own manservant and chambermaid because I trust no one else to attend me or my rooms, no one else to oversee my food over any period of time. Distrust is something Belgadt understands."

"Enter us," Joshua confirmed.

"He considers me an eccentric, but that, too, is something he understands. You'll need to attend me as if I'm as strange as I've portrayed, but I also want you to fraternize with the other servants. I'm assuming they know whatever goes on at the estate—especially those who've been there longest. Do what you can to get close, get them talking. Keep your eyes open for anything we can use in court. If we're able to prove they're selling or transporting women over state lines for purposes of prostitution, we can nail them."

"The Mann Act against human traffickin'," Maureen remembered, as Madame swatted wisps of hair from her shoulders. "The girls at Darcy's spoke of it."

"I'm just hoping it's enforceable—it's new legislation, so we've no precedent to predict success." Curtis frowned. "There's no way to guess the extent of political or police involvement in human trafficking; we only know it exists. Even if we compile sufficient evidence to make a case, I don't know what will stick or what kind of ruling we can realistically expect. No doubt the judge appointed will carry the day."

"The risk—" Joshua began, but Curtis cut him off.

"If we gain enough evidence to bring them to trial, and if, through exposure, we can raise a public outcry, that might just be enough to shut them down—ruin the operation at the source of its power and money and begin to bring down those in office who are criminally involved. For them to fall like dominoes—that's the best, the highest hope. Though it may not be realistic." He sighed. "It's all a gamble."

"Suppose we gamble and fail—suppose they discover us . . . what will stop them from comin' after us?" Maureen couldn't hold back the question any longer.

Curtis met her eye. "Nothing."

"Then she's out of it," Joshua stated flatly. "I'll not have Maur—"

"We need a woman in the house," Curtis insisted, "to search places neither you nor I could gain access to. The more of us there are, the less able Belgadt's people will be to keep tabs on each of us—especially with all the coming and going during these events."

Madame pulled a stocking cap over Maureen's scalp, then a wig over her eyes, and jerked it back to her hairline.

"I've no idea exactly what we're looking for or where we'll find it. But if they're keeping captives at the estate, they must be feeding them," Curtis went on, "which might be noticeable in the amount of food prepared by the kitchen each day."

"If they're feedin' them well," Maureen cautioned.

Curtis nodded. "If their purpose is to make the women's existence totally dependent on complying with their jailer's demands, they're not likely being treated well."

"No," Maureen replied quietly, remembering. "They're not."

"But whatever they're feedin' them," Joshua said, "they must be carryin' food somewhere—if not within the mansion itself, then somewhere on the estate. And that's somethin' to look for." He frowned again.

He doesn't like this any more than I do. At least there will be three of us there, and, Joshua Keeton, I'm more than glad you're one of those three.

"The house is huge and, from Belgadt's boasts, probably riddled with hidden passageways and false cupboards," Curtis continued.

"He told you that?"

"He told me—boasted, in fact—that the mansion and surrounding area, with its hiding places and tunnels, were built by a slave smuggler early last century when it became illegal to import slaves. Belgadt claims it's the perfect place to keep his 'merchandise in storage' until he's ready to transport." Curtis sat back, his shoulders suddenly rounded. "Finding the captives he's holding there now is one thing and perhaps, after all, will be the easiest. But we mustn't forget the bigger picture. We need documentary evidence to present in court—Belgadt's records. That's as much our goal as finding the women. Otherwise, we're only saving a handful at best."

"Records?" Joshua objected. "The women can't be more than inventory to him."

"Which is why he's bound to have details regarding when and where he bought or picked up his goods; his contacts for buying and selling; costs in feeding, clothing, transporting. He's a businessman, and white slavery is, for him, a very lucrative investment. There may be no actual names, but Belgadt's a man who keeps his fingers on everything and everyone." Curtis leaned forward again. "And we must consider just how and where we'll find such documents. I'm assuming he keeps them under lock and key."

"A desk? A safe?" Joshua suggested.

Curtis opened a bag on the table between them, pulling out three flat pouches of thin tools and three small, thick bottles with stoppers and seals. "These are the tools of our temporary trade in the event we come across such a treasure."

"For pickin' locks, are they?" Maureen asked, opening one of the pouches, certain she was in over her head and yet somehow thrilled to be part of something daring.

"That would be ideal. If it's a combination lock, we'll likely need to use acid—a risky but quiet method of entry." Curtis handed each of them a bottle and pouch. "Not something you want to open on a whim."

Maureen picked through her slender tools. "I'm more adept with a long hairpin."

Joshua's brows shot up.

She smiled in return, happy to have surprised him.

"If Belgadt's kept records of the women he's trafficked—anything at all—then we stand the added chance of finding those women and helping return them to their families, even if they . . . even if they've been heavily drugged or badly used." Curtis stopped, as though the intense energy of his mission had suddenly blown away, and said quietly, "And if we can't find them, perhaps we can determine what happened to them."

Maureen glanced up at Joshua, whose concern for his employer was etched on his face. *What have they not told me?* She was vaguely surprised by the thought. *And what happens if we find them—if their families don't want them back or if they have no families? What will we do with them then?*

"Whatever happens, we must each maintain our roles at all times. I'm sending Drake on a wild-goose chase for women in Washington. If he comes to the dead end it is before we find what we need . . ." Curtis looked up and, imitating Madame's earlier gesture, mimicked, "Then 'the jig is up.'"

CHAPTER FORTY-EIGHT

CURTIS HAD SECURED a private railcar, both to continue their ruse of an eccentric millionaire traveling with his trusted domestics and so they might continue laying their plans.

Maureen had never ridden a train, nor had she seen such a vast land. Paved streets, concrete buildings, and all semblance of energy fell quickly away once the tracks left the city. The thrill of the ride itself was more than enough.

But Curtis demanded her attention and recitation from each of them detailing their fabricated history as siblings who had immigrated to America four years before. Backward and forward, much as she and Joshua had practiced their new duties, they rehearsed their background stories.

"It's hard-pressed I am to be thinkin' of you as my sister." Joshua half smiled.

"Better than as your wife," Maureen responded dryly.

"Oh, I don't know." He grinned.

She felt herself blush.

Curtis passed each of them a packet of letters, written as if from family members still in Ireland. "Easy to falsify. Not so quick or simple to check. Read them, trade, and read them again, then pack your own group among your belongings. Your luggage will certainly be searched sooner or later. You've an hour to come up with a half-dozen family traditions and stories based on your new parents and siblings."

"Who would be askin' such questions?" Maureen would rather look out the window, so new was the experience.

Curtis pulled the shade, shutting out the swiftly passing landscape and capturing her full attention. "We don't know, and that could be the very slip that ruins us—all of us." He stared at her for a moment. "Watch what you say—remain in character at all times. You never know who might be listening or how. Be especially careful of Harder, Belgadt's butler. There's something in the man—something that takes pleasure in cruelty. I'm sure he and all there stand vigilant. Belgadt would have it no other way."

Maureen sobered and opened the first letter.

After they'd read and traded letters, Joshua prayed aloud for the success of their venture and God's protection on each one. Curtis prayed for the safe restoration of the women to their homes and families, nearly choking, so earnest were his pleas. Maureen prayed silently that the Lord would hear the prayers of these good men. She doubted He would hear or heed her own. But just in case, she prayed for Katie Rose, for Eliza, for Alice, trusting them to a God she barely knew and equally feared.

Half an hour before the train slowed, Curtis opened a bottle and poured three drinks. After handing them round, he raised a toast. "To Mary and David Carmichael, émigrés of Dublin, oldest children of Keith and Ailene Carmichael, and first in their family to set foot in this fair land, with the hope of bringing younger siblings along. Hence—" he smiled— "your strict devotion to a wealthy and eccentric dandy. May your lucrative employment be short, safe, and accomplish its purposes. May your wits be sharpened, your powers of perception clear, and all our exits swift."

Three crystal flutes clinked.

CHAPTER FORTY-NINE

"WELCOME TO SEDGEBROOK, Mr. Morrow." The too-young, broad-shouldered butler in full uniform bowed smartly, stepping back from the doorway.

Curtis strode through the marbled foyer. Removing his gloves, he said, without turning, "My entourage, the Carmichaels. You'll see to their needs that they might see to mine."

"Very good, sir. Mr. Belgadt has informed us to expect your staff."

"Excellent." Curtis removed his hat, but before Harder could take the hat and gloves, Joshua smoothly retrieved them.

Harder shifted his jaw, a flash of slight in his glance. "Mr. Belgadt is expecting you. This way, sir."

An hour later Maureen had settled into her new duties. Between them, she and Joshua had made the agreed-upon adjustments to their employer's bedchamber: books, papers, and writing instruments positioned at exact angles across the desktop; toiletries lined in a row with labels facing forward; suits hung two inches apart, matching shoes directly beneath—all designed to give the impression of an eccentric and fastidious character, a man of habits, accustomed to having his demands met.

"Pity the woman he marries!" Maureen chuckled.

But Joshua frowned sharply, raised a finger to his lips, and shook his head.

Maureen nodded in return, accepting his rebuke. *It's no game we've entered, and no tellin' who might be listenin' at doors.*

"We'd best make our way to the kitchen," Joshua said plainly, "meet the staff, and see to the master's meals."

"Yes, sir," Maureen responded obediently, for although they portrayed brother and sister, she knew his position as gentleman's gentleman was well superior to hers as chambermaid.

He quickly squeezed her hand and motioned "chin up."

Maureen returned his smile, stopped by the looking glass to adjust her wig with a slight forward tug, and followed down the stairs.

Curtis had timed their entrance for the middle of the afternoon, shortly before they were expected, knowing it would give Maureen and Joshua an opportunity to settle in and liberty to observe the room assignments of arriving guests.

Once his simple needs were met, he begrudgingly offered Belgadt the supplemental services of Mary and David Carmichael, saying he wished to help alleviate strain on the harried household staff.

Waiting for the other guests to join them, Curtis and Victor Belgadt shared drinks in the library.

"Good of you to offer your staff, Morrow," Belgadt observed. "You can appreciate why I would not want to bring in outside help for this occasion."

Curtis nodded. "The very reason I travel with my own people."

"Sure of them, are you?"

"Four years."

"I envy you that. It's always a risk—what they know, who they know, their sense of loyalty."

"Not when you own their father's farm."

"Here? In Ireland?"

Curtis snorted softly, swirling his drink. "I told you my assets are far-reaching. Nothing like the Atlantic and the dependence of their parents and siblings to ensure discretion."

"Particularly among the Irish—clannish lot." Belgadt laughed. "I like you, Morrow."

Curtis lifted his brows and raised his glass.

Dinner for thirty-one went smoothly. Harder and "David Carmichael" waited table.

"Mary Carmichael" assisted the Sedgebrook maids in running hot dishes up the kitchen staff stairs and soiled ones down. She stayed until the last platter was washed, earning grudging thanks from the cook, Mrs. Beaton, and undying appreciation from Nancy Small, the scullery maid.

"I never thought we'd get that lot washed and put away." Nancy pulled her sopping apron from her shoulders.

"Just in time to set the table for breakfast?" Maureen tied a fresh apron round her waist.

"Oh no, miss! Mr. Belgadt's very strict. No dishes in the dining room till morning."

"But he wants breakfast served by eight, you said."

"Aye, but he uses that great, long dining room table to stage his auc—" Her eyes widened as she caught herself. "To entertain, some evenings," she whispered at last.

"They smoke and take brandies in the dinin' room?"

"What's that?" Mrs. Beaton asked.

"It's nothing," Nancy spoke up quickly. "I just told her we don't set table for breakfast till morning."

"That's right, we don't. You've a problem with that?" Mrs. Beaton challenged Maureen.

"No, of course not. I'll be down by six, shall I, and lend a hand?"

Mrs. Beaton stared but didn't respond.

"I'll finish my duties for Mr. Morrow and say good night, then." Maureen warmed a cup of milk for her master on the stove, conscious of the weighted silence behind her, and headed for the stairs.

She'd barely turned the corner when she heard Mrs. Beaton hiss, "Watch what you say, you little fool!"

"But she's been brought in to help us. She surely knows why they're all here, don't she?"

"I don't know what she knows, but if you value your tongue, you'll keep it behind your teeth."

Nancy, Maureen thought with a smile to herself, *we must have a little chat.*

The night had run late for Joshua and taxed everything he'd learned in the last weeks. He and Harder had been on duty since the first guests arrived that afternoon, fetching and carrying, pouring drinks and lighting cigars, not only for their own masters, but attending every gentleman's whim.

The full-story clock in the downstairs foyer struck two before the last guest retired, and then only because Belgadt had had the women escorted away, promising to bring them out to prance and play the next evening.

The butlers had been left to set the room to rights and then attend their masters.

Once he'd left Curtis for the night, Joshua locked the door to his servants'-quarters room above stairs behind him, pulled his collar and tie from his shirt, and heaved a sigh. *At least I've not been billeted with that slime, Harder.* He sank to his knees and poured out the contempt he'd barely kept hidden.

It sickens me, Lord, this shameful exploitation of the crown of Your creation. I know we're here to cut this abomination off below its knees. I know that if we're to do that, these men must be made to feel safe and important enough to reveal their secrets, or they'll never lead us to their victims. But I don't know that I can long look on these men without showing them the anger and disgust I feel. And forgive me, help me, Lord, in my thoughts and in the surrender of my flesh to You, this night. For I'm a man, and that's all I am.

Protect Maureen, Father. Protect her from the hurt these men would cause her. Protect her heart and sensibilities. Remind her that what she does, she does for the good of her friends, her sister, and for other women so they'll never know the cruelty she's known. And most of all, Lord, let her know Your love. Reach out to her, and draw her heart to Yours. Let her know the joy of bein' Your daughter.

Thank You for Curtis and his plan. Thank You for giftin' him with the ability and the resources to do this work. Strengthen our arms and spirits. Make us successful in this fight. Help us free these women in bondage so that You might show them a life they've not yet imagined. Help us reunite them with those who love them, and open the hearts of their families to receive and restore them. Through Jesus, who came to set us free, amen.

CHAPTER FIFTY

THREE LONG DAYS LATER Curtis spit into the snow, then said, "Night after night of throwing to these bloodhounds the most expensive caviar and liquor money can buy, soirees to rival pre–Civil War slave auctions, and all Belgadt's sales talk—and we've whittled our 'guest list' to seventeen." He spit again as though he couldn't get the nasty taste from his mouth. "Seventeen men who would willingly sell their sisters for a price, and some who've already sold their wives to brothels."

"But no progress on our end." Joshua followed close on Curtis's heels, the picture of the manservant obediently trailing his eccentric master during a midday constitutional, but also providing their only opportunity to speak freely.

"No." Curtis marched faster, fury evident in his stride.

"I'm at the beck and call of the lot of them, so I've had no opportunity to look for ledgers or accounts or where they keep the women. Maureen's found nothin'."

"Nor have I," Curtis sighed. "Belgadt sticks to me like glue."

"And Harder to me. I'm thinkin' that's his assignment."

"No doubt."

"Some are scheduled to leave by tomorrow mornin's train. It'll not be easier to search when they've gone."

"No." Curtis slowed. "We need some sort of distraction—an upheaval of sorts, to throw things off-kilter—to give you and Maureen freedom to search. And we need it tonight."

"Somethin' they're not prepared for," Joshua mused.

"Exactly."

"Leave it to me."

———————— ❦ ————————

"You want me to what?" Maureen gasped, her hot iron in midair.

"You're not deaf, lass; we need a distraction," Joshua insisted, slipping her a small vial.

"Well, that will distract them, if it doesn't kill them. Not that they deserve better." She pocketed the vial and shook the shirt she'd been pressing for Curtis.

"Just a little in the soup and the cuttin' of the trunk wires in the attic. I'll show you after we serve drinks. You can meet me there," Joshua pushed, leaning closer. "Can you manage it?"

"I suppose. But if I'm caught, Mrs. Beaton will kill me before that demon Belgadt ever catches me!"

Joshua winked and kissed her on the cheek. "Well then, we'll dance from the gallows together, Miss Carmichael."

Maureen might have slapped him, but he was out the door before she could think to raise her hand. Instead, she touched softly the place of his kiss upon her cheek.

———————— ❦ ————————

It was half past six when the winds of a violent snowstorm howled through the lanes of the estate, whistling and rattling panes of glass as Maureen ladled creamed oyster chowder from the stove pot into china tureens under Mrs. Beaton's watchful eye. She'd half filled the first, smiled at Mrs. Beaton, innocent as a babe, then looked sharply again, spreading her eyes wide in horror at a point just over the woman's left shoulder. Her bloodcurdling scream rent the steamy kitchen air. The sturdy woman jumped and turned as Maureen's ladle flipped high, showering scalding soup over Mrs. Beaton's arm and hand, then sent the first tureen crashing to the floor.

Mrs. Beaton bellowed in agony. Nancy dropped to the floor in terror, desperately trying to corral the spreading rush of imported oysters with her tea towel. Maureen deftly tipped her small vial into the pot.

"Look what you've done, stupid girl!" Mrs. Beaton screamed again, dousing her hand in water. "That tureen's come from France—part of a matching set! It's worth more than three years of your wages!"

"I'm ever so sorry," Maureen cried as mortified as she could be. "I saw a rat run across the shelf—just there."

"There are no rats in my kitchen!"

"But I saw one, and I'm that terrified of them!"

"Stupid, stupid girl! How you ever made it out of the scullery and above stairs is beyond me."

Maureen began to sniffle. "I said I'm sorry, and I'm sorry." Then penitently, she retrieved the ladle from beneath the stove and handed it up. "Perhaps you'd best do the soup, mum. I'll help Nancy clean up."

Cook jerked the ladle from Maureen's hand. "Call Harder to come for the tureen. Shorthanded or not, I'll not trust either of you simpletons to carry it up the stairs."

"Yes, mum." Maureen lowered her head, curtsied, and turned to do as she was bid.

"And when you've done that, get out of my kitchen! Don't come back until the meal's done, clumsy girl! We'll save you the pots to scrub!"

"Yes, mum." Maureen hid her smile until she was out of sight.

"Well, their families will have to manage without them! You should have insisted the live-out staff remain with a storm brewing. We can't afford to be shorthanded tonight," Belgadt berated Harder.

"I should have thought ahead, sir."

Belgadt waved him away in contempt. "Get every maid and groom on duty. I want you and Carmichael in the dining room at all times. Bring up some of those girls with domestic experience and put them in uniforms—the strongest ones not dancing tonight. I want the house to look staffed to the rafters. Now that we've skimmed the less than committed, I intend to convince our potential investors we're wallowing in diamonds."

That evening, over an elaborately planned banquet, Belgadt announced, "With our mutual investments, gentlemen, we can more than double our playing fields. Morrow has agreed to match us dollar for dollar and inventory for inventory, the proceeds to be divided by all."

Murmurs of surprise and approbation ran both sides of the banquet table.

"All that you see, gentlemen—" Belgadt spread his hands before the lavish feast and wider, to include the estate—"is but the beginning for all of us."

Glasses were raised.

The first course had just been served when the lights flickered from the storm. Belgadt motioned to Harder, who nodded to Joshua. The two butlers produced candelabras for the sideboards and along the banquet table. Before they had set them all in place, the electric lights went out.

Once accustomed to the change in lighting, Belgadt initiated toasts. Half jests, vulgar boasts, and running speculations regarding the extent of financial possibilities and the necessity for personally "testing new merchandise" peppered the second and third course.

It wasn't until the fourth course was removed that the stomach cramping began—a grimace here, a puffing of the cheeks there. After the second man excused himself from the table, Belgadt received wary glances from his remaining guests.

The fifth man to clutch his stomach exclaimed, "What is this, Belgadt? You trying to poison us?"

Belgadt smiled and huffed at the insult but was taken aback by Curtis's furious and accusing glance as he clasped his napkin to his mouth, excused himself quickly, and motioned for Joshua to follow.

When retching was heard from the hallway, Belgadt called Harder to his side and ordered that the remaining Sedgebrook staff abandon their duties and attend their guests.

The order was barely given when Belgadt clutched his stomach and stumbled from the table.

Washbowls and seldom-used chamber pots, sloshing and stinking with the leavings of heaving guests, flew up and down the dark stairs between the arms of a frazzled staff. Indoor toilets, flushed too many at a time, backed up into bathrooms.

"Can you give me a hand, Carmichael?" Harder called from the upstairs landing, a chamber pot in either hand.

"When I've attended Mr. Morrow," Joshua called back. "You'd best bring in a doctor, lest your employer boast a houseful of corpses!"

A door flew open at that, and a guest, stripped to the waist and clutching a towel before his mouth, ordered, "Tell Belgadt he'd best get a dozen doctors out here at once! Tell him I'll sue for this!"

"Make the call, Harder," Belgadt ordered weakly as he topped the stairs, his face ashen, just before his stomach emptied upon the landing.

Harder slammed his lamp onto the marble-topped table in the downstairs hallway and madly tapped the telephone's cradle. "Operator . . . Operator!" He swore, then tried again.

"Is someone coming?" Joshua demanded from behind him, not sorry that the contents of the bowl he carried slopped onto Harder's livery and shoe.

"The lines are down!" Harder raked his hands through his hair, not seeming to notice that he reeked. "Do the best you can. I'll get the groom and send him for a doctor."

"I just saw him below stairs. He's down with it too—must have sampled the feast. Where's the rest of your staff, man? We can't manage alone!" Joshua challenged, barely able to hide his glee.

Harder looked desperately from Joshua to the front door and back.

"I'll have to go for the doctor myself. I'll bring the women to help you." He swore beneath his breath. "At least the swells'll die smiling."

Maureen had searched Belgadt's room during the first course. Finding no ledgers, no safe, no secret panels, and no women, she'd visited two of the guest bedchambers during toasts and Harder's room after cutting the trunk and telephone wires coming in through the attic.

As the men took to their rooms, groaning and swearing, she waited silently in the small storage room beneath the stairs, the door barely cracked to let her observe the comings and goings of all who passed through the open hallway.

She never moved until Harder had thrown the telephone receiver against its cradle and, taking up his lamp, pushed open his employer's study door. She shadowed Harder, just out of the lamp's range, and crouched behind an overstuffed leather chair, watching him fumble before the fireplace. Awkwardly, he turned the right andiron. A single bookcase slid smoothly open behind another. Harder passed through, turned, and raised his hand somewhere beyond Maureen's line of vision. Less than a moment passed before the bookcase slid back into place.

Holding her breath and a flashlight, Maureen searched the bookcase for a seam, a sign of the hidden door. There was none.

Having no idea how long before Harder might reappear or if she'd have warning, Maureen searched the drawers of Belgadt's desk. The very fact that not one drawer was locked convinced her that she'd find nothing incriminating. But she paid special attention to the dimensions and depth of each drawer, in search of secret compartments, as Curtis had instructed her. She ran her hands along the backs, seats, and bottoms of his chairs, along the chair rail that ran round the room. She was halfway through reading the spines of his books upon the shelves when she heard the shuffling of feet beyond the bookcase. As the bookcase opened, Maureen clicked off her flashlight and slid beneath the desk.

CHAPTER FIFTY-ONE

"ARSENIC, if I don't miss my guess," a weary Dr. Bates diagnosed, closing his bag in Belgadt's drawing room before dawn. "Not enough to kill you, but certainly enough to make the lot of you deathly ill."

"Thank heaven it wasn't my oysters after all!" Mrs. Beaton nearly cried. "I was so afraid they might have turned."

The doctor peered at her over his spectacles.

"But of course—" she colored suddenly—"I couldn't see how. They looked fine, smelled fine, felt fine. It's just . . . it was during dinner they all took so violently ill."

"Did you taste the stew?" Dr. Bates demanded.

"Right before I dished it up."

"And you suffered no ill effects?"

"Not one."

"Your staff—any of them taste the stuff?"

"Just the groom. I saved him out a bowl, for when he come in from the cold. He did come down a bit, but he'd been nursing a cold anyway. Of course it mightn't have been the same as Mr. Belgadt's gentlemen." She twisted the hem of her apron, the lie on her face.

"What about the wine?" He looked up and down the row of assembled staff.

"No." She drew herself up. "I don't allow nips of this and nips of that in my kitchen."

"Of course not." Dr. Bates smirked. "Who . . . ?"

"Harder and I served the dinner, sir," Joshua spoke up. "But I assure you, nothin' was amiss. We performed our duties in the dinin' room."

"For all to see?" the doctor baited.

"Yes, sir. As always, sir."

"You're new here, aren't you?"

"Yes, sir. My sister Mary—" he tipped his head toward Maureen—"and I attend Mr. Morrow, his personal staff."

"I see. And did you carry the stew from the kitchen to the dining room?"

"No, sir," Joshua said but glanced at the floor as if reticent to speak.

"Why, Harder did, sir, and he chose the wine," Mrs. Beaton said with a fleeting widening of her eyes.

"Tea and toast, that's all the dandies want for breakfast," Mrs. Beaton huffed to the minimal staff eating porridge in her kitchen. "And not all of them trust that, as if poison is everyday fare on our menu!"

"What do you think they'll do to Harder?" Nancy whispered, ladling hot water into teapots. "I heard they'll be taking him with them when they go."

Mrs. Beaton shook her head. "It'll be the end of him, I'm afraid. Men like those don't take kindly to being dealt such a blow."

"But why would Harder do such a thing?" Nancy pleaded.

"God only knows." Mrs. Beaton momentarily closed her eyes.

"It's insanity, sure enough!" Maureen vowed, setting cups on the trays. Joshua bumped her foot. She bit her smile.

"I heard they found a pouch of diamonds in the linin' of his coat." The groomsman imparted his knowledge with self-importance.

"They never!" Mrs. Beaton gasped.

"I always knew he was a fool," the groomsman gloated. "Always parading around, above himself."

"A distraction!" Nancy's eyes lit with the knowledge. "He wanted a distraction so he could steal the diamonds!"

"A case for hanging!" the groomsman pronounced.

"Well—" Mrs. Beaton pushed herself up from the table, weariness evident in every movement—"they'll all be gone before noon. But keeping their lordships waiting won't improve their tempers. Get these trays upstairs, the both of you!"

"I'll give you ladies a hand," Joshua offered, tossing his napkin to the table.

Maureen shot Joshua a more than grateful glance before she realized that its warmth might not be construed as sisterly.

CHAPTER FIFTY-TWO

AN ARMY OF LOCALS shoveled the road into town by late afternoon, and all the guests, save Curtis and his staff, departed.

It was another day before the electricity came on, thanks to Curtis's surreptitious trip to the attic. No sooner had the road been cleared but temperatures rose and a new storm, a wild northeaster, swept through with driving wind and rains. The river ran high, and creeks off the Hudson overflowed their banks.

Joshua and Maureen made themselves indispensable to Victor Belgadt and his house. The schedule kept the two trusted employees busy but gave them free access to search all the rooms without Harder peering over their shoulders. Still, they found nothing.

By noon of the fourth day, telephone lines were repaired and service was restored. As Joshua served late-afternoon martinis and Maureen delivered trays of cheeses, caviar on ice, and finger fruits to Belgadt's study, Curtis convinced the estate's owner of his need to see proof of profit figures for his brothels and out-of-state trafficking if he was going to merge operations. "It's down to you and me, Belgadt. Take it or leave it."

Belgadt drummed his fingers on the arm of his chair and glanced indecisively toward the far wall. He heaved a sigh as the telephone rang, making every other person in the room start. But Belgadt ignored the ring. He'd just risen and headed toward the opposite wall when a knock came at the door.

"Come," Belgadt ordered, stopping in the midst of the room.

Collins, the new underbutler, bowed. "Mr. Drake Meitland on the line, Mr. Belgadt. He insists that it's urgent he speak with you."

"Meitland? What now?" Belgadt grumbled.

"Shall I handle it?" Curtis offered congenially.

But Belgadt ignored him and lifted the receiver from his desk. "Meitland, what is it?"

Curtis knew Belgadt's silence went on too long. He heard the low rumble through the phone's receiver and the staccato punctuations, urgent, though he could not make out the words.

Belgadt glanced up sharply, and Curtis knew he stood accused.

"Is there a problem?"

Belgadt pulled away from the receiver. "There doesn't seem to be a Madame Trovetski or a Thaddeus Skyver in Washington. The address you gave Meitland for the brothel doesn't exist."

"That's impossible!" Curtis exerted every bit of superior indignation he could muster. "Let me talk to him." He reached for the phone, but Belgadt held back.

"This had better not be a setup, Morrow." Belgadt held the receiver by his side. "As a matter of fact—"

Curtis jerked the receiver from his hand.

Belgadt was not used to such presumption.

"Drake, Curtis here. Did you go to the office on Green like I told you? . . . No—that's impossible. . . . Of course he's not going to admit it—he's no reason to trust you. You're right; I should have thought of that. . . . No, stay where you are. I'll come down first thing tomorrow. . . . Yes, bad storm here, but trains are running again. Where are you staying? Right, just hold on."

Belgadt pushed a pad and pen toward Curtis and watched as he scribbled an address.

"Yes, I'll meet you in the hotel lobby tomorrow night. Don't talk to anyone else. I don't want you scaring them off. The operation's made to shut down at a moment's notice. Wait for me. I'll contact you when I get there."

Belgadt reached for the receiver, but Curtis replaced it—a little too quickly, Belgadt thought. A mistake? He wasn't sure. "You don't want to cross me." Belgadt studied the man before him.

"Meitland's ineptitude had better not have cost my DC operation," Curtis threatened in return. "Need I remind you that I'm the one who's lost most, thanks to Harder's sticky fingers?" He jerked his cuffs below his jacket sleeves. "Now let's finalize our business before I go. I'll catch the first train tomorrow. Where are those ledgers?"

Eyes narrowed in concentration, Belgadt rounded his desk and settled slowly into his swivel chair. "I think our business can wait until you—and Meitland—return." His fingers drummed the desktop. "That will be time enough to lay our cards on the table."

CHAPTER FIFTY-THREE

ALTHOUGH EVERY WOMAN had warmly welcomed her, Mrs. Melkford still felt awkward speaking or voting in the Ladies' Circle. She didn't fully understand young women, let alone wealthy young women. But she believed their hearts true and eagerly supported Hope's motion to purchase and staff a building in lower Manhattan for the purpose of training immigrant women in employable skills.

"They must have the opportunity to learn English," Julia insisted. "Speaking the language will make all the difference in whether or not we'll be able to find jobs for them."

"That's true, but there are a number of schools that already offer those evening classes. We can't do everything—or everything in one building," Isabella argued. "I think we should focus on domestic service training and sewing and tailoring. Those skills are always needed, and most immigrant girls have at least some experience with a needle, some much more."

"Please." Julia dramatically rolled her eyes.

"There's nothing dishonorable about those skills," Isabella reminded her.

"Of course not. And for some women that will be just the ticket. But we have to offer women more opportunities than they have now. We absolutely must offer training in sales clerking and secretarial skills, including use of the modern conveniences—like the telephone. And record keeping, teach them some basics about budgeting and finance. And all of those skills require speaking English in New York."

"Might I say something?" Mrs. Melkford timidly raised her hand.

"Of course, Mrs. Melkford." Olivia turned toward her. "What is it?"

"You all mean so very well. These are wonderful ideas and will make such a difference in the lives of these young women."

"But?" Julia demanded.

"But they desperately need a place to stay from the moment they leave Ellis Island. They need sponsorship—someone to take responsibility for them, to prove they won't become a public charge. If women don't have that, they'll not be allowed into the country."

"Sponsorship?" Agnes clasped her hands together. "But that means providing housing."

"That's quite another thing," Dorothy responded.

"It would mean providing a live-in situation, a safe place, and accountability," Mrs. Melkford replied, doing her best to make eye contact with each woman without singling out Dorothy. "Those are the things most difficult to find."

"Don't most women know they won't be allowed through Ellis Island without family? Wouldn't that deter them from coming in the first place?" Isabella asked.

Mrs. Melkford looked at Katie Rose, hoping she would speak up, but the girl appeared to be studying her cuticles. "Yes, it keeps many from coming, but not all."

"Then perhaps they shouldn't come," Dorothy persisted, much to Mrs. Melkford's dismay.

Mrs. Melkford hesitated, framing her words. "Sometimes they don't understand that rule before they come, and for some there is no choice but to leave their country. Victims of starvation, war, abuse, and forces beyond their control—they come to America for so many reasons, almost always because life was not tolerable in their home country. And sometimes—" she moistened her lips—"it would be better, safer, for young women to be with other young women, rather than with their families."

Dorothy, paler than usual, looked away. Mrs. Melkford wondered if the young woman was unwell or if the topic upset her more than it had the others.

Mrs. Melkford knew she was treading on delicate ground with women of protected sensibilities who, she was certain, knew little of the world of poverty, but she added, "You may be aware that some girls are forced into less than desirable forms of employment in order to provide for their families—even *by* their families."

Eyes widened. The women said not one word. Katie Rose's face flamed.

"In that case," Miranda said at last, "they should refuse."

"You know that's not always possible," Carolynn reprimanded softly. "They've nowhere to go, no one to help them, no money. In many cases they speak no English to ask for help."

"Precisely why we must teach English!" Julia insisted.

"And why we must consider taking some into our homes," Olivia added, turning to Mrs. Melkford. "That's what you meant, isn't it? That we must take them into our homes?"

"Jesus said it best," the older lady replied, smiling softly. "'I was a stranger, and ye took me in.'"

The quiet that followed gratified Mrs. Melkford. *At least they're not bolting, Lord, and they are taking it in. They'll need time to talk with their husbands and families, time to make arrangements. But it's a start. Thank You, Lord, for giving me the courage and the opportunity to speak for our sisters, to help bridge this gap between. Thank You for opening the hearts of these women. Infuse their hearts with Your love to open their homes and lives, as well as their purses.*

"You're right," Hope said. "We need to think about life in New York from their point of view—and that begins with a safe place to stay. But we can't stop there. It's not only what they physically need when they first come to a strange country, but what they need to know—and we must help them learn it quickly. Everything from how to count money to the tools and products they'd use to clean in wealthy households, locations of the markets, what foods they'd be expected to prepare, where to go for help—medical or spiritual—or . . . everything. Everything will be different."

"I can help with that part," Katie Rose little more than whispered. "There were a hundred things I wished I'd known when I first stepped off the boat."

"It's a good thing you and your sister came together!" Isabella encouraged. "Think how hard it must be for those without family."

"Not so different—" Katie Rose shifted stiffly in her seat—"dependin' on who your family is."

It's hard not to contend with such ingratitude, Lord, Mrs. Melkford prayed, her patience with Katie Rose wearing thin. *Child, you've no idea how hard Maureen worked for you. I'm not sure I do.*

"That's it, then. We must treat them as if they are our family, as if they're our sisters, and not strangers we're helping," Julia affirmed.

"We clearly have a great deal to consider," Agnes sighed. "Mrs. Melkford, we'll be looking to you for guidance; you've worked with so many young women. But in the meantime, I believe I speak for all of us when I say we want to begin making arrangements. All in favor of taking pledges of means and service to purchase and staff a building in lower Manhattan, to be used for the purpose of teaching immigrant women and girls English and life skills, and for training them in domestic service, sewing and tailoring occupations, sales clerking, and secretarial work, show your hands."

"Unanimous!" Julia squealed. "It's a bold plan to go right into the thick of things. We'll need a site where the girls are likely to look for housing, an area they'd find affordable to live permanently so they won't have a huge distance between home and training and employment."

"You're out of order," Miranda teased the effervescent Julia.

But Agnes lovingly, patiently prayed for the Lord's guidance and blessing on the project, on each woman there, and adjourned the meeting.

"We'll need to staff the different departments, but we must also consider staffing security for the building round the clock," Hope advised as the women collected their coats and hats.

"Security for that area will add to our expenses," Agnes cautioned. "We'd best see what the building will cost, estimate our operating budget, and get busy right away raising pledges."

"Dorothy, your husband's in real estate, isn't he?" Carolynn asked. "Perhaps he could help us find what we're looking for—something suitable but within our means."

Dorothy's pale cheeks flushed at the question. "Drake's been away on business a good deal lately. I can ask him, but it might be better if we don't wait for him."

The women turned toward Dorothy, brows raised.

Mrs. Melkford sensed the young woman's discomfort and turned to

Olivia. "Perhaps Mr. Morrow could help us? I understand that he's begun investing in real estate."

But Olivia would not meet her eye. *Whatever is going on with these sisters and their young men?*

As they walked through the foyer, Mrs. Melkford pulled Olivia aside. "I've not heard a word from Maureen for nearly two weeks. Is she still traveling with her new employer?"

"I—I'm afraid I don't know," Olivia stammered. "We've not heard from her."

"No?" Mrs. Melkford hoped the alarm she felt was unjustified. *Maureen's a sensible, capable young woman. She's just busy with her work and can't get away. Or this dreadful weather is to blame.* "Well, I'm sure that if Mr. Morrow found her the position, she must be perfectly all right." She fumbled with the buttons of her coat, wondering if she should venture to ask. Curiosity won. "Perhaps you've heard from him?"

But before Olivia could respond, Katie Rose intruded. "We've not heard from either of them, nor from Joshua, for that matter." She pinned her hat into place, her color rising. "I told you both that Maureen was up to no good, that her reputation precedes her—once a snake, always a snake—but you wouldn't listen." Angrily she grabbed her purse and swept through the door, hissing none too quietly, "Well, now you see, don't you? Two good men—your sweetheart and mine—and my sister. All missin'. What do you think of that?" The door slammed behind her.

Mrs. Melkford, horrified by Katie Rose's outburst, would have given no credit to such a childish display, but for the quick tears that sprang behind Olivia's eyes.

Please, Lord, keep Maureen safe; keep her pure. Hold her in the palm of Your hand. She tucked her arm through Olivia's as they walked through the door together. *And please, Lord, above all, help these young ones trust You.*

CHAPTER FIFTY-FOUR

MAUREEN PUSHED WIDE the draperies of Curtis's vacant bedchamber and watched as the only two men she trusted were driven to the train station in the downpour.

"Keep them safe, and hurry them back, Lord," she whispered as she stripped the sheets from the bed, collected soiled bath linens, and handed them off to the young maid in the hallway. *Here I am, prayin' again. As though You listen to me.* She shook her head. But she hesitated, duster in hand. *Are You there?*

To stall for time apart from Belgadt and his staff, Maureen swept the floor and beat the carpets, oiled and rubbed the mahogany found in the furniture and woodwork, polished the lamp brass and andirons, scrubbed the washbowl, and trimmed the lamps—all she could imagine to ready the room for Curtis's return. *Oh, that they could have taken me with them!*

With Drake Meitland's phone call, Curtis had given up the search for documents; it was too risky to remain. The most they'd dared hope was to leave the house and bring in authorities that very day to release the women being held, exposing Belgadt and his operation through the passageway that Maureen had discovered the night she followed Harder into the study. Such an arrest would not penetrate the web of the organization, nor would it enable them to trace the whereabouts of women already trafficked. Indeed, it put them all at risk for Belgadt's retaliation. But it would at least free the group of women being held at the moment. Maureen had prayed that Eliza and Alice were among them, alive and well.

But Victor Belgadt had foiled even that plan. Maureen and Joshua had been packed and waiting by the door when, at the last moment, Belgadt had insisted Curtis leave Maureen as collateral.

"Collateral?" Curtis had played the unbelieving and indignant guest. "You jest."

"I never jest." And Belgadt had clearly meant it, revolver in hand. "Until you return with Meitland and our new shipment is secured." He'd motioned the underbutler to return Maureen's luggage to her room.

She'd seen the protective rise in Joshua's chest and known he was about to protest. But realizing that all their lives and the lives of the women beyond the bookcase were at stake, she trusted them to return for her and stepped quickly forward. "I'll make certain your room is ready for your return, sir."

She'd turned before another word could be spoken and climbed the stairs to Curtis's room, taking refuge in her duties.

If I'd not stayed, all would have fallen apart in the moment, and Mr. Belgadt would have surely moved the women before we could return—might do so yet.

If they bring the police to release the women today as planned, I'll be rescued. But if Curtis truly goes to Washington in an attempt to keep Drake Meitland out of the way longer, I may have another day to wait—and search. But how or where? The moment Drake telephones, the moment he cries foul . . . the women in the tunnel will be moved. We'll all be exposed. Curtis and Joshua will be tracked down. She dared not guess their end or her own, though frightening images stole through her brain.

She drew a deep breath, pushing the air down into her belly, held it for a count of five, then allowed it to escape her lips in a slow and steady stream—a strategy she repeated throughout the morning in an effort to maintain her sanity.

If they don't return with the police by midafternoon, I'll know their plans have changed. I'll play this out as long as I can.

By two o'clock Maureen had made her decision. *If I must stay the night, I'll risk searchin' for the safe. There must be one on that far wall. Mr. Belgadt's eyes shot there as he was tryin' to decide what to do—just before the phone call. We all saw.*

But what if I find it? How will I get ledgers out of the house and safely away in this weather?

As windswept torrents of rain continued to pour and beat against the house deep into the afternoon, Maureen's brain whirred. By the time she served Mr. Belgadt's late afternoon drink, her head ached with an intensity she'd never known. Every muscle in her neck and back and shoulders screamed.

"You seem troubled, Mary," Belgadt crooned sympathetically.

"It's nothin', sir. Just a headache." She gave a feeble smile.

"Pity," he soothed, rising from his chair.

She stepped back, but her reticence did not deter him.

He motioned for her to sit down.

"I'd best help Mrs. Beaton with dinner, sir."

But he placed his hands on her shoulders and guided her firmly into the nearest chair. "No, Mary. Not tonight. Nancy can give her all the help she needs. I won't hear of you working when you're not feeling well." He began to massage her shoulders, her neck, her temples. "We must make certain you're in fine condition for your employer's return." He ran his hands down her arms and up again. "Mustn't we?"

Maureen heard the simpering smile, the knowledge of power in his voice. Her stomach turned.

His hands finally rested on her shoulders, a brace surrounding the base of her neck. "Feeling better, Mary?"

"Yes, sir." She swallowed, willing her voice to remain steady, willing her skin not to crawl into a shiver, praying her wig did not slip.

"Perhaps you'd like to go to bed early tonight. Too much tension isn't good for a woman."

Her heart flipped into her stomach. She felt the panic rise as bile in her throat. "I'm afraid I'm not well and ever so likely to be sick, sir." She coughed loudly, then bolted from the chair, gagging, apron to her mouth, not waiting for his response.

It was not hard to plead a sick stomach and pounding headache when Nancy came to her locked door. "Tell Mrs. Beaton I'm sorry; I'm ill and cannot serve tonight. I've gone to bed." *At least it is my bed, and I'm alone.* But when Nancy's footsteps had faded down the hallway, she rose, trembling, and checked the lock again.

CHAPTER FIFTY-FIVE

DISGUSTED, DRAKE MEITLAND threw the unread *Washington Evening Post* to the dining car seat beside him and pushed cramped fingers through his hair. His head pounded from too much whiskey and the knowledge that everything he'd worked to build with Belgadt was skating a thin edge.

He knew better than to trust another living soul. Why had he let his guard down with Curtis Morrow?

The man was smooth—Drake gave him that—suave and courtly with Olivia, daring and a good bluff with Belgadt. But the resemblance, now that he thought about it, was striking: dark-brown eyes, curling hair, tall and slim, and that nearly alabaster skin. *It just looked better on a woman.* He shook his head. *How did he find me? How did he know it was me? It was finished three years ago. She swore her family was dead.*

Drake narrowed his eyes, thinking you could never trust a woman, certainly not a desperate one. Then he groaned inwardly at his own stupidity.

If only he could take back his words over tonight's dinner, when he'd confided that it was ironic he'd returned to DC for his biggest coup, since that was where he'd gotten his first lucky break in buying and selling women. Curtis had encouraged his boasting, free with the bottle.

Drake grimaced as he recalled his words.

"Started a few years ago with a girl I picked up outside a restaurant. Down on her luck, hungry—she'd had some kind of row with her parents up in Georgetown and run off. But she was prime and clean—to start." Drake had chuckled, the wine doing its work. Still, he was careful, as always, not to mention names. "Told her I needed a wife and a mother for my two kids. Gave her a full-fledged sob story that my wife had died the month before of consumption, said I was lonely and desperate—needed somebody who understood, or my kids would be sent to live with strangers."

I should have noticed his shift in demeanor, but like a fool, I went on.

"Didn't take much—a three-dollar gold band and two dollars to a justice of the peace I dragged out in the middle of the night—and voilà: Mrs. Meitland."

"Dorothy?" Curtis had asked incredulously.

"No!" Drake had laughed aloud, thinking that was the funniest thing he'd ever heard. "No, before I married Dorothy. Mrs. Dorothy Meitland, now, she's the real thing. Purebred—came with papers, license. Wealthy father, bound for inheritance—the works. The other one was a business deal, but a real looker."

"So you sold her?" Curtis had been sawing through a prime rib when he asked, and Drake had taken the flush in his face as a response to the chef's letting a tough cut slide through his kitchen.

Still, something about the purpling vein in Morrow's neck had given him pause. But he'd kept on, glad for an audience. "When I was done with her. She fetched a tolerable price in the brothels in the city—that was before the big raids. But by then she was used up—dirty, you know." He'd lit a cigarette, uncomfortable with the details. He'd never liked details. "So I married Dorothy—Papa Wakefield's money and all that."

He'd shifted the talk to the plans for the morning and the high-class brothel Curtis still maintained existed. Drake had wanted to go that night, was eager to close the deal. He'd already wasted a week running in circles and needed to get back to New York. Every day he was away, he was losing money—money he couldn't afford to lose, money he owed Belgadt. A lot was riding on this deal, both to maintain Belgadt's good graces for having introduced him to Curtis and because Drake's debts had long outgrown his income.

But Curtis was clearly in no hurry and claimed they couldn't interrupt during the brothel's business hours. If he didn't know better, Drake would have thought the man was stalling.

Curtis had just signed for their bill and they were leaving the table when the question casually came.

"So what happened to her?"

"Happened?"

"To Lydia, your brothel wife."

Drake caught himself just in time and, shrugging, feigned a slump of regret, a curse that she'd run off, ungrateful as she was. He'd willed his face and hands steady when he told Curtis he'd meet him in the hotel lobby the next morning at ten.

Drake had tried phoning Belgadt from behind the hotel desk but learned that though the lines in the area were operating, Belgadt's line was out of order once again. It had taken Drake less than five minutes to return to his room, load and pocket his revolver, throw a few essentials into his bag, and slip unseen down the hotel's fire escape. He'd caught a cab to the station and run to catch the night's last train to Manhattan.

Now the waiter removed Drake's cold, untouched coffee. Drake tamped and lit another cigarette, cursing himself again for his boasting, wishing he could will the train to pick up speed, desperate to reach Belgadt before Curtis did, and wondering for the twentieth time who else was in the game.

As the train drew closer to Penn Station, Drake decided he'd have enough time before the morning train to Cold Spring to make it home and pick up a peace offering for Belgadt—or a bargaining chip for his life.

Despite her dread and fear, Maureen had fallen asleep sometime after the downstairs clock bonged eight.

She woke when someone tried her door—once, twice. Then came a half grunt and steps faded away. A door down the hallway opened and closed. A lock clicked, and all was silent. She waited for the clock to strike the half hour and then one.

Breathing slowly in and out, she waited until it struck one thirty, then two, and two thirty. Maureen rose, threaded the slender lock-picking tools through her wig, pushed the small vial of acid deep into the lining of her cloak, and pocketed in her uniform a small flashlight. She moved silently down the stairs to Curtis's empty room, carefully pulling the door behind her. Glimpsing through the drawn draperies, she caught no reflection of light outside Belgadt's study.

Maureen waited another thirty minutes before slipping from the room. She hesitated by Belgadt's door, registered his soft but steady snore, then crept down the stairs, keeping to the wall. No lamp burned in the hallway below. But as she stepped onto the main floor, a male voice not fifteen feet away demanded through the dark, "Who's there?"

Maureen's breath caught. She didn't move, didn't speak.

"I say, who's there?" The voice demanded again, this time more forcefully and identifiable as Collins.

Her heart in her throat, Maureen nearly stepped forward, but from the end of the hallway came the swoosh of a door as it swung open. A pale light shone on slippered feet.

"It's just me, sir—Nancy," a second voice whispered.

"What the devil are you doing down here, creeping about the house this time of night?" Collins demanded gruffly, but the feet stepped quickly forward.

Maureen pressed her back against the wall and slid round to crouch at the side of the stairs.

"Mrs. Beaton told me you'd be keeping watch tonight," Nancy simpered, "and I thought you might like a sandwich and a cup of coffee to keep you company."

"You did, did you?" Collins sounded pleased. "You stayed up all this time just to fetch me a snack?"

"I couldn't sleep, that's all," came the coquettish reply.

"Well, seeing as how I'm not sleeping either, how about *you* keep me company?"

"Thought you'd never ask." The giggle in Nancy's voice was muffled by the door's soft swoosh.

Maureen peeked round the corner of the stairs and saw the pale light bob beneath the door as if going downstairs toward the kitchen.

In less than a minute Maureen slipped through the study door, closed it behind her, and pulled the flashlight from her pocket.

The targeted wall held five life-size portraits. How she would lift even one from its hanger to open a safe on the wall behind, Maureen couldn't imagine. She forced the panic down, forced herself to breathe again. *Finding the safe is the first thing. One step at a time.*

She tipped the corner of the first painting. Finding no safe behind, she tipped the edge of the second, the third, and the fourth. "This is it, then," she whispered as she pulled back the corner of the last. But there was only wallpaper.

How can that be? He was surely headed for this wall!

She thought back to the moment Belgadt's eyes glimpsed the wall. She pictured him in his overstuffed chair beside the fire, imagined again the conversation. She tiptoed across the room, sat in the chair herself, looked up as Belgadt had done when speaking to Curtis, then rose and headed for the wall.

She stepped around the long, ivory-inlaid credenza that ran beneath the portraits, ran her hands along the seams of the wallpaper, hoping for an unseen edge. But there was nothing. *Think, think! The house is riddled with hidey-holes. The tunnel was hidden by a bookcase, its lever in the andiron. If there's a safe, it must be accessed by something in plain sight—something normal or useful.*

She swept her light over the wall and then the credenza again, slid open its doors. She pushed, hoping to glimpse the wall behind, but it was too heavy to move—unnecessarily heavy.

Maureen ran her hand over the sideboard's end, then the opposite end. She stepped back, frustrated, and ran the light over the entire piece once more. *Something's not right. What is it?*

Then it registered. The piece was not entirely symmetrical, at least not inside. The doors opened in the middle of the piece, but there was more than an extra hand's breadth of storage space on one side than the other. And yet the interior wall was solid. Maureen ran her fingers along each interior edge. No buttons or levers, no indentations to gain a handhold.

She closed the doors, running her light round the edges of the piece, letting her fingers follow. Just beneath the back corner on the short end, her palm caught a tiny, raised button she could feel but not see. One press and it popped the outside end panel open. *So here you are, you hide-and-seeker!*

Maureen sat back on her knees, studying the lock. *My "hairpins" won't do for this, more's the pity.* She pulled the small vial of acid from her cloak. Holding her breath and bracing the light against the base of the credenza, she twisted the cap and released the stopper.

Maureen prayed that Collins was busy with Nancy, that he'd stay in the kitchen below stairs, that his nose would not pick up the unusual scent. She'd never prayed so many prayers in all her life. And now she prayed that Someone was listening.

She was not prepared for the number of ledgers Victor Belgadt had accumulated or for the extent of his "property holdings." She knew there was no time to decide which were the most pertinent, the most incriminating.

In the end she creased random pages near each book's spine, then swiftly, quietly, tore two or three from each one. She folded the lined pages into tight rectangles and forced them through the lining of her cloak.

Maureen hid the ledgers behind books in the bookcase's far corners, on shelves as high and low as she could reach so they would not all be in the same location. Belgadt might discover someone had been there, but he would not be so quick to find what she hoped the police—or better yet, Curtis and Joshua—might find when Belgadt was arrested.

She closed the safe door, no matter that a hole had burned through its metal large enough to pull out the lock. She closed the wooden panel of the credenza. Then she swept the light across the carpet, making sure no sign of her work remained, and turned toward the fireplace's andirons.

CHAPTER FIFTY-SIX

OLIVIA HAD VOWED to do everything possible to honor her sister's wishes and maintain her privacy. But Dorothy needed medication and medical attention. It was the middle of the night, and she tossed and turned as her fever raged. Olivia was certain her sister had lost ten pounds in the last month, and the dark circles beneath her eyes had deepened. But Dorothy had made her promise not to call for the doctor again, nor alert the staff.

"There's nothing they can do, and the fever will pass. It always passes," Dorothy had weakly protested.

Olivia wrung the cloth into the china bowl on the bedside table and wiped her sister's brow.

"Drake," Dorothy mumbled, nearly delirious.

Drake is the one who got you into this. Why isn't he the one suffering? Perhaps I should regret or feel shame for such a thought—a wish, in fact—but I don't. He might as well have put a gun to her head.

And then Olivia wept silent tears of anger and frustration for Dorothy, the sister who'd thought she was marrying a prince—someone who loved and cherished her, someone who wanted to father a child with her. *My precious Dorothy, you wanted children nearly more than life itself. There will be no children now nor ever.*

And where is Drake? He's been gone at least ten days with no word—no letter or telephone call, no telegram. Dorothy had said he'd left after giving her a peck on the cheek and a casual "Business trip—nothing to worry your pretty head. I'll be back in a few days. Don't give away the furniture while I'm gone."

It was a petty but serious remark, reminiscent of his displeasure upon learning that Dorothy had contributed her last year's overcoat and gloves to the Immigrant Aid Society, still desperately in need of warm clothing.

Olivia forced herself to mentally berate Drake, to focus on fury he so richly deserved. But into the back of her mind crept images of Curtis as they had done constantly of late: Curtis smiling. Curtis offering to help her find Maureen. Curtis sitting beside her in church. And then Curtis telling her he was going away with Maureen and Joshua, asking her to keep it all a secret, guaranteeing they would be back within the week. But none of them were, and the days were passing.

With each day, Katie Rose shredded the remnants of her sister's reputation anew, grinding both Joshua and Curtis into the dust, casting them as fools lusting after a woman's skirt.

Dear God, was I a fool to believe him?

The clock in the hallway had just bonged four when Maureen heard footsteps outside the study door. The knob turned as she dropped behind a hearthside leather chair. A light played slowly over the room, flicked off, and the bearer closed the door.

Maureen lay still until she heard the scrape of a chair outside the door and the faint, off-key hum of a satisfied Collins.

With two hands she gripped and pushed the andiron. One bookcase slid behind the next, and Maureen slipped through the opening. Running her hands above the lintel as she'd seen Harder do, she found the small lever. Barely a touch, and the bookcase slid closed, clicking into place.

Maureen stood in the cold dark and buttoned her cloak, praying that Collins had not heard.

She pressed against the stone wall, swept her light down the steeply spiraling steps, and took them one at a time.

How far she descended she could not guess but was certain she'd burrowed at least two floors beneath the main floor of the house, into an under cellar of sorts—where the stairs stopped short, hit a rough landing, and turned a sharp corner. She shone her light ahead. The path shot forward, tunneling through the dark.

CHAPTER FIFTY-SEVEN

IT WAS FOUR THIRTY. Olivia half dozed in a chair by Dorothy's bed. She'd not heard the door open and was startled awake when a sharp thud came from Dorothy's adjacent dressing room.

She'd risen and was about to admonish the maid to keep quiet, to lay the fire later and let poor Dorothy sleep, when she realized it was not the maid after all, but a man in overcoat and hat going through her sister's vanity. And yet, the figure was familiar.

"Drake?" Olivia bit her lip to make certain she wasn't dreaming.

Drake dropped the necklace he'd plucked from the open jewelry case but scooped it deftly from the floor.

"What are you doing with Dorothy's pearls? What are you doing here at this hour?"

Drake's face blanched, but he composed himself so quickly, and with such sarcasm, that Olivia felt two people stood before her.

"I live here, in case you've forgotten, Sister-in-law. In fact, I must ask you the same question."

"I'm here, Drake, because Dorothy is ill."

"I thought surely she would have rallied by now." He sounded critical, as if Dorothy's constitution was a deserved judgment upon weak character. She watched as he slipped the pearls into his coat pocket as though she could not plainly see him.

"She did rally but is down again." She stepped closer. "Those are the pearls Father gave Dorothy on her eighteenth birthday." Pieces of a puzzle began to slip into place in Olivia's mind as she watched her brother-in-law: Drake's annoyance over Dorothy's generosity; the pieces of silver Dorothy maintained Drake had packed away for safekeeping, as if their staff had not always been completely trustworthy; Dorothy's diamond earrings that had suddenly gone missing. "If you need money, Drake, I'll gladly advance you some. Please don't take Dorothy's pearls."

"Don't be ridiculous," he snapped. "My train got in early. I promised Dorothy I'd have her clasp attended to before she loses the pearls, and I mean to do it before another day goes by." He made to brush past her, but Olivia stood in the doorway.

"I don't believe you."

He stopped. "You're out of line, Little Sister, and quite beyond your realm. It's time for you to go home and put your wild imagination to penning schoolgirl novels."

"Gladly," Olivia said and, despite his demeaning and spiteful barb, meant it. "But I cannot leave Dorothy. Do you understand how ill she is? Do you know her condition, her . . . her prognosis?"

"I understand that she's my wife and therefore my responsibility, not yours." He moved toward her. "Now, shall I have George call for your car?"

"Drake?" Dorothy moaned from the bedroom.

Olivia stood aside, but Drake made no move to go to his wife.

"You've become meddlesome, Olivia."

"And you've become cruel and irresponsible. Do you—?"

But Dorothy cried again, "Drake, are you there?"

Drake pushed past Olivia, locking the bedroom door behind him.

Olivia's heart caught for her sister, but she admonished herself. *He won't openly strike her. He wants too much from her.* She clasped her temples. *Dear Lord, please help Dorothy. Please show me what to do.*

She hesitated, hoping for a clear answer. Tempted as she was to listen at her sister's door, she knew she could not, that Dorothy wouldn't want it.

Olivia left the dressing room by the hall doorway and walked slowly down the stairs, already regretting her challenge to Drake. *If I'm to help Dorothy, I can't afford to alienate him.*

She waited at the bottom of the stairs another twenty minutes, not wanting to leave before she knew Dorothy was all right. George appeared with her coat.

"You shouldn't have waited up, George."

But the older man simply smiled and nodded. He'd just called for her car and driver when Drake descended the stairs.

"Still here?" He didn't look pleased.

"Please, Drake. I don't wish to quarrel. I'm worried about my sister."

"She's under the weather." He sounded as though he were speaking to a child. "She'll be fine in a day or two."

"Is that what she told you? Have you spoken with Dr. Blakely?" Olivia pressed. "Because this means you're both infec—"

"You forget yourself." Drake drew himself upward. "I've tolerated your meddling and forward remarks because you're Dorothy's sister and she loves you. I love my wife, Olivia—though you don't seem to think so—and I indulge her where you're concerned. But don't cross me if you wish to remain welcome in my house."

Olivia swallowed. She knew she'd gone too far and that Drake could and likely would forbid Dorothy to see her. No matter what, she couldn't let that happen. "I'm sorry, Drake. You're right. I've overstepped my bounds."

Drake looked as though he didn't believe her.

"It won't happen again."

He hesitated, buttoned his coat, then smiled indulgently with the victor's magnanimous condescension. He leaned forward, curling a stray wisp of hair from her forehead round his finger and tucking it behind her ear.

She felt her face flame, felt his breath feather her hot cheek.

"You need someone—a husband of your own—to keep you occupied, dear Olivia. As soon as I've taken care of my own business, I'll see what I can arrange."

A sharp retort was on her tongue when the front door opened and her chauffeur bowed discreetly. "Your car, ma'am."

Relieved, but still holding her breath, Olivia turned her back on Drake and pulled on her gloves. "Thank you, Ralph."

"New driver?" Drake asked.

"What?"

"You fired your foundling Irishman?"

"No, and Joshua's hardly a foundling. He only drove for me until he began working for Curtis. He and Maureen are both working with Curtis the past week or so," Olivia replied. Even as she said it, she remembered

Curtis's warning to tell no one that Maureen was connected to him in any way, that it might endanger her. *Surely he didn't mean Drake. They're working together, aren't they?* But she wondered again that Maureen had not returned to Morningside, that Curtis had not been in touch. And though she didn't want to believe Katie Rose and her cruel accusations, she feared the growing relationship between Curtis and Maureen. *How could a man work so closely with a woman as striking as Maureen and not notice her?* "You've been working and traveling with Curtis too, haven't you—for business?"

"Is that what he told you?" Drake smirked, his jaw and eyes hardening.

"I assumed." *Something's not right.*

"Did you?" Drake buttoned his coat, pulled on his leather gloves, jerking the fingers into place, and walked out the door.

Maureen's waning light danced crazily up and down the tunnel walls as she stumbled along its uneven path. *Please don't let the light give out, not here!*

She could not guess how far she'd come but felt at last a slight stirring, a breath of air against her face. She stopped, burying the light in the folds of her skirt. Muffled voices, some soft and moaning, others gruff and coarse, came from a short distance ahead. Maureen reached a flat wall, where the tunnel turned sharply. A pool of light lay on the path round the first corner, and beyond the next a flight of stone steps, leading down into a rock and earthen cavern the width of three Pullman cars and the length of two.

Maureen pressed back against the tunnel wall as her eyes adjusted to the dim light of the damp room. Three double-sided rows of what looked like barred animal pens—the bars three finger widths apart—ran the length, each ten to twelve hands high, with a perimeter big enough to stall a cow or a couple of sheep.

Maureen crept closer. Broken boards and fragments of boards stood between the locked stalls, and tattered blankets hung crooked over the fronts, isolating the cages from one another. To the top of each cage was wired a small board, with a number crudely drawn: 28, the next 29, the next 30. A hole the width of a rolling pin and perhaps a hand high was cut into the front door of each pen near the floor. As she stepped nearer, tin cups, clutched by clawlike hands, pushed through several holes to the aisle.

The hairs on Maureen's arms rose. She peered both ways, then gingerly pulled a corner of blanket from the door of the first stall. She stared but couldn't credit what her eyes were seeing. She leaned closer.

Half-asleep, and curled like a newborn calf, lay a woman, her hair knotted, her skirt and waist torn, soiled beyond redemption. The woman looked up sleepily and crooked her finger. "Take me; I'm good." Her head dropped toward her chest, but jerking herself awake, she repeated in rote, "Come—take me."

The next young woman, not older than Katie Rose, looked up with a blackened cheek, covered her face with her arm, and moaned, "No, no," curling her limbs into her torso. It was not so much an answer, Maureen thought as she dropped the blanket into place, as a response to anything or anyone that came near. She bit her lip and pressed forward.

Hands trembling, Maureen pulled the blanket from the front of the next stall and the next—on down the line until she pressed her fist against her mouth to keep from vomiting at the sight of the women and girls, some barely twelve, some beaten, their faces marked and eyes, jaws, lips, or fingers swollen.

The farther down the line she crept, the cleaner and healthier, less bruised but also less aware the women became. She recognized two of the women who had been brought up to serve the night of the poisoning.

As she stepped in front of one of the cutout holes, another hand shoved a tin cup through the small door, rattling it against the floor, begging for water. Dozens more women followed, shoving hands through their small doors, banging cups against the stone floor. Beyond the aisle she walked, Maureen heard more stamp their cups.

"Knock it off! You crazy—" a crude voice cut the air. Maureen froze, prepared to run, but a man twice her size rounded the corner. "Well, well, what have we here?" He leered. "You don't look much like our general merchandise, missy."

Maureen backed away, sorely tempted to make for the tunnel and the long trek back to the house. But she sensed that another came around the opposite end of the aisle, behind her, cutting off escape. And so she bluffed.

"Mr. Belgadt sent me down."

"Not his usual method of adding inventory," the voice behind her grated. "But we're willing to oblige. He wanted us to break you in, did he?"

"He wants you upstairs, all of you. He told me to keep watch while you're gone."

"It'll have to wait. We're shipping the lot out as soon as Flynn gets here. We've already started druggin' the best ones."

Maureen shrugged, forcing her voice above the din of rattling cups. "He said now."

"Shut up!" the beefy one bellowed, slamming a wooden club against the cages.

Maureen jumped. The clamoring stopped.

"Go tell him if we don't get 'em outta here before the water's over the bags, they'll drown. Not that I care, but it's a stinkin' waste of inventory."

"I'm not one to waylay Mr. Belgadt's plans." She looked at them pointedly. "That was a mistake Harder made."

The men glanced guardedly at each other. "So what's he want with us? We didn't have nothing to do with that, didn't even know about it till Cook told us."

"He knows that," Maureen soothed, "but he wants to lay before you his change in plans. He said to wait at the end of the tunnel until he opens the door. He'll call you when he's ready."

"Boss is consultin' us now?"

"Why don't we just go up through the cellar, like usual?"

Both men frowned, and she knew she'd overstated herself.

"He's had investors in and out this whole week," she patiently explained, doing her best to sidestep the water streaming across the cave floor. "He doesn't want them to know where he keeps the women, so you have to wait until he's alone in the house and can open the bookcase." She wrinkled her brow and peered down the aisle. "It's just the two of you to look after all these women? I thought there'd be more."

"Flynn's comin' out from the city. Ought to be here before the tide rises. He's expectin' to get 'em out before daylight."

The first man hoisted his suspender over his soiled shirt. "If he gets here before we get back, tell him to wait. Just in case the boss changes orders."

Maureen nodded, steeling herself against her choking fear of Jaime Flynn.

"'Shave and a haircut, two bits,' against that door." He pointed to an indentation at the far end of the room, a tunnel less than a broomstick long that led to a solid-looking door. "That's his signal. Don't open to nobody else for no other reason."

Maureen squinted into the darkness. "He's got no key?"

"It only opens from this side—we don't need no visitors. And don't open till he knocks. Flynn knows to watch the tide. We've got sandbags on the other side. But with this storm and the tide comin' in soon, they ain't much good. The whole place is gonna flood—door or not. That's why we've gotta get 'em out, and soon."

"But where can Mr. Flynn take them in this storm?" Maureen did her best to sound nonchalant, but the men exchanged an uncertain frown, and she knew she dared ask no more.

"Know Jaime, do you?"

She shrugged. "We're from the same county—a long time ago." Maureen forced herself to return their stare.

"Never mentioned anybody he knows workin' in the house."

"Would you?"

The taller one hesitated, then motioned toward the cages. "Keep these locked. They'll beg and carry on. Let 'em."

Maureen shivered involuntarily but crossed her arms, lifted a jutting chin, and nodded as though he'd addressed a hardened woman of New York's underworld.

CHAPTER FIFTY-EIGHT

Maureen waited until Belgadt's men had climbed the stairs and the echo of their footsteps died in the tunnel before she began pulling back more blankets.

"Alice?" She whispered at first, running down the aisle. "Eliza?" From cage to cage she ran, forcing herself to push away the faces of misery in hope of finding her friends.

But it was no good. More than half of the women responded.

"Here!" one cried.

And "Help me! I'll be Eliza if you want!" called another.

Hands reached through the small doors, clawing the ground, begging with outstretched fingers.

After a dozen false hopes, Maureen knew that the names she called meant nothing to the women desperate to escape and that doors without begging hands housed women likely too weak or beaten, too intimidated and frightened, too sick or malnourished to plead.

Eliza and Alice could be behind any one of these blankets, or they might not be here at all. But how can I leave these women here—any of them?

She gripped the bars of a cage door and shook it until her teeth rattled; not a bar gave way. "Keys . . . keys . . . there must be keys," she whispered, flashing her light across the cages. And then louder, "Where are the keys? Do any of you know where they keep the keys? Help me, tell me, and I'll let you out!"

But the room had gone silent.

"I'll help you, I swear it, but you must help me before they come to take you away!"

A timid voice called, uncertainly, from across the room. And then another and another.

"Maureen?" a voice, thick and husky but familiar, separated itself from the others.

"Alice? Eliza?" Maureen cried.

"Maureen?" the voice came again, closer.

"Alice? Alice, where are you?" Maureen could not believe her ears or the hope that beat in her chest. "Keep talkin'. I'll come to you!"

"My cage is against an outside wall; that's all I know. I've no idea where they keep the keys, but I've heard them hang them near my cage."

Maureen ran in the direction of the familiar voice, but as the two called to each other, a life, a fervor, passed from cage to cage. Women cried, then screamed for help, the room exploding in a riot of calls that curdled Maureen's blood.

"Come to me—to me!"

"Help me!"

"Open the door!"

Maureen could no longer distinguish between one voice and another, could no longer hear Alice above the rest.

Help me, Lord!

Find the keys. That voice in her head came clearly, above the rest—not an audible voice, but a voice of reason and stability in the midst of chaos. The insistent voice that had counseled her before.

Holding her flashlight steady, she fanned its light across the walls of the cave, floor to ceiling, coming to rest on a heavy brass ring. "Keys," she whispered in relief, pulling the ring from a post rammed high into the wall.

She prayed, as she fumbled with the first lock, that the key would fit all the locks, open all the cages. But the key stuck, jammed into the first lock. She tugged and twisted it back and forth until she was able to pull it free.

But even after she jerked wide the door, the woman cowered in her sodden cell corner, her face and eyes shielded by her arm as though she feared Maureen might strike her.

"Come out! Come out!" Maureen pulled the woman's arm.

The woman burrowed deeper into the corner of her cage. Maureen finally left her, fearful of the passing of time. For every turning of the key

340

and opening of the lock, for every swinging wide the door of their prison, not one woman in three ventured through her open door.

She pleaded with them to come out, but she understood too well the absolute terror written on their faces. *They trust no one—not even freedom.*

Maureen, helpless to help them believe they were free, shed silent tears of frustration for them, came close to cursing, as she continued to unlock cages.

"Maureen? Maureen, is it truly you?" The feeble, hopeful plea came from behind a blanket and locked door near the end of the first row.

"Alice!" Maureen dropped the keys in her excitement, then scrambled across the puddling floor to retrieve them. She fumbled with the lock, twisted and turned the key. Nothing. She groaned, jerked the key from its lock, tried again, and the stiff lock pulled open.

The cell door flung forward. Maureen grabbed her friend by the arms, dragging her to her feet. "Alice! Alice!" she wept. "Oh, thank God! Thank You!"

Alice was thinner by half, cheek bruised, hair matted, her waist and skirt wet and torn, but she was alive, and Maureen rejoiced in the wonder of her friend.

"Have you seen Eliza? Do you know what they've done with her?"

Alice shook her head miserably. "I think they took her away—somewhere. I heard her once, but I couldn't help her, and after that . . ."

"We've got to get you out." Maureen pulled back, still grasping her friend's frail arms, desperately trying to rub strength and life into them. "Those men will be back any minute, and the one who took you—Jaime Flynn—he's comin' by boat to clear the cave."

"They don't mean to take us all—the boat's too small. He never takes more than a dozen at once."

"There's a storm. The river's risin' and it will flood the cave—everyone must be moved."

"They'll only move the healthiest. I heard them talking before you came."

"But—"

Alice covered her face with her hands as if shutting out an image too horrible to bear. "We've got to get out of here before they lock us in again."

"There's nearly fifty of us. If we band together, we can run them over."

"We're too weak," Alice argued, "and too afraid. There won't be time to unlock all the cages. They'll come with guns—and cords! We've got to get out!"

"The tunnel leads back to the mansion, and—"

Alice shook her head wearily, and Maureen knew every word cost energy her friend couldn't sustain. "Beyond the door—" Alice pointed to the door where Flynn was expected—"we can climb over their sandbags and up onto a ledge. There's a side tunnel beyond that. It leads up to an opening—into a copse of trees."

"You're sure?"

"It's how he brought Eliza and me in—by truck, into the trees, then marched us down through the cave. I can lead us out. But it's a narrow climb—one at a time."

Maureen bit her lip. She wanted to hold tight to Alice, to run with her, but the pressure in her heart insisted, *Help them.*

If I help them, we'll be caught!

Trust Me.

But—

Trust Me.

Maureen ordered, "I'll unlock the doors, and you coax them out. Then lead them through the tunnel. I'll push from behind."

"There's no time, I'm telling you! Come with me now!"

Despite the fear weighting her feet and legs, Maureen shoved the key into the next lock and the next. *What if Katie Rose were one of these? What if Eliza is here somewhere? Dear God, I know I cannot leave them. I cannot leave even one!* "You go!" she whispered, the conviction in her heart growing. Then louder, "Go!"

But Alice stayed by her side. As quickly as Maureen unlocked the doors, Alice pulled prisoners from their cages. Only when she stumbled did Maureen slap her awake and shove her toward the tunnel. "You've got to lead them out. I don't know the way!"

Still Alice balked.

"I'll be soon behind you. Go!" She turned back to her work, trusting Alice to do her part.

The women, once outside their cages, stood, unbending their limbs, dazed and uncertain. Some, though still strong, were drugged beyond grasping their opportunity. Maureen pointed them toward the door and Alice. Stumbling, a few formed a sluggish human train—boxcars disconnected.

Maureen worked quickly, from one lock to the next. But the locks were stiff and some were rusted.

The weight of her cloak slowed her down. She tore at its buttons, yanking it off and shoving it high on a ledge, desperate to save the precious ledger pages hidden in its lining from the water that streamed through the doorway, a quickly rising tide. She went back to work.

When Maureen glanced up again, she saw the train of women slipping in the rushing, ankle-deep water, exhausting fragile stores of strength to regain their footing and move forward. "Grab hands!" she called.

They trust no one enough to reach for them—not the woman before or behind.

"Join hands! Join hands so you don't fall!" Maureen screamed, pushing women forward. "Form a chain!"

Most of the women ignored her, each staying her own course. But one here and there reached for a woman behind her or for a skirt in front of her, pulling herself and the next woman along.

Maureen unlocked another door and unceremoniously dragged the frightened captive to the aisle. She'd opened but half the cages. The emaciated woman in the next cage had been terribly beaten, her clothing and bedding soiled and stained with blood. The woman closed her eyes and turned her back on her rescuer.

Though Maureen urged and tugged and pulled, she knew that for this woman there was no reason to live, no freedom great enough to rouse the energy to run. Still she begged, "Please, please come with me. I'll help you. I swear it!"

Jaime Flynn didn't like winter boat runs, and he didn't like it that Belgadt's phone line had been dead so long. All he could do was follow his last set of orders, no matter that the weather made those nearly impossible.

He thought Belgadt overly cautious about using land transportation after a storm. *Who's out in this mess to care about tracks in mud and snow?* But he also knew it was Victor Belgadt's penchant for detail and cover that had kept the operation secret and lucrative.

Flynn stood behind the boat captain and stared into the Hudson's predawn fog. He shrugged. *I suppose I've made enough gaffes of late. Best not to stray from his lordship's good graces. I might as well indulge the hand that feeds me.* He tugged lower his checkered cap.

The boat pulled deftly into a nearly hidden tributary above Cold Spring. Ice chunks crowded the banks, but the center flow was clear. The cave lay dead ahead.

CHAPTER FIFTY-NINE

JOSHUA KEETON SET the binoculars on the farm window's ledge and kneaded the base of his neck. Willing away the crick there, he forcibly opened wide his eyes. It had been a long night, ever since Curtis had telephoned that Drake Meitland had flown the coop in Washington.

It had seemed an excellent plan to have Joshua wait and keep an eye on the comings and goings of any in Belgadt's house. Most importantly he'd be closer to Maureen, should it appear that things were getting out of hand.

Joshua knew it would take Drake hours to make his way back to New York and Cold Spring, but neither he nor Curtis knew whom he might have contacted in the meantime. Confirmed doubts about the legitimacy of Curtis's operation would surely trigger a mass evacuation of Belgadt's "inventory" by land or river.

As Curtis's contacts watched the river, Joshua watched the only road into or out of the estate from the window of a couple all too willing to assist in the downfall of Mr. Belgadt, the pompous neighbor who'd sent his lackeys to coerce them into selling their farm. All the while, Joshua prayed for Maureen.

He started at the soft nudge against his arm.

"It's after six, Mr. Keeton." Mrs. Bramwell, the farmer's wife, handed him a steaming mug of coffee.

"Ah, thanks, Mrs. Bramwell." He stretched and sipped the bitter brew—strong enough to stand a spoon in and scalding. Keeping awake was no longer a challenge.

"Try this bit of sweet bread while you're watching. I'll fix a platter of eggs and sausages when Hiram comes in from the barn."

Joshua smiled his thanks, his mouth watering at the prospect of a hot breakfast, and turned back to the window.

But Mrs. Bramwell didn't move. She leaned into the windowpane, peering over Joshua's shoulder, her breath near enough to tickle his ear. "What in the world?"

"What? What do you see?" Joshua adjusted his lens.

Mrs. Bramwell pointed to a distance far to the east. "Now, what do you suppose those girls are doing traipsing through the woods this time of the morning, so wet and bedraggled?"

Joshua aimed his binoculars in the direction she pointed. "Two girls—no, three—five . . . They've no coats!" He adjusted the lens for a closer view. "Nor shoes . . . I don't like the looks of this." He dropped the binoculars to the table behind him as he pulled on his coat. "Make the call, Mrs. Bramwell. This is it."

A half mile into the cave, the tributary divided. Flynn and his men bore a hard right. Rounding two bends, they came to a makeshift dock and cast their lines ashore.

Flynn frowned, pulled the straps of his fishing boots over his shoulders, and hopped to the narrow ledge. *Water must be two feet above high tide.* He swallowed, realizing that the sandbags ahead could provide no match for the swollen river.

Gripping the damp rock, he made his way round another bend, expecting to glimpse at least the tops of the bags. But they'd disappeared beneath the current—he couldn't tell how deep. The lapping, sloshing water covered not only the bags but the rock-hewn stairs above them and poured through the metal door, standing wide open.

They can't be sending sixty women up through the cave! Flynn grimaced. He didn't fancy slogging or swimming through the freezing pool only to discover that Grimes and Mercer had already moved the inventory by land. He swore. *Belgadt will blame me if his cover is blown, no matter what those idiots do.*

That was when he saw two women across the pool, struggling to help each other maintain precarious footing as they crept along the narrow ledge that led up into the hillside tunnel.

Before Flynn could determine his next move, another woman pushed through the doorway, then another. *This is foolishness! Where's Grimes? If it's that desperate, why aren't they taking them up through the house?*

Freezing or no, Flynn slipped into the water, gambling that the river would not fill his boots like cement blocks, and waded through the deep. Within earshot of the human chain, he bellowed, "Grimes! Mercer!"

His shouts initiated screams of recognition and terror from the women, but no familiar face emerged from the holding room. Flynn swore again and groped for the steps, shoving the woman in his path into the freezing water.

<hr />

Joshua's calls for Maureen grew desperate. He recognized four or five of the women from Belgadt's nights of entertainment. *But where is Maureen? They couldn't have escaped on their own.* He knew that Belgadt would not be sending them away on foot or unescorted. Most of all, he wagered this was just the kind of desperate and unexpected break Maureen might have initiated.

He pushed against the growing tide of terrified, river-sodden women as they poured from the copse of trees. He pitied them, would help them, but only after he found Maureen.

He called for her again and again, turning the shoulders of every raven- or flame-haired woman to search her face. Following the line, he reached at last the tunnel's hidden entrance. A young woman, so weak she could barely stand and soaked to her skin, pulled captives one by one from the narrow pass.

"Maureen—have you seen Maureen O'Reilly or a woman called Mary Carmichael?" he begged her.

"Maureen?" The woman whitened.

"Please—have you seen her?"

"She's . . . she's unlocking the cages before the boat comes to take them away!"

"Cages?" But Joshua sensed there was no time to ask. "This tunnel—will it take me to her?"

"Yes." The bedraggled young woman looked suddenly relieved. She grasped Joshua's arm. "Help her—please, please help her!"

Joshua needed no encouragement. Pulling the next woman up and into the light, he squeezed into the pass and began the winding trek downward.

"Come—come." Maureen pulled another woman from her cage as the water swirled about their waists. She pushed the lagging group toward the tunnel and door, now half-filled by the water rushing into the lower room.

A few empty cages had come loose from the floor and tipped, like barges unmoored, confounding the women. Maureen herded the group round them, for the women were too dazed and weak to reason and weakening faster in the frigid water.

"Go! Follow the ledge!" she cried and turned back to tackle more locks. The next door she pulled open, the woman was already dead, her eyes rolled back in her head, her limbs quickly stiffening in the cold water. Maureen wept and cursed because she'd wasted precious moments on the dead. She wept anew because the woman had not lived to taste freedom, all the while forcing her stiffening fingers to work the next lock.

But when she looked up, the human train had stopped again. Women stumbled backward, into the water, into the room.

"Go! To the ledge and the tunnel! You must move forward!" Maureen cried. "I promise I'll help you!"

But the women continued to fall back, whimpering.

"Well, now, what have we here? We ought not promise things we can't deliver; don't you agree, sweet Miss O'Reilly?" From atop the rushing threshold, the too-familiar Irish brogue sneered.

Maureen's veins froze. *Breathe in, breathe out, breathe in . . . God, help me. . . . Deliver me. . . . Breathe out . . . Deliver these women. . . . Breathe in . . .* The prayer gave her power, and she bluffed her way forward.

"Mr. Belgadt wants his inventory saved, and you're late! They've got to go up through the tunnel or they'll drown. Help me get them out," she shouted above the swirling water's roar and turned to the next lock.

"You're working for Belgadt?" Flynn shouted, clearly not believing.

"I'm working to save these women, Mr. Flynn. Help me, or you'll have Mr. Belgadt to answer to." She pushed another woman through the door, calling, "Follow the ledge!"

He stepped round both women, blocking Maureen's return to the cages. She tried to brush past him, but he caught her arm. "He doesn't want all—only the fittest."

She jerked free. "There's no time for this—no way to know who's fit and who's not. Help or get out!"

"What I know, Miss O'Reilly, is that you'll fetch a brighter penny than any of these used-up wretches." He laughed and caught her tight in his grasp, but she pulled back, and the lunge forced her into the water. She went under and came up coughing, gasping for breath.

He reached for her again, but she jerked a cage door between them, ramming its corner against his face.

Disbelief, then fury, flashed through his eyes. He clasped a hand to his bleeding mouth and hurled the metal door aside.

Maureen scrambled for the open door, pushing her heavy skirts through waist-high water. She'd barely reached the threshold when he caught her by the legs, dragged her back, and thrust her down into the water.

She fought and kicked, but he was stronger. Even in her panic she knew she could not gain the upper hand. She twisted, turned, and bit his arm, sinking sharp teeth nearly to the bone.

He bellowed but grabbed her by the hair.

Maureen pulled his feet from under him and wrenched herself free, leaving the sopping black wig in his hand.

She'd gained the door, the mound of sandbags, the ledge, daring to believe she might outrun him, when he grabbed the hem of her skirt and caught her up, ripping the sleeve of her waist. She beat him with her fists, but he threw her over his shoulder and let her beat and kick away.

Flynn stumbled, hauling her over the bags, and shoved her in the water. Before she could gain her feet, he grabbed a fistful of hair and, dragging her through the water, beat and slapped, kicking her ribs until he'd forced her into a cage, jerking her petticoat beneath her.

Please, God, she begged, *don't let him. Don't let him!*

He slammed and locked the door, smirked as the water covered her shoulders. Dripping and triumphant, he ripped her petticoat, wrapping a strip round his bleeding arm.

"It's sorry I am that I've no time to sample your feminine virtues,

Miss O'Reilly," he gloated. "But the tide waits for no man, not even Jaime Flynn." He tipped her a salute and slogged through the water toward the flooding doorway.

CHAPTER SIXTY

MAUREEN GRABBED the iron bars of her cage, jerking and pulling, pushing and pounding, but they did not budge. She shifted her weight from side to side, throwing her body against one corner and then another to maneuver her cage through the water, toward the door. But it was no use. An inch or three, and the incoming water swept her back, swelling round her neck. She shook with cold so terrible she could no longer feel her feet or legs or torso. The women screamed around her. And the water continued to rise.

Joshua reached the bottom of the tunnel and lowered himself onto a ledge into a foot of water. The women he'd passed nearest the top of the tunnel had told him to turn right and follow tight against the wall to the open door. But it was so dark. Though he'd been told that more women climbed, he'd not passed another in the tunnel for several minutes, if he was able to gauge the time.

He squinted. At last his eyes made out a pale light far ahead.

A motor, that of a boat, gunned and roared to life from somewhere beyond the bend, far to his left.

Dear God, don't let them have taken Maureen! Help me find her here— before it's too late!

He repeated the prayer as he groped his way forward, gasping in, gasping out. Twice he slipped into the freezing water, clutched at the cliff again, hoisted himself onto the ledge.

"Maureen! Maureen!" he called until he was hoarse, until he scrambled over sandbags two feet below the water and reached the flooding gateway, the open door the fleeing women had described.

Dozens of cages crowded the cave-like room that was nothing but a cesspool filled with rags and debris sloshing back and forth on the captured tide. He strained to see, to understand the horror before him—some cages with faces upturned in terror, gasping for last breaths before being covered in water. Other faces, bodies, floating dead just beneath the surface, illuminated by wall lanterns that would soon be doused. "Maureen?" he whispered. He couldn't believe, wouldn't believe she was there.

He glimpsed stairs at the far end of the room and prayed that she'd gone back through the tunnel, to the house and higher ground, that he could reach her before she let herself into Belgadt's accursed study. He aimed for the door, praying aloud. "Maureen—please, God. Please!" But hope was failing.

"Joshua?"

He stopped, listened, held his breath.

"Joshua?" the voice, weaker yet, came again.

"Maureen? Maureen, where are you?" He threw iron and rags aside, desperately searching through the morbid sea of cages.

"I'm here! I'm here!" she cried.

He followed her voice until he found her cage, her face upturned, red hair spread in a streaming fan. He grasped the lock, jerked it to no avail, and croaked, "The key!" He grabbed the bars of her cage, shaking it in his impotence.

"Flynn took it. He's gone!"

"The wall—the wall by the door," the woman in the nearest cage cried. "There's another by the door!"

Joshua forced his way back to the door. Lamps extinguished one by one as the water rose to lick their wicks. It was too dim to see, but he ran his hands over the doorposts and lintels, up and down the sides of the door, and then again, a foot from the door. At last he grasped a small brass ring with a single key, but in his hurry it fumbled to the floor.

He drew a breath and plunged into the water. Groping, feeling the edge of the ring, he pulled, but it slipped, catching between the bars at the bottom of an open cage door. He struggled, twisting and turning the key and its ring, found his footing at last, and pulled through the water.

Maureen's nose was barely above the water level when Joshua ducked beneath it, forcing the key into the lock. It jammed. He pulled it out and tried again, turned the key upside down, and pushed yet again. At last it slid into place, the tumblers fell, and he jerked the lock open.

He dragged a sputtering, coughing Maureen from her cage, determined to get her to higher ground before the water rushing through the doorway filled the space and made their passage across the ledge and up the tunnel impossible.

But she fought him. "Help them! Help them!"

"Make for the door!"

"There are women in those cages! Give me the key!"

"It's too late!"

"Give me the key!"

"They're dead, Maureen!"

Maureen pushed against him and stumbled back to the woman's cage beside hers—the woman who'd told them of the second key. But water had risen over the top of the cage, and no face, no fingers, reached up to plead.

Joshua grabbed Maureen round the waist. "She's dead—they're all dead. If we don't go now, we won't get out!"

He pulled her toward him, away from the cage, but she turned and lunged again toward the cage, taking hold of the board atop it. "The plate! Give me the plate!"

With no idea what she meant, Joshua ripped the board she clung to from the woman's cage, pressing it into her hands. He wrapped his arms around her again, pulling her from the flooding, roaring room with barely time or space to pass beneath the lintel, barely time to push her through the surging water to the ledge. Together they slipped, groping their way into and through the steep tunnel, up, into the light.

CHAPTER SIXTY-ONE

MRS. MELKFORD received word by a newsboy messenger:

Meet me at Morningside. Come quickly; Maureen needs you.
                                    Curtis Morrow

She paused only to fill a basket with apples, the carrot muffins she'd just pulled from the oven, and a jar of apple butter—Maureen's favorite—from her pantry.

Though the poorly clad newsboy led her faithfully through the trolley system bearing her burden as he'd been hired to do, he spoke not a word. Once they were securely seated on the crowded trolley, he eyed her basket, inhaling deeply. Mrs. Melkford slipped him a muffin and an apple.

The largesse loosened his tongue, but he could not tell what he did not know. "All I know," he confided, "is what I seen down near the station—and that's a lady, all a-muck, laid out on a stretcher like she was near dead. They was soaked, her and the gent with her, what was shaking in his boots for the cold. But the man that hired me was all right—dry and scrubbed. Bit of a dandy, if you ask me. Still, I'm not one to bite the hand that feeds me." And he gave her basket another longing gaze.

She waited for more information.

"And he seemed right worried for the lady," the boy added feebly, his eyes hopeful.

Mrs. Melkford passed the boy a second apple.

He grinned. "Couldn't really tell if she's gonna keep ole Scratch away. Might be a close shave yet."

Mrs. Melkford sat back against her trolley seat and closed her eyes, praying through her fears, praying for Maureen, for Joshua, for Curtis, for whatever had happened now.

Maureen could not open her eyes, but she could distinguish voices, and the first she heard was Mrs. Melkford's.

"Bring her to me," Mrs. Melkford urged. "I love her as a daughter. I can't take in all those poor girls, but I can take in Maureen."

But Curtis disagreed. "It's not safe, not for you and not for her. We've separated the other women into small groups, all in undisclosed locations, and will keep them guarded until after the trial. At least that gives them a chance to recover before we look for their families."

"Guarded? But they're not prisoners, Mr. Morrow! They need care and a bit of mothering."

"I understand, and I agree—completely. Mr. and Mrs. Bramwell took the lot of them in right away—hot breakfast, dried them by their fire . . . They offered to keep a few for recovery there, too, but we just can't risk it—for their sakes or for the women. Belgadt and Drake have been arrested, but their network is broader than that. You've no idea the people we've enraged—the lengths they'd go to in order to keep Maureen and those women from testifying. No," Curtis argued, "I can post greater security here than I can in your apartment building, and I owe it to Olivia."

Testify? Maureen heard the word, and her mind conjured images of her village in County Meath, of the day she'd spoken against Lord Orthbridge, begging the priest to take her from the English landlord's service, giving him enough lurid details from the secrets of the grand house to disgrace and ruin most men.

But she'd not been pitied, not been taken from Orthbridge Hall and restored to her family. She'd been accused and condemned by priest and villagers as a harlot, a shame upon her family and church and community. Far from bringing Lord Orthbridge to account, they'd twisted her testimony and cast her out of the church as a leper, a pariah no parishioner would touch.

Testify? Never again.

And she did not open her eyes.

356

ONCE THE POLICE had gone, once Maureen was settled and Mrs. Melkford with her, once Joshua had been placed in Grayson's capable hands for a hot bath and dry clothing, Olivia showed Curtis to her drawing room and indicated a place on the settee nearest the fire. She took a chair across from him. "Of course Maureen can stay for as long as she needs, as long as she wants. I've told you both that before."

"Mrs. Melkford's determined to stay and oversee her nursing. I'm afraid you'll have two of them."

"Mrs. Melkford is always welcome," Olivia assured him. But she couldn't stop the words that flowed from her heart to her lips, could not keep the edge from her voice. "What I don't understand is why you couldn't trust me, why you didn't tell me what the three of you were doing."

"I couldn't put you at risk—" he leaned toward her—"and I couldn't risk you confiding in Dorothy. Drake was my only link—my main suspect. I knew the position that would have put you in. I'd have done anything to protect my sister and her heart. I knew you would do the same for Dorothy."

She bristled. "You thought deceiving me, using me as part of your ruse to foster Drake's trust, was better?"

Curtis flushed and lowered his gaze, taking a sudden apparent interest in the carpet between his feet. "I've done a lot of stupid things, Olivia." He looked up. "Not trusting you with the full story may have been the stupidest of all. I'm sorry. Truly sorry."

"You've no idea how willing I would have been to help you bring Drake Meitland to justice, how glad I am that he's locked up." She swallowed to regain her composure. "But you used me. And I have to know . . ."

He looked eager to answer.

"Was it all a pretense? Everything?"

"Of course not!" Curtis looked dumbfounded, even wounded. "Let me explain about Lydia, and then I know you'll understand."

"The woman the police said Drake had married?"

"Yes—as hard as the truth is, thanks to the ledgers Maureen found, I at least know what happened to her." Curtis's jaw tightened. "Lydia was everything to me, to my family."

"You loved her?"

He looked offended. "With all my heart. She's the reason I've done all I've done. If any sort of redemption can be brought to her death by bringing Drake and his low-life cohorts to trial, then—God be praised—it was worth it."

"And now you love Maureen?"

"Well," he floundered, "I care very much for her, certainly."

"In the way you loved Lydia?"

Curtis looked more confused. "I suppose . . . similarly. I hadn't thought about it like that." He blinked. "I certainly feel responsible for all she's been through and will do whatever it takes to make certain she's well and cared for."

"And loved."

"She's already loved." He smiled, clearly on more confident ground. "I don't think there's any question about that."

She couldn't sit any longer but rose and walked to the window. *How could I have been such a fool? How could I have so misunderstood his words, his actions? Or did he use me in that, too—play me for the fool?* She pulled back the drapery as though intent on the avenue before her. But it was no use. *I hate that I love you, Curtis Morrow. Would that I didn't—and more that I never did!*

She closed her eyes. *Is this what You want of me, Lord? To be a sister to Maureen and Curtis—the sister Father intended I be to Morgan O'Reilly's children? I thought . . . I'd hoped . . . I'd hoped so much. Oh,* she all but groaned, *if this is what You want, You must help me, Lord. I can't do this alone.*

At last she cleared her throat. "Of course, you're welcome to visit Maureen anytime. But I must ask you to go now."

He stood immediately and walked to her side. "Must you?"

Why does he sound so puzzled, so hurt?

"I'm afraid so." She clutched the drapery with her fist as if it would provide a lifeline against her own drowning. "You will show yourself out, please."

"Olivia?" He touched her arm.

His presence was enough, but the touch of his hand completely undid her. *I will not cry. I will not cry!* "Please go, Mr. Morrow."

"Olivia, I'm so very sorry that I didn't confide in you. It was not only stupid of me, it was wrong. I regret it in every way. I'd hoped we—"

But she could hear no more and ran from the room.

———————— ❧ ————————

Floating in and out of consciousness, Maureen's body became a ship gliding westward, racing the sun. The fiery ball danced ahead, just out of reach, dappling its light upon the water. She pushed on, splintering waves, casting a foaming wake behind. But the globe ran faster yet, spreading its sparkling highway across the sea until it poured, a liquid gold, into the waves.

She closed the distance. Beneath the water the ball was no longer golden but black. A swirling, whirling tunnel, an underground cellar, lined with rusted, water-filled cages. Fingers clawed through the cages' topmost bars. Long tresses floated, streaming in stark manes, encircling the beautiful, terror-filled faces of women.

And then Maureen was no longer a ship, but one of hundreds of women swimming, swimming against the tide with brass keys wrapped round their necks.

She struggled to lift her key to unlock cage doors, but the keys were too big and the locks too small. All the while the water continued to rise, to her chin, to her nose, to her eyes, until she could not breathe, could not see, could hear nothing but the roaring of the tide.

At last, a voice—the still, small, insistent voice she'd come to know—mingled with Mrs. Melkford's soft, melodic reading, pushing back the roar. Through the depths, the voice became clearer, until the roar subsided and all she heard, all she saw, was light.

"'Save me, O God; for the waters are come in unto my soul. I sink in deep mire, where is no standing: I am come into deep waters, where the floods overflow me. I am weary of my crying: my throat is dried: mine eyes fail while I wait for my God.'"

Yes, that's how I feel. I'm weary of cryin'. I can't stand on my own, and these waters, these troubles, are too deep for me.

"'They that would destroy me, being mine enemies wrongfully, are mighty: then I restored that which I took not away.'"

Yes, they are powerful, these enemies. I tried to help the women they'd stolen. I tried to restore them—but I failed. I wasn't fast enough, strong enough. Oh, God! I don't even know their names!

"'O God, thou knowest my foolishness; and my sins are not hid from thee. . . .'"

Nothin' is hidden from You. You've seen everything I've ever done or let be done. It's that knowin' that keeps me from You, makes me hide in my shame.

"'I am become a stranger to my brethren, and an alien unto my mother's children.'"

Katie Rose has disowned me. I wanted to help her, to save her from my hell. I thought by savin' her and the other women, I could make her love me, make You love me. But I've failed in that, too.

"'But as for me, my prayer is unto thee, O Lord. . . . O God, in the multitude of thy mercy hear me, in the truth of thy salvation. . . . Let me not sink. . . . Let not the waterflood overflow me, neither let the deep swallow me up.'"

I've no one to turn to but You, Lord. Have mercy on me! Forgive me . . . help me!

"'Hear me, O Lord; for thy lovingkindness is good: turn unto me according to the multitude of thy tender mercies. . . . Draw nigh unto my soul, and redeem it. . . . I looked for some to take pity, but there was none; and for comforters, but I found none.'"

But You saved me when all my enemies would see me dead, when even my family turned their backs. You sent Joshua and Curtis and Mrs. Melkford and Olivia—and the voice, my Comfort.

"'I will praise the name of God with a song, and will magnify him with thanksgiving. . . . For the Lord heareth the poor, and despiseth not his prisoners. Let the heaven and earth praise him, the seas, and every thing that moveth therein.'"

You heard me in my deepest sorrows when I was poor, in my desperation, locked as a prisoner in a cage, and drownin'. You saved me.

A single tear trickled from the corner of Maureen's eye, down her cheek, and onto her neck. *Could it be that You love me, Lord? Could it be that You've saved me, no matter that I've failed to save the others?*

Mrs. Melkford did not leave her patient's side for five long days. Spoonful by spoonful, she slipped hearty broth through her patient's half-open lips, urging her to swallow, no matter that she'd not opened her eyes. Mrs. Melkford was not deterred. She read aloud to Maureen—the whole of Psalms and every chapter and verse she knew that expounded the Lord's forgiveness for those who seek Him, His all-encompassing love and mercy.

By the time Maureen opened her eyes, her face was awash in tears—tears Mrs. Melkford counted precious, tears she knew the Lord gathered in a bottle.

CHAPTER SIXTY-THREE

EACH TIME MAUREEN heard a footfall outside her door, her heart rose. But when the door opened, revealing solicitous visitors bearing gifts, she pasted a grateful and welcoming smile across her mouth as her heart quietly fell, for not once was the visitor her own sister.

She'd been told that Katie Rose had been moved to Dorothy's home, that they'd not told her the entire story because it was crucial that no more details be leaked to the press or the defense before the case went to trial. Now that Drake was safely locked away, Curtis thought those ladies safe, though he'd posted guards at every door. Olivia assured Maureen that Katie Rose was the perfect companion for Dorothy. By not knowing all that had happened to Maureen, Katie Rose could continue to go to work and lead a more normal life. Once the trial was over, she could be told everything.

Maureen tried to understand, mustered the bravest face she could, but knew that they were all shielding her from the fact that Katie Rose had also refused to see her.

By the middle of the second week, Maureen was sitting up and feeding herself. Though she felt perfectly capable of walking and resuming minor activities, the daily visiting physician, Mrs. Melkford, Curtis, Olivia, and Joshua all insisted that she remain confined to bed and chair rest.

By the third week she felt more a prisoner than a guest. When the five—Olivia, Mrs. Melkford, Curtis, Joshua, and she—met over dinner in Olivia's dining room to discuss the coming trial, Maureen demanded her freedom.

"Aren't you comfortable?" Curtis asked—too innocently, Maureen was certain. "I'm sure Olivia will provide more novels if you like." They all looked to Olivia, who nodded helpfully, before Curtis went on, "Perhaps Mrs. Melkford could come more often."

"Certainly, if you—"

But Maureen cut Mrs. Melkford off. "I want to go back to work." She spoke slowly and plainly as if Curtis had a hearing problem. "I'm perfectly well. You promised me a job—a respectable job—and I want to get on with it. I hold you to our agreement, Mr. Morrow."

"We'd best tell her," Joshua said quietly.

"Just another week of rest," Curtis insisted.

"Tell me what?" Maureen straightened, taking in the glare Curtis directed toward Joshua.

But Joshua ignored him and took Maureen's hand. She tried to pull away, but he held tight as he said, "There have been threats."

"Threats?"

Curtis assured her, "We've men stationed at every door and on every floor, in the yard, and in the street. Belgadt's ogres don't stand a chance of getting past my men. They're trained security, to a man."

Maureen remembered a new face in the hallway but had thought nothing of it. "But why? Why do I matter to them now?"

"They fear your testimony."

"I've already told you, I'll not testify. Besides, you said you found the ledgers and the pages I hid. You have enough evidence without me."

But she saw the momentary hesitation between the two men.

"You did find the ledgers after the police raid?"

"Exactly where you said they'd be," Joshua reassured her.

"Well then?" She glanced back and forth between the four before her but was conscious that Olivia looked away. "You said if we found those ledgers, it would be more than enough to hang them."

Curtis sighed. "The ledgers irrefutably link Belgadt and Drake to Darcy's Department Store. It's clear they used the store as a front, and a number of employees and well-connected men have already been arrested. But so much of what we're able to make stick depends on the judge." He threw his napkin to the table. "Whose payroll he's on or how or if he's linked to Belgadt. The man is even better connected than I'd thought."

"It seems so impossible." Mrs. Melkford shook her head. "The idea that those reprobates might not be held accountable for the crimes they've committed, that they might be freed to go back to committing such horrors against other women and children—it's unthinkable!"

"Surely that won't happen." Olivia laid her hand over Mrs. Melkford's.

Curtis shrugged. "It's happened before." He leaned toward Maureen. "That's why your testimony—everything we can possibly throw at them—is vital."

Maureen sat back, conscious that her hand remained in Joshua's.

"I won't lie to you. They'll likely tear you apart on the witness stand."

Maureen stiffened. It was what she'd dreaded, what she'd feared. "How do you mean?"

"They'll try to make you out as one of Drake's girls who's eaten sour grapes because you didn't get the money you wanted or the customers you wanted. They may say you're an immigrant who came here for purposes of prostitution. They'll use Jaime Flynn's testimony against you—say you took money from him for services rendered."

The knot twisted in Maureen's stomach.

"They'll say you went willingly to the address he gave you, knowing it was a front for prostitution." Curtis sat back. "They'll surely bring up the theft you were accused of at Darcy's and the letter of reference you forged. They'll have the personnel manager and floor supervisor from Darcy's testify against you."

Maureen could not keep at bay the ring of heat spreading round her neck. "If you know this, why do you want me to testify?" *Why would you put me through such public shame?*

"Because you were an eyewitness—the only eyewitness to every phase of Darcy's and Belgadt's operation," Curtis urged. "From Jaime Flynn at Ellis Island directing homeless girls and women to Darcy's prostitution ring, to his and Drake's kidnapping women from the store, women you knew! You even witnessed the involvement of the cop—what's his name?—Flannery, on the corner! You saw firsthand what went on at Belgadt's, the extent of the ring of trafficking connections. You found the ledgers, the tunnel, the women imprisoned in cages. You saw it all—nearly every step of their operation. You can expose them in a way no one else can."

"But you said they'll discredit me no matter what I say. Isn't Alice's testimony enough? She knows as much about Darcy's as I—perhaps more!"

"Your testimony will verify the partial testimonies of Alice and others. The judge and jury can't ignore every witness, and yours ties them all together." Curtis let out a long sigh, a deflated balloon. "If we don't stop Belgadt and Meitland and the heads of the rings connected with them, if we don't stop the Darcy's front for prostitution, then they'll do it again and again and again—if not at Darcy's, then the same operation under another name in another location. No woman, no child, is exempt from their exploitation—immigrants or American born."

"Like Lydia," Maureen said, recognizing the pain in Curtis's eyes. "Joshua told me."

"Like Lydia," Curtis replied, his voice breaking momentarily. "Or Dorothy—" he glanced at Olivia—"or Katie Rose."

"Or Katie Rose," Maureen repeated. *Will she ever speak to me again? If I do this, if I bring the shame of this public trial—this spectacle—upon us, will she disown me altogether? Would that be different from the way things stand now? Should that even matter when so much is at stake?*

Maureen didn't realize she'd been staring at Olivia as she pondered. But when she blinked, returning to the moment, the pain in Olivia's eyes sparked a bond between them. "What about Katie Rose and Dorothy—are they in danger?"

Curtis shook his head. "I told you I've posted men at Meitland House, and Drake's facing a string of charges a mile long all on his own. He'll be locked away for years. As for Alice and the women freed, they're under protection until they testify and are probably safer away from you."

Maureen knew that should be a comfort. She rubbed her temples, trying to think, to sort it through.

She remembered the woman who'd saved her—the woman who'd told Joshua of the key. The woman neither she nor Joshua had been able to save. *Too late! When did she realize he couldn't save us both? But her cry helped Joshua save me. Her cry saved my life.*

Maureen closed her eyes. She remembered the board attached to the cage, number 37, the board she'd struggled to save when she could not save the woman. Testifying would not help that woman now. Testifying would mean public humiliation, possibly deportation if they twisted her words and deemed that she'd entered the country as a prostitute. But perhaps her voice could save others like her who just wanted a chance at life. This was what the insistent voice that lived inside her would do. She knew. No matter that she didn't want to do it.

She drew a long breath. "Yes. For Lydia and Dorothy, for Katie Rose." Her voice broke. "For number 37."

Joshua squeezed her hand and pressed her fingers to his lips. Maureen opened her eyes and was warmed by the love and pride shining in Joshua's. Refreshment flowed through her veins. She felt herself blush at Olivia's openmouthed gape and the young woman's glance of urgency between Joshua and Curtis.

"For our sisters." Curtis raised his coffee cup in a toast.

"For all our sisters." The toast rounded the table, though Maureen noted that Olivia's cup barely left its saucer and that she barely sipped.

Olivia swallowed. *This is surreal. Curtis and Maureen toast with camaraderie and respect, but neither evidence the love she proclaimed for him—the love he considered he has for her.*

Olivia rubbed her temples. The tension of hosting the woman Curtis loved was bearable, until they were all present in one room. *How will I do this for a lifetime?*

Before Joshua left for the evening, he promised Maureen that he would check on Katie Rose. *As if he reads her mind . . . How is it that she so commands the attention of two fine men? Oh, dear Father—I'm not jealous of any attention she gives or receives from Joshua. But . . .*

But then she saw him lean down and heard him whisper in the other woman's ear, "Katie Rose'll come round. There comes a time we each must stake our claim in life and do with it what we will, what we know God wills for us. Everything else follows."

Olivia bit her lip. *Such good advice! Help me take that advice, Lord.*

Joshua embraced Maureen lightly. Olivia felt herself stiffen. *Surely there's nothing improper in that—not after all they've been through together—but still . . .*

Olivia glanced at Curtis, trying to judge his reaction. And in that moment Curtis looked up, not even mildly affronted by Joshua's advances toward Maureen but miserable just the same. *At me! He looks miserably at me!* Olivia thought her throbbing temples might burst. She felt herself scowl at Maureen. *He might not love me, but he certainly deserves better than those glances Maureen throws Joshua's way!*

Mrs. Melkford left soon after. The sudden awkward silence between the remaining three lay thick.

"I should be going." Curtis rose. He took Maureen's hand respectfully. "I'll send my attorney round tomorrow. He'll do a preliminary interview with you, and then I'm sure we'll all be working on the case together. I know this will not be easy, but I thank you from the bottom of my heart. My parents will thank you."

"You've told them?"

"Some. Not everything. It would be too painful for them to know the details. But they know she's dead and that they mustn't search anymore. They must let go now. Thanks to what we've all done, what we've learned, they can."

He glanced at Olivia but did not step nearer. "Drake as good as murdered Lydia. I hope Dorothy understands that she's well rid of the man."

Olivia drew in her breath. "It's been a shock, of course. But she had some inkling that he was not what he said. I think she realizes he was using her, misusing her. She just didn't want to believe it. And then to learn that he was already married—still married—when they stood in church for their wedding . . ." Olivia hesitated; she didn't know if she truly wanted to tell Curtis, but she could not bear the burden alone any longer. "There's a greater concern. Dorothy's not well. She was not well before Drake left."

Curtis paused, frowned. Olivia saw knowledge, understanding, and alarm cross his face. He started to speak, stopped, and started again. "I don't know how else to say this, but she must see a doctor. Right away."

Olivia shook her head, tears filling her eyes, threatening to spill forward. She did her best to compose herself. "She's being treated."

"Curse the man!" Curtis's fists clenched. Olivia knew it was only the company of women that kept him from smashing the table with his fist. The muscles of his jaw worked in sharp contrast to the pity that filled his eyes. "I'm so sorry. So very sorry . . . If there is anything I can do—anything at all . . ."

But Olivia shrugged helplessly. "I don't know what to do," she whispered as the tears coursed her cheeks. "I don't know . . ."

"The best doctors . . . ," he began.

"Are seeing her now," she finished. "Drake's given my sister a death sentence."

Curtis nodded. "As he did mine."

"Yours?" Olivia felt the blood drain from her face. She glanced, barely comprehending, from Curtis to Maureen and back again. "Lydia . . . was your sister?"

Curtis looked puzzled. "Yes, of course."

"You loved Lydia—as your sister." Olivia felt that scales were falling from her eyes.

"With all my heart," Curtis vowed. "Much as I care for Maureen and Joshua, much as I would give all I have to help Dorothy."

Olivia caught a light of growing understanding in Maureen's eyes, her half smile. Her heart too full to speak, Olivia placed her hand in the one Maureen extended.

Olivia glanced at their clasp of hands in wonder as Maureen pressed her fingers. "I'll be excusin' myself now. I'm tired, and tomorrow promises a full day." Smiling, Maureen slipped quietly from the room.

Olivia knew Maureen had spoken, but she could barely take in her words for staring at Curtis.

Yet no sooner had Maureen closed the dining room door to the hallway than Olivia forced herself to her feet and jerked it open. "Wait, please wait." She pulled the door closed behind her.

Maureen turned. Olivia had not been running, but she couldn't catch her breath, couldn't steady her runaway thoughts, her tied tongue.

But Maureen waited, still smiling.

"I asked once if you love him, if you thought you might love him."

Maureen started, looked taken aback, as if trying to place the memory.

A memory that all but seared my soul! "Before you and Joshua and Curtis left to work together—the night Curtis's note came." Olivia mustered her courage. "You said . . ."

Maureen blinked, the light of understanding rising in her eyes. "Joshua. I thought you meant Joshua."

Olivia clasped her hand to her heart as if holding it there might keep it from bursting through her chest. "Joshua," she said, breathless. "You love Joshua."

Maureen's head tilted ever so slightly. Her shoulders lifted; her smile began with the turning up of the corners of her mouth and radiated, as if from the inside out, until her eyes shone and she glowed with a beauty Olivia had not seen before. Maureen whispered, her voice growing stronger, more certain, with each word, "Yes. Yes, I love Joshua." She bit her lip and squared her shoulders. "And he loves me."

Olivia smiled in return, her tears welling to match Maureen's own. Both women laughed softly, conspiratorially, like sisters.

Maureen clasped Olivia's arms, kissed her cheek. "Go to him. He's waitin'. He's been waitin' for you."

CHAPTER SIXTY-FOUR

FOR THREE WEEKS Maureen, Joshua, Olivia, and Curtis conferred with the prosecuting attorney.

Though white slavery was a topic of frenzy in the news, Maureen was cautioned by Curtis and warned by the prosecutor that the jury and the courtroom, packed by men, might be largely unsympathetic to her cause, might even be connected by various means to the roots of the tangled web.

They coached her to remain calm under fire, to anticipate heckling and harassment, to imagine she had a bull's-eye target posted on her chest—but one that could deflect poison arrows.

The coaching took its toll. But day after day, Joshua reassured her of his belief in her by his gentle encouragement and moral support, of his care for her heart by the tender compassion he showed for the weight of her load, and he shared that load by the quiet strength his nearness imparted. Though Maureen could have basked in the warmth of that sun forever, she dared ask him the thing she knew would test his heart.

One late afternoon, after the attorney had gone, while Curtis and Olivia walked in the winter garden, Maureen asked Joshua about Katie Rose.

"She's still at Dorothy's—safe and sound as a bell, goin' to work at the Triangle day by day, guarded by good men she doesn't even know are there. Nothin' to worry your mind."

"I mean her heart. I need to know her heart."

"Give her time. You know Katie Rose." Joshua shrugged. "She's green with envy over the attention you're gettin'—from Mrs. Melkford, Olivia, from the women of the circle."

"From you?" Maureen asked softly, knowing her sister, knowing the answer.

"Probably." He didn't look at her. "She'll come round. She's got to find a life of her own."

"But what if she doesn't? She's in love with you, you know."

"She's in love with love. I'm the only man she's known, the only man she's been allowed to know. She'll find her own life in time. Let her grow up."

"She'll claim I've stolen you from her."

"And have you?" he asked, smiling, but Maureen saw the urgency of the question in his eyes.

"I don't want to hurt Katie Rose."

"Nor do I. But it's you I love. It's you I've always loved, from the time you were a slip of a girl, from the first day I saw you walk through the fields to Lord Orthbridge's house and into service."

Maureen felt the warmth begin in the too-fast beating of her heart and radiate through her torso and arms. She felt the heat rise, with fearful hope, into her face until her eyes smarted and filled. "How could you love me? Did you not know what Lord Orthbridge—?"

But he pressed two fingers to her lips. "Have I not told you? It's you I've loved and never stopped lovin'—just waitin', hopin' you'd look my way."

Maureen swallowed. *Is love truly like that, then? Does it see only what is good and not the evil? Charity—love—"is kind . . . thinketh no evil . . . is not easily provoked . . . beareth all things, believeth all things, hopeth all things, endureth all things"—isn't that what Mrs. Melkford's Bible says? Is that the way you see me, the way you love me?* She tried to speak, failed, swallowed, and tried to speak again. "You love me." She formed the words and said them aloud, foreign though they were.

"In every way I can." Joshua took her fingers and pulled them to his chest. "But I must ask you now, for it's too long already that I've waited to ask. Do you love me?"

She couldn't catch her breath, couldn't speak.

"I must know now: do you love me, Maureen O'Reilly?"

Tears overflowed their bounds and spilled down her cheeks. The love she'd realized for this man filled every space in her soul, and if she didn't confess it, she knew she would burst—and yet . . .

"Is it that hard to say?" He looked as if she'd shot a poison arrow to his heart, and let go of her fingers.

The unexpected cold—the fear of losing him—that flashed through her chilled her to the bone. "I do love you, Joshua Keeton, with all of my heart, but—" She couldn't finish.

"But?"

"But what about Katie Rose? She'll blame me . . . she'll blame me for—"

"For what? For lovin'? For bein' loved? And if she does? Does that change anythin' between us?"

It was the question Maureen had pondered each night before she fell asleep. It was the question she could not answer. She sighed. "I don't know what will happen after the trial."

"None of us do." He pulled her into his arms.

She leaned her head against his chest. "But what if—?"

"The prosecutor is painting the worst possible picture, just so we'll all be prepared."

But the prosecutor hadn't, and that was what frightened Maureen. Not once had the man addressed the problems she'd face if they deemed her a woman who'd passed through Ellis Island for purposes of prostitution, if they sent her back to Ireland. *There'd be no one to watch over Katie Rose, no one to protect her from the Jaime Flynns prowling the streets of New York.*

She sighed, wishing she could stay there forever. But she left the warmth of his embrace and folded Joshua's hand between her own. "Promise me."

"Anything." He smiled, leaning very near her cheek.

"That you'll stay close to Katie Rose—now, before the trial, and during. Close enough to know she's not desperate, that she's not alone. And no matter what happens, you'll stay in New York. You'll watch over Katie Rose."

Joshua pulled back. "We'll stay. We'll watch over her together."

"Promise me," she insisted.

But he held his ground.

Maureen anticipated Mrs. Melkford's frequent visits. She knew her friend would come every other day, as regularly as clockwork, just as soon as she'd finished her work at the Missionary Aid Society. Though Maureen regretted the toll the sum of events had taken on Mrs. Melkford, there was something entirely healing and loving about the older lady's presence that helped repair the damage the grueling prosecutor had done to Maureen's spirit—something she couldn't imagine doing without.

"It's demoralizing, this pounding against your character!" Mrs. Melkford insisted.

"He's only trying to prepare me for the worst, to harden me."

"He'll not harden your heart. I know you won't allow that." Her friend smiled. "Snowdrops never harden. You have a heart like spring rain, and nothing's going to change that."

"If I do," Maureen laughed, "it's thanks to you."

"It wasn't me," Mrs. Melkford replied.

Maureen smiled in return, knowing she was right. It was the voice that spoke within. It was the quiet affirmation of the Lord's unfailing love for her, His complete forgiveness of all her past and all her present—the things she'd done and let be done, the things she'd failed at and been unable to do.

In the days before the trial, Maureen dug into Mrs. Melkford's Bible, especially the account of her Lord's last week—His betrayal, His arrest, the moment His closest friends deserted or denied Him, His mock trial, His beating, His crucifixion.

"He knew what was coming," she whispered two days before she was to give testimony, "but He did it anyway. He did it for us because we couldn't do it for ourselves." She swallowed her tears. "He did it for me."

Maureen sat a long time that evening, thinking, praying. When morning dawned, so did a resurrection in her heart, born of one nearly two thousand years before.

Before she left for the courthouse to testify, Maureen prayed on her knees for strength. She remembered Jesus in the garden of Gethsemane. She remembered that He'd begged for the cup of suffering to be taken from Him. But when it wasn't, He'd walked forward.

The day passed in a blur. The faces of the courtroom swirled before her—hard faces, leering, condescending, suspicious. But in their midst she recognized Joshua—smiling, encouraging, worried; Olivia—brave, determined; Mrs. Melkford—believing, but slightly more frail than before, constantly moistening her lips for courage; Curtis—the face of an older brother, protective. As she took the stand, she noticed more familiar faces, women from the circle—Agnes, Julia, Carolynn, Hope, Isabella, Miranda—all sitting in the third row. Knowing it was considered nearly scandalous for reputable women to attend a trial, Maureen was taken off guard by their presence.

She remembered in a rush the things Katie Rose had said to her and about her to the circle, things she was certain had singed the ears of those proper ladies. Maureen quailed, sure they'd come to witness and gloat over her downfall.

But a look of fierce determination linked their countenances, encouraging warmth in their expressions, a solidarity in their posture. Maureen knew, in that moment, that she was not alone, would never be entirely alone again, no matter the outcome of the trial. She was embraced by an entire battalion—made up of these she could see and others she could not.

She was asked her name, told to place her hand on a Bible. As she made her vow to tell the truth, the whole truth, she knew that this was exactly what Jesus would do.

CHAPTER SIXTY-FIVE

THE PROSECUTOR and Curtis had rightly anticipated the false witnesses from Darcy's, even the paid false testimony of Officer Flannery. Over the next two days, they ripped Maureen's reputation to shreds, discrediting or reinterpreting everything she said.

But not even the jaded prosecutor had anticipated the damning letter the defense had extracted from her village priest in County Meath, let alone a shaming false dismissal from Lord Orthbridge of Orthbridge Hall, signed and sealed with his signet ring.

The only part of her testimony that appeared to bear weight were the cold, black figures written down in Belgadt's ledgers. Even those the calculating defense minimized, misrepresented, redefined.

Mrs. Melkford broke down on the witness stand when forced to testify to Maureen's early lies. If Maureen regretted anything, it was her actions that led to hurting her dearest friend.

Jeered from the courtroom at the end of the third day, the judge's gavel pounding for order in her ears, Maureen held her head high, squeezed Mrs. Melkford's stooped shoulder as she passed, and walked out into the late afternoon sunshine, free at last.

※

"But for how long?" she asked Joshua as he took her arm to begin the long trek to Morningside from Mrs. Melkford's that evening. "What if they decide to send me back?"

"We're small potatoes to them." Joshua squeezed her hand to his side as they entered Washington Square. "They'd not bother nor wish to bear the scrutiny of the fuss Curtis and Olivia would rouse in this city, let alone your Ladies' Circle." He chuckled. "I do believe those women could move mountains, once they put their voices together for a cause."

She sighed wearily. "Then I'm ever so glad to be small potatoes."

Joshua stopped, and she with him. He turned to her. "You truly don't mind? Wouldn't you rather have the grand life—a life like Curtis is offering Olivia?"

Maureen snorted. "I'd not know what to do with it. It's wearying to think about. I just want a fire and a home and a—" She stopped, blushing.

He guided her to a nearby bench, pulling a small box from his coat pocket. "If being small potatoes is all right with you, Miss O'Reilly, then perhaps you won't mind sharing that fire and home and those small pratties with a Paddy like me."

The soul Joshua poured into Maureen's eyes stole her breath.

He opened the blue velvet box, revealing a ring, a golden band engraved with leaves and rose of Sharon, delicately cut in filigree.

She couldn't speak for the joy set before her. *To think he loves me—Joshua—and heaven, too!*

"I take that unprecedented silence as consent." And he slipped the ring on her finger.

Before God and all of Washington Square, he kissed her. And when she gasped, he kissed her again and again, until she nearly rose off her seat for kissing him back.

When a matron strolled by shaking her head, Maureen pushed him away and straightened her hat.

Joshua laughed out loud.

That was when she saw Katie Rose walking arm in arm with her friends, just off work from the Triangle Waist Factory.

"Isn't that your young man?" one of the girls beside Katie Rose asked loudly. "Is that your sister he's with, the one from the trial?"

Katie Rose paled. The spears of fury she shot toward Maureen found their mark, piercing deep into her heart.

"Katie Rose." Maureen made the first move, but Katie Rose backed away.

"Don't touch me." Katie Rose pulled her friends back the direction they'd come. "I want nothing to do with a liar and a thief."

"Katie Rose!" Joshua started, but Maureen shushed him.

"She's taken you in, Joshua," Katie Rose said, pleading in her voice. "You should read the papers. They're full of the trial, full of her slander and the truth that found her out!"

"Katie Rose, don't," Joshua cautioned.

The girls beside Katie Rose backed up in wide-eyed wonder. But one reached her hand to Katie Rose. "You can't believe everything the rags say. It might not—"

"Shut up, Emma! You don't know her as I do." She turned to Maureen. "All my life you've taken whatever you wanted, whatever *I* wanted. I thought in America things would be different. But you can't change—you won't change! I never want to see you again! Never!"

"But we're sisters," Maureen pleaded.

"I have no sister!" Katie Rose turned on her heel and fled toward the factory. Her friends ducked their heads and followed, but the one called Emma stole a last pitying glance.

CHAPTER SIXTY-SIX

OLIVIA FINISHED READING the account of the trial and the judge's sentencing to the silent Ladies' Circle gathered in the dining room at Morningside. She folded the newspaper and closed it away in the sideboard drawer. A minute passed.

"A slap on the wrist, and that barely," Hope fumed.

"At least they've closed Darcy's," Carolynn said, "and that brothel down on Orchard Street."

"Darcy's was nothing but a front," Julia retorted. "They'll open another before the week's out. It's all big money—enough to hire dishonest lawyers and pay for bribed and false testimony. They must be brought down." She thumped her cup into its saucer.

"And they will be—another day," Isabella said. "But this is a start."

"It doesn't matter what they say," Agnes insisted quietly. "We know the truth. We all know the truth."

"Maureen's taken it very hard." Olivia searched their faces.

"Did you tell her we recognized some of those policemen—the same liars who abused our picket lines for the shirtwaist factories last year? Tammany Hall's payroll—that's what they are!" Julia's voice rose.

"Her heart's broken." Olivia glanced round the room. "But it's only partly the trial and its outcome—the deeper cut is Katie Rose."

Agnes shook her finger. "That girl needs a good—"

"That won't help," Mrs. Melkford intervened, "or I'd have done it."

"Maureen will be down in a moment." Olivia counseled, "Please, everyone, please make this all we can for her. It's the one thing we can do."

Maureen had not wanted to join the circle meeting that afternoon. She'd appreciated the plethora of kind and supportive notes and letters from the women, each expressing sympathy over the harsh words and undermining she'd received on the witness stand and in the papers, assuring her of their love and faith in her, even admiration and thanksgiving for all she'd been brave enough to do.

But they were not Katie Rose, and no matter how much they seemed to want to embrace her, it grated her heart anew that these women would take her in, make her their sister, when her own sister would not.

When Olivia had told her Carolynn's idea for the memorial service, however, she could not refuse. This was something Maureen wanted to do, something she could do that no one could take away or diminish; it was not for her, not of her.

When she walked into the dining room, a collective cheer rose from the women, a standing ovation. Maureen's heart quickened, surprised by how glad she was to see them and how genuinely glad they seemed to be to see her.

"This way." Olivia escorted her to the center of the table.

Maureen gasped. Every leaf had been laid to extend the table the length of the room. A pale damask cloth had been spread, and a line of marble plaques with brass plates had been set, engraved with the numbers from the cages. Into each plaque was chiseled a rose—a delicate, thornless sketch of beauty.

"These will go in an open pavilion, a memorial in the church cemetery. Reverend Peterson has arranged everything," Carolynn whispered. "There will be a pillared flame, kept burning, in their midst."

"We thought it best to include every number because we don't know which belonged to those who escaped," Isabella interjected, "and which to those who didn't. We couldn't omit one—not one."

"Nor could I." Maureen could not say more but embraced each precious woman by turn.

They prayed for those who'd been saved and for the memory of those who were lost. They read the names of the certain dead aloud, names Curtis had gleaned from the ledgers and confirmed with women who lived. For all the rest they spoke aloud the numbers that had been torn from empty cages, for someone, surely on Belgadt's payroll, had stolen the bodies before the police had searched the cavern after the storm—a cruelty Maureen found hard to let go.

As they were about to light the first candle and set stones of remembrance, Dorothy entered through the hallway, worn looking and flushed.

"I'm sorry to be late—so sorry to interrupt, but I had to come. I couldn't miss this. I just couldn't . . . get myself ready in time."

Olivia wrapped an arm around her frail sister and escorted her into the room. "You came. That's all that matters."

But Dorothy pulled herself from her sister's arms and walked to Maureen. "I'm so sorry I ever doubted you. I'm so sorry I for one moment did not make you welcome in my home. Forgive me, please."

Maureen reached out, and Dorothy clung to her. Still, Maureen had to ask, for she had so hoped her own sister would have come. "Katie Rose?"

"She's working today, and Joshua's meeting her—something about a surprise." Dorothy glanced round the room. "I'd hoped they might be coming here."

"Joshua?" Maureen could not imagine.

"She's not with me." Joshua stood suddenly in the doorway, a bouquet in hand. He walked to Maureen, handing her the flowers. "My plans are to honor my fiancée and help carry these plaques and stones to the cemetery. Curtis will be here to help any minute."

"There must be some mistake, then," Olivia said.

"No," Dorothy insisted. "Katie Rose was nearly beside herself with anticipation—she even bought a new hat and waist." She concentrated on Joshua. "She said she'd received a note—from you—saying you couldn't wait to meet her by the Garibaldi statue in Washington Square. The note said that she should give notice at the Triangle—that you had plans for a wonderful life together." She looked confusedly to Maureen, then back to Joshua. "I thought it strange and forward because I thought the two of you . . . I mean, I thought . . . I was surprised, but Katie Rose said it meant that at last you must have realized who loves you best. I tried to slow her down, but you know Katie Rose." Dorothy paled further, held her hands out to Maureen. "I knew you all trusted Joshua, so I . . ." She couldn't finish.

"Who would do such a thing?" Olivia stammered.

Maureen felt the color drain from her face. "Jaime Flynn. He boasted once that he could take Katie Rose anytime he wanted. It's the sort of thing he might do—in retaliation."

"Thank the Lord he's in prison!" Miranda said.

"He's not. He was released yesterday with a paltry fine and a slap on the wrist," Joshua countered.

Maureen reached for his arm.

But Joshua dropped the flowers to the table and charged out the door, yelling behind him, "Get Curtis! Meet me in Washington Square!"

"Grayson!" Olivia called. "Have the car brought round! Dorothy—telephone Curtis; tell him to meet us in the square!"

But Maureen could not wait. She grabbed her coat and took off after Joshua on foot. In no time Olivia matched her pace. The two women raced through Gramercy Park toward Fifth Avenue until Ralph appeared behind them, laboring on the automobile horn. They picked up Joshua, already five blocks ahead. In minutes they reached East Ninth, only to find their way slowed to a crawl by abandoned horses and carriages, poorly parked automobiles, and pedestrians clogging the streets, all pointing and swarming toward Washington Square.

Joshua stepped from the car; Maureen and Olivia crowded behind. Sirens, shrill whistle blasts, and a relentless clanging of bells could be heard in the distance over the mayhem.

Joshua pulled a boy of ten or eleven aside from the surging tide. "What is it?"

"The Triangle—she's burning!" The boy jerked away, rushing ahead.

Maureen's heart plummeted to her feet. She pushed past Joshua and joined the throng, running, weaving her way toward her sister's place of employment. *Please, God! Not Katie Rose! Not Katie Rose!*

But Joshua grabbed her hand, pulling her from the crowd, and led her through the back alley of Washington Mews, across University Place to Greene Street, skirting Washington Square.

They'd nearly reached the Asch Building, could see the plume of smoke billowing above the roof, when another horse-drawn fire wagon, this one from the Lower East Side, broke through the crowd. As it clattered to a stop, its firemen hit the ground, connecting hoses and raising ladders. But the ladders, fully extended to the sixth floor, couldn't reach the enflamed windows.

Maureen tucked herself behind Joshua, who shouldered his way through the crowd, pushing toward the burning building. Just as they hoped to break through the lines, they were stopped short by a row of policemen who, with clubs drawn, pushed back the frantic masses. Joshua pulled her round the block until they crowded with onlookers diagonal from the burning building.

"They're jumping—get back. Get back!" the policeman before them yelled.

Maureen screamed for her sister and screamed again. But her cries were nothing in the wails and keening of the watchers. Flames licked the spring air, dancing through open windows of the top three floors, eight, nine, and ten stories high. Women shrouded in smoke appeared on the roof, too near the edge, where flames torched the edges of cornices.

From the corner of her eye Maureen saw a dark bundle plummet, as if fabric had been thrown from a window. It hit the ground with an unnatural thud. She couldn't make out what it was, but Joshua pulled her head to his shoulder. Maureen jerked away.

And then they came. Girls, women, even a boy stepped through windows draped in smoke, backlit by flames. One by one, feet gripping the ledge, they stepped gingerly along the narrow precipice.

Firemen spread their nets below. A girl jumped, and they tipped her out. She took a few steps and collapsed. Two jumped together, breaking the net—as though it were paper being ripped.

No matter that the nets could not—did not—hold, they stepped into the air, dropping to the ground, one by one or two by two, arms linked, hands clasped. One young woman stretched her hands toward the early spring air, another toward heaven as if relinquishing her spirit.

The crowd surged forward again, screaming, "Don't jump! Don't jump! Wait!"

But the Triangle Waist Factory workers jumped anyway, some crashing through the sidewalk skylight to the basement below, their clothes and hair in flames. Some stepped into the windows, prepared to jump, then changed their minds, stepped back, and surrendered to the inferno.

A young man, a perfect gentleman, helped young women through the window and into space as if handing them into a carriage. Last came the woman he loved, or so Maureen believed, for they embraced and kissed before he let her fall. And then he joined her.

The last girl Maureen watched did not fall far—grabbed as she was by a steel hook protruding from the sixth floor, caught by the fabric of her dress, hanging like a rag doll in midair.

If only she can wait until the ladders reach her! They can reach that high!

But in moments her dress burned, and the weight of her body propelled her to the stone walk below.

The fire was fierce, and the firemen fierce and brave. It was over in minutes. But for Maureen it was an eternity; she could not move.

Joshua gently shook her, pinched her arm. "Take hold. We don't know anythin' yet."

But she couldn't speak.

An hour passed. The police wouldn't let them near enough to view the bodies, to identify loved ones, but Maureen knew in her soul that Katie Rose was not among the corpses lining the street, that she couldn't be.

Darkness crept in. A gentle breeze drove the worst of the smoke away. Makeshift lights rigged inside the building burned unnaturally bright and eerie through empty windows where the fire had been contained, exposing their caverns. Firefighters rigged block-and-tackle sets outside the building.

"They'll be lowering the corpses soon," an onlooker said.

Joshua pulled Maureen through the crowd. She followed, stumbling, tripping on the walk, on her own feet. He slowed, wrapped his arm around her, and helped her cross the street into the faintly lit square.

"She might not have been in the buildin' if she met someone in the square. And if she was, she might have gotten out in time. Let me take you home. If Dorothy's not heard from her, I'll come back. I'll stay till they let me check each one. I swear it."

Maureen gritted her teeth, determined to stop their chatter. "I won't leave until we find her."

Joshua tried to embrace her, but she pulled back, stumbling into a young woman behind who cried out in anguish.

"I'm sorry." Maureen turned to the girl, whose clothing reeked of smoke. "I'm so sorry. Did I hurt you?"

The girl, shivering, seemed about to cry, couldn't seem to speak. Her face was streaked with soot and her hair fallen down and singed, her hands and one arm wrapped in bandages, yet she looked vaguely familiar.

"Katie Rose—you were with Katie Rose in the square last week, weren't you?"

The girl stopped, appeared to try to focus on Maureen's face, and nodded, her smoke-reddened eyes filling with tears.

"Did she get out? Did Katie Rose get out?" Maureen would have shaken the girl if it would have made her speak faster.

But the girl shook her head slowly, wearily. "I . . . .I don't know. I don't . . . I don't think so."

"Oh, dear God!" Maureen cried.

"When did you see her last?" Joshua urged.

The girl shook her head yet again as if trying to remember. "She went out with Emma—at noon—to meet someone." She looked at Joshua, clearly confused. "I thought she said you—" She stopped. "They came back, but late, and the supervisor . . ."

"The supervisor what?"

"The supervisor separated them from the other girls—gave their machines to new girls, said he would dock their pay and they were lucky to have jobs at all. He sent them somewhere—upstairs, to snip threads with the nursery girls. I don't know where, but I didn't see them with the others when we came out." The girl's eyes filled. "I'm sorry. I'm so sorry." She swayed. "I've got to go home."

Stepping back, Maureen let her go. "We can't let them take the bodies away without knowin'. We can't—"

Joshua took her arm and led her toward the building. By that time the bodies were being gently lowered by davits, forlorn bundles followed by searchlights, and pushed carefully, one by one, by policemen, away from the building. Each time a body was lowered, Maureen pressed as near as she could, praying that by some telltale sign she would know it was not Katie Rose.

Though Maureen begged to be allowed closer, and Joshua implored, the police told them they had to do their best to identify the bodies, record the details, and tag them before they could be released to families.

"Go on home now, miss. It's after ten and we'll not be done for another hour or more. Come down to the pier in the mornin'. We'll have them laid out proper enough. You can look for your sister then."

It was only when they knew the policeman would not relent that Joshua guided Maureen back through Washington Square. Somewhere a clock bonged eleven. They'd not quite reached the Garibaldi statue when Olivia and Curtis, Carolynn, Hope, Julia, and Agnes met them, enfolding Maureen in their arms.

"Come, dear," Olivia whispered. "Ralph has the car waiting; we'll go home."

"We couldn't find her," Maureen muttered, closing her eyes.

"Take her home," Joshua whispered. "I'm goin' to stay."

"Joshua?" Maureen clutched his coat sleeve, needing him beside her.

"They're bound to need help gettin' the bodies to their makeshift morgue. It's somethin' I can do to help, and I can look for her at the same time."

Maureen swallowed and, nodding, let him go.

"I'll come with you," Curtis said, but he squeezed Olivia's arm. "You'll be all right?"

Olivia nodded too.

The cluster of women formed a shield around Maureen against the milling crowd. The night breeze picked up as they walked her through the square toward Washington Arch, forging a path between men and women, boys and girls wandering, anxious, numb, dazed, still searching for their own loved ones.

They'd just passed the last wooded area of the park within the square when Maureen heard what sounded like a whimpered chanting, over and over. "I'm sorry. I'm so sorry, so sorry."

Maureen stopped and listened. She couldn't tell the direction of the sound, but it seemed to have come from the darkness to her right.

"Forgive me, forgive me. God, forgive me. I'm sorry, so sorry." The muffled voice came again.

Maureen pulled away from Olivia. She pushed through her human shield and followed the voice down a small side path, out of the light of the streetlamp. She stopped and listened again.

No words, but heartbreaking sobs, half-choked, came from somewhere beyond the shrubbery.

"Who's there?" Maureen dared not voice her hope. She crept forward.

"What is it, Maureen?" Olivia asked.

But Maureen motioned for silence and strained to listen, strained to separate the whimpering pleas from the drone of hundreds. The crying stopped. She stepped deeper into the shadows. "Katie Rose?" she whispered, then more loudly, "Katie Rose? Is that you?"

Nothing.

"Maureen, no one's there." Julia wrapped her arm around Maureen, pulling her back to the path. "Come, let's go home. We'll search in the morning."

Maureen pushed her away and waited, but no sound came from the darkness. She buried her face in her hands and sobbed until she thought her heart would break—five minutes, ten . . . a hundred years—until Olivia folded her in her arms and led her away.

They'd reached the lit path at last, were nearly to the arch, when a voice behind them softly pleaded, "Maureen."

Maureen turned, and there, in the half-light and shadows, stood Katie Rose, barely more than an apparition. Her face streaked in black soot and tears, her eyebrows singed, her hair burned on one side and torn from its bun, her skirt and waist blackened and half-burned away, wearing one shoe and no coat.

"Katie Rose!" Maureen gasped and took a step, stumbling forward, picked herself up, and stumbled again.

But Katie Rose ran, limping, to meet her, falling into her sister's arms.

"Katie Rose!" Maureen cried. "Katie Rose! Thank You, God! Thank You!"

Maureen cradled her sister's head to her chest, kissing its crown again and again, wrapping her tight in her arms, fearful to breathe lest she disappear.

Katie Rose clung back, surrounded by women who loved her.

❧ CHAPTER SIXTY-SEVEN ❧

IN THE DAYS FOLLOWING the fire, Maureen and Katie Rose, with thousands of New Yorkers, attended funeral after funeral, in churches, at gravesides, in the downstairs rooms of tenement houses, sometimes two in an afternoon. Of the 146 dead, Katie Rose knew only a few. But the one she'd known and loved best was Emma.

The newspapers listed no services for her friend, but Katie Rose was not surprised. She leaned her head against the overstuffed chair in Olivia's parlor and lamented to the circle women gathered there, "Her parents don't speak English. How they would even know what to do, I don't know."

"Someone must speak English, or someone must have helped them. They claimed her body," Maureen said quietly.

Katie Rose turned away. "It's not enough."

"No," Maureen replied, reaching for Katie Rose's hand, "it isn't. What do you want to do? I'll help you do it."

Katie Rose let out a small sob and clasped her sister's hand. "I want to tell them I'm sorry. I want to tell them it's my fault that Emma died."

"Katie Rose—"

"If she hadn't gone with me to meet Joshua—I thought it was Joshua, but it was James. But if Emma hadn't gone with me, that man would have taken me. I could never have fought him off alone." Katie Rose swallowed her grief, determined to tell the truth at last. "And I knew . . . I knew that's how it must have been for you, with no one to help you . . . I'm so sorry I didn't believe you. I'm so sorry I said all those hateful, spiteful things."

Katie Rose sobbed but pressed on. "Emma was so good to me—she didn't shame me or hate me, even when we lost our machines. She told me to go to you and to Joshua, that you would take me back, that you would love me because we're family, because that's what her family would do."

"She was right."

Katie Rose covered her eyes with her fists. "Because of me, we were late gettin' back to the factory. I tried to tell the supervisor what happened, to explain that it wasn't Emma's fault, but he wouldn't believe me. He said I was cheap and that cheap girls get cheap jobs. He sent us to snip threads—the lowest of the jobs. And when the bell rang to quit, we couldn't get our pay envelopes because we were on the wrong floor."

Maureen knelt beside her, but Katie Rose pushed her sister away. She paced the floor. "Don't you see? That's why we didn't get out in time. That's why we missed the elevator!"

"Why didn't she go to the roof with you?" Julia asked.

"She was afraid to go up. She'd seen Jewish women herded to a roof in her village to burn. She said the firemen would come for her if she waited inside, that they won't let you burn in America. I told her I'd make sure it was safe and come back for her, but I didn't." Katie Rose coughed, choked, burrowed her fists into her stomach.

"You couldn't. You couldn't go back."

"No, but I left her there. Don't you see? The university students ran their ladders to our roof, and we climbed up. They got us out through their buildin'. I got out and I left her there!"

Maureen closed her eyes and saw clearly, just as clearly as she'd seen number 37 floating in the water when Joshua pulled her to safety. For number 37 she could do nothing but inscribe a marker. She didn't even know her name.

But Katie Rose knew Emma's name, knew where she'd lived, knew that her family had lost a daughter and a sister. And lost a paycheck that Maureen knew could mean the difference between eating and not eating, between having a place to sleep and having no place, between selling your labor and selling yourself.

The next day the sisters went to the Bowery together. They found Emma's street, Emma's apartment in a tenement building. They heard high-pitched keening on the other side of the door and what must have been Emma's father chanting prayers in a language they didn't understand. Maureen placed a hand of support on her sister's shoulder as she knocked on the door.

The keening stopped. The chanting stopped. But no one answered. Katie Rose knocked again and, after a minute, once again.

At last the door opened a hand's breadth, just enough to reveal a pair of reddened eyes in a small woman's lined face.

"My name is Katie Rose, and I'm a friend—"

But the woman's eyes filled. She shook her head and began closing the door.

"Of Emma. Please, I'm a friend of Emma's, from the Triangle!" Katie Rose pushed forward.

But the door clicked firmly into place. A bolt slid behind it. Katie Rose looked helplessly to Maureen.

Maureen knocked again. The keening started up once more, the chanted prayers resumed, but the door did not open.

Maureen cradled Katie Rose's elbow as if to lead her away, but Katie Rose stiffened.

"No," she whispered. "This isn't enough."

Moments passed as the two stood outside the door. Finally Maureen nudged Katie Rose, taking up her purse. She pulled from it the envelope her sister had prepared. A letter, written in English—with the hope that the family knew someone able to translate—explaining Katie Rose's great love for Emma, telling how Emma was her first friend in America, how she'd helped her find her way at the factory, how she had saved her from the kidnapping and likely slavery by an evil man, and how that wondrous gift had led her back to her own sister. A letter recounting the ways Emma loved her own family, loved her faith and the traditions of that faith, how she'd wanted, more than anything, to leave the Triangle and become a shopgirl one day.

Tucked inside was every bit of money Katie Rose had saved since she'd come to America, as well as money Maureen, Joshua, Curtis, and the women in the circle had added to help the family.

"Push it under the door," Maureen urged.

"But I want to tell them . . . I want to tell them how good Emma was," Katie Rose pleaded. "How much I loved her."

Maureen placed a hand on her sister's shoulder. "They know."

On April 5, in a cold spring rain, thousands of outraged and grief-stricken New Yorkers thronged the streets of Manhattan in a massive silent funeral procession for Triangle Waist Factory workers burned beyond recognition—the unidentified victims no one could claim or no one came to claim.

Dorothy, Olivia, and Maureen flanked Katie Rose, marching arm in arm through the downpour. Behind them marched the Ladies' Circle—women who'd picketed with the strikers in life and now mourned them in death.

For five hours the populace of New York marched through the Washington Square Arch behind white horses outfitted in black netting.

Blame for the fire was cast and recast. Workers' rights and workplace safety reforms were demanded by the International Ladies' Garment Workers' Union, by politicians eager to step on a new bandwagon, and by an enraged public. But no amount of investigation, blame, accountability, or even reforms could bring the Triangle workers back to life.

As the tragedy of the fire filled the headlines, the outrage against Victor Belgadt and his cohorts—the owner and management of Darcy's Department Store—and public cries to investigate the ring's connections to Ellis Island were swept from the front pages of newspapers and soon fell out altogether.

"Of course, reforms are desperately needed—better wages, shorter working hours, safer conditions," Agnes pointed out at the circle meeting at Morningside, the Saturday afternoon before Easter Sunday.

"But those reforms won't automatically change the basic face of poverty or the way immigrant women are treated when they first enter this country," Hope insisted. "They might help workingwomen in time, but it's getting those jobs in the first place that concerns me."

It concerned Olivia, too. No matter what they did or how hard they tried, they couldn't change the way others treated women—immigrants or native born. They couldn't make them train or hire women who were not qualified for positions. *We can't even make them hire women who are qualified! And how many can we help?* She rubbed her temples. *Twenty? Fifty?* It was too little for a problem so great.

As though her sister could read her mind, Dorothy whispered in her ear, "Courage, dear. Do you remember Father's literary trio?"

Olivia stared in return, thinking her sister had surely gone mad. *What has that got to do with anything?*

"One for all and all for one?" Dorothy clasped Olivia's fingers within her own and whispered again, "We're not meant to do this alone. We need a greater band of women and men to be the hands and feet of Christ in this fight for abolition of white slavery. So you'd best get started."

Olivia narrowed her eyes in concentration, taking in Dorothy's words and their implications. *"One for all and all for one" . . . That is the point, isn't it? Father knew that. . . . It's the point of the Musketeers and of our growing, inclusive band of women. It's what truly loving one another means.* A flicker of hope marched up her spine. "I understand, but what can I do—?"

Dorothy cut her off. "You can dust off those social justice writing skills you and Father used to revel in and use them to rouse the troops. With Curtis's help, of course. People can't help if they don't know the need. Once they recognize the need and understand what they're capable of doing to help stop this injustice, they'll join the fight—just as we have."

Olivia stared at her sister—the sister whose timid heart had, with Drake's arrest and the revelation of his crimes, not been destroyed but been transformed into the heart of a lioness, despite her failing health.

Olivia's own heart pounded as the idea took hold. *Could I truly write something useful? Something that would glorify God by inspiring a movement for abolition and healing?* She remembered how *In His Steps* had changed her life, her father's life, and the lives of all this band of women. She swallowed, barely able to focus on the faces around her for the unexpected fire surging through her bones. Isaiah's response to the Lord's call rushed through her mind: *"Here am I; send me."* Tears sprang, unbidden, and she knew the Spirit's voice. *Thank You, Lord! Thank You!*

"I still say women who can't speak English are at a terrible disadvantage and a terrible risk," Julia interrupted her thoughts, "whether they're working in the garment industry or wherever they are. Employers can take all kinds of advantage of them."

"So we're back to where we started," Carolynn concluded. "We still need to provide housing and classes, services to help women find better, safer jobs. And we need ways of intertwining our lives with theirs."

"Not entirely back where we started," Isabella insisted. "We've taken into our homes the rescued women who are still looking for families."

"You'll have some of them forever," Agnes said quietly. "You know their families won't all take them back."

"Then I'll have them forever." Isabella bravely smiled. "It's finally a good use of that great house."

How far we've all come!

"I can help at last," Dorothy said.

The women turned. Olivia held her breath, knowing what was coming, knowing what her sister's offer had cost her.

Dorothy smiled tentatively. "I'm donating Meitland House as a home for young women who will train and work as sales clerks."

Women shifted in astonishment.

"I've already talked with Reverend Peterson and one of the members of our church who owns a major department store in the city. He's willing to take the girls in at entry level, with an eye to promotion—as long as they can read and speak English, as long as we prepare them to work with the public, and as long as we guarantee they're living respectably."

"But where will you live? What will your husband say?" Hope asked.

Dorothy drew a deep breath. "It turns out that Drake is not my husband. He was married to Curtis's sister, and she was still living when he fraudulently signed our marriage certificate."

Someone in the group gasped, but Dorothy lifted her shoulders and braved ahead. "Meitland House was Father's wedding gift to me, given and received in good faith. But I don't want to live there anymore. And I've prayed, asking what I should do, what Jesus would do in my situation."

Katie Rose slipped her hand into Dorothy's.

Dorothy clasped it and smiled. "Being on 34th Street will give the women perfect access to the stores on Fifth Avenue—the best stores in the city for employment. Katie Rose and I are going to move back to Morningside with Olivia and Maureen. We can all run it together."

"We're calling it Emma's House." Katie Rose smiled.

One for all and all for one. Olivia shook her head softly and in wonder.

The meeting had not quite finished when Curtis and Joshua arrived, papers in hand, both looking as pleased as cats following a canary lunch.

Agnes whispered, "I've been dragging my feet ten minutes! I thought you'd never get here!"

"Curtis?" Olivia asked. "What is it?"

Curtis grinned and pulled Olivia to her feet. "Wait till you see!" He spread rolls of paper blueprints and official-looking deeds across the dining room table. "Wedding gifts," he proudly announced. "Those tenements on Orchard Street that Drake sold me—the ones I bought to convince him of my interest in his scheme—I've deeded to the church. Close enough to the Battery and the factories to provide easy access for women working on the Lower East Side. One is destined for an employment and living skills training center for immigrant girls and women, and one for housing, to be overseen, of course, by you ladies. I've talked with Reverend Peterson and given notice to the bar owner on the first floor. They'll be available for us to begin renovations by the first week in June."

The room erupted in cheers.

"We're in business!" Julia shouted.

Curtis turned to an astonished Olivia. "Do you like it?"

But Olivia did not seem to know how to respond.

Curtis looked surprised, confused, deflated, and concerned by turn. "Olivia? Say something."

"I—I don't know what to say." She picked at her broach.

Agnes coughed a cough meant for the stage.

The couple turned toward her.

"Did you say 'wedding gifts'?" Agnes asked pointedly. "Do you think you might have put the cart before the horse, Mr. Morrow?"

Joshua smirked and took a seat beside Maureen, lifting her ringed finger to his lips before one and all. Then he raised curious eyebrows toward Curtis, still standing with Olivia in the center of the room.

Curtis's complexion rivaled the bright roses in Olivia's centerpiece. He stammered, stopped, started to speak, and gave it up.

When his eyes found Olivia's, he turned brighter still. It took a moment, but he bowed slightly and respectfully asked, "Miss Wakefield, may I speak with you in the garden?"

Joshua's appreciative chuckle was cut off by Maureen's playful but reproving "Hush now!" But the moment she pushed his fingers away, she reconsidered and tucked hers back into his strong grasp.

Curtis gave Olivia his coat just before they slipped through the French doors.

Members of the circle smiled knowingly at one another, took up their purposeful and animated conversation, and discreetly turned from both blushing couples.

But from the corner of her eye, Maureen sensed more than saw the nearly imperceptible shift in her sister's shoulders. She caught the momentary strain in her forced smile, the too-bright shine and flash of hunger in eyes that followed Olivia and Curtis through the glass doors. She saw Katie Rose blink—almost wince—as the latch clicked behind them, then quietly separate herself from the group of women and creep closer to the glass doors.

Maureen squeezed Joshua's hand, bade him stay, and followed Katie Rose. She stopped just as she realized her sister's mission, watched her lean against the doorframe, saw her spy as Curtis ushered Olivia through the early spring garden. As she stepped closer, Maureen, too, could see Curtis swipe his handkerchief across a low wrought-iron bench and carefully settle Olivia there. Framed by a budding purple and white wisteria, he knelt, taking Olivia's hands in his own.

It was a beautiful but private moment, one that Maureen knew neither she nor Katie Rose should share. She reached out to chide her sister to come away when she saw Katie Rose lick her lips and swallow hard. Something in her younger sister's vulnerability, in her all-consuming fascination with the scene before her, stayed Maureen's hand. She watched Katie Rose's reactions to Curtis's upturned face—a face transformed into light by his love for Olivia. She saw the hunger in Katie Rose as Curtis's lips moved, surely asking the all-important question, and as Olivia's hands cupped her lover's face.

Katie Rose swiped a renegade tear, and Maureen could wait no longer. She stepped closer and wrapped her arm around her sister's waist, drawing her to her side.

"I'm glad for them—I am," Katie Rose stammered.

"And so am I."

"It's just . . . it's just that I want that too. I want someone to . . . And it's what Emma really wanted. But she never had the chance—and what if . . . ?"

Maureen buried her face in her sister's hair, whispering with a kiss, "We're safe now, sweet Katie Rose. We're safe, we're loved, and we've all our lives ahead."

But Katie Rose shuddered, her shoulders trembled, and the tears Maureen knew her younger sister had held back began to fall, a cleansing rain. Maureen held her close, praying silently for her spirit, willing strength into her fragile frame.

At last Katie Rose heaved a sigh, coughed, and breathed more evenly. Maureen kissed her forehead, then pushed damp tendrils from reddened eyes and wiped the face she loved with her handkerchief.

Katie Rose sniffed and drew a nearly clean breath before braving a wobbly smile, replete with the determined brightness Maureen longed to see. "We do." She sniffed again, her arms encircling Maureen at last. "We've all our lives ahead."

Caught suddenly in the fragility and wonder of that truth, Maureen felt her heart and smile swell until both breached their bounds—*We do! Thank You, Jesus!*—and embraced her sister in return.

NOTE TO READERS

I'D PLANNED TO WRITE a historical novel about female immigrants who were hounded in the late 1800s by traffickers lurking near Castle Garden, New York—gateway to the New World—and members of the settlement house movement who came to their aid. I'd planned to include the story of Jacob Riis, his exposé of the extreme poverty found in New York City, and his crusade for change through rousing the social conscience of his time. But while I was busy making plans to tell a story, the Lord shaped a vision to ignite a cause dear to my heart.

I discovered that my agent, Natasha Kern, shared my passion for helping women and children caught in modern-day slavery. I learned that my editor, Stephanie Broene, was fascinated by Ellis Island and the immigrants who'd poured through those doors. And I learned through crusaders and research that today, in this twenty-first century, there are far more people trapped in bondage, more people exploited and enslaved in every way, than at the height of the transatlantic slave trade.

Remembering a challenge my son once made ("Why don't you write about a current need?"), but without a story, I went to New York and sailed on the earliest morning ferry to Ellis Island. I read everything I could beg or buy, asked innumerable questions, and left on the last ferry of the day. I spent two days at the Lower East Side Tenement Museum and three days trekking through the Lower East Side, taking multiple tours, loading my bag with books and emptying my wallet of their purchase price, in search of a story.

There were fascinating accounts at every turn, but none that bore my name, none that connected with the growing frustration in my spirit over the gross injustices I discovered—those taking place today and those recorded in the pages of history. The problem of human trafficking simply loomed too big. It was not enough to state the problem, to paint a picture of grief—there had to be an answer, at least the beginnings of an answer.

Finally I returned to my hotel room, weary but satisfied with the extent of my research. I trusted that once I'd rested up and read my bounty of materials, one of the many tales I'd heard would emerge in some new and fictionalized form in my brain. But morning after morning came, and the story didn't. By the time my stay in New York was nearly at its end, I was on my knees to the Lord, begging that He show me what He wanted me to write. *Whatever it is, as long as it is Your story, that's what I want and all I want.*

Because I knew I'd be searching, I'd taken two books with me to the Big Apple: one that is my guide and stay—my Bible—and one that set my feet on the path to consecration of my life to the Lord many years before—Charles Sheldon's book *In His Steps*. In between the books I write, there's something profound and revitalizing about returning to the roots of my journey, about seeking again the place of Christ's strength made perfect in my weakness.

It had been a number of years since I'd read *In His Steps*. It's odd that I would have packed it in an already-full suitcase. But after days of walking the history-laden streets of New York and researching dozens of story angles to no avail, discouraged, I closed the door to my hotel room and picked up my age-old friend.

I wasn't through the first chapter when I knew that this book embodied the only question that mattered about human exploitation or modern-day slavery or how we treat immigrants or, in fact, any other issue in life: *What would Jesus do?* It's the only question that matters because in Him is the only place we find answers.

If we all truly do what Jesus would do, slavery will end. Jesus never exploited men or women. He never used children or child labor for ease or gain. He never bought or sold baby girls to fulfill the "bride needs" of one-child cultures favoring boys. He never bought or sold human organs or fetuses or body parts. He never lied to immigrants, never enslaved them, never threatened their families or their loved ones or their lives if they did not comply with His demands, never coerced or forced, never shamed or punished a single person into submission to His will. But in every way He set a moral compass, employed divine compassion to the brokenhearted and broken-bodied, and held to account any and all who victimized others.

Band of Sisters is a mild story in the world of human trafficking and modern-day slavery. The realities are far more grim—at the time the story took place and certainly today. But I pray this is a voice—one voice—that evokes a platform for discussion.

If we unite, if we all raise our voices in a demand for change, we will create a clamor that can't be resisted.

To see what other groups and individuals are doing to raise awareness and to learn how you can help create that change, please visit my website and connect to the links for sites fighting modern-day slavery and sites that are holding out a hand of hope and help. The opportunities are there. Dozens of organizations are in place. But "we, the people," are desperately needed.

Let me know what you think and what you're doing to help. I'd love to hear from you at www.cathygohlke.com.

CATHY GOHLKE is the two-time Christy Award–winning author of the critically acclaimed novels *Promise Me This*, *William Henry Is a Fine Name*, and *I Have Seen Him in the Watchfires*, which also won the American Christian Fiction Writers' Book of the Year Award and was listed by *Library Journal* as one of the Best Books of 2008.

Cathy has worked as a school librarian, drama director, and director of children's and education ministries. When not traipsing the hills and dales of historic sites, she, her husband, and their dog, Reilly, make their home on the banks of the Laurel Run in Elkton, Maryland. Visit her website at www.cathygohlke.com.

DISCUSSION QUESTIONS

1. Why is Maureen so resistant to Joshua Keeton's help at the beginning of the story? At what point does she start to realize that maybe his intentions aren't malicious after all? What still keeps her from accepting his help? Have you ever wrongfully doubted someone's intentions?

2. Olivia had misgivings about Drake from the beginning, even though she had no proof of her suspicions. Keeping in mind the social restraints of her day, do you think she was wrong not to confront Dorothy about him earlier? Have you ever been in a similar situation? Without giving too much detail, how did you handle it?

3. In his book *The Three Musketeers*, Alexandre Dumas made famous the line "All for one, one for all." Douglas Wakefield kept the literary trio (busts of the three musketeers, Athos, Porthos, and Aramis) in his study. Do you see a relationship between the philosophy of these characters and the way in which Douglas Wakefield lived his life? How did Olivia and Dorothy understand and embrace their father's philosophy?

4. Much of the distance between Maureen and Katie Rose is initially due to assumptions they've made about each other. What other conflicts and misunderstanding arise as the story progresses to drive them further apart? As the elder sister, should Maureen have handled these situations differently? Do you think it would have made a difference?

5. In the midst of her conflict with Katie Rose, Maureen thinks, *You've made a god of your fear and jealousy, Sister. For what is a god but what*

we go to again and again? (p. 276). Do you agree that Katie Rose has made a god of her negative feelings? Have you ever found yourself returning again and again to a similar "god"—whether a person, achievement, emotion, etc.?

6. When Olivia expresses doubts about using her love of writing, Curtis asks her, "Why would God gift you with a love of something—and an ability, I have no doubt—unless He intended for you to use it?" (p. 115). Do you agree with his perspective? Have you seen God bring connections between your abilities and His purposes for your life? Are there passions you possess that haven't yet found an outlet?

7. Do you think most of the women in the Ladies' Circle grasped Olivia's early challenge to ask, "What would Jesus do?" in every situation? If not, what initiated the change, and what factors influenced their decisions about what to do? What do you think about accepting the same challenge? How would it change your life?

8. Many characters in *Band of Sisters* struggle with issues of social justice and how to personally address them. Do you? How do you think the Lord looks at issues of social justice, and why? Are there Scriptures, Bible stories or principles, or other factors that help you draw your conclusion?

9. It has been reported that the number of humans trafficked in its many forms today is greater by far than the number trafficked at the height of the transatlantic slave trade. Does that surprise you? Discuss the various forms of modern-day slavery and human trafficking of which you are aware.

10. The characters in *Band of Sisters* operated within the legal and (sometimes) social restrictions of their time and within the opportunities they perceived as theirs. In what ways did they use their influence and opportunities to create change? (Consider the women in the circle, the immigrants, the women working at Darcy's, Curtis, Joshua.) What opportunities do we have that the characters didn't? In what ways can we influence change on a local, national, or global level to end slavery?

11. Among some of the women in the circle there was an attitude that the poor bring their poverty, abuse, and exploitation on themselves and that they should be grateful for whatever they receive from benefactors. The women also expressed fears or reservations about bringing the poor into their lives and homes. Have you ever shared feelings like these? If so, why? After reading and discussing *Band of Sisters*, have your views changed?

12. How did Jesus respond to women who were caught in forms of bondage or were hurting or broken? Consider the woman with the issue of blood (Mark 5); the Samaritan woman at the well (John 4); the woman accused of wasting valuable spikenard to anoint Jesus rather than selling it to give to the poor (Matthew 26); Martha and Mary at the death of Lazarus (John 11); Mary Magdalene, from whom seven devils were cast (Mark 16, John 20). Can you think of other examples that display God's heart toward women?

13. Once men, women, or children are freed from slavery, they often need help to heal and adjust to society. What organizations do you know of in your community to help support these individuals? What needs continue? How can you personally contribute?

14. Do you believe the church has a responsibility in working to end modern-day slavery? Why or why not?

15. How did the men in *Band of Sisters* reflect the worth of the women around them—both positively and negatively? What are some examples you've witnessed of the ways men value or demean women? How can we (men and women) help to encourage the boys in our lives and communities toward healthy perspectives on women?

Turn the page for an exciting preview of . . .

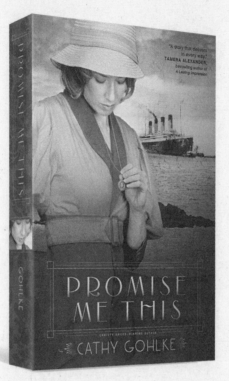

"Stunning. Simply one of the best—if not most powerful—books I have ever read."

Julie Lessman, author of *A Heart Revealed*

CHAPTER ONE

THE GREAT SHIP RETURNED late from her sea trials beyond the shores of Carrickfergus, needing only her sea papers, a last-minute load of supplies, and the Belfast mail before racing to Southampton.

But in that rush to ferry supplies, a dockworker's hand was crushed beneath two heavy crates carelessly dropped. The fury and swearing that followed reddened the neck of the toughest man aboard the sturdy supply boat.

Michael Dunnagan's eyes and ears spread wide with all the fascination of his fifteen years.

"You there! Lad! Do you want to make a shilling?"

Michael, who'd stolen the last two hours of the day from his sweep's work to run home and scrub before seeing *Titanic* off, turned at the gruff offer, certain he'd not heard with both ears.

"Are you deaf, lad? Do you want to make a shilling, I say!" the mate aboard the supply craft called again.

"I do, sir! I do!" Michael vowed, propelled by wonder and a fear the man might change his mind.

"Give us a hand, then. My man's smashed his paw, and we've got to get these supplies aboard *Titanic*. She's late from her trials and wants to be under way!"

Michael could not move his feet from the splintered dock. For months he'd slipped from work to steal glimpses of the lady's growing. He'd spied three years ago as her magnificent keel was laid and had checked week by week as ribs grew into skeleton, as metal plates formed sinew and muscle to strengthen her frame, as decks and funnels fleshed her out. He'd speculated on her finishing, the sure beauty and mystery of her insides. He had cheered, with most of Belfast, as she'd been gently pulled from her berth that morning by tugboats so small with names so mighty that the contrast was laughable.

To stand on the dock and see her sitting low in the water, her sleek lines lit by electric lights against the cold spring twilight, was a wonder of its own. The idea of stepping onto her polished deck—and being paid to do it—was joyous beyond anything in Michael's ken.

But his uncle Tom was aboard *Titanic* in the stoker hole, shoveling coal for her mighty engines. Michael had snuck to the docks to celebrate the parting from his uncle's angry fists and lashing belt as much as he'd come to see *Titanic* herself. He'd never dared to defend himself against the hateful man twice his size, but Michael surely meant to spit a final good-bye.

"Are you coming or not?" the dockhand barked.

"Aye!" Michael dared the risk and jumped aboard the supply boat, trying for the nimble footing of a sailor rather than the clunky feet of a sweep. Orders were shouted from every direction. Fancy chairs, crates of food, and kitchen supplies were stowed in every conceivable space. Mailbags flew from hands on dock to hands on deck. As soon as the lines were tossed aboard, the supply craft fairly flew through the harbor.

Staff of Harland and Wolff—the ship's designers and builders—firemen, and yard workers not sailing to Southampton stood on *Titanic*'s deck, ready to be lightered ashore. The supply boat pulled alongside her.

Michael bent his head, just in case Uncle Tom was among those sent ashore, though he figured it unlikely. He hefted the low end of a kitchen crate and followed it aboard *Titanic*, repeating in his mind the two words of the only prayer he remembered: *Sweet Jesus. Sweet Jesus. Sweet Jesus.*

"Don't be leaving them there!" An authoritarian sort in blue uniform bellowed at the load of chairs set squarely on the deck. "Bring those along to the first-class reception room!"

Michael dropped the kitchen crate where he stood. Sweeping a wicker chair clumsily beneath each arm, he followed the corridor-winding trail blazed by the man ahead of him.

He clamped his mouth to keep it from trailing his toes. Golden oak, carved and scrolled, waxed to a high sheen, swept past him. Fancy patterned carpeting in colors he would have wagered grew only in flowers along the

River Shannon made him whistle low. Mahogany steps, grand beyond words, swept up, up to he didn't know where.

He caught his breath at the domed skylight above it all.

Lights, so high he had to crane his neck to see, and spread wider than a man could stretch, looked for all the world to Michael like layers of icicles and stars, twinkling, dangling one set upon the other.

But Michael gasped as his eyes traveled downward again. He turned away from the center railing, feeling heat creep up his neck. Why the masters of *Titanic* wanted a statue of a winged and naked child to hold a lamp was more than he could imagine.

"Oy! Mind what you're about, lad!" A deckhand wheeled a skid of crates, barely missing Michael's back. "If we scrape these bulkheads, we're done for. I'll not be wanting my pay docked because a gutter rat can't keep his head."

"I'll mind, sir. I will, sir." Michael took no offense. He considered himself a class of vermin somewhat lower than a gutter rat. He swallowed and thought, *But the luckiest vermin that ever lived!*

"Set them round here," the fussy man ordered. Immediately the first-class reception room was filled with men and chairs and confounding directions. A disagreement over the placement of chairs broke out between two argumentative types in crisp uniforms.

The man who'd followed close on Michael's heels stepped back, muttering beneath his breath, "Young bucks busting their britches." A minute passed before he shook his head and spoke from the side of his mouth. "Come, me boyo. We'll fetch another load. Blathering still, they'll be."

But as they turned, the men in uniform forged an agreement and called for Michael to rearrange the chairs. Michael stepped lively, moved each one willingly, deliberately, and moved a couple again, only to stay longer in the wondrous room.

But as quickly as the cavernous room had filled, it emptied. The last of the uniformed men was summoned to the dining room next door, and Michael stood alone in the vast hall.

He started for the passageway, then stopped. He knew he should return to the deck with the other hands and finish loading supplies. But what if he didn't? What if he just sat down and took his ease? What if he dared stay in the fine room until *Titanic* reached Southampton? What if he then walked off the ship—simply walked into England?

Michael's brow creased in consternation. He sucked in his breath, nearly giddy at the notion: to leave Belfast and Ireland for good and all, never again to feel Uncle Tom's belt or buckle lashed across his face or shoulders.

And there was Jack Deegan to consider. When Deegan had injured his back aboard his last ship, he'd struck a bargain with Uncle Tom. Deegan had eagerly traded his discharge book—a stoker's ticket aboard one of the big liners—for Uncle Tom's flat and Michael's sweep wages for twelve months. As cruel as his uncle had always been, experience made Michael fear being left alone with Jack Deegan even more.

To walk away from Uncle Tom, from Jack Deegan, from the memory of these miserable six years past, and even from the guilt and shame of failing Megan Marie—it was a dream, complex and startling. And it flashed through Michael's mind in a moment.

He swallowed. Uncle Tom would be in the stoker hole or firemen's quarters while aboard ship. Once in Southampton he would surely spend his shore leave at the pubs. Michael could avoid him for this short voyage.

"Sweet Jesus," Michael whispered again, his heart drumming a beat until it pounded the walls of his chest. He had begged for years, never believing his prayers had been heard or would be answered.

Michael waited half a minute. When no one came, he crept cautiously across the room, far from the main entry, and slid, the back side of a whisper, beneath the table nearest the wall.

What's the worst they could do to me? he wondered. *Send me back? Throw me to the sharks?* He winced. It was a fair trade.

Minutes passed and still no one came. Shrill whistle blasts signaled *Titanic*'s departure from the harbor. Michael wondered if the mate who'd hired him had missed him, or if he'd counted himself lucky to be saved the bargained shilling. He wondered if Uncle Tom or Jack Deegan would figure out what he'd done, hunt him down, and drag him back. He wondered if it was possible the Sweet Jesus listened to the prayers of creatures lower than gutter rats after all.

※ ※

"I simply cannot keep the child alone with me any longer," Eleanor Hargrave insisted, stabbing her silver-handled cane into the pile of the Persian carpet spread across her drawing room floor. "While I am yet able to travel, I am determined to tour the Continent. My dear cousins in Berlin have been so very patient, awaiting my visit while I served my father, then raised your father's orphaned child."

It was the story of martyrdom Owen had heard from his spinster aunt month after month, year after year, designed and never failing to induce guilt. It was the story of her life of sacrifice and grueling servitude, first to her widowed and demanding father, whom her younger sister had selfishly deserted, and then to the orphaned children of that sister and her husband. His aunt constantly referred to that sacrifice as her gift to his poor departed father, though no mention was ever made of her own sister, Owen and Annie's mother. Owen tried to listen patiently.

"It is unfair of either of you to presume upon me any longer. You simply must take the girl and provide for her or return here to help me look after her. If you do not, I shall be forced to send her away to school— Scotland, I should think."

"I agree, Aunt. I'll see to it immediately."

"You cannot know the worry and vexation caused me by—" His aunt stopped her litany midsentence. "What did you say?"

"I said that I agree. You've been most patient and generous with Annie and with me—a saint." What Owen did not say was that he, too, was aware that his sister grew each day to look more like their beautiful mother—the sister Aunt Eleanor despised. It was little wonder she wanted Annie out of her sight.

"You will return here, then?"

He heard the hope in his aunt's voice.

"I've made arrangements for Annie to begin boarding school in South-ampton."

"Southampton? You mean you will not . . ." She stopped, folded her hands, and lifted her chin. "No one of consequence attends school in Southampton."

"We are not people of financial consequence, Aunt. We are hardworking people of substantial character, as were our parents." Owen had yearned to say that to his aunt for years.

Her eyes flashed. "Your pride is up, young man. My father would say, 'Your Allen Irish is showing.'"

Owen felt his jaw tighten.

And then his aunt smiled—a thing so rare that Owen's eyebrows rose in return.

She leaned forward to stroke his cheek. "Impetuous. So like Mackenzie. You grow more like him—in looks and demeanor—each time I see you."

Owen pulled back. He'd never liked the possessiveness of his aunt's touch, nor the way she constantly likened him to his father. And now that he'd set his sights on the beautiful, widowed Lucy Snape, whose toddler needed a financially stable father, it was essential that he establish his independence.

Eleanor sniffed and sat back. "It is impossible. Elisabeth Anne must remain in London. It is the only suitable society for a young lady. You will return to Hargrave House." She took a sip of tea, then replaced her teacup firmly in its saucer. "Your room stands ready."

"Not this time, Aunt." Owen spoke quietly, leaning forward to replace his own cup, willing it not to rattle. "I will support Annie from now on."

"On gardener's wages. And send her to a boarding school—in a shipping town!" She laughed.

"A convenient location for those going to sea." Owen paused, debating how to proceed. "Or those crossing the sea."

"The sea?" His aunt's voice took on the suspicion, even the menace, that Owen feared. But he would do this, afraid or not.

Owen leaned forward again, breathing the prayer that never failed him. "Do you remember Uncle Sean Allen, in America?"

She stiffened.

"He and Aunt Maggie offered Father half of their landscaping business in New Jersey after Mother died."

"A foolish proposition—a child's dream! The idea of whisking two motherless children to a godforsaken—"

"It was a proposition that might have saved him from the grief that took his life—if you hadn't interfered!" Owen stopped, horrified that he'd spoken aloud the words harbored in his heart these four years but delighted that at last he'd mustered the courage.

She drew herself up. "If it was not an accident that sent him to his grave, it was his own ridiculous pining for a woman too silly to help him manage his business! I offered your father everything—this home, my inheritance, introduction to the finest families. He needn't have worked at all, and if he had insisted, I could have procured any business connections he dreamed of in England. I can do all of that for you, Owen. I offer all of that to you."

And it would be the death of all my hopes for Lucy—or even someone like her—just as you were the death of Father's hopes and dreams. "I'm grateful for the roof you've given Annie and me these four years, Aunt. But it's time for us to go. Uncle Sean has made to me the same offer he made to Father, and I've accepted. I sail Easter week."

"Easter!" she gasped.

"As soon as we turn a profit, I'll send for Annie."

"He has been in that business these many years and not succeeded?" She snorted scornfully, but the fear that he meant to go did not leave her eyes.

He leaned forward. "Do you not see, Aunt? Do you not see this is a chance of a lifetime—for Annie and for me?"

"What I see is that you are foolish and ungrateful, with no more common sense than your father! I see that you are willing to throw away your life on a silly scheme that will come to nothing and that you intend to drag the child down beside you!" Her voice rose with each word, piercing the air.

Owen drew back. He'd not hurt Annie for the world. At fourteen, she was not a child in his eyes; that she remained so in Aunt Eleanor's estimation was reason enough to get her away from Hargrave House.

Eleanor's face fell to pleading, her demands to wheedling. "Owen, stay here. I can set you up in your own gardening business, if that is what you want. You can experiment with whatever you like in our own greenhouses. They will be entirely at your disposal."

Owen folded his serviette and placed it on the tea tray. The action gave him peace, finality. "I'm sorry you cannot be happy for us, Aunt. But it is the solution to our mutual dilemmas."

A minute of silence passed between them, but Owen's heart did not slow.

"Leave me, Owen, and I will strike you from my will." The words came softly, a Judas kiss.

Owen stood and bowed.

"My estate means nothing to you?"

"It comes at too high a price, Aunt." Owen breathed, relieved that the deed was done. "I'll stay the night and then must get back to Southampton. I'll return to collect Annie and her things early next week." He bowed again and walked away.

"There is something more. I had not intended to tell you—not yet."

Owen turned.

His aunt folded her hands in her lap. "It was your grandfather's doing."

※ ※

Annie knelt beside the stair rail, her nerves taut, her eyes stretched wide in worry. When at last Owen stepped through the parlor door, she let out the breath she hadn't realized she was holding.

But Owen didn't move. Annie leaned over the railing for a better look at her brother. His hands covered his head, pressed against the doorframe, and she was certain he moaned. She stood back, biting her lower lip. She'd never heard such a sound from her older brother. "Owen? Owen!" she whispered loudly into the hallway below.

At last he climbed, two stairs at a time, but she'd never seen him look so weary.

"I could hear her shouting all the way up here. What has happened?" Annie met him at the landing and rushed into his arms.

"Come, close the door, Annie." Owen spoke low, pulling her into her room. "Pack your things, everything you want to keep. We'll not be back."

"Pack my things? Why? Where are we going?"

But her brother would not meet her eyes. He pulled her carpetbag from the top of the cupboard and spread it open. He picked up their parents' wedding photograph from her bedside table. "You'll want this."

"Whatever are you doing?"

Owen wrapped the frame in the linen it sat upon and placed it in the bottom of her bag. "I'll tell you when we've settled for the night. Now you must pack, and quickly."

"Am I going to live with you?"

He shook his head. "Pack, Annie."

"Is Aunt Eleanor sending me away?"

"She knows we're going. She—"

They both started when Annie's door swung wide.

"Jamison!" Annie gasped.

The old butler's bent frame filled the low doorway. He looked over his shoulder, put a finger to his lips, and motioned Owen closer. "Do you have a place for Miss Annie, sir?"

Owen ran his fingers through his hair. "In Southampton, as soon as I can arrange it. I don't know what we shall do tonight."

Jamison nodded and pushed a crumpled paper into Owen's hand.

"Jamison!" Eleanor Hargrave bellowed from the first floor.

"What's going on?" Annie begged.

"Take this round to my old sister, Nellie Woodward. Her address is on the bottom. She will do right by you for the night," the butler whispered.

"Jamison! Come—at once!" Annie heard their aunt rap her cane against the parlor doorframe.

"Good-bye, Miss Annie." Jamison's ever-formal voice caught in his throat.

"No." Annie shook her head, confused, disbelieving, and reached for Jamison. "I can't say good-bye like this!" Her eyes filled. "Someone tell me what's happening!"

The butler took her hands in his for the briefest moment, coughed, and stepped back. "God take care of you both, Mr. Owen. Write to us when you get to America. Let us know you are well, and Miss Annie, too." He nodded. "You can send a letter to my Nellie. She'll see that I get it."

"America?" Annie gasped. "We're going to America?"

Jamison caught Owen's eye, clearly sorry he'd said so much, and looked away. But Owen wrung the butler's withered hand. "Thank you, old friend."

Jamison turned quickly and crept down the polished stairs.

"Owen," Annie began, hope rising in her chest.

"Don't stop to talk now, Annie! Hurry, before Aunt Eleanor sends you off with nothing!"

Annie whirled. "America! Where to begin?" She plucked her Sunday frock from the cupboard; Owen grabbed her most serviceable. She tucked in stationery and coloring pencils; Owen packed her Bible, *The Pilgrim's Progress*, and the few books of poetry their mother had loved.

"You must wear your spring and winter cloaks. Layer everything you can."

"It isn't that cold!" Annie sputtered.

"Do it," Owen insisted.

They stuffed all they could into her carpetbag and a pillow slip. Ten minutes later they turned down the lamp, slipped down the servants' stairs, and closed the back kitchen door softly behind them.